BOOK THREE

A TALE OF RIBBONS & CLAWS

CHECK
Mate

RACHEL E SCOTT

Check-Mate, A Tale of Ribbons & Claws Book Three

Copyright © 2024 by Rachel E. Scott

All rights reserved.

Cover by Miblart.

Interior art by Rachel E. Scott

For Irene. Thank you for giving me my love of romance and always blushing when I talk about kissing. I love you, Mr. Wallace's Golden Girl.

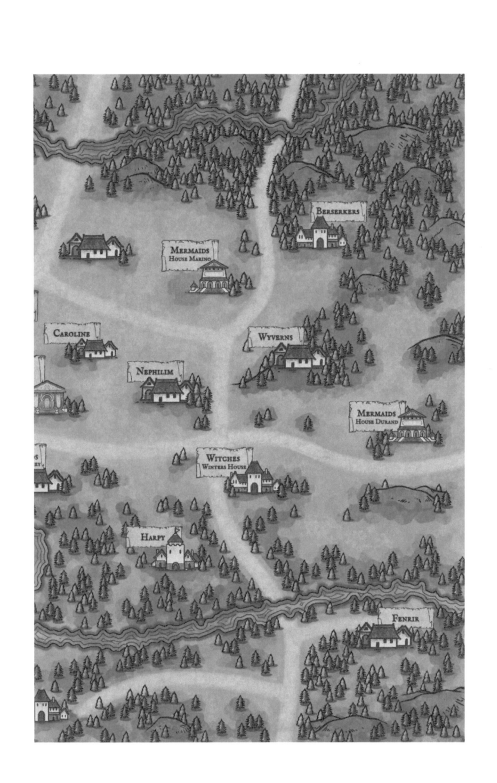

Also by Rachel E Scott

Contemporary
The Grinch Next Door

Fantasy
Legends of Avalon: Merlin
Legends of Avalon: Arthur

A Tale Of Ribbons & Claws
Stale-Mate
Bond-Mate
Check-Mate

Welcome to Autumnvale
Book One Coming Autumn of 2024

Plot Twist
Bonding With the Bodyguard (Coming winter of 2024)

Do you like to listen to playlists while reading? I've got you covered. Here's my personal playlist for
A Tale of Ribbons & Claws
https://open.spotify.com/playlist/3FtDbSH38NRnforYV8kaXe?si=e98f71ee2a91
41bf

Content Warnings

All of my books are clean reads, but here are some things to note before you begin reading:

- Age gap between love interests (10 years)

- Mention of death of past loved one

- Mention of cancer (past)

- Basic violence (nothing descriptive or graphic)

- No sex

- Kissing that stays sweet and swoony

- Mild innuendos (Ex: 'that's what she said.' No vulgar jokes.)

Note: This book is the final in a trilogy and contains a tied-up story with a happy ending.

Contents

Last Time on A Tale of Ribbons & Claws   XVII

Creatures of Shifter Haven   XIX

1.   Chapter 1   3

2.   Chapter 2   13

3.   Chapter 3   27

4.   Chapter 4   33

5.   Chapter 5   39

6.   Chapter 6   51

7.   Chapter 7   65

8.   Chapter 8   73

9.   Chapter 9   85

10. Chapter 10   93

11. Chapter 11   103

12. Chapter 12   115

13. Chapter 13   123

14. Chapter 14   135

15.	Chapter 15	149
16.	Chapter 16	157
17.	Chapter 17	163
18.	Chapter 18	169
19.	Chapter 19	181
20.	Chapter 20	187
21.	Chapter 21	193
22.	Chapter 22	201
23.	Chapter 23	211
24.	Chapter 24	219
25.	Chapter 25	225
26.	Chapter 26	237
27.	Chapter 27	251
28.	Chapter 28	269
29.	Chapter 29	275
30.	Chapter 30	285
31.	Chapter 31	297
32.	Chapter 32	305
33.	Chapter 33	313
34.	Chapter 34	319
35.	Chapter 35	323
36.	Chapter 36	329
Also by...		341
Acknowledgments		343
About the Author		345

Last Time on A Tale of Ribbons & Claws

C aroline Birch has been the vigilante of Shifter Haven for the better part of three years, but when Morgan Hohlt shows up, that all changes. Morgan and Caroline started off on rocky terms. With his reputation as the scariest Berserker Chief in the country and her secret lineage, they were a recipe for disaster...or chemistry.

Same thing.

But over the past few months, they've become more than teammates or even friends. They're partners. Mates. And these lovers will do anything to keep each other safe.

But that turns out to be a little more challenging than they thought. After taking down the Dragon Queen who had been hoping to sell Caroline—the only living Elf—to the highest bidder, they quickly realized that the Dragon Queen had merely been a chess piece in someone else's game.

Because somewhere out there is someone who knows that not all the Elves were killed off in the civil war centuries ago. Someone who wants to buy Caroline.

Morgan, however, isn't willing to part with his mate. And when a stranger comes out of the woodwork to help them, they aren't sure whether to call him friend or foe...

Volund is a Dark Elf who's been trailing Caroline for months, claiming that their parents once knew each other. But amongst his pleadings that he only wants to offer her a community, the Dark Elf is riddled with secrets. One of which being that he isn't the only Dark Elf alive, and he just so happens to be the prince of all the survivors.

When Volund shows his true colors, Morgan, Caroline and the gang face him and his army of Dark Elves in a final showdown. But when Caroline gains the upper hand and takes Volund prisoner, he insists that he's not the one she can't trust. But our heroine knows better than to trust a snake.

Nearly killing herself with the effort, Caroline takes Volund down, the good guys win, and all is right in the world. Or so they thought.

Just as things seem to be settling down, Caroline receives a package containing her inheritance from her birth parents. A letter and an address. To the surviving Light Elves...

The Shifters of Shifter Haven & Their Most Identifying Abilities

Alfar—Light Elves (powers unknown)

Berserker—can shift into bears.

Dragon—can shift into dragons.

Fenrir—can shift into giant wolves.

Firebird—can control fire.

Harpy—can control air.

Kelpie—can shift into black horses.

Mermaid—can read minds.

Minotaur—can shift into large, heavily muscled people with horns.

Nephilim—Dark Elves (powers unknown)

Pixie—can control nature.

Sphinx—can shift into large cats (lions, tigers, cheetahs, etc.)

Witch—can perform spells.

Wyvern—can shift into a wyvern.

Chapter 1

CAROLINE

As a spy with three years of experience under her belt, I could confidently say that breaking into places that required your boyfriend to change into a stolen uniform was a *great* idea.

I watched as Morgan tugged his shirt up over his head and handed it to me, fumbling with the new shirt we'd taken from the security guard who lay passed out on the floor. Although Morgan made quick work of the change, in my mind, he might as well have been moving in slow motion.

The hard planes of his stomach called out to me, and I knew from experience that they were just as firm as they looked. Would he yell at me if I touched them now? Part of me wanted to find out.

My eyes slowly traveled up the solid surface of his chest, pausing to admire his lovely pecs. *Such an underrated muscle.* Then there were his shoulders, big but not too big. And those arms, defined and strong, but slender enough that he could easily wrap them around me. *And don't even get me started on his forearms.* Man, how I loved those things.

"Caroline," he said, a warning in his voice, "We cannot make out here. We'll get caught."

But his words just drew my attention up to his face. His beautiful, terrifying face. He was an intimidating looking man by nature. With his steely grey eyes, firm bone structure and dark hair. A Milo Ventimiglia doppelgänger with an even more devastating smolder. But with the white scar that trailed across his left eye and over his right cheek, he was like a nightmare come to life. A really handsome nightmare. Oh, how I wished we were alone in the dark for different reasons right now.

"Oh, come on. You don't think the guards would believe that we're just two young lovers getting into trouble?"

"Well considering that you *are* trouble," he teased, pulling down the new shirt so it covered his beautiful torso, "They probably would."

I wrinkled my nose at him and shoved his shirt into my backpack. "You like that I'm trouble."

Mor stepped close and kissed my temple. "Yeah, but I'm an idiot for you. My judgment can't be trusted where you're concerned."

"Hm. I'm not sure if I should feel insulted or flattered."

"Whichever one makes you want to kiss me when we get home."

"Oh, spicy. I like it. In that case, let's get this show on the road."

I winked at him and encouraged my magic forward. My ability to read emotions was like coaxing a cat to behave, but changing my appearance with magic was like pulling the chord on a curtain. In a blink, my body had shifted, and I no longer looked like me. I felt the same, but when I looked down, I nodded at the guard uniform I now wore, the end of a dark ponytail trailing over my shoulder instead of my natural auburn hair. "That'll do."

When I glanced up, Morgan's eyes were steeped in emotions, and the sweet affection I felt swirling around inside him through our mate bond made my insides go warm and cozy.

"Care," he whispered, setting his hands on my cheeks, "I know you don't need me to tell you how amazing you are, but I am so proud of you right now."

I smiled, knowing exactly what he meant. Since I could remember, I'd avoided using my magic unless absolutely necessary. And even though I'd broken into places dozens of times, I almost never changed my appearance to do it. For years, I'd believed that I needed to prove my value. And using magic always felt like a shortcut. Like it cheapened my ability or my worth if I used it. Now, I knew that was a lie.

Although I still sometimes struggled to really believe it.

"Thanks, Bear Man," I replied, reaching up to kiss his cheek.

Normally, I would've gone for his lips, but I didn't love the idea of another woman's mouth on Morgan's. Even if they were actually my lips disguised as someone else's.

Our disguises taken care of, we turned and headed further down the darkened hall. The Human Services Department Building was quiet, with no patrons around this early in the morning. And unlike the Shifter Alliance Building across the street, this building only had a few security guards, all stationed at specific areas rather than roaming the building. It was a much easier place to sneak into.

"Do you have the bug?" Mor asked, sliding his palm along mine and twining our fingers together.

I held up the USB drive Mike had given me before we'd left the Berserker house. According to him, the bug was programmed to delete all the footage for every day that I broke into the Alliance Building. Which was a lot.

Part of me missed being a vigilante. There was a satisfaction in being able to take down bag guys without worrying about all of the red tape that prevented law enforcement from doing it themselves. Now that I was the significant other to a Regional Council Member, I wasn't sure how I'd be able to keep fighting to make Shifter Haven a safer city. But maybe with Morgan's connections, we could do more than I ever did as a lone vigilante.

"One bug to wipe all incriminating evidence, ready to go," I announced, winking as I slid the USB back into the pocket of my black pants.

"Say that louder, why don't you?" Mor complained, but I sensed his teasing attitude.

"Why would I? You're the one who likes to yell."

"I don't yell."

"And I'm not addicted to processed food."

He rolled his eyes but didn't release my hand. "Alright, let's get this over with. We'll distract the guards, plant the bug, and get out."

"Then Frank's."

Morgan shot me a knowing look, one full of concern and vague disapproval. Meanwhile, I tried to pretend that I was fine. That I wasn't still reeling from the revelation that other Light Elves still existed. That it didn't totally freak me out that I was their queen.

I knew I wasn't fooling Morgan. He was too observant, too tapped into me to be so gullible. Unfortunately, our nightly routine clued him in to my true emotional state. That and the mate bond. But since I didn't know how else to cope with my new reality, we just kept up the same routine, and he just kept waiting for me to move forward.

"I promise I'll deal with it soon," I whispered as we neared the guard room where the door was propped open and a conversation about baseball filtered into the hall.

"You don't have to promise me anything," Morgan said, tugging on my hand until I looked at him. "If this is what you need right now, then that's fine. We'll keeping doing it until you're ready."

Sweet as his offer was, I wasn't quite sure if I ever would be ready. So instead of replying, I just smiled and nodded, knowing he saw right through it.

"Mm," I hummed loudly as we strode into the guard room, Morgan and I's hands no longer connected, "You guys should go try the cake in the break room."

"Cake?" The larger of the two men in the room perked up, looking between Morgan and me with bright eyes. The guard room was small, with a bank of monitors showing the rest of the building. Little did these guys know that their cameras currently weren't live.

"Yeah, someone must have brought it in yesterday," I shrugged, leaning against the door frame. "It's one of those big sheet cakes with the really good frosting. There wasn't much of it left though. So, if you want a slice, I'd do it soon."

The two guards looked at each other with raised eyebrows. Then they were launching to their feet, practically running out the door. "Be back in a sec," the smaller man shouted back at us.

Crossing my arms, I grinned at Morgan, who was watching the men jog down the hall with a look of severe disappointment on his face. "Our law enforcement at work."

"Technically, they're only security guards, not cops," I pointed out, walking over to the monitors.

"Still, for once I'd like to see a guard who's genuinely dedicated to their job. Someone who takes it seriously."

"In their defense, I'm wearing the face of their friend."

"I think they still would have left even if you hadn't shifted. Anything for a slice of poison."

"Question," I said, inserting the USB into a computer, "For your birthday, will you even want a cake? Or is there some kind of nasty tasting healthy thing posing as a dessert that you want instead?"

I watched as a green bar travelled across the screen, marking the progress of our footage-deleting bug.

"Not all healthy foods taste bad," Mor argued.

"No, but usually the ones parading around as sweets do," I said, slipping the USB in my pocket now that the screen showed that the footage had been deleted. "So, what'll it be for your birthday? Cake or tofu?"

I smiled and Morgan glared. "I do like sweets, you know," he defended, taking my hand and leading us down the hall in the opposite direction the guards had gone. "I'm just very conscious of how often I eat them."

"Alright, so then what do you want for your birthday?"

"You do know that my birthday isn't until October?"

"Yes, but as your girlfriend, I should know what kind of cake you'd want."

Morgan dropped my hand and moved to the exit, holding open the side door of the building for me. I smiled at him as I stepped out into the darkness of the early morning, the streetlights our only illumination. Now that we were outside,

I released my magic and let my appearance shift back to normal, barely feeling a thing.

"Alright," he said, winding an arm around my shoulders, "I want cheesecake for my birthday. And I'm assuming you want a smorgasbord of desserts rather than one cake for yours?"

"You assume correctly. Now, I'm sorry, but did you just say you want a cheesecake? Is it a special no sugar kind? Or some kind of vegan concoction?"

He shook his head and opened the passenger door when we arrived at the SUV where it was parked along the quiet street. "Nope. Just regular cheesecake. My mom's recipe."

All the teasing went right out of me at the mention of his mom. He didn't talk about her often, and when he did, it was always with a mixture of wistful happiness and a weathered sadness. And while I loved that he still had happy memories, I also hated how melancholy they made him. But that's how grief works. Even when you're healed and happy, it taints every memory and every place our lost loved ones ever touched.

"Why cheesecake?" I asked gently, turning to look up at him where he leaned one arm against the doorframe.

"I'd had a really good one at a diner one time," he said, shrugging like it was no big deal. "After that, I asked my mom if she could make it for me herself. So, she did, but I insisted that it didn't taste like the one at the diner. She ended up trying at least four different recipes and had to tweak one over and over until I finally declared it good enough. I was such a brat, but she humored me anyway." He shook his head, a faint smile on his lips. "Although she did warn me that it would be her last attempt, and if I didn't like it, I could kick rocks."

He chuckled quietly and I smiled at the sound. "Sounds like she was a good mom."

"She was. And she would have loved you," he whispered, grey eyes studying me with sweet adoration. "You two probably would've been in cahoots against me."

"Me plotting against you?" I gasped, pressing a hand to my chest. "Never!"

Morgan grinned and kissed my forehead, nudging me toward my seat. "Oh, just shut up and get in."

"Bossy," I complained, winking at him as I sat. "I like it."

His eyes dropped to my lips, and from the attraction blazing to life inside him, it seemed he was considering kissing me. But then he seemed to think better of it, shaking his head and muttering 'no time'. Then he shut my door and went to the driver's side.

We stopped by Frank's and got some fries and shakes—Morgan, claiming he was only eating it because he was under duress. And by the time we pulled up to the same street we'd been staking out for a week, the mood had dimmed remarkably.

It was the ideal neighborhood, with big trees lining the street, well-kept landscaping, basketball hoops in the driveways and cheery looking front doors. No one was out yet at this time of the morning, except for the occasional person going to work. But they didn't notice us here parked along the street under an oak tree. They never noticed us.

And a part of me hoped they never did.

"How are you feeling today?" Mor asked quietly, no judgment in his voice.

He'd been good about that lately, being patient with me and giving me space to process. It made it all the more frustrating that I didn't have a real answer to give him.

"I don't know," I admitted with a sigh, swirling the straw in my milkshake. "What do you think I'm feeling?"

It wasn't a facetious question, and he knew it. I was actually asking him to name the feelings I couldn't quite put words to. And since he could sense them through the mate bond, he could at least guess at my emotions, even if he didn't always know the details.

"Anxious," he replied, eyes focused out the windshield. "Sad, curious...jealous."

I listened as he voiced my own feelings aloud, wondering why it was so hard for me to do it myself. He was right, of course. I was feeling all those things.

"They've had this," I whispered as we watched an Alfar woman wearing scrubs walk toward her car. "They've all grown up with this community, this safe haven where there aren't any secrets. They have no idea what it's like to carry it all alone."

Morgan was quiet for a moment. "No, they don't know."

"But?" I prompted, turning to study the knowing look on his face.

"But they've had an entire community to impose opinions on how they behave with the world. How they protect their secret and who they interact with. I doubt anyone here has ever been allowed to even dream of doing what you've done as a vigilante. It's too dangerous."

I didn't argue with him. He wasn't wrong. My life had its own baggage cart, but so did everyone else's. *Different bags, same weight.*

"You think I should come forward," I sighed, leaning my head against the seat.

Morgan took my hand and held it in his lap, his fingers warm over mine. "I think you should be nicer to yourself. I know you're feeling a lot of self-doubt—"

"Because I'm supposed to be a *queen*, Mor. How can I be a queen? I can barely work as a team," I argued—whined, actually.

"Like I said, you need to be nicer to yourself. You're way more capable than you think you are." When I rolled my eyes, he gently squeezed my hand. "I have no problem with you waiting as long as you want before you come forward to the Alfar. I just don't like that your reasons for waiting are so self-deprecating."

"I know," I said, giving him an apologetic smile. "I'm sorry I've been so unfair to your favorite person."

"You joke, but you *are* my favorite person, Red."

Then he leaned across the console and slid one big hand along my cheek. I wasn't feeling particularly impressive at the moment, but when Morgan's eyes grew warm and his face neared mine, I felt treasured and precious.

"I love you," he murmured, just before his lips met mine.

They were warm, soft and inviting. Like wrapping yourself in a blanket fresh from the dryer after being chilled to the bone. I clung to him, reaching up to grasp his shirt in my hands, pulling myself closer.

I knew that kisses and comforting touches were only so strong, and they couldn't actually fix things. But there was something so healing about Morgan's kisses. Like with every caress of his lips on mine, every stroke and brush and tug, he was speaking to me. Marking me. Precious. Loved. Important. Wanted. Needed. His touch wasn't a cure, but it did help ease some of the negativity from my mind.

"I love you too," I whispered as he pulled back just far enough to tilt his head the other direction, our lips still brushing. He didn't reply, but he didn't have to.

His kiss claimed me, proudly declaring me 'lover', and 'partner'. And I gave back as good as I got. My movements were slow and tender, measured by the gentle appreciation I felt for all his patience and faithfulness. But Mor wasn't disappointed by my lack of fire.

He captured my lips again and again, his hand on my face so sweet and reassuring. And when he pressed a closed mouth kiss to my lips, and leaned his forehead against mine, we were both a little out of breath.

"See, you're capable of so much," he teased.

I tugged on his shirt, leaning up to kiss the corner of his mouth. "If only I could rule an entire society with just a kiss."

Mor growled and I smiled. "No, that kind of authority is reserved for me. As for your people," he leaned back, looking me in the eye, "I think all you need is you, Red."

Such a simple sentiment, and yet it penetrated the insecurities in my mind in a way that I hadn't anticipated. Maybe Morgan was right. Maybe it was time I stopped being scared and start taking on my role as Alfar Queen.

But as I watched a few more Alfar walk to their cars, heading off to work, I wondered if I couldn't put off introducing myself for a few more days...

Chapter 2

MORGAN

Care bumped my hip with hers, standing next to me in the kitchen. Pancake batter swirled in the bowl she was stirring, while my homemade protein balls lined a cookie sheet on the counter.

"So domestic," she teased, leaning up to kiss me. I kissed her back, snaking an arm around her waist to tug her closer. "Mm, but I can't say I'm fond of that taste. Protein balls are nasty."

She pulled back and licked her lips, scrunching her nose in displeasure. But I wasn't deterred. I just captured her lips again. "You just need to get used to the flavor. I can help with that."

She laughed but kissed me back, and I marveled at how bizarrely wonderful it was that after four years of believing that I'd never get to feel this kind of happy again, I was so blissful that it made me stupid.

"Have I told you today how grateful I am that I kidnapped you?" I whispered, squeezing her hip.

"We've definitely got to come up with a fake story to tell our kids," she replied, smiling as she shook her head. "The last thing I want is for them to tell their teachers that Daddy kidnapped Mommy and now they're married."

My ears perked up at the sound of her mentioning kids and marriage, but just as I opened my mouth to pester her with questions, Clint walked into the room.

"Uh, Morgan," he interrupted, looking very confused, "There's someone at the door, and I think they're here for Caroline."

"What?" Care spun around, caution and skepticism running through her. "It couldn't be my parents, could it?" she asked, looking up at me.

Her mom had been over the moon when Caroline told her about our relationship, and I got to meet both her and Care's dad over Facetime. Her mom was friendly and excited, crying half the time and smiling for the rest of it. Her dad was likewise happy, but he'd had the girls leave for a few minutes so he could give me the standard 'if you hurt my daughter, I hurt you' speech. And as Caroline and Ariel predicted, I actually found Ariel more terrifying than their father.

But I doubted that they would've shown up here. We'd explained our situation to them, and made it very clear that their involvement would only cause more danger for Caroline. As proven with Ariel's abduction just a few weeks ago, Care's loved ones were prime targets, and the further away her parents were from the conflict, the better.

"I don't think this guy's your dad," Clint said, shaking his head.

My muscles went rigid at his words, and I felt my protective instincts stand at attention. "Why not?"

"Because he asked to see his queen."

Care and I shared a panicked look, and then without a word, we made a beeline for the front door.

But as she reached for one of the double doors, I stopped her, my hands on her shoulders. "Wait, this could be a trap."

"You're right," she replied calmly, "But I've got you, Clint, and Grey all here in the house to help protect me if it is."

"True...although I would've loved for you to say that you're sure it's not a trap and I'm being silly."

"Sorry. Let me try again." She pasted on a bright smile and laid her hands against my chest. "Morgan, you're being silly. Of course, this isn't a trap. Better?"

"No, I know you're lying."

Care rolled her eyes and then without warning, she yanked the door open.

A man stood on the other side; a stack of papers clutched in one hand while the other was tucked into the pocket of his slacks. He was wearing a blue suit vest with a black tie and a white shirt rolled up to his elbows. White hair was trimmed short, and a beard contoured his lined face, trimmed to a perfect point at the chin. A pair of blue eyes slid across Care and I both, assessing but not surprised.

"I'm Harold," the older gentleman said, holding out a hand toward me. I stared at it for a moment before I finally shook it. "I'm your logistics advisor and a fellow Alfar."

"You're..." Care blinked, seemingly at a loss for words for the first time ever. "What—how..."

"You've been watching our neighborhood," Harold explained, understanding Care's unfinished question. "I recognized Chief Hohlt immediately. And as for you Queen Caroline," he paused, a sentimental look in his eyes, "You look like your mother."

Caroline was silent, but I saw the moisture gathering in her eyes, and the simultaneous pain and joy that squeezed her heart. Without a word, I slipped my hand around hers and gave it a gentle squeeze. She looked up at me, and whispered, "He's not lying."

And given that she could sense emotions, she would know if he was.

"I hope you don't mind," Harold said, though the stubborn look in his eyes told me he wouldn't really care if she did mind, "But after I recognized you, I took the liberty of arranging a few things. Clearly, you're hesitant to announce your position to our people. Which is fine, but I figured that having both a proper base of operations and a knowledge of how our society functions would help you gain confidence in your position."

"Base of operations?" I asked, not sure that I liked the sound of that.

"Yes, I bought you a house to conduct Alfar business from. And don't worry, it's just down the road from here. I gathered that you two are quite attached to each other and assumed you'd want to work closely."

"You bought me a house?" Care asked, looking from Harold to me, her eyes wide.

"Well, the entire Alfar community technically paid for it," Harled shrugged nonchalantly, "With previous rulers, there was never a proper place to conduct business and it wasn't practical. Now there will be a place for you to live and for us to hold functions and meetings."

"Practical," Care parroted, her voice losing all inflection.

"Yes. Practical."

As Caroline's emotions began to whip from confused to scared to shocked to completely overwhelmed, I held her hand tighter and drew my eyes to Harold.

"How did you know her name?" I asked. I trusted Caroline's judgment that he wasn't lying. But that didn't mean I trusted Harold. There were very few people I trusted when it came to my mate.

Harold's blue eyes held a twinkle of mischief. "I looked into you, and you have a car listed under her name."

I felt more than saw Caroline turn toward me. "What car?" When I didn't immediately answer, she pinched my arm with her free hand. "Morgan, what car?"

"A beautiful mint green Jeep, completely updated with all the bells and whistles." Harold answered for me. "A 1997, I believe."

"You *bought* me a Jeep?" Care nearly shouted. I resisted the urge to clap a hand over my ear. "Why would you do that? You don't need to be buying me expensive things, Morgan Gareth Hohlt."

"You needed a car, Red," I defended, looking her in the eye. "I knew that eventually you would take on the role of queen and you'd need a way to get back and forth."

"And instead of buying me some used car—or better yet, having me buy my own—you bought me a vintage—and I'm sure *expensive*—Jeep?"

I shrugged. "What do you expect me to do? I love you, and I want to treat you to nice things sometimes. I mean, it was supposed to be a surprise..."

I turned a scowl on Harold, and he had the good sense to look contrite. "Sorry."

Caroline's glare slowly faded, and she shook her head at me. But when she kissed me on the cheek, I knew her wrath had come and gone.

"Fine, you can buy me a car," she said, as though it were a big hardship, "But no more expensive gifts until next year!"

"None?" I traced the base of her left ring finger with mine and watched with immense pleasure as her cheeks turned my favorite shade of red.

She bit her lip, barely holding back a smile, and quickly turned her attention back to Harold. "I appreciate your thoughtfulness in buying a house close to Morgan, but I haven't exactly decided what I'm going to do about being queen."

But Harold wasn't going to be shot down so easily. "Well then let me help you decide. Come see the house, meet the staff, let me explain how our leadership functions, and then you can make an informed decision."

I felt Care's anxiety humming through the back of her mind, but what caught my attention was the hope that seemed to spark inside her. Excusing us for a moment, I shut the door and grasped her shoulders.

"Talk to me, Red. What's going on in there?" I nodded to her head.

"I don't know..." She studied me like she might find all the answers in my eyes if she just looked hard enough. "He knew my mom, Morgan. He must have if he says I look like her. Maybe he has stories about her, or at least some pictures I could see..."

I felt for her. After everything we'd been through, after all the revelations and heartbreaks, here was a living breathing link to her birth parents. Not just a letter or a photo, but someone who actually knew them. She'd be crazy *not* to jump at the chance to ask every question she could think of.

"And what do you think about being queen?" I asked, knowing that her eagerness to learn about her birth parents wasn't the problem. Her resistance to taking up the role of leadership was.

This question she was much slower to answer, looking at the door, my shirt, her shoes. And although I could sense her emotions, it wasn't a perfect science and the shades between emotions were hard to decipher. Especially when she was feeling so many things, all jumbled together like they were now.

"I want to do it," she whispered, as if she were afraid of who might hear her. "I want to do right by my birth parents and lead as well as they did."

"Is that the only reason you want to do it?"

She met my eyes again, hers a little glossy with emotion. "No. I also miss it—being the vigilante. I miss having an impact and actually helping people. I'm a creature of action—I know, big surprise." She smiled and I rolled my eyes. "But I miss being in a position to act. I know I can't go back to being the vigilante now that I know someone else might get blamed for my crimes. But being queen is an opportunity to be helpful again..."

"So, what's been holding you back?" I was baiting her, and she knew it. We'd had this discussion more than a few times in the past week. And I planned to keep having it until she truly believed that she could do this. That she was enough.

"Me," she answered, albeit a little petulantly. When I raised my eyebrow, inviting her to go on, she sighed dramatically. "I've been the one holding me back with all my self-doubt and insecurity. Which, to be fair, I feel is pretty reasonable given that I'm supposed to be a *queen* all of a sudden."

I shrugged but didn't argue. It was fair to feel insecure, but as someone who loved her, I wished she never had to.

"But I guess it's like they say," she went on, "'If you can't beat the fear, then do it scared'."

I let a smile slip across my lips, proud to see her fire burning bright.

"Exactly," I whispered, tucking her against my chest, her face pressed under my chin. "You don't have to get over your insecurities today. Or tomorrow, or next week. Every day you push against them, they'll get smaller and smaller until one day they'll be more of a whisper than a yell."

Caroline hugged me tight, taking a deep breath. And when she breathed out, her shoulders were a little less tense, and her hold was a little less desperate. After a few moments soaking up the peaceful silence, she stepped back and nodded. Ready to face the world.

Or at least the rest of the Alfar.

***

Half an hour later, we were standing in front of Caroline's new house. If it could even be called that.

"*This* is my house?" Care demanded, her face frozen between shock and confusion.

Harold just smiled at us like he was having some kind of private joke. "It is."

"How the heck did you find a castle in the middle of the valley? Who built it? And why?" she asked, staring up at the monstrosity with wide eyes.

The castle—because Care was right and it absolutely was a castle—was like something out of a movie or a video game. It was a little bigger than our house and much taller, with alabaster walls instead of the classic grey stone, and wood trim that curled around the balconies and diamond-paned windows. A wide staircase led up to a large, curved stone landing that was roofed by an especially large balcony. And high above that were spires of dark wood and metal sloping rooflines. The place was set far back from the road, surrounded by tall trees and a manicured lawn and garden, and just a stone's throw to the left was the river.

"A man named William Bailey had it built in 1986," Harold explained as Caroline, Clint and I all looked at the castle with complete confusion. "He was determined to start a renaissance festival here, but unfortunately at the time, city ordinances prevented such an event. He did use the place as a personal vacation house for a long time, but once his health declined, he stopped using it. When I approached him with an offer to buy the place and explained that it would be used by a Shifter queen—don't worry, I didn't say which species," he added quickly when we all glared at him, "He was all too happy to sell the place at a decent price, excited that it would be used as a castle and not just a bizarre Airbnb."

"A bizarrely cool Airbnb," Clint muttered.

Caroline, however, was much less enthused, staring up at the castle like it was her greatest nightmare. When Harold suggested we go inside and look around, Care nodded, but said nothing, her face drawn in terror.

"This is the formal entry," Harold explained, in full tour guide mode as he led us into the house. "There's also a formal dining room, a kitchen, a parlor, a study, a living room, a small ballroom, three smaller bedrooms, and a garage on this floor."

"*Just on this floor?*" Care squawked, spinning to stare open-mouthed at Harold.

The older Alfar nodded, still with that glint of entertainment in his eye. "The second floor houses more bedrooms, an office, a living area, and a library. Of course, William was happy to sell the place completely furnished, but you're more than welcome to make whatever design changes you like, Queen Caroline."

When Care looked at me with a stricken expression, I wasn't sure if it was the massiveness of the house that freaked her out, or hearing someone call her 'Queen Caroline'.

"Well, I guess now you're a snooty mansion owner just like the rest of us Shifter leaders," I teased, bumping her shoulder as Harold showed us to the master suite upstairs. And more importantly, the master bathroom. Which was about the size of a small bedroom, with a big clawfoot tup, cathedral style windows with frosted glass, and shiny marble floors.

"Shut up," she growled, shoving my arm.

I knew that Caroline liked pretty things, but she also hated injustice, and I had a feeling that living in such an opulent house was going to bug her. It probably wouldn't be long before she was selling off unnecessary pieces of furniture or decorations and using the money on other people. *Once a vigilante, always a vigilante.*

"This is absolutely obscene," she grumbled as Harold led us down to the dining room. "I may own enough shoes to fill the giant bathtub upstairs, but no one needs to be *this* fancy. It's excessive and selfish."

"Are you going to sell your castle then?" I asked, smirking when she flashed a scowl my way.

"No. If I did that, some other rich idiot would just move in and live like a king. No, I'm going to simplify this place. No excess for me, and no unnecessary bougee living for the Alfar. Maybe we'll even turn some of the bedrooms into temporary living spaces for people who need it. Or rent them out cheap to small businesses or something."

When I just grinned at her, she furrowed her brows. "What?"

"Nothing," I shook my head. "I'm just really glad that you're you. No one else I know would have become a vigilante and put their life in danger in order to help people of other races. No one else would be trying to figure out ways to take their luxury and turn it into support for other people." Sliding my arm around her shoulders, I tugged her close and kissed her temple. "You may be snarky and a pain in the butt sometimes, but you're a woman of action, Red. You don't just think about doing the selfless thing, you *do* the selfless thing. It's one of my favorite things about you."

Care's green eyes grew warm, and she wrapped her arm around my back. "Once we're alone, I want to hear the rest of your favorite things about me."

"Throw in a promise to try one of my paleo cookies and you've got a deal."

She scrunched up her nose and shook her head. "Heck no. I love you, but there's no one I would eat those for."

"I agree," Clint said, crossing his arms, "I love you too, bro, but you eat some gross stuff. I'm all for eating healthy, but I also want to *enjoy* eating."

"I enjoy eating!" I insisted, but neither Caroline nor Clint were convinced.

We were all three still arguing in whispers when we followed Harold into the dining room and found a line of people waiting for us.

The dining room was large—imagine that—with a long table and high-backed chairs. Credenza's, fancy paintings, and big potted plants lined the walls, some of the summer sun filtering through the many windows. And standing on the other side of the table were eight strangers.

"Queen Caroline," Harold announced, waving a hand toward the lineup, "I'm pleased to introduce you to your staff. You have a cook, a gardener, a housekeeper, and a valet who will see to all your vehicles."

"I also serve as a handyman," the valet, a man in his late thirties said with a friendly smile, stepping forward to shake Care's hand. He had a welcoming face, with a mop of wavy brown hair and a quiet voice. "I'm David."

"Nice to meet you David," she managed to squeeze out, her smile a little frozen as the panic in her body kicked up a notch.

I'd dropped my arm from around her shoulders so she could properly greet everyone, but I remained close by, letting my large stature and resting murder face speak for me. *Mess with my mate, and I'll mess with you.*

Everyone seemed to get the message regardless of my silence, sizing me up with wary expressions. There were few times in life when I was grateful for my imposing reputation. And this was one of them.

"And I'm David's wife, Torrie," the cook greeted cheerily, also shaking Care's hand. "Not that I'm trying to mark my territory or anything. I mean, if you make a move on him, I'll kill you," she paused, giggling nervously and running her hands across her apron. She was a short plump woman, with light auburn hair pulled into two short pigtails. And with her rosy cheeks and ready smile, I determined her unthreatening. "Oh my gosh, I didn't mean that!" she gasped, eyes wide. "I was just kidding, I swear!"

"It's okay," Care said with a laugh, her posture finally beginning to relax. "I knew you were joking."

"You did? Okay good! Because I say stupid things a lot...and I babble a lot. But I'm never trying to be annoying or rude or anything, I'm just..." she sighed, looking embarrassed, "Clumsy."

Caroline's responding smile was bright and unburdened, her emotions clearing up a little for the first time this afternoon. "Don't worry about it, Torrie. You're honest, and I like honest people. No matter how 'clumsy' they are."

Torrie visibly relaxed, thanking Caroline profusely before stepping aside for the next person to introduce themselves. Next was Stefan, the groundskeeper. He was probably in his mid-twenties, with a strong jaw and thick hair styled in that purposefully messy way. Based on the way the housekeeper's eyes followed him, I gathered that women found him attractive.

Not sure that I liked that notion, I glanced at Care, trying to discern whether or not she found him attractive too. But after she greeted Stefan, she latched a hand onto my bicep and flashed her sassy green eyes at me.

"Don't worry, Bear Man," she whispered, "You're the only man I'm interested in. Please don't Berserk out here in my new house before I have a chance to sell off some of these expensive items."

I resisted a laugh, not wanting any of the Alfar to think that I was friendly. Better for them to be a little bit wary of me for the sake of Caroline's safety.

The housekeeper, a pretty brunette with blue eyes and a shy smile, was the last of the staff to introduce herself. After she stepped back, our eyes all turned to the four other people still standing behind the table.

While a few of them looked welcoming, there were others who set me on edge with the judging glint in their eyes.

"These are your advisors," Harold announced, motioning to the four remaining people. "There are five of us in total. We hold no authority over anyone, but simply provide our leader—you—with advice on our various departments. Mikael is our justice advisor. He works as a police captain in the city and helps us make decisions regarding rules and regulations."

Clint, Caroline and I all watched as a man in his sixties gave Care a brief nod, looking vaguely unimpressed. He was poised and a little cold, dressed in black. I made a mental note to watch out for him.

"Millicent is the treasury advisor," Harold went on, pointing to a woman who couldn't have been too much older than Caroline. She was pretty, with long blonde hair, although her smile was a little overzealous. "She works for the city planning office and helps us track our finances and make financial decisions."

The woman nodded; her attitude slightly superior. But at least she was trying to be friendly.

"Jude is our health and safety advisor," Harold said of a young Alfar in his mid-twenties, with a head of wavy black hair that went to his shoulders. He was a little pale, with angular features and an ever-present scowl. "He's a Shifter Alliance employee. And here he gives advice about the health and safety of our people."

Jude said nothing, didn't even bother to nod his head. Although I couldn't tell if his indifference was personal toward Caroline, or if he acted that way toward everyone.

Harold waved a hand toward the final Alfar, who was a young man about my age, with rust colored hair and a five o'clock shadow. And unlike the rest of the advisors, the smile he flashed at us seemed genuine.

"I'm Tristain," he said with a surprisingly deep voice, "I'm the diplomacy advisor. I work in the mayor's office, and I help the Alfar navigate relationships with other species. Sorry Harold," he added, smiling at Caroline's logistics advisor, "Didn't mean to steal your thunder."

"You did," Harold pouted.

Tristain smiled, entertained. "Ignore him. It's nice to meet you, Queen Caroline."

Care nodded and after a moment, all eyes turned to her, silent and expectant. Despite their intense attention, she stood there, shoulders back and chin level to the ground, appearing like the Elven queen she was.

But I knew her better than that. I felt her squeeze my arm tighter, sensed her lean further into my side. And I felt the anxiety and fear coursing through her. She was scared, but she was doing it anyway.

If we hadn't had an audience, I probably would have kissed her.

"It's likewise nice to meet you all," she said, managing a smile. "I'm Caroline—"

But she was cut off by a bang, quickly followed by shattering glass.

Shouts erupted, and I felt something whizz past my shoulder as I shoved Caroline to the ground, cradling her against me. Sometime during our descent, she'd wound her arms tightly around my waist, her head tucked against my neck.

"Are you okay?" I was aware that I was barking at her, but I was too panicked to care.

"Are *you*?" she screeched, releasing her hold on me only to run her hands across my body, checking me for injuries.

"Me? I don't care about me! Red, *are you hurt*?"

"No! I'm fine. Are you hurt?"

I shook my head, letting my knees hit the floor on either side of her. Then I took her face in my hands and pressed my lips to hers. It wasn't a gentle kiss. It was hard and desperate and grateful that the woman of my dreams was still breathing.

She kissed me back, both of us understanding the weight it could've been to lose each other. Though it was a fierce kiss, it wasn't long. Not meant to be the start of anything more, just a kind of thanks for surviving.

As we pulled away, I looked around the room at the chaotic scene. Clint, David and Jude were already headed outside to try and catch the shooter. Stefan and Tristain were trying to clean up the mess, and Torrie was consoling Charlie, the crying housekeeper.

But Harold was inspecting the bullet hole in the wall.

"Thank God they missed," he said, glancing at Care and me.

"They weren't aiming at me," Care argued, shaking her head. "I was on Morgan's other side. If they were shooting at me, then they were a really crappy shot because they were a full two feet off."

Confused, I looked down at my mate, who was still lying on the floor, propped up on her elbows. "Then who were they shooting at?"

"You."

Chapter 3

MORGAN

"Could we get our hands on some Kevlar?" Care asked, frantically pacing the length of my office.

She'd been doing that for nearly a half an hour, refusing to sit down or take a breath. It was strange, seeing her react like this. It was usually my job.

"Morgan should start wearing it at all times," she went on, not pausing long enough for anyone to comment.

Even Daisy Mae seemed anxious about her mom's behavior, the little brindle colored dog sitting on her dog bed, watching Caroline walk back and forth. Logan, Mike, Clint, Grey, and Ariel had all gathered in my office to discuss the attack from earlier. Of course, no one had actually been able to do any discussing with Caroline going on and on.

"We should probably hire a bodyguard too," she said, not bothering to notice that no one had yet been able to comment. "And I would suggest that we do bullet proof glass at the castle, but I'm not sure how possible that is with so many diamond-paned windows...Maybe Merida could spell them not to break?" She shook her head. "No, she wouldn't have enough strength to do that many windows. We could ask if her charges would be willing to help—I'd even pay all of them."

"Care," I pleaded, trying to catch her fingers as she made her way behind the couch where I sat. But she paid me no mind, continuing on her route, arms crossed and expression hard and threatening.

"I did some research on the bullet," Mike offered, trying to get Care's attention.

"And?" she turned wild eyes on him.

Everyone traded concerned looks, no one quite sure what to do. Caroline was usually the one calming *me* down. We'd never had to deal with a panicked, overprotective Caroline before.

"Care, why don't you sit down while we talk it out?" Ariel suggested, gesturing to the empty spot on the couch between her and I. But Caroline just shook her head and continued pacing.

"What'd you find, Mike?" she asked, a dog with a bone.

Mike sighed and shrugged at me, apologetic. I waved him off, it wasn't his fault Care was so on edge.

"Well, the bullet came from a pistol," he explained, "Likely a Smith & Wesson pistol—but since it's the most commonly owned gun in the U.S., I doubt we'll have any luck finding the specific gun that fired it."

Caroline ground her teeth, fuming as she strode across the floor. "Logan?"

Logan sat up in his chair, glancing over at Ariel for guidance. But Caroline's adoptive sister just shrugged helplessly, like even she didn't know what to do with her sister.

"Um," Logan babbled, "Well the castle only has cameras on the exterior doors, and none facing the surrounding woods. So, we didn't get any footage of the shooter. However, I've got a company coming tomorrow to install more cameras throughout the interior and exterior of the building."

Caroline nodded, but didn't even spare a glance at Logan, the wheels turning behind her eyes. "Ariel? Any luck with the Alfar?"

Ariel looked at Logan, and then the rest of us with a concerned expression. But no one had any solutions for how to calm Caroline, so we all silently shrugged.

"I talked to your staff," Ariel said with a sigh, watching her sister pace around the room, "And your advisors. No one saw anything before the gunshot. They were all looking at you and Morgan. Then, after the shot went off and people looked outside, the shooter was already gone. And according to Torrie, they've never had anyone attacked like that."

"Really?" Logan asked. "All these centuries of hiding and they've never dealt with attacks?"

"She said they have scares sometimes where someone gets close to figuring out that Elves still exist, and in decades past they've had to relocate, but they've never been hunted like this."

"This shooting wasn't about the Alfar," Care mumbled, biting her thumb nail as she walked across the room, her eyes focused on the floor.

"What makes you say that?" Grey asked, scribbling on his trusty clipboard. The thing was like an appendage, I was pretty sure his body would go into shock without it.

Care looked at me, her worry blazing through the mate bond. I hated seeing her so panicked, but she was too focused on the fear to be calmed down. I would know. It was usually me in her shoes.

"They shot at Morgan, not me. They weren't there to hunt Elves," she explained. "They were there for Morgan. We need to look into Mor's enemies. Not just people who don't like him, but anyone who actually wishes him harm." She tapped her lips, still too focused to bother looking at me. "Francine obviously wishes you didn't exist."

As she made her way around the room, I grabbed her wrist and pulled her around the couch, plopping her down beside me. She glared at me but didn't fight me off when I put my arm around her waist and pulled her close.

"You need to calm down before we can make a plan," I insisted, tucking her auburn hair behind her ear.

"*Calm down?*" she roared; eyes narrowed dangerously. "You want me to *calm down*? Morgan, someone shot at you! I can't calm down. You have no idea how terrified I am right now!"

I gave her a sympathetic smile and ran my fingers along her jaw. "Actually, I do," I gently corrected. "You see, normally it's you who's being attacked and me who's freaking out. So I know exactly how this feels, Red. I know how scared you are, how panicked. I know that you think if you can just control something, then you'll feel better, and I'll be safer. But I also know that you can't control things and that freaking out is only going to make you more stressed and more tired."

She furrowed her eyebrows, lips puckered in a pout. "You're not supposed to be right when you tell me to calm down. I'm supposed to yell at you for it."

"You can still yell if you want."

Care sighed, leaning further into my hold. "No, you're right. I need to chill. It's just…" she paused, her green eyes watching me with so much sadness and fear that it nearly broke my heart. "I almost lost you."

"I know."

"I don't know what I'd do without you."

"I know." I kissed her forehead.

"You can't die, Mor."

"I won't," I promised, her chin grasped in my fingers.

She nodded and I gave her a quick kiss, mindful that we had an audience, but more concerned with my mate's wellbeing than the opinions of anyone else in the room.

"Now as for my enemies," I said, getting us back on track now that her emotions were evening out again, "I know Francine hates me, but I'm not sure that she's the type to hire a hitman. If she wanted me dead, I think she'd be a lot less careful about it."

"What about the gambling dens?" Clint suggested, seated in an armchair. "They've hated you longer than anyone."

"Thanks for the reminder," I smiled, eyes narrowed at my baby brother.

He shrugged, unfazed.

"But haven't the gambling dens been framing you for their murders for years?" Ariel pointed out, pushing her glasses back up her nose.

I nodded. "They have. Which makes them very unlikely to be the ones trying to kill me now. If I'm dead, then they don't have a scapegoat anymore."

"What about my buyer?" Care asked, tilting her head back against the couch as she looked up at me. "They've been trying to get their hands on me for months. If they decided that you were too much of an obstacle for them, they might want you gone."

She wasn't wrong. If the person who'd been trying to get their hands on an Elf wanted one bad enough, they might kill me to make their path easier. But until we got more information or I was attacked again, we didn't really know enough to go on.

As everyone traded ideas and discussed the possibilities of who our shooter was, Care seemed to slip out of the conversation. She sat curled up beside me, but her eyes were focused somewhere else, her mind not keyed into our discussion anymore.

"Care?" I whispered, not sure how I felt about the plotting look in her eye.

She blinked up at me, a little wary. I felt my body go on defense, ready for bad news.

"There is someone who might have an idea about who's after you or why..." she said carefully.

I shook my head, knowing where this was going. "No, absolutely not."

There was no way I was going to let her anywhere near *him* again.

Chapter 4

CAROLINE

We stood outside the bedroom upstairs for four whole minutes, just staring at the door. Morgan said nothing, only growling to show his displeasure.

"We have to actually open the door—"

"I know," he said through a scowl.

"Mor, he's bound to the room. He can't leave, and no one's giving him a Minotaur artifact to break out with this time. Please stop worrying."

Morgan turned his pinched expression on me, unimpressed. "And if the tables were turned and I was about to meet with my attempted kidnapper, how would you feel if I told you to stop worrying?"

I sighed. He was right. I'd been in his shoes this morning when that bullet flew past his shoulder. I hadn't known at first that the shot had missed him. All I saw was a bullet bust through the window and aim itself at my mate. And then we were on the floor and my every thought was consumed with whether or not he was okay.

And even though he wasn't injured now, it didn't mean things would stay that way. Because now Morgan had an attacker out there hunting him. And I was finally understanding just how scared he'd been for me all these months.

"I'd be upset," I admitted, looking at the closed door, knowing that our prisoner was likely standing with his ear pressed against it right now. "But just remember that I'm here with you, so I'm not alone. And we already defeated him, so we know we could do it again. Plus, he's cursed not to hurt me. We'll be okay."

"Promise?" he asked, turning those imploring grey eyes on me.

"I promise."

He nodded and opened the bedroom door.

Sure enough, Volund stood on the other side, clearly eavesdropping. He was dressed all in black, as per usual. After I'd defeated him, we brought him back here. He wouldn't tell us where his people were, but we did find his things in one of the bedrooms of the house he'd been hiding in.

I seriously considered telling him that he could have one item of clothing for every truth he told us. But in the end, I gave him the clothes. Only a monster would hold clothes for ransom.

"Cousin," he greeted, his expression neutral. He still wore his chin length black hair perfectly styled. The dark scruff on his face was perfectly trimmed, and his outfit was perfectly in place. Our traitorous Ben Barnes lookalike was just as insufferable as ever.

"Volund," I responded, knowing it would annoy him for me to *not* acknowledge him as family or friend. "How's captivity treating you?"

"The service is snarky and a little slow. But the uniforms do wonders for my figure."

"How are you doing on your bougee shampoo?" I asked, arms crossed as I studied his hair, narrowing my eyes like I had found something wrong with it.

Volund stood straighter, brown eyes flashing between Morgan and me. "I'm getting low...why?"

"What would you say if I brought you a case of it?"

His face lit up, but his eyes remained skeptical. Volund may be our prisoner now, but the prince of the Nephilim wasn't stupid. He knew a bribe when he saw one. "What do you want?"

"Information. Morgan was attacked earlier today. What do you know about it?"

Volund pursed his lips and turned away, walking over to sit on his bed. With one leg crossed over the other with his ankle on his knee, he leaned back and studied us both with that neutral look on his face.

Ever since we'd captured him, he'd been playing this game. Pretending that he wasn't our enemy, but rather an ally. None of us were buying it.

"Cut the theatrics and answer the question, Volt," Morgan snapped, both his muscles and his emotions going tense.

"I thought nicknames were a rite of passage," the Dark Elf pointed out smugly. "Something you do for friends. Does that mean—"

"We still hate you," Morgan quickly interrupted, smiling.

"You've always said that," Volt pointed out.

Seeing that this was quickly going to turn into a battle of wills that we didn't have time for, I decided to step in. "Volund, do you have any idea who would attack Morgan or not?"

Volund sighed, looking like a little boy who'd had his toy stolen. I tried not to be too giddy about ruining his fun. The last thing I needed was to annoy him. Arrogant Volund was a pain, but annoyed Volund was insufferable.

"I don't have that information at my disposal. If you haven't noticed, I've been locked in my room," he complained, albeit much less petulantly than I'd expected.

"Listen here," Morgan started, stepping closer to the open doorway. But I put a hand on his chest to stop him, my eyes latched on Volund.

Power seeped through me, my magic responding quickly to my call. Without a word, I sent it toward Volund. But I didn't tug on his preexisting feelings, manipulating them until they were what I wanted them to be. That skill I'd used my whole life, but recently, I'd discovered that I could force whatever feeling I wanted on someone.

Though it wasn't without great cost.

"Tell us what you know," I demanded, feeling the magic drain my energy as I poured it toward Volund.

"I don't know anything," he insisted, resisting the pressure of my magic.

I ramped up my power, knowing it was stupid but too desperate to protect my mate to care. As magic left my body, it took my strength with it, making my body begin to quake. "You're hiding something," I hissed. "I can feel it. Now tell me what it is!"

Volund gritted his teeth as he stood, glaring me down. "There's nothing to tell."

Knowing it was stupid, I pushed the rest of my strength into the magic. The last time I'd done magic like this, it put me to sleep for three days. There was no telling what kind of damage it would do a second time. But I needed answers. I needed to know how to protect Morgan.

But I would never get them. Because Morgan slammed the bedroom door shut and swept me up into his arms, only putting me down once he'd moved us to my bedroom.

He was gentle as he set my feet on the ground, but that gentleness faded the moment he was assured that I was okay.

One might think that a Berserker in bear form was the most terrifying thing, but Morgan in his human form, staring down at me with such intensity was much more terrifying. He crowded my space, pressing me back against my bedroom door. Planting his hands on either side of my head, he caged me in, his burly forearms making for a lovely prison.

"Never," he rasped, the fury in his eyes shifting to reveal the fear underneath, "Do that again. Remember what we just said? That we both understand the panic of almost losing each other?"

"I'm sorry," I breathed, caught off guard by the tenderness in his voice. "I just thought—"

"I know. But we already knew that trying to control Volund's emotions was a dead end. Last time you tried it, you almost didn't survive. Please promise me you don't do it again."

I nodded, eager to do whatever I could to remove the fear on his face. "I promise."

Anything else I might have said was thrown far from my mind as Morgan's lips suddenly found mine.

He was gentle, coming and going. As if tasting me for the first time. There was no fire, nothing rushed or fierce like I expected from a moment like this. Instead, his lips cradled me, soothing, coaxing, comforting.

My fingers found the front of his shirt, and I tangled it in my grasp. His hands skimmed down my arms, passing my ribs before settling on my waist. His grip was strong, holding me in place against the door, but never squeezing too tight.

I let the door hold me up, my body turning to liquid as the kiss deepened. Still slow, still gentle, but with every move, I felt my soul crack open a little wider. It was Morgan's for the taking, and with the way he held me like I was precious, I knew he was mine.

"We'll keep each other safe, Care," he whispered, setting his forehead against mine. "But not at the risk of losing each other."

I nodded, struggling to find my words after a kiss like that. It took me a good twenty seconds to actually speak.

"Deal," I rasped, holding him tight. "No self-sacrificing. No stupid risks."

He nodded and kissed the top of my head, pressing me close against him, my head snuggled under his chin. "No stupid risks."

Chapter 5

CAROLINE

"I can't believe you live here," Ariel screeched as she waltzed into my new master bedroom, her blue eyes bright behind her glasses. "It's like a movie set!"

She wasn't wrong.

My room, like the rest of the house, was ridiculously fancy. The ceilings were at least fifteen feet tall and sponged with gold. A crystal chandelier hung above the large bed that was decorated with varying hues of blue. The tall windows were trimmed with stained wood and gold accents, letting in plenty of sunlight. Antique wallpaper lined the room, accented by various pieces of artwork and gilded mirrors. And a—probably very expensive—painting of a meadow hung above the upholstered headboard.

I intended to sell most of it and use the profits to help whichever areas the Alfar were suffering the most. And I needed to look into business licensing to see how it would work to rent out some of the unused bedrooms to small businesses or struggling families. After all, the place was mine to do whatever I wanted.

"Technically, I don't just live here now. I own it," I explained, taking a jacket from the suitcase I had sitting open on the giant bed. "The house belongs to a trust, and that trust gives ownership to the current heir. Which means that as queen, it belongs to me."

"Oh, does that mean that yours is the only permission I need in order to hold a Comicon here?"

I paused in my unpacking and glanced at her. An event where thousands of people paid to see writers and actors and artists involved in books and film wouldn't be a bad idea. It could be a great way to get my people some business, and a good way to get some positive PR. "If you sign a contract saying that you'll employ only Alfar vendors, then yes. But you'll have to wait until after we come out of hiding. Which might take a while."

Especially since I hadn't exactly told any of the Alfar about my plan yet.

"That's fine, I'll need time to work up the nerve to contact the Comicon people anyway," Ariel said, waving her hand as she sat on the bed.

"Why don't you just have Logan do it?"

"Because as much as I love his willingness to help me, I need to stop using him as a crutch."

I shot her a sisterly look, sensing her insecurity. "He's not a crutch, he's your partner. He's good with people, and people make you nervous. Why not let him use his strengths to shore up your weaknesses?"

Ariel narrowed her eyes at me. "Since when did you get so wise about relationships? Does owning a castle magically make you more queenly or something?"

Ignoring her jab, I pulled a metal tin from my suitcase and handed it to her. "No, this is how I got so wise with relationships."

She opened the tin and stared at it for a moment before pinning me with a sentimental expression. "Oh my gosh," she sighed, pulling out a few sticky notes. "This is freaking adorable. How long has he been doing this?"

I smiled at the tin full of sweet notes Morgan had been leaving me since I'd found out about the mate bond. Even after I told him I loved him and forgave him for keeping the bond a secret from me, he still kept leaving me the notes.

I picked up one from the many in the tin.

Reason #21 that I love you:
when you smile at me like you
have devious plans. I always
hope they're about kissing.
Usually they're about
conning me into eating junk
food.
     Which still usually entails
          Kissing ☺

"Ever since I found out about the mate bond," I said, scratching Daisy Mae's head as she jumped up on the bed and started sniffing the tin of sticky notes. "I was scared that the magic convinced him to love me, so he started leaving me these notes. In my room, on my snacks, every few days I still get another one from him."

"Oh, you two are nauseatingly in love." Ariel smirked, giving into Daisy's begging and scratching her back. My brindle-colored pup arched her back, her lips pulled back in pleasure.

"You're one to talk," I pointed out. "You and Logan are no better. I swear, if I catch you guys making out again in a public space, I'm going to start using a spray bottle on you."

"Pot meet kettle! You and Beast Boy kiss all the time."

"Yes, we *kiss*. As in one or two kisses, not a continuous make out complete with sucking sounds."

"We do *not* make sucking noises—"

"Who doesn't make sucking noises?" Ariel and I both turned to see Logan entering the room. Morgan had assigned him as my official bodyguard now that he and my sister were boyfriend and girlfriend instead of charge and bodyguard. All the boys had a room in my new home, but Logan was the one who would be here every single day that I was here.

"You two and your prepubescent make outs," I said, sending a snarky smile at my sister.

She glared at me, but when Logan's arms encircled her shoulders, pulling her back against his chest, a grin tipped her lips.

"Oh, we're definitely noisy," Logan scoffed, kissing the top of Ariel's head. "And we make out way too much in front of others. If I were other people, I would hate us. But I'm not, so I don't care."

He smirked and I rolled my eyes.

"Of course, when we go visit my mom, we'll have to tone it down a little," he added. "If she sees us being too affectionate, she'll be demanding grandkids."

"But," Ariel sputtered, her cheeks going pink, "We're not even married yet."

Logan leaned close to her ear and whispered loud enough for me to hear. "I'm sorry, all I heard was 'yet'. Glad to know we're on the same page, Sprite."

Touched and thankful that my sister was so happy, I turned my attention back to my unpacking to give them a little privacy. Now all I needed was to have Morgan here giving me similar attention, and all would be right with the world. Well, except for the attempts on his life, the missing Nephilim, and the fact that all Elves were still in hiding. But other than that, it would be perfect.

My thoughts were halted as my phone buzzed. Glancing at the screen, I picked it up off the gaudy nightstand.

Bear Man: We're not currently kissing and I'm not shirtless, so what are you so happy about?

Smiling, I typed out a reply.

Me: As if your lips and pecs are all that makes me happy in life.

His response came almost immediately.

Bear Man: That and Frank's food.

I laughed. He wasn't wrong.

Me: *GIF of Creed from *The Office* nodding and pointing his finger at the camera*

Me: My happiness could be pushed over into ecstatic territory if only I had a boyfriend who sent me a picture of said pecs *smirking emoji*

Bear Man: No.

Me: Do you want me to salivate over you or not?

Bear Man: I don't trust you with pictures of my half naked body.

Me: *GIF of Kevin from *The Office* saying 'I bet you like it'*

Me: *GIF of Dwight from *The Office* saying 'Do it now'*

I paused, sensing his entertainment even from two miles away courtesy of the mate bond. Ariel and Logan were still canoodling like teenagers when Mor finally texted me back.

Bear Man: *picture of Morgan holding up his shirt to reveal lovely pecs and a firm stomach*

I would know, I'd felt it.

I grinned at the photo and the scowl he was wearing. He might be doing it under duress, but he was doing it. And I warmed, knowing that he wouldn't be so quick to sway for anyone else. It felt good to know that I had that kind of power over him. Because he certainly had the same sway over me.

Me: *GIF of Kevin from *The Office* saying 'nice' creepily*

I smiled at the exasperation I felt in him and silently slipped out into the hall as I dialed his number.

"You're banned from using GIFs," he growled in lieu of a greeting when he picked up.

"You love it," I teased, meandering mindlessly around the wide empty hall. A gaudy chandelier hung above me, and ridiculously expensive paintings lined the walls. But even their offending presence couldn't steal my happiness. "I know you secretly sit around waiting for me to say or do something ridiculous so you can pretend to be annoyed. Meanwhile, inside you're a big ball of warm fuzzies, completely besotted with me."

He didn't even hesitate. "One hundred percent true."

I grinned, big and stupid, and headed toward one of three staircases in the mansion. Because every house needs multiple staircases. How else would they have gotten all the expensive furniture and useless décor up to the second floor?

"I miss you," I whispered, knowing that Charlie, the housekeeper, could be just around the corner. None of my staff seemed particularly untrustworthy so far, but I really didn't want to give any of them a reason to tease me by overhearing my sappy conversations with Morgan. "I was thinking of having the castle moved right next door to you. There's enough space if we take out a few trees."

"Brilliant idea. Totally worth the millions of dollars it would cost," he said seriously. "And while we're at it, why don't we build a connected balcony between our bedrooms for clandestine meetings?"

"Hu uh, Mr. Hohlt. My bed has its own TSA check point, and a wedding band is required to get through."

"I have TSA pre check," he teased, his whisper just as effective as if he'd been right there with his breath on my ear.

I stumbled as I reached a wide staircase, grasping the polished wood banister to keep myself from falling down the stairs. "You're not my husband," I squeaked.

It was pathetic how easily he got to me. Pathetic and incredibly hot.

"*Yet*. But I've got plans for you, Red."

"Yeah, what kind?"

It was playing with fire, teasing like this. But I'd always been a touch first, ask questions later kinda gal.

"Big ones," he said, his voice low and rough, for my ears only.

"Mm..." I hummed, trailing slowly down the stairs, biting my lip to keep the stupid grin from my face.

"Lifelong ones."

"Mm..."

"Overnight ones."

"Morgan!" I admonished, though my voice was a little too breathy and my neck a little too warm to bother pretending that I was actually mad. We were both committed to waiting to be intimate until we'd promised each other forever. Which was incredibly masochistic when I had the most gorgeous, grumbly beast of a man so madly in love with me, always at my fingertips.

And thoughts about bedrooms and overnights did *not* help the waiting process.

"What?" he growled.

I paused at the bottom of the stairs, staring hard at a landscape painting on the opposite wall to keep my mind from wandering where it shouldn't. "You can't torture me like that! *I'm* having a hard time behaving, and I'm a woman. It's gotta be even worse for you."

"It is." He sighed, loud and annoyed.

I shook my head and smiled. "Then I guess you'd either better hurry up and marry me, or keep your mouth shut."

"Is that a challenge, Red?" he asked, a grin in his voice.

"Absolutely it is."

This time, I didn't try to hold back the wide smile that split my face, letting it beam and proclaim my immense, ridiculous happiness.

"Queen Caroline?"

I screamed and jumped at the interrupting voice, turning to see Harold watching me from a few feet away. Three unknown women were standing behind him in the entry way. All watching me either with blushes and smirks or scandalized expressions. *Great. They heard everything.*

"Mor, I gotta go," I whispered into the phone, my cheeks hot with embarrassment. "I have an audience."

"Yeah? Who is it?"

"Harold, and I think the applicants for the position of my assistant?" I said louder, looking to Harold for confirmation. He nodded his head.

"Alright, go be a boss Elf Queen and I'll call you in a bit," Morgan said, affection warming the bond between us.

"Okay, I love you."

"I love you too. Oh, and Care?"

Sensing a bit of mischief from the scary Berserker Chief, I turned my back to Harold and the applicants. "Yeah?"

"If you have a chance between interviews, I need to know what kind of rings you like and what side of the bed you want. I usually sleep on the left side, but so do you. So, we might have to flip for the right side. Or we can just share the left. I am a big fan of spooning. But it's your call. Think about it and let me know."

Then, before I could scold him, he hung up.

"Little brat," I mumbled, shoving the phone in my pocket.

For someone with such a terrifying reputation, Morgan was quite the tease. Ever since he realized that he could make me blush and stutter and act generally stupid by saying or doing cheeky things, he'd been a menace.

A sexy, endearing, wonderful menace. *Dang me and my freaking sappy heart!*

"Queen Caroline?" Harold interrupted, and I turned to see him watching me with a straight face. Except for the evil twinkle in his eye. "If you and Chief Hohlt are done fornicating over the phone, the applicants are ready."

I narrowed my eyes at him while one of the girls coughed to cover a laugh. "You know I could fire you."

"You won't," Harold said with a shrug. "You need allies and so far, you deem me trustworthy. Plus, I think you prefer people who are a little ornery."

I laughed, unable to hide my approval. "I do. So, who's up first?"

Harold smiled and handed me the applications, stepping aside so I could fully see the three women. One was a bit older, with a severe expression matching her severe bun pulled tightly from her face. She watched me openly, her nose wrinkling like she could smell the rebellion on me.

The second woman was young, with wild hair pulled back into a stylish ponytail. She looked much more approachable, even with her slacks and ballet flats, but the way she kept nervously touching her hem made me hesitant. Nerves were fine, but I'd also need someone who could hold their own in dealing with the other Alfar.

My eyes drifted to the last girl, a tall brunette with hair the color of wet sand. It was straightened to perfection, and her pencil skirt and edgy black blouse were likewise without a single blemish. And unlike the other young girl, this one held my gaze with a determined look in her eyes.

"What's your name?" I asked, stepping closer to the trio. I wished I'd known they were coming today—I would've dressed a little more professionally. But my jeans and faded Dunder Mifflin crewneck sweatshirt would have to do. I'd definitely have to up my game though if my assistant was determined to be so polished every day.

"Lizzy," the young brunette answered, and if I wasn't mistaken, her eyes narrowed just a bit in a silent challenge, as if she had a chip on her shoulder.

I pursed my lips, flipping through her application thoughtfully. She had no previous work experience as an assistant, but her references were impeccable. And while applications matter, I was a woman who followed her intuition. And I had a gut feeling about Lizzy.

"Would you please come with me?" I said, nodding toward a connecting hallway.

Lizzy nodded and silently followed behind me as I led the way into my office. It was nothing like the office I had at Morgan's house—which I would always consider my real home. But it was beautiful. Even if it was a little too ostentatious for me.

The room was a little larger than my office at home, with big diamond paned windows stretching toward the high ceilings. A few walls held artwork, but two of them had floor to ceiling bookshelves, complete with a balcony running halfway up where another section of bookshelves was housed. The room had come furnished with a big black desk, ornate rugs and old, intricate couches and chairs. But most of it wouldn't be staying if I had anything to say about it.

"Please, have a seat," I said, gesturing to one of the chairs across from my ridiculously huge desk. Seriously, the thing was nearly the size of a twin bed.

Lizzy sat across from me, controlled and collected as she set her bag down by her feet. I studied her for a moment, trying to discern what it was that made me so interested. But when she squared her shoulders and tilted her chin down, brown eyes bright with fire, I knew. Lizzy had something to prove. And as a woman who'd only recently began deconstructing my own need to prove myself, I couldn't help but empathize.

"Why do you want this job?" I asked, leaning back in my chair.

The young Elf watched me for a moment before answering. "I guess the normal answer would be that I want it because I'd be good at it. I'm organized, highly motivated, observant, and I'll do what it takes to get the job done."

"And the non-normal answer?"

"I'm twenty," Lizzy replied almost resentfully. "I'm young and inexperienced, and I know it. I have a lot of life to live and a lot of things to figure out, but I do know that I want to help my people. Serve somehow and make a difference. It's cheesy, but I want to have an impact."

"So why not work your way up to being an advisor?" I asked, crossing my arms as I studied her. "You could've been an assistant for one of them before now."

Lizzy smiled ruefully, the expression making her already pretty features even more beautiful. "I could've tried, but no one would've hired me. I'm too young, too innocent—"

"Too pretty," I prompted, a sense of kinship lighting in my chest, "Too girly to be capable?"

She nodded, leaning forward in her chair. "I got this interview because I know Harold, but I want you to hire me because you really think I can do this job well."

"Can I trust you?"

"Yes, but I imagine you won't really believe that until I have the opportunity to prove it."

I considered her silently, knowing that some of my advisors would balk at hiring her. But honestly, that just made me want to do it all the more.

"You're hired." Grinning, I held out my hand to her and she shook it.

"Thank you, Queen Caroline," she replied with a bright smile and a humble look in her eyes. "You won't regret it."

"I know I won't," I said, looking around for the paperwork she needed to fill out.

"How? I haven't done anything yet."

I paused, meeting her eyes. "Yes, you have. You've shown me that you have better motivation than anyone else to do this job. You're not here for the money or the benefits or to have a potential influence on my rule. You're here to find your purpose and prove to everyone that you can do it."

Lizzy frowned as I opened one of the desk drawers. "And that makes you confident in hiring me?"

"Yes, because once upon a time, I was you. In some ways I still am. Still proving myself, still fighting to be respected, still figuring out what I'm meant for. There's no purer motivation than honestly wanting to serve a purpose."

My new assistant nodded thoughtfully, and I caught the glint of a sparkle in her eyes. "Well, I also want everyone who's ever told me I wasn't enough to eat their words."

I laughed and opened another drawer, still searching for the forms. "Lizzy, I think we're going to get along just fine—"

A gasp tore from my lips as something flew out of the drawer. I ducked backward, just barely avoiding being hit in the face as whatever it was sprung up and lodged itself in the ceiling.

"What on earth?" Lizzy demanded, both of us standing to get a better look at what was clearly a dart. "Queen Caroline, are you okay?"

"I'm fine," I sighed, looking back down at the drawer. A note lay inside.

"What is that?" Lizzy asked as I picked it up.

I silently showed it to her.

"You shouldn't be here," she read, lifting her wide brown eyes to me. "Do you have any idea who would have done this?"

I shook my head. "No, but I'm going to find out."

Chapter 6

MORGAN

"Morgan, I'm fine," Care called from her bedroom in the Alfar mansion. She was right of course. The dart that had shot out of her desk a few days ago hadn't nicked her at all. But she wasn't so lucky in my mind. I kept seeing her, hurt and lying on the floor. Imagining what would have happened if she hadn't moved back just in time to avoid the dart.

"We should cancel," I insisted, leaning against her doorframe to make sure she heard me. Harold, Lizzy, Mike, Clint, Logan and I were all in Caroline's adjoining sitting room, waiting for her and Ariel to be ready to go down to Caroline's official coronation. Technically, she was already queen of the Alfar. The ceremony was just a tradition, one that we were hoping would encourage the Elves to welcome her rule.

"I have a cancelation plan in place," Lizzy said matter-of-factly, an electronic tablet clutched in her hands. "Just give me the word and I'll take care of everything."

"We can't cancel," Harold argued, sitting on the couch. He, like the rest of us guys, was wearing a fancy suit for the occasion. "There are two hundred people downstairs waiting to officially welcome their queen."

I straightened from the door and glared at him. He might be one of Caroline's advisors, but I was her mate. And if there was anyone I was willing to use my scary Berserker Chief status for, it was Care. "And my mate was attacked with a poisoned dart five days ago. If we decide that her safety is in jeopardy, we're canceling."

I was pleased when Harold sat a little further back in his seat, looking wary. *That's right, Harold. I'm in charge around here.* Well, technically I was second in command behind Caroline. But the point was the same.

"We're not cancelling," came Care's voice from behind me. "I need to make a good impression on my people. And besides, the poison in the dart wasn't even lethal."

"As if that's supposed to make me feel better—" All words fled from my mind as I turned and saw Caroline standing in the doorway.

I'd never understood why women spent so much money on fancy dresses they would only wear one time. But as I stood there staring at my mate, I suddenly understood.

Care was wearing a deep red dress that fit snugly around her waist before flaring out to the floor. Thick straps sat below her shoulders, wrapping around to crisscross in the front, creating a sweetheart neckline.

She fidgeted as I stared, and the skirt of her dress shifted to reveal a slit that showed her right leg. My already racing heart began to pound like a war drum at the sight, and my hands shook. *Easy, boy. Ring, vows, then ravage.* But that order was hard to follow with my pea sized cave man brain in control.

Shaking my head, I drew my eyes up to her face and felt an ache form in my chest. She was beautiful, with her auburn hair swept up into a fancy updo. A few loose tendrils of hair trailed along her neck and temples, curled to a perfect wave. I had the sudden urge to make a game out of kissing every spot where her hair touched her skin.

A flush stained her cheeks as my gaze roved over her, and between her slightly darker than normal eye makeup, the bold shade of color on her lips, and the elegant swoop of her hair across her forehead, I was smitten. Then, when her green eyes flashed at me with want, I was completely breathless.

"Should we leave you two alone?" Clint teased, and I didn't have to look to know he was smirking.

"Yes," Care and I both said in unison.

"No time for funny business. We have a coronation to get to," Grey argued, looking down at his ever-present clipboard.

"Yes, listen to your Second," Harold nodded, standing from the couch. "Besides, we have five Berserkers, a Witch and a Wyvern all watching for danger tonight. Everything will be fine."

"He's right," Mike said, walking toward the door to the hallway, checking the gun on his hip. "Merida and Asher are posing as guests, so no one will suspect that they're on duty. And we're all more than capable of dealing with an attacker."

Normally, we didn't carry weapons—having super strength and the ability to shift into bears kind of made it unnecessary. But it was too likely that one of Care's own people had planted the dart that she found in her desk. So, we were taking more serious measures. And since he'd begun training for Mayor Fitz's Task Force a few weeks ago, and part of the training required him to be armed at all times while on the job, Mike was the most comfortable with it.

"Yeah, the key tonight is to find out *who's* attacking," Clint agreed. "And with this many eyes watching, it shouldn't be too much of a challenge."

While I agreed that catching the attacker was important, nothing trumped Care's safety. Stepping toward Caroline, I slid my arm around her waist and tucked her close to my side. "We're trying to catch the attacker, but it *will not* be at the expense of Caroline. Her safety comes first. At the slightest sign of danger, we're getting her out of there. I don't care how close you are to identifying the attacker, if she's in danger, she's the priority. Understood?"

No one argued, silently nodding. I knew it was unnecessary for me to be so gruff with them. They all cared about Caroline. But I'd almost lost her too many times to play nice.

"You're not going to fight with me about it?" I whispered, looking down at Care as everyone began to file out into the hall.

She set her hand on my chest, smoothing out the lapel of my suit jacket, looking completely serene. "Nope."

"Who are you and what have you done with my girlfriend?"

She rolled her eyes, but her expression remained gentle. "You forget that not too long ago, you were the one on the floor of the Shifter Alliance Building, blacking out and in pain. I know what it's like to worry that I'm about to lose you. So, if me being extra careful and everyone being armed gives you peace, then I'm okay with it. Your peace is worth a little sacrifice."

Touched by her thoughtfulness, I leaned down and kissed her. She immediately leaned in, giving me full control and I resisted the desire to pull her closer and pull the pins from her hair. We had an audience waiting for her arrival, and while smudged lipstick and messy hair might be on my list of things to do, the crowd probably wouldn't appreciate it.

Using an impressive amount of restraint, I squeezed her hip and gave her one last slow kiss before pulling away.

"Tease," she complained, a little breathless.

When her eyes fluttered open, a little unfocused, my chest swelled with manly pride. "I've got to keep you interested."

She smirked. "Mission accomplished."

Everyone but Logan was already gone by the time we made it out to the hall. He dropped back just behind Caroline's shoulder as we all made our way to the stairs that Caroline would descend in front of the gathered Alfar. He was Caroline's new bodyguard, and he was now officially on duty. And just as soon as we could find enough trustworthy people, I intended to hire her an entire security team.

"This is as far as I go," I said, coming to a reluctant stop at the top of the stairs, the crowd just out of sight below us.

Care nodded; eyes fixed on the first floor where a constant hum of impatient conversation made its way up to us.

"Hey," I whispered, sliding my palms along her cheeks, "You're going to be fine."

"I might trip," she argued, her voice soft and timid in her anxiety. "I'm a sneakers girl, I never walk in heels like these. I'm going to fall flat on my face in front of two hundred people."

"You're not going to trip. And if you do, it's okay, because you're part Nephilim. You'll right yourself too quickly for anyone to notice."

She nodded; my suit jacket fisted in her hands. I doubted she even realized she was holding me so tight, her eyes glazed over with panic.

"Red, look at me," I pleaded, and she lifted her eyes to mine. "You're a vigilante. You're an Elf queen. You're the mate of the scariest Chief in the U.S. You are Caroline Felicity Birch, the most capable, compassionate, clever person I know. I know you're scared, and that's okay, but you *can* do this."

She shook her head, eyes wide. "I don't think I can, Mor. I'm used to working alone—I barely know how to work with other people. And I certainly don't know how to lead an entire species!"

"You don't have to know how. All you have to do right now is go down those stairs, repeat the vows Harold says to you, and wear the crown. That's it."

"And then you'll hold my hand and not leave me all evening?"

I chuckled. While I loved that she wanted to lean on me, I knew she didn't need it. Even if she didn't see that yet.

"I promise I won't leave you. Let's just get through the actual coronation part, okay?"

"Okay..." She took a deep breath, smoothing out the wrinkles she'd made in my suit, and stood a little taller. "Wait, did you just do to me what Pam did to Michael in *The Office* when he started the Michael Scott Paper Company?"

"One hundred percent. Making a list of the easiest tasks is a great way to stop someone from freaking out. Now go kick butt and I'll see you at the bottom of the stairs." Then I kissed her forehead and scurried down the stairs like a coward.

If it weren't for the crowd that was gathered, everyone shifting a step back as I joined them, I knew Caroline would have chased after me. But she was a queen now, and queens didn't chase their boyfriends down the stairs. At least, not in front of their new subjects who potentially wanted to do her harm.

I caught Lizzy's eye over the throng of people and gave her the signal. She nodded and tapped her tablet. Music began playing, and a moment later, the hem of Caroline's dress could be seen on the steps.

She came gliding down the stairs, holding the wooden banister with one hand, her fingers relaxed despite the anxiety I felt rolling around inside her. With her shoulders back, chin down and her steps slow and measured, my mate looked every bit the queen she was.

And when her eyes caught mine and stayed, anchoring me to the spot, I felt a flame spark to life in my chest. She was scared, but confidence radiated from her anyway, and I saw everyone in the room study her with awe. *As they should.*

As she'd practiced this morning, Caroline stopped on the third to last step, and Harold walked up to meet her, a crown clasped in his hands. It was beautiful, layered with swooping silver designs layered with white, glistening in the light of the small ballroom. When Care had tried it on yesterday, it looked a little silly paired with her ratty old T shirt.

But now there was nothing silly about it.

She dutifully repeated the vows Harold spoke and ducked her head for him to set the crown against her hair. She looked appropriately regal, the silver and white contrasting with the warmth in her auburn hair. Then she turned and faced the crowd, her head held high, and repeated the final words.

"To you, I swear my fealty," she said, her voice projecting easily across the mute audience who stood watching their new queen ascend the metaphorical throne. If there had been an actual throne, Caroline would have already donated it to some public-school drama program or something. "I swear my every protection, my strength, my life, and my service."

Care swept her eyes across the room as a pregnant pause filled the space. And just when her stress seemed to spike, she looked at me and winked and an 'I'm stupid and in love' smirk tilted her lips.

"Alfar," Harold announced, though I was too busy looking at Caroline to pay him much attention, "I present to you, your new leader, Queen Caroline."

A heartbeat of silence passed before applause erupted around the room. Who'd started the clapping, I didn't know. Didn't care. All that mattered was that Caroline got to have this moment where she got to see—and hopefully believe—what I saw. A true queen.

***

"Honey, I understand feeling jealous—believe me, I do—but I don't think threatening your people is the first impression you want to give them," I warned quietly as Caroline sent a sugary smile to a young Alfar woman.

Now that the coronation was complete, people were mingling throughout the small ballroom, dancing and eating food. Most of the guests introduced themselves to us, curious to lay eyes on their queen and her scary mate.

But some were more than just curious.

The woman standing in front of us now with her friend was admittedly a little too interested, her eyes never leaving me. But this one unwanted admirer was nothing compared to the men who'd actually *touched* Caroline. It was one thing to shake her hand, but some men had even kissed her knuckles or touched her arm like they actually had a right to. Luckily, they were always quick to step back with one glare or growl from me.

Care, on the other hand, had just gone straight in and verbally threatened my lurker.

"Nice to meet you ladies," I said louder, smiling apologetically to the two young women as I silently motioned them along.

The friend of my admirer watched Caroline, wide eyed and uncomfortable. But the other woman just smirked and gave Care some kind of strange nod that I was pretty sure I didn't have enough estrogen in my body to understand.

"What was that?" I asked once they were gone. "You literally told her that for every part of my body her eyes touched, she would get bruises in the same place.

Then suddenly you two are giving each other a weird nod and smiling like you're friends."

Care shrugged; her hand tucked into the crook of my arm. "She wanted what's mine, but now she respects my subtle claim on you. I like her. I think we could be friends."

I stared at her, unsure if I should be worried or weirdly turned on by her need to claim me. "You don't actually think that was subtle, do you?"

"Did I throw furniture or rip out her pretty blonde highlights?"

I thought back to Care and I's first interaction. Zip ties, thrown chairs, name calling. *Yeah, this reaction was pretty tame.* "Fair point."

Care smiled and glanced around the room. The party had been going for over two hours now and there were no signs of it slowing down anytime soon. We'd already spoken to almost everyone in the ballroom. And even though Lizzy had sent out an email earlier in the week to all the Alfar, introducing Caroline and announcing the coronation, nearly every guest had plenty of questions for Care and me both.

'What strengths do you feel you bring to the role of queen?'

'Chief Hohlt, how will you help Queen Caroline in her position?'

'Is it wise to be dating a man whose reputation is second only to Richard III?'

Honestly, that one was a little theatrical for me.

But my personal favorite was, 'are you two monogamous, or is it a more open relationship?' I almost throttled the man who said it. With any luck, we were done with triggering questions for the evening.

"Incoming," Logan whispered from his dutiful position behind Caroline. "It's that advisor. The red headed one."

"Tristain?" Care perked up, lifting her chin to look over the crowd.

"A little excited, aren't you?" I taunted, only feeling mildly territorial as the young advisor made his way over to us. He certainly seemed like the nicest of Care's advisors other than Harold, and there weren't any piggish qualities in the way he looked at Caroline as he approached.

But masculine etiquette still demanded that I remind him who had Caroline's heart. So, I dropped my arm and snaked it around Care's waist, pulling her flush against my side. But instead of rolling her eyes or shaking her head like I expected, Care just curled closer.

"What, you're not going to get on my case for being too territorial?" I whispered as the young advisor approached.

Care smirked at me. "Why would I? I like it when you get territorial." Then, before I could forget that we had company, she turned a cheery smile on the newcomer. "Tristain, it's good to see you again."

"Queen Caroline, it's nice to see you," Tristain replied with a friendly smile. "You look stunning tonight." Care thanked him and he turned to me. "I'd compliment your appearance too, but something tells me you wouldn't appreciate it as much."

"Good to see you, Tristain," I said, surprised to find that I actually meant it as I shook his hand. "Enjoying the party?"

The young Alfar glanced around the room, pursing his lips as if unimpressed. "Eh. It was incredible to see the coronation. But I'm not much of a mingler, so the actual party part of the evening isn't my favorite. I can be chatty, but small talk grates on me after about twenty minutes."

"Ah, something you two have in common," Care teased, patting my stomach.

Tristain chuckled good-naturedly and raked a hand through his slightly messy hair. "There are worse things than despising small talk."

"True," Care replied with a nod. "I'll have to do my best to keep the chit chat short during meetings with the other advisors so you won't suffer too much."

"I knew I was going to enjoy your reign," Tristain said with a smile. "Although this is definitely an added bonus."

Tristain hadn't given me a particular reason to doubt his kindness. In fact, he seemed genuinely interested in talking to us. But I couldn't stop myself from prodding him just a little to see where his loyalties truly laid.

"What exactly made you think you would enjoy having Caroline as queen?" I asked. And although I kept my tone conversational, Tristain's eyes narrowed and he pulled his shoulders back, clearly understanding the point behind the question.

"Honestly, I'm excited for all the reasons some other people are terrified," he replied evenly. "Because in the short time you've been here, Queen Caroline, you've already proven that you're inherently honest. Your candidness and authenticity scare some people—and rightfully so." He smiled ruefully. "So, I'm excited to see how your approach to leadership affects both us advisors and the Alfar as a whole. Hopefully it brings out some honesty in all of us."

Care pursed her lips thoughtfully, and I felt her pleasure and curiosity. Tristain's words were good, but it would take time to see if he lived up to them. "Thank you for saying that," Care said. "I'm curious though who you think is so scared of honesty."

"As far as I'm aware, none of your advisors are up to anything nefarious or illegal," he said, a look of understanding in his eyes. "But we've been operating without much oversight in the last twenty plus years. So, some advisors are going to struggle with having someone to report to again."

Caroline and I shared a look. That didn't sound good, but we'd known that not everyone would be receptive to Care's rule. This wasn't exactly a surprise.

I gave Care's hip a gentle squeeze, but instead of responding in kind, her brows drew down in confusion.

"Red? You okay?" I asked, but when she opened her mouth to respond, nothing came out.

Her eyes widened and she looked as though she was gasping, but she made no sound. When she started to clutch her throat, shaking her head, I waved Merida over.

"Is it that you can't speak or can't breathe?" I demanded, her panic matching my own as it swelled in my chest.

Care shook her head and mouthed 'breathe'. Needing no other explanation, I swept her up into my arms and made a beeline for the door. "Make up an excuse," I heard Logan say to Clint as we passed him. But I was too busy worrying over my mate—who wasn't breathing—to pay them much attention.

Once Logan, Merida and I were in the hall, I set Care's feet on the ground.

"What happened?" Merida asked. Her hands were already drawing invisible spells in the air like she was conducting an orchestra. As the magic took effect, her eyes became a bright gold, her black hair turned to a pearly white, and an unearthly glow seemed to emanate from her skin.

"She can't breathe," I snapped, angry that for all my super strength, there was nothing I could do to help in a moment like this.

But Merida wasn't fazed. She continued drawing spells until suddenly Caroline started coughing. A shimmering pink powder worked its way out of her mouth, drawn by Merida's magic into the air.

"Pixie poison," Logan spat, swearing under his breath, eyes scanning the area like the danger was still imminent. And although there was no one currently in the hall with us, I was grateful he was taking his bodyguarding duties so seriously.

"We need to get you to the hospital," I growled, moving to pick Care up.

But she stopped me with a hand on my chest. "No, I'm okay." Unconvinced, I glared at her. "Really, Mor. I'm okay. I'm not in any pain and Merida got the poison out."

"I also don't sense any lingering damage," Merida said, backing up Caroline's claims as she finally ceased her magic and lowered her hands.

"No one asked you," I growled. Caroline gave me a reproachful look, but I wasn't done freaking out yet. I was getting really sick of people trying to assassinate my girlfriend. "Logan, we need to start interviewing guests. The poison had to get into Care somehow. Merida, inspect the food and drinks, please—"

"Subtly," Care interrupted, looking at Merida. "Can you inspect the food from a distance, so no one sees you using magic?" Merida nodded, poured the Pixie powder into her pocket, and slipped back into the ballroom.

"Red—" I began, but she stopped me with those pleading green eyes.

"We need to go back in there," she insisted. I hated how easily moved I was.

"Someone just tried to poison you!"

"Yes, and believe me, I'm pissed about it. But whoever did it needs to see that I'm not ruffled by it. That I'm not so easily cowed. I won't let them think this method of intimidation is going to work, otherwise they'll just keep doing it."

I bit my lip, wishing I didn't admire her decision. "Please don't ask me to be reasonable about this," I begged quietly.

"You don't have to be reasonable," she said, slipping her hand into mine. "You can keep worrying, just trust me enough to go with my plan while you're at it."

I sighed, loud and petulant. "Fine, but we're officially in protective mode. Logan," I said, turning to my best friend, "Tell Asher to take up position beside you guarding Care. I want him close enough to sense if she's in danger. Then tell Mike and Clint to split up and watch the entrances. I don't want any guests planting other traps anywhere in the house."

"Got it," he nodded, already typing away on his phone.

"You good?" Care asked, gently squeezing my hand.

I took a deep breath. "You're an Elf Queen who shouldn't exist, and you're dating the scary Berserker Chief with a very long list of enemies. No, I will probably never be good again."

Chapter 7

CAROLINE

Is there anything sexier than an attractive man carrying a pizza? Because the sight of Morgan bringing in my DoorDash order of Little Ceasar's was *definitely* doing it for me.

"You've never been hotter," I teased as he closed my bedroom door behind him.

We were staying at the Alfar house for the night—much to his chagrin—and even though I wasn't injured from my earlier poisoning, he'd insisted on staying with me.

"You know you can't eat this until I taste test it, right?" he said, standing beside my bed, holding the pizza just out of reach. He'd forgone his suit a while ago and was now dressed in a T shirt and sweatpants. I'd likewise changed out of my dress and into pajamas the moment the guests were gone. While I loved my coronation dress, there is nothing better than taking off your fancy clothes at the end of the night.

"And you know you're going overboard on the whole protective boyfriend thing, right?" I teased, rising onto my knees and slipping my arms around his neck.

He hummed, his free arm winding around my waist as he pressed his lips to mine.

I should have been used to his kisses by now. Newbie to the kissing game or not, my body should be getting bored now that the experience wasn't new. But no matter how many times he kissed me, I still felt it all the way down to my toes.

His hand was warm on my back and his stubble was rough against my chin. But the beard burn was *always* worth it. When his arm tightened around me, a growl rumbling in his throat and his lips working mine into a deeper kiss, I took my shot and snatched the pizza box from his hand.

"Ha!" I exclaimed, crawling quickly to the other side of the bed before he could catch me.

"Caroline!"

"Don't 'Caroline' me," I argued, taking a slice of cheese pizza from the box. "We both know that you don't need to taste test anything. Merida gave me an anti-potion to use. One drop and any poison on this pizza will be useless."

Taking the corked bottle from my nightstand, I poured one drop onto the pizza and then took a hearty bite. A few moments passed as I waited. Morgan just stood there, arms crossed and fuming, but nothing happened.

"See?" I smiled. "I'm totally fine."

Mor's only response was a grunt.

"Come on Bear Man," I pleaded, setting the pizza aside and crawling back over to him. Once on my knees and almost at eye level with him, I ran my hands across his chest. "I'm sorry I tricked you."

"No, you're not," he pouted.

I flashed my eyes up at him, knowing—sensing—that he was wavering. "I'm sorry that I wasted the opportunity to make out with you in order to do it."

"Serves you right."

"Maybe, but I don't think you should let me off so easily."

"No, I shouldn't." But he didn't stop me when I tipped myself against him and grasped his shoulders.

"In fact, I think you should teach me a lesson," I whispered, smirking at him. "If you don't, I'll never learn."

He shook his head, but he couldn't stop the smile from spreading across his handsome face. "I love you too freaking much."

I opened my mouth to reply, but he cut me off. Never had I been so happy to be interrupted.

This kiss wasn't quite as slow to ramp up as the last one. I could tell by the way that Mor's hands fisted in my sweatshirt that he was trying to make me think he was annoyed. But I knew better.

The gentle way his lips stroked mine in a constant rhythm and the way he brought one hand up to tenderly tilt my face to the side gave him away. But I also felt his joy, his euphoria and his relief.

But once that relief and pleasure started to burn hotter with less and less control, I pulled back and hid my face in the crook of his neck. We were both usually pretty careful not to get carried away. But making out on my bed wasn't going to help matters.

"I hate that your people don't all love you," he whispered, a tremble of frustration in his voice as his arms held me tight to his chest. "I hate that anyone would ever consider hurting you. But especially your own people. Don't they know how lucky they are to have you? How much you're giving up to lead them? How good of a queen they have in you?"

"I think some of them just see a complication when they see me," I replied, breathing in the scent of him as I nuzzled closer. "My sudden appearance means that they'll have a lot less freedom."

Morgan scoffed. "People only fear leadership when they're afraid of getting in trouble. And since you haven't changed any laws, the only rules they would be breaking are their own."

I didn't disagree, but I also knew that he didn't need any fuel for his fire. He was plenty lit up about it without me agreeing with him.

"Sit," I insisted, tugging him down beside me on the bed.

Crisscrossing my legs, I grabbed the pizza box and offered him a slice. He was so caught up in his soap box moment that he didn't even comment about the unhealthy effects of gluten on the body or how many chemicals were in the cheap processed cheese.

"I get that change is hard," he went on as I grabbed my remote and pulled up *The Office* on the TV on the opposite wall. "And I understand that they might feel unsure about not knowing what their new leader's plans are yet. But to actually *poison* you?"

"Calling it a poison is a little extreme," I argued with a mouthful of pizza. "Merida said the liquid in the dart was only meant to make me hallucinate. And it was a low dosage, so it wouldn't have done much to me. And the Pixie powder that made me unable to breathe was also a small dosage and would have faded on its own within two minutes."

I felt more than saw Morgan glare at me.

"Someone planted a dart to drug you instead of kill you, and somehow that's supposed to make me feel better?" he demanded, deadpan.

I leaned over and kissed his cheek. "Yes, because it means that whoever we're dealing with isn't trying to kill me. They're trying to scare me. And while I would *love* to have my people be excited about having me as queen, I can't blame them for being wary. I have to prove myself to them, Morgan."

"No. No more proving yourself to anyone." His expression was so earnest and concerned. It made my heart swell.

Feeling sentimental, I grasped his chin and tugged him closer. He met me halfway, kissing me sweetly. "I love you for that," I whispered, whipping a bit of pizza sauce from his cheek with my thumb.

"And I love you. I've already seen you expend so much of yourself trying to prove things," he said, his hand on my knee. "I hate watching you smother yourself or hide yourself in order to prove points to people whose opinions don't matter."

"I know. And I promise I won't go there again. But the Alfar have a right to be worried. They don't know me yet; they don't know what kind of queen I'll be.

So, while you're right—I don't need to *prove* anything—I do need to give them a chance to see what kind of leader I am."

"Maybe...but they're hardly giving you a chance."

"Since when do I need anyone to give me an opportunity to be myself? I make my own opportunities." I kissed his nose and went back to eating my pizza. "And before you go freaking out about my safety, might I remind you that someone tried to shoot you the other day."

"True. We're really going to have to do something about that. Especially since the shooter tracked me here."

"Yes, but that is a tomorrow problem. Tonight, you're going to cuddle your girlfriend and watch *The Office*."

"Oh, I am, huh?"

I nodded, turning my eyes back to the screen. It was one of my favorite episodes. Michael Scott was finally proposing to Holly. It was one of those proposals that goes completely askew, but in the most charming, romantic way possible.

And as I watched Michael kneel in front of the love of his life and ask her to marry him—using his own version of the Yoda voice from *Star Wars*—I found myself tearing up.

"How many times have you watched this?" Mor asked, his smile sweet and gentle as he looked at me.

"Dozens." I sniffed, sweeping a few renegade tears from beneath my eyes.

"And you still cry?"

"It's just so sweet, you know? Someone being *that* in love with you. Wanting to spend the rest of their life with you. Making a fool of themselves because nothing is too crazy or too humiliating if they get you in the process."

Morgan's gaze softened and he reached out to swipe a lone tear from my cheek. "And what if I proposed to you and it went that sideways like that? Would you mind?"

Smiling, I shoved the pizza box aside and wrapped my arms around him. Mor followed my lead, leaning back against the pillows and pulling me close. I snuggled my head on his shoulder and tangled my legs with his. His hum of contentment as his hand latched around my waist sent a feeling of warmth all through my body.

"So long as I get you, I don't care how it happens," I whispered, closing my eyes.

"You don't even care whether or not you get fed at some point during the proposal?" His tone was light and teasing, a smile in his voice.

"As long as you feed me within an hour, I'll be fine. I mean, I get you out of the deal. What more could I want?"

He kissed my forehead. "Duly noted."

Morgan's breaths and the beat of his heart beneath my ear were the last things I remembered before I fell into the most peaceful sleep of my life.

Chapter 8

CAROLINE

"This is the last of it," Torrie said, setting a *fifth* plate of snacks on the giant table in the dining room of the Alfar house.

"You really didn't have to do all this, Torrie." I smiled gratefully as she nudged a plate of brownies my way.

"Yes, I did. You've had enough drama since you got here," Torrie insisted, standing there in a dirty floral apron, a pink bandana holding back her short red hair. "The least I can do is cook up some snacks for you and your friends."

The entire gang was at the Alfar house today to go over our plan of attack. Morgan sat across from me—Asher insisted that we not sit next to each other, or we'd just kiss the whole time. He wasn't wrong.

Lizzy sat beside me, tablet at the ready, and Grey was next to Morgan. Mike, Clint, Asher, Merida, Logan and Ariel were also seated around the table, already digging into our smorgasbord of food.

"And the friends greatly appreciate it," Clint smiled, stacking a handful of pigs in a blanket on a small salad plate until they were close to falling over.

Mike slapped his baby brother's hand. "Dude, seriously? Pace yourself."

Clint started to shove Mike's arm, but paused, his eyes flying to Lizzy.

Both brothers had been completely enamored with my new assistant since the moment they laid eyes on her. While Clint was about as subtle as a gun, always staring and making stupid comments, Mike was the definition of shy. He only ever looked her way when she was otherwise engaged, and he rarely ever spoke to her unless it was absolutely necessary.

I glanced down as my phone buzzed, seeing a group text from Ariel.

Ariel: Alright sis, what's the deal here? Which brother should I be betting on?

I glanced up at her and saw Logan glaring at her. His text came in a moment later.

Logan: *GIF of Naill Horan shaking his finger* No cheating! Everyone has to bet without hints!

Grey: Hints are unnecessary if you just pay enough attention.

Ariel: Alright stone face. What's your bet then?

I looked over at Grey and found him smirking.

Grey: I bet $15 that she picks Mike.

Me: What makes you guess that she'll pick Mike?

Grey: She takes more notice of Clint, but based on the judging look in her eye, I don't think she's impressed.

I shrugged. He wasn't wrong. The first time Clint saw Lizzy, he knocked over a *very* expensive vase and blurted 'holy hotness'. She wasn't entertained.

Mike, on the other hand, had turned bright red and suddenly became fascinated with the floor. While he had yet to actually make a direct comment to Lizzy that wasn't work related, at least he wasn't overtly hitting on her.

Bear Man: Yeah, but you're assuming that Mike will make a move. I've seen ice bergs move faster than my brother.

Ariel: $5 says he decides to man up and go after the girl!

Logan: I'll take that bet!

Me: I'm gonna say five bucks that he makes a move, and an extra five if she says yes.

Bear Man: $10 that Clint asks her first.

Logan: Deal.

Even with my ability to sense emotions, I was still betting somewhat blindly. Yes, Lizzy was attracted to both Mike and Clint. And yes, both boys were interested in her. But while she often seemed annoyed with Clint, Mike stayed so far in the background that she didn't notice him very much. So really, it was anyone's guess which man—if either—she was interested in.

"Someone should start talking," Asher the Wyvern King said, making a formidable figure with his dark shaggy hair and nearly black eyes. "I think Merida is about to stab Tweedledee and Tweedledum over here." He nodded at Mike and Clint, who were quietly arguing over the food.

"Yes, your man children are making me feel particularly stabby," Merida sighed, shadows under her eyes. It wasn't until recently that we discovered the reason our Witch friend always seemed so stressed and exhausted was largely because while Witches had the right to live at the house they belonged to, they could also just send their kids to live there. And since Merida was Headmaster of Winters House, she was responsible for the handful of young Witches who lived there.

"Do you want us to watch the kids sometime this week?" Ariel offered, her blue eyes shining with empathy from behind her glasses. Over the last few months, we had Mike, Clint and Logan go over to Merida's to watch the kids a couple times. And the kids had helped Merida rescue Logan and Ariel when Volund had his people abduct them. So, we all felt a fondness for the young Witches.

"No, you don't have to do that." But even as Merida said the words, a yawn roared out of her mouth.

"Oh, stop being stubborn and take them up on it," Asher sighed.

"You're one to talk, lizard boy," Merida snapped.

Asher abandoned his usual enigmatic look and narrowed his eyes. "Really? Lizard boy?"

Merida shrugged. "What do you want from me? I'm tired."

"Fair enough," Asher conceded, then he turned to Morgan and me. "So, what's on the agenda for this meeting?"

Morgan, who'd been more invested in having this meeting than I had, was quick to respond. "We need to deal with whoever is coming after Caroline. So far, nothing they've done has been lethal, but I'm not willing to bet that it stays that way."

"And we also need to figure out what to do about whoever shot at Morgan," I pointed out, glaring at my boyfriend. He could pretend all he wanted, but I was not the only one dodging attempts on my life these days.

"Someone shot at you?" Merida demanded; her blue eyes wide. "Where? When?"

"About two weeks ago." I sent Morgan a smug look, and he glared at me. "It was the day Harold brought us here. Actually, the bullet came through that window back behind Clint."

Everyone turned instinctively to look at the diamond paned window that had already been replaced. There was no evidence of the shooting left in the room, even the hole in the wall had been patched.

"Did you see the shooter?" Asher asked, leaning forward and resting his elbows on the table.

"No, but we were able to ID the gun," Mike answered, having been the one to research the bullet. "Unfortunately, it came from one of the most common hand-guns, so it would be impossible to track down the specific gun. We've installed a top-of-the-line security system now and I have an algorithm running through the security cameras that will notify me if it sees something that resembles a gun. It's unlikely that the shooter will try the same method twice, but it's still good to cover our bases."

"Impressive," Lizzy muttered beside me, too quietly for anyone else to hear.

Curious, I glanced at her. Lizzy was beautiful, with her soft brown hair and matching eyes. But the severity of her serious expression usually kept people from looking her way for too long. Right now, though, there was a softness in her expression as she watched Mike that I hadn't seen before.

I smiled, already brainstorming ship names for them. *Mizzy? Like?*

"We may not have any idea who the shooter was," I added, looking at Morgan, "But we do know that they were shooting at Mor. They missed him by a hair."

"Why would someone want to kill you?" Lizzy asked, typing a list on her tablet.

Morgan laughed bitterly. Mike, Clint and Logan followed suit. "How much time do you have?" Mor said dryly. "To the public, I'm a murderous Chief who's killed over a dozen people. And to the city officials, I ask too many questions and cause too many problems. A lot of people would want me dead."

"Sure," my assistant shrugged, unbothered by Morgan's callous attitude, "But while a good percentage of the public think you're a bad guy who does bad things, I'd say the majority consider your alleged killings to be the acts of a vigilante. It's gambling den members that you've been accused of murdering, and while they're gruesome deaths, most people aren't sad to see those men gone. So really, while the public might fear you, I doubt they want you dead."

Mor was silent for a moment, a look of utter bewilderment on his face. I sensed his emotions shifting from a little insecure to surprisingly pleased.

When his eyes turned to me, I gave him an encouraging smile. It was true that people were scared of Morgan. But in all my research as a vigilante, I'd never found any reason to launch an attack on him. Because even if the rumors were true and he had killed those people, it was for the greater good. Even when painted as a bad guy, Morgan never quite fit the bill.

"I never thought of it that way," he murmured, giving Lizzy a grateful look. "Thank you."

She nodded and smiled. "You're welcome. Now as for your real enemies, is there anyone who has a more personal issue with you? Not just a general fear or wariness, but a genuine hate?"

"Francine hates his guts," Clint suggested through a mouthful of donut. *Way to win the girl, buddy.* Lizzy only quirked an eyebrow and then turned her eyes to her list.

"I kind of doubt she'd hire an assassin though," Merida said thoughtfully. "She's such a combative person. If she wanted to take you out, I think she'd do it herself."

"And she would probably do it politically rather than actually killing you," I pointed out, recalling all the nasty things she'd said to him during council meetings. If anyone wanted to make Morgan's life miserable, it was the Minotaur representative. Which she couldn't do if he was dead.

"There's always the gambling dens," Ariel suggested, stealing a scone off of Logan's plate. "Clearly they hate Beast Boy enough to frame him for all their in-house murders."

"I can look into it and let you know what I find," Asher offered, already taking out his phone. And while I appreciated that he was so willing to help, I didn't want him or Merida to think that they were only here to give us favors.

"Thank you, Asher," I said, hoping he knew I meant it. "But that's not why I invited you or Merida here."

Merida shared a quizzical look with the Wyvern King. "Then why?"

Suddenly feeling a little embarrassed, I twirled my pen in my hand. In the weeks since coming to the Alfar house, I'd done my best to hide my anxiety. And so far, it was working. Even Morgan didn't know the extent of my fears. Whenever I could tell he was sensing my worry, I tried to shift my focus or explain the feelings away as something else. But I didn't think I could keep dealing with these feelings by myself.

"Well..." I hummed, pointedly avoiding Morgan's gaze. "I actually asked you two to come today because I wanted your...advice."

"Advice?" Merida asked, clearly confused.

"Yeah. You two both lead your own factions, and you have a lot of experience, so..."

"Morgan also leads his own faction," Asher just had to point out.

Reluctantly, I finally met my mate's gaze. He was glaring daggers at me.

Whether it was because I'd withheld my anxiety from him or because I was asking for everyone else's advice *except* his, I wasn't sure.

"Morgan's a great Chief," I said earnestly, wanting Morgan to know that I meant it, "But he's biased when it comes to me. And while he makes great decisions for the Berserkers, I'm afraid any advice he gives me will be skewed toward my safety rather than what's best for my people."

Mor seemed to digest this, sighing heavily, his eyes never leaving mine. I felt his disappointment and anger, knowing he would definitely be giving me a lecture later about hiding things from him. But he didn't seem angry *at* me...

"You're not wrong," he finally gritted out. "But you and I will be having a discussion later."

"Ohhh," Clint and Mike both cat called, winking at me.

"I know," I agreed, then stuck my tongue out at Thing One and Thing Two.

Mor nodded, letting the issue pass for now.

"So, what kind of advice are you looking for?" Asher asked. I still couldn't get a clear enough read on his emotions to know what he was feeling, but he seemed thoughtful.

I squared my shoulders, forcing myself to set aside my pride and be honest. "I want advice for what kind of queen to be. Some of my people seem excited to have a queen after so long without one..." I trailed off, thinking of the empty space in leadership that my parents had left vacant with their deaths. Now that I'd stepped into their old role, I'd done my best not to think of them too much. I was already struggling with the stress of the job. I didn't think I could handle the heaviness of their memory along with everything else.

"But not everyone is happy that I'm here," I went on, looking between Merida and Asher. "And I can't decide if I should be soft and empathetic to encourage those who don't already hate me, or if I should be fierce and intimidating to scare the crap out of the ones that do. I don't know what kind of queen they need me to be."

No one spoke for a moment, and the silence felt deafening with the words of my insecurities filling the space. I hesitated to look at anyone but the two leaders. I wasn't usually one to be vulnerable with other people. At least, not with people other than Morgan. And even his silence felt heavy to me.

"In my experience," Merida finally said, her voice kind and gentle, "Trying to be what other people want is never helpful. Because no matter what you do, you can't please everyone."

"Merida's right," Asher agreed. "There will always be someone who thinks you're doing it wrong. You can't do the job well if you're doing it for other people."

"So, then what do I do?" I begged, unashamedly whining now.

"What do your instincts tell you?" I pouted at his simple question, hating that he was turning my own request for advice back on me. "What kind of queen do *you* want to be?"

I shrugged helplessly. "I don't know. Sometimes I want to be empathetic and approachable, and other times I want to snap and put people in their place. Let them know they can't mess with me."

"So do that," Asher said simply. As if it were that easy.

"Just—what? Be inconsistent? The Alfar are going to think I have a personality disorder if I do that."

"It's like a parent with their kids," Lizzy explained. "With one child they might have to be heavier handed, and with another they need to be easier going. Your leadership style *should* depend on which people you're dealing with."

I considered her words and glanced over at Morgan when his foot brushed against mine. "You should know better than anyone," he said, a look of faithful support on his face, "That you don't have to fit into a certain archetype. You don't have to be the scary queen or the nice queen. Just be you and you'll be fine."

"That's so cliché," I teased, trying to cover up the emotion that was suddenly clogging my throat. "But you might be right."

Mor reached across the table and took my hand, his fingers warm and comforting over mine. "It happens every once in a blue moon."

I smiled and squeezed his hand, and he squeezed back. I didn't want to get too mushy in front of the group, but my new role had been weighing on me since the moment I'd opened my parents' letter and discovered that there were actual people for me to lead.

I barely knew how to handle myself, let alone an entire species. But as always, my thoughtful boyfriend was right. I was putting too much pressure on doing it right, when really, I just needed to do the job. Whatever that looked like for me.

"You good?" Mor whispered.

I nodded. "Yeah, I'm good. Thank you."

The sweet moment was ruined by Asher's sigh. "Great. So now that we've sufficiently pepped you—"

"Now that we've 'pepped' her?" Merida mocked.

"Yes, pepped." Asher scowled. "We gave her a peptalk, she's fine. Now we can get down to business."

"Alright fine," Morgan said, smiling at the Wyvern King, "We'll do what lizard boy says and get back to business."

"See what you've done?" Asher snapped, looking at Merida. "I have a nickname."

She grinned. "You're welcome."

"Were you ever able to get any leads on the Pixie potions used against Care?" Logan asked once we were all finally back on topic.

Merida shook her head. "No, with Fitz's—I mean Mayor Fitz," she stuttered, a blush staining her pale cheeks.

I winked at Morgan. Her blunder was evidence that I was right, and she was into our darling human mayor. *Mitz will sail.*

"Yes, tell us about Mayor Fitz," Ariel taunted, fluttering her eyelashes.

Merida was not impressed. "Since he started the Task Force, production for black market magic has slowed. None of the faction leaders want to get caught doing anything illegal while they're all being investigated. So, whoever used the Pixie potions must have had them for a while before they used them."

"And there's really nothing else we can do to track down a possible gunman?" I was not okay with the idea of Morgan's shooter running around planning another hit.

Mike shook his head. "No. If they try again, we'll be better prepared to ID them, but something tells me they won't try the same way twice."

They might not come to us, but that didn't mean we couldn't go to them...I pursed my lips, an idea slowly forming in my mind.

"Red?" Morgan said warily. "What's that look for?"

I smiled. "I do look good in black; don't you think?"

He scowled as realization slowly dawned on his face. "No."

"Yes."

"We wouldn't even know who to watch."

I rolled my eyes. "We can start with the gambling dens and work our way down your list of enemies."

"Caroline..."

"Morgan, you'd be saying yes if this was about me."

But he sat there fuming, grinding his jaw and glaring at me. He couldn't argue with me about that. "Fine. But the usual rules apply. We don't leave each other's side and we don't get out of the car unless both of us agree."

"I'm confused," Clint interjected, his plate of snacks finally cleared as he dusted crumbs from his shirt. "What are we talking about?"

Morgan groaned, rubbing a hand across his face. "A stakeout."

Chapter 9

MORGAN

"Pringles?" I said, offering the tall green can to Caroline.

She gasped, staring at me with false shock. "You brought Pringles? But you hate my obsession with them!"

"I do. But that's only because I'm concerned about what the chemicals will do to your body in twenty years." I shook the can. "Now do you want some or not?"

"Do I want some? Are you insane? Of course, I do."

She snatched the can from my hand and dove right in. She'd convinced me—curse her puppy dog eyes—to stakeout a diner downtown that was a well-known hangout for gambling den members from the east side of the city. How she planned to find out if the den was involved in the attempted shooting, I wasn't sure. But as far as I was concerned, we weren't going to be leaving the car.

"You know," Care whispered, trailing a finger along my bicep, "We could still go with my plan."

I snatched her hand and tugged. She tipped closer to me, and I closed the gap. Our noses brushed, her eyes out of focus as I pressed her hand against my chest, my heart beating beneath her fingers.

"I said," I whispered, my lips feather light against hers, "No."

Then I sat back in my seat.

"Not fair!" she exclaimed, throwing a chip at my shoulder. "You shouldn't tease me like that. It's rude."

"You tease me all the time." But I was already leaning forward to grasp her chin between my fingers. "How come you can play dirty, but I can't, Red?" Then I pressed a short kiss to her lips and sat back again.

She smiled smugly and touched her tongue to her bottom lip. "Because you always give in too fast."

I didn't argue. She was right. For someone with super strength, I was a weak man where she was concerned.

"And you act like my plan was terrible," she complained, munching on another chip.

"It wasn't terrible, it was dangerous."

She shrugged. "It was easy though. I shift into a different body, go inside the diner and listen to the den members' conversation. Easy peasy."

"Easy peasy?" I deadpanned. She nodded. "Caroline Felicity Birch, you suggested going into a building with *seven* gambling den members. These are people who have framed me for *four* murders. And that's not including all the deaths I've been blamed for by the rest of the groups! Imagine what they'd do to you if they found out who you were."

"They're not going to find out that I'm an elf."

"That's not what I'm talking about. You're *my* girlfriend, Red. There's a risk that comes with that. I have enemies, and they will use you as a pressure point if they think it'll get to me."

Care watched me for a moment, silent and contemplative. I could feel her, the curiosity and empathy that swirled in her chest. I could be a beast sometimes, but she always saw through the bluster. She knew what I didn't say.

"You're not going to lose me," she whispered.

Who knew six little words could completely undo a grown man. Suddenly I was pushing back tears, memories flashing through my mind of the last time that someone I loved didn't survive the gambling dens.

I was so busy trying to control my reaction that I didn't notice Care set aside the Pringles and unbuckle her seatbelt until she was crawling across the console and into my lap.

"We should be watching," I complained halfheartedly. But my arms were already banding around her.

"I'm paying attention," she shrugged, snuggling close so my head was under her chin, holding me like a child. "I'll know when the guys' moods shift. Plus, I can still see the front doors. I'll let you know when they're getting ready to leave. Now talk to me. What's going through your head?"

I sighed, squeezing her tighter, my cheek against her neck. "I don't know. I'm happier than I've been in years..."

"But?"

"But being happy also makes me scared. My dad was a crummy excuse for a man," I admitted, remembering how easily he had traded his family for money. "But my mom always went above and beyond. And then she died. And for years, I thought that if I had been stronger, or just a little older, I could have killed that gambling den boss faster and been able to save her in time—"

"No." Care shook her head. "You did what you could. In the end her fate wasn't yours to decide, Mor. She knew that."

I nodded. She was right, but while I understood that logic, it didn't always feel true. "I know. But I blamed myself. Still do sometimes."

Caroline kissed my forehead, the empathy in her eyes so strong that I could've drowned in it. "You're human—well, kind of," she smiled, "You're not going to be perfect. Not even when it comes to your own healing."

"I know, but I was miserable about it for a long time. And then Gen came along, and I was happy again. Until she died. I know it's a childish thought, but after you lose enough people, you start to wonder if it's just a never-ending cycle."

I sat there, tense and anxious as Care patiently listened. I'd made a point in the years since Gen's death not to get introspective very often. Analyzing my pain and its causes was a hurtful process, so I did it as little as possible.

But now I had Caroline. And while an injured man alone didn't do a lot of damage, I knew that if I didn't start dealing with my crap, I could very easily injure her. And nothing was worth that.

"You've never had a love that wasn't taken from you," she said after a moment, her voice free of judgment. "It makes sense that you would be tight fisted with me."

"I don't mean to be." And I didn't. It wasn't intentional that I often acted like a bear where she was concerned. Granted, she provoked me plenty, but I hated how obsessively protective I was. I felt like I was smothering her sometimes.

"I know. It makes sense that you're scared." She bit her lip, studying me thoughtfully. "And honestly, I don't really know that I'm that different. I've never had a relationship that made me feel safe. So, I tend to be a little possessive of you—of us—because I don't want to lose it."

"So how do we let go of all the fear then, if we're both always terrified to lose the other?"

"Easy. We do our best."

I quirked an eyebrow at her. "That's it? We do our best?"

"Yeah." She smiled. It was that clever, 'I'm up to something' smile. *My favorite.* "Whenever I feel the fear step in," she explained, "I'll do my best to remind myself that I can't control the outcome. And that strangling you with my possession isn't worth the measly peace of mind it gives me."

"And when I feel terrified that I might lose you, I'll do my best to remember that in trying to control the outcome, I'm not letting you be you. And the last thing I ever want to do is smother your flame. It's one of my favorite things about you."

"Because it keeps you warm?" she teased, quoting one of the notes I'd left for her during our very brief semi-breakup.

I leaned forward, my lips touching hers. "Sure does. It's the real reason I call you Red."

She chuckled, but just as I was pressing myself closer to give her a real kiss, she pulled back. "They're coming."

Then, she shifted her appearance and suddenly Logan was sitting in my lap.

"Not cool," I complained, dropping my hands from her waist. Er, *his* waist. I shook my head. *Weird.*

"What? It's still me," Care taunted; her attention fastened on a group of men walking out of the diner.

I stared at her, deadpan. "It's not the same and you know it."

She chuckled and I watched as a younger man from the group walked over to the sleek black car next to us.

"You were right that this is one of their cars," Caroline said.

"Young members are always too eager to flash their status to everyone."

"So, what do you think? Should we do good cop, bad cop?"

I nodded, checking that the knife at my hip was still secured. "I assume you're good cop?"

"Oh, I think your naturally sweet disposition and positive, peppy attitude would make you the perfect good cop." I glared at her, and she winked. "I love you."

If she hadn't been in the form of my male best friend, I would have kissed her.

Care, however, had no reservations about being physically affectionate in our current forms. She leaned forward, kissed my cheek, then slipped out of the car before I could stop her.

"Little imp," I grumbled, stepping out into the cool evening air. Care was already standing at the front of the other man's car, so I went around the back.

"Hi," Care greeted cheerily, Logan's voice coming out of her mouth as the young man reached for his door.

"What do you want?" he snapped, his entire manner brimming with immaturity.

"Now is that any way to talk to a lady?" I growled, and the man spun to find me standing right behind him.

"You," he stuttered, his gaze fixed on my scar. "I...uh..."

"So, you know who he is then." Care waltzed up, arms crossed and smiling. "Good. That will make this a lot easier."

The man opened his mouth, looking ready to argue, but it was no use. Caroline had already tapped into her magic.

It rolled around the man, an invisible thick cloud playing with his emotions. I couldn't sense the finer details of the magic; how she manipulated the emotions or which ones she pulled at. But I could feel the power around her, toying with him.

The man's face tensed as the magic tethered to his emotions. He couldn't tell that magic was in the air, but he likely sensed something strange going on inside him.

"What do you know about the shooting?" Caroline asked, her smile sharp and threatening.

"I don't know what you're talking about," the man grunted, resisting her.

But it was a futile effort. Only Volund had ever been able to escape her magical influence. And I had a suspicion that it was because manipulation didn't work quite as well on other Elves.

"Now let's try that again," Care said sweetly, and I sensed her magic intensify. "What do you know about the shooting?"

The man winced and I nudged him in the back. "I'd answer if I were you."

He clenched his jaw. "We were paid to do it."

"By who?" I demanded, stepping closer.

"I don't know. All we were told was that someone paid us to attack you, but not kill you."

My eyes turned to Care, and I saw my own anger and confusion reflected there. After all these years of using me as their scapegoat, why were the gambling dens suddenly interested in taking a job to come after me?

"But why would they—" Caroline's words were cut off as the man used her moment of distraction to break free of her compulsion and launch himself at her.

He shoved her back against his car, and I flinched when she grunted at the impact.

All at once, my instincts went online, completely taking over my body. My fingers gripped the man's hair and yanked so hard that he fell to the ground. Then, before he could stand, I dropped and shoved my knee into his gut, put a hand to his throat, and pressed him down against the pavement.

"Wrong move, buddy," I seethed, unphased as he clawed at my arm. "Your fight is with *me*. Now, because I'm a merciful man, I'm going to let you live, but you're going to give your bosses a message for me." I leaned closer, watching him cower. "They can come for me all they want, but if any of you touch my family again, the next murder I'm blamed for in the news will be theirs."

When I stood, the man didn't waste a second, immediately bolting to his car. It took him three tries to open the door, and he watched me with wide, terrified eyes as he sped off into the dark.

"Did he hurt you?" I demanded, turning to Care and taking her face in my hands. Thankfully, she'd shifted back into herself, otherwise I would feel a little weird.

"No, I'm okay. But what about you?" She grabbed at my hands, her face going rigid when she saw the red marks on my arm.

"Hey, I'm okay, Red. He didn't draw blood."

She nodded and smooshed herself against me, her arms banding tight around my waist. I held her close, pressing one hand to the back of her head, smoothing her hair beneath my fingers.

"They're not going to hurt you again, Mor," she hissed, "I promise."

I smiled despite the panic I felt at the thought of her putting herself in danger. My mate may be little, but she was *fierce*.

"They aren't going to hurt *either of us*." I didn't care what it cost. No one was going to steal love away from me a third time.

Chapter 10

CAROLINE

The picture on the wall stared back at me, invoking a swirl of confusing feelings in my gut. It hadn't been there when I went to bed last night, but when I walked into my office in the Alfar house this morning, a cup of hot tea in my hand, there it was. Just...staring at me.

"What do you think, Mae?" I sighed, reaching down to scratch Daisy between her ears. She was adapting well to the Alfar house. It took her a minute to warm up to the staff, but now they loved her. Stefan kept buying her dog toys, David talked to her in baby talk when he thought no one was listening, and Charlie always took the opportunity to cuddle with her in between cleaning, but Torrie was the worst. Every morning she greeted Daisy with homemade dog treats and even made her dinners from scratch. It was no wonder the chef was Daisy's favorite person.

"Yeah, I don't know what to think either," I hummed thoughtfully.

"I wasn't sure if it would be a welcome surprise." I glanced up as Harold entered the room. Since hiring Lizzy, I no longer needed him to fill the temporary assistant role. But he still came by frequently anyway.

From what I understood, he and his wife were never able to have kids. So, I had a sneaking suspicion that he was basically adopting us as his surrogates.

"You did this?" I asked, pointing to the large picture of my birth parents that hung in a black frame on my wall.

"I thought you might want something to remember them by. I know you haven't asked much about your parents since you moved in. And I figured that if you had questions, you would ask when you were ready, but it seemed wrong for you to take up their mantle and not have something in the house to honor them. But I can take it down if it bothers you," he rushed to add, concerned.

"No, I don't want you to take it down," I assured him, willing myself not to tear up. "I really appreciate you hanging it. The only reason I haven't asked questions about them is because it was already hard taking on a completely foreign role. But thinking of them—asking questions about them—made me feel like I would be trying to live up to their legacy. And that was just too much pressure."

"There's nothing to live up to," Harold said sternly. "You're different people. You'll rule differently—as you should. And I know for a fact that they would be proud of what you've done here so far. Of who you've become."

I looked up at the picture. The faces were the same as the ones in the photo I'd treasured my whole life. The one where my birth parents held their infant daughter, wearing faces that I'd always believed weren't theirs.

"I have a photo of them," I whispered, thinking of the framed picture on my dresser at the Berserker house. "I always thought that they'd shifted their faces for it. But this is exactly how they looked."

"I'm surprised you didn't guess that their appearance was real. You look so much like your mother. Except that you have your father's eyes."

It was true. In this photo, my parents were standing side by side, looking so bright and happy. My dad had sandy brown hair, but his green eyes were just like mine. Mom's hair was a brighter red than my auburn, her eyes more of a grey like Morgan's. They looked so hopeful, so young and vibrant and healthy.

It killed me that two people with so much life ahead of them had died with so much of it left unlived. That although I now had people to talk to who had known them, I would only ever know my own parents through stories and photos. *But at least I have stories to hear now.* And I would always have my adoptive parents.

I mourned the fact that my birth parents were gone, but my adoptive ones had more than filled that gap. Even with my losses, I felt rich.

"What were they like?"

"Your dad was an energetic person," Harold said, smiling fondly at the picture. "Full of life and ideas. But your mom was quieter, more easy going. But if you dared push her too far, she could be a force to be reckoned with. I've only known you a few weeks, but already I can guess that you've got fire like your dad, and stubbornness like your mom."

"Me, stubborn?" I scoffed. "Never."

Harlod chuckled, but as the sound faded, a heaviness filled the room.

"They wanted to keep you, know."

I glanced at the advisor, saying nothing.

"They thought about keeping you when they first found out your mom was pregnant," he went on. "But at the time, there was some concern about discovery, so they decided that you would be safer elsewhere. Most people didn't know your mom was pregnant, so even if we'd been found out, you would have been safe with your adoptive parents. When they died in a car accident a few years later, those of us who knew about you had no idea where you were. But your parents wanted it that way."

I nodded and stared at their faces behind glass. "They wanted to give me my best chance. I can't fault them for that."

I tried not to squirm under the weight of their frozen gazes, unsure what they'd think of my plans. I'd already been coronated in front of the entire Alfar community, but somehow today's events seemed scarier. Like there was a bigger chance for backlash.

"Would they do this?" I asked, unsure of myself.

"That's not the question that needs answering."

"Then what is?" I stood and Daisy scampered off to beg Harold for pets.

He scratched Daisy's back and then straightened. "The question is whether *you* think you should do this."

I groaned and headed for the door. "Seriously? You couldn't have just answered the question instead of getting all psychological on me?"

"I could have." He shrugged. "But that would be a lot less fun."

I glared at him, but he just smiled wide. *Old man needs a hobby.* "Some advisor you are," I complained as we walked toward the back entrance of the house.

"Would you rather have me be evasive or insert myself into every decision you make?"

Hm. "Good point. You can keep doing what you're doing."

We paused in front of the double doors that led out to the backyard and I took a deep breath. I would have preferred to have Morgan with me when I made my entrance. But he'd insisted that my people needed to see me walk out on my own, so they'd know that I didn't need him.

But it's a lie. I do need him.

"Ready—where are you going?" I demanded as Harold strode off down a connecting hallway.

"Outside through the side door."

"You're not coming with me?"

Harold rolled his eyes. "Queen Caroline, we're both going out to your backyard where your boyfriend and your family are waiting. You'll be alone for all of three seconds."

I pouted and crossed my arms. "A very long, uncomfortable three seconds."

The old man waved a dismissive hand in the air and walked off. "You'll be fine."

But would I be? There was a yard full of Alfar waiting for me. *Probably angry ones.*

"But I'll be fine," I assured myself, looking down at Daisy. "You're not going to leave me, right?" She licked my hand. "I'll take that as a yes."

A moment later, the doors opened, and I stepped outside.

The August sun shone brightly above the gathered Alfar, sparkling on the river that rippled just beyond them. The yard was mostly perfectly trimmed grass, but various shrubs and well-maintained roses lined the huge deck that wrapped around the back of the house.

A beautiful carved banister curved around the deck, and similarly carved columns rose up to support the balcony above me. The wood was stained and inlaid with beautiful designs—the stone floor even had scrollwork engraved in its smooth surface. And gathered around the long, wide stairs that led down to the lawn, was a crowd of Alfar.

I couldn't tell at a glance how well I was being received. And although I could sense that no one present was feeling fully hostile toward me, I was reminded that while I could feel their emotions, they could also feel mine. Which meant that they could tell how petrified I was. *So much for being a fearless leader.*

Clasping my hands together to keep my fingers from shaking, I glanced over at Morgan. He and the rest of our band of misfits were waiting for me on the grand back deck, standing off to the side. I wished they would stand beside me, but they had all agreed that while they needed to show their support, I also needed to show the Alfar that it would be me leading them, and not my loved ones.

I grudgingly agreed.

"Thank you all for coming to our first combat training," I began, thankful when my voice came out strong and confident despite my anxiety. "I'm sure many of you are curious and maybe even concerned about doing this."

A murmur broke out across the crowd and the scrutinizing look in people's eyes seemed to intensify.

"Are you planning to take us public?" Jude, my health and safety advisor asked. Despite his overall brooding appearance, his question wasn't rude or snide. Just curious.

He wore half of his shoulder length dark hair back in a man bun, and his arms were crossed over a black T shirt, but the kindness in his eyes gave him away as an ally. It was the one thing he shared with his brother Tristain.

For a moment, I considered not answering him. I was their queen after all, I didn't have to explain myself. But I wanted to. Being honest was the kind of queen *I* wanted to be. And that was all that mattered.

"Yes," I replied, trying to meet the eyes of as many people as I could. "My plan is to take the Alfar public within the year," I admitted, a hum of whispers immediately rippling through the crowd. "Which is why I want to train you all to fight."

"Are we staging a takeover?" Mikael, the older justice advisor asked. His question, unlike Jude's, was definitely intended to be snide. I couldn't say I was surprised.

Somehow, I managed to keep my voice level, though I let a dark, threatening note enter my words. "Let's not be naïve. Once we go public, there *will* be people who want to cause us harm. Some of the other factions may feel threatened, others will think we're at the bottom of the food chain and easily intimidated. We need to be prepared for any outcome."

"Maybe we shouldn't go public then," someone called out, the owner of the voice indiscernible from the crowd.

The whispers grew louder, and I sensed the overall nerves in the area begin to climb. My own panic started to spark. Anxious, I turned to look at Morgan. His grey eyes were already focused on me, and I knew he felt my fear, and yet all I felt from him was complete confidence.

'You've got this,' he mouthed. Then he winked at me.

I smiled. 'I love you.'

He mouthed it back and I turned to the crowd, feeling my resolve strengthen. "You don't know me yet," I said, my voice loud enough for even the people in the back to hear me. "But you'll learn soon enough that while my flaws are numerous, I am the most determined person you'll ever meet. I want all of you to live whatever lives you want to live. I want you to be free from secrecy. To be able to marry whoever you love without the other person carrying the burden of your secret. I want you to pursue whatever your passion is, to have just as much opportunity as everyone else in the world. I want all of you to live, not just survive. And in the words of the great Lorelai Gilmore, I usually get what I want."

The expressions of the people in the crowd became thoughtful, though I sensed their lingering doubt. "You might be able to offer us freedom," a middle-aged woman further back in the crowd called out, a young preteen girl at her side. "But at what cost? Is it really worth our safety?"

A few people nodded their heads in agreement and all eyes turned to me. Accusing. Waiting.

"You forget that I'm also an Alfar," I snapped, allowing my frustration to show. I intended to be a nice queen, but I needed their respect just as much as their affection. "But unlike you, I didn't have the luxury of a community. I grew up alone in my species. No one other than my family had any idea what I was. And yet someone still found me. How long do you think it will take for whoever's hunting me to find you—a large group of Elves hiding in plain sight?"

No one replied, but many of them shrunk back a little, properly chastised. *Good. They need to take this seriously.*

"Do you really want to sit around and wait for the day that someone finds us and sells us off like trophies on the black market?" I went on, frustrated that in their blessings, the Alfar had become complacent and placid. That they'd forgotten to value their own freedom. "Or do you want more? To stand up for yourselves? To have a voice on the Shifter Council? Would you rather fight to earn your place in the world, or wait until we're snuffed out and sold off?"

The silence that followed was taut and sharp. The gazes of the crowd ranged from angry to curious to anxious. But amongst the fear and frustration, I felt it. A bit of hope. And like a spark in a dry summer, I knew just how powerful that one flash of heat could be. *That's all I need...*

"What would training look like?" I turned my eyes to a young woman at the front of the crowd. She was probably in her early twenties with silky dark hair thrown up into a messy bun and an aged ACDC T shirt hanging baggy and wrinkled from her shoulders.

For this question, I looked over at Mike and Clint who were going to be in charge of training the Alfar. A decision I was seriously rethinking when Clint winked at some of the younger women, and they smiled back at him.

"For today, we'll start with very simple self-defense," Mike explained, rolling his eyes at his baby brother.

"But in the future the goal is to train you in hand-to-hand combat," Clint added, puffing out his chest. I sighed. *That's testosterone, folks.* "As well as some simple weapons training, and we'll teach you how to spot threats."

Mike nodded, too annoyed with his brother to bother with his own nerves for the moment. "Those of you who finish the self-defense training and are interested in going beyond it can apply to be a part of the new defense team. This team will be responsible for ensuring safety for all the Alfar. If someone is assaulted or threatened, they'll go to the defense team. This team will also be led by a new advisor that will be chosen after everyone who wants to has completed their training."

The murmurs that broke out across the yard now were contemplative and curious rather than fearful. *Progress.*

"Alright," I said, clapping my hands together, "Let's start the training. Who would like to start us off by being the first volunteer?"

"I'll do it." It didn't surprise me to see the young dark-haired girl stepping forward, a determined look on her face. I knew that look. I respected that look. I'd worn it for most of my life.

A young man behind her mumbled something I didn't hear, and based on the glare she shot him, I gathered it wasn't kind. "Oh yeah?" she barked. "And what would you have us do, Carmine? Keep living in silence? Bring up the next generation in a world where they can't have relationships with anyone who's not an Elf? Where they can't stand out, can't be special. Always have to look over their shoulder." The man sneered but said nothing. "If I have to endure a little bit of discomfort so they don't have to, then I'm more than happy to do it."

"Oh, I like her," I whispered to Mike and Clint.

"Like calls to like," Mike sassed. I bumped his shoulder and he chuckled.

The boys and I made our way down the wide steps and stopped in front of the fiery young girl. "What's your name?" I asked.

She straightened her shoulders, her blue eyes flashing. "Allie."

"Nice to meet you, Allie." I smiled and offered her my hand. "I'm Caroline."

She eyed my fingers for a moment. "It's nice to meet you." Then she shook my hand.

And for the first time since taking on the role of queen, I felt hope. Maybe I could do this after all...

Chapter 11

CAROLINE

"Alright, that's enough. You're cut off," I said, snatching the tablet from Lizzy's hands.

"Oh, come on," she whined, her brown eyes somehow getting bigger as she turned them on me. "I don't have that much more to do."

"Lizzy, I love how good of an assistant you are, but I invited you to come down here to join us for girl's night, not so you can work while we enjoy girl's night."

"Yeah," Ariel agreed, combing her curly blonde hair up into a messy bun. "There's no work allowed on girl's night. Only boy talk, gossip and junk food are allowed."

My young assistant rolled her eyes and let out an impressively deep growl that could've put Morgan to shame. She had moved into the Alfar house with us after she was hired as my assistant. And as one would expect, she was the perfect roommate. Very organized, always courteous, never too loud. But as in control as she was, she still packed a fair amount of sass.

"Fine, but I expect to get paid overtime for this," she said dryly, shoving her hands in the pocket of her pristine sweatshirt. Yeah, even her loungewear was perfectly put together.

"Deal," Ariel agreed for me. I raised an eyebrow at her, and she shrugged. "What? It's not like you can't afford it." She wasn't wrong. "Now Lizzy, it's time to tell us which Hohlt boy has caught your attention. I need to know which ship to root for."

"Oh, are we finally going to find out who Lizzy has the hots for?" Torrie teased, grinning wide as she came into the kitchen carrying a bag of groceries, Charlie, the housekeeper, trailing behind her.

Lizzy's expression grew dark at our taunting, but Torrie only giggled. The boisterous chef was too positive of a person for even my intimidating assistant to dampen her spirits. Charlie, however, was not so unaffected.

The young housekeeper stood by the island, helping Torrie take the groceries out of the bags. But every few seconds, her eyes would flick toward Lizzy as if she expected her to combust at any moment.

"What about you, Charlie?" I said, sitting at one of the barstools that lined the island.

I would have offered to help Torrie make the pizzas for tonight's meal, but it would be useless. Torrie didn't like for anyone to use her kitchen except herself. I would never forget the lecture she gave me when I baked cookies one night. They were from a tube, so I only needed to use the oven. But she was insistent that it was her job to cook for me and that if she was going to be paid to be the chef, then she should be the one to cook. She promised that she was more than willing to make me anything I wanted, but that I wasn't to do the cooking myself. I hadn't touched the stove since.

"What about me?" Charlie asked, her wide eyes turning to me. She was a beautiful girl, with thick brown hair and big blue eyes. But she was also so shy and unsure. *Not for long though.* If I'd broken through Morgan's exterior, I could get through anyone's.

Of course, with Morgan, I'd mostly flirted and teased him until he caved...I'd have to try a new tactic with Charlie.

"How are things with Stefan?"

Charlie blushed at my question, completely flustered. But when she realized that everyone was watching her with the same knowing look, she sighed. "Am I that obvious?"

I shrugged. The groundskeeper was hot, so who could blame Charlie for not being cool about it? "To us, but probably not to him."

"That's because he doesn't even know I exist," she sighed, immediately deflating.

"I see you two talking all the time," Lizzy pointed out, tugging on the end of her light brown ponytail. "You're friends."

"Exactly." Charlie rolled her eyes and sat on a stool. "He only knows me as a friend and a coworker. He doesn't know I exist as anything more."

"How long have you known each other?" Ariel asked, stealing a pinch of cheese from the bag Torrie had set on the counter.

Charlie hummed. "A couple years. He worked for a landscaping company and one of the houses he worked at was my boss'. We would talk every time he came by, and when the jobs here became available, he said he was going to apply and asked if I would do it with him. He knew that my last job wasn't my favorite..."

I shared a look with the other women and Torrie gave me a wink like she knew exactly what to do in this situation. She couldn't have been more than forty at most, but she had the energy of a mom to a bunch of teenagers. Sweet, patient, but a little wily.

"You know," she started, rolling out the dough I'd seen her prep earlier, "I had to engineer David and I's relationship."

"What do you mean 'engineer?'" Lizzy narrowed her eyes at the chef.

"I mean that I masterminded it, Taylor Swift style." Torrie grinned. "He lived two blocks down from me and I'd seen him around but never talked to him. What I needed was a *reason* to talk to him. So, I made one."

We all laughed and munched on the various pizza ingredients laid out on the big island. "Alright, Taylor," I sassed, "What'd you do?"

Torrie smirked. "I broke my car."

"You what?" Ariel grinned.

"David was a mechanic," Torrie explained, swirling some sauce over the pizza dough. "But I knew nothing about cars, so I had nothing to talk to him about. And one day as I was driving by, I saw him out working in his driveway, his T shirt all stained and his arms messy with grease..." she paused, a faraway look in her eyes.

"Earth to Torrie!" I tossed an olive at her.

It bounced off her cheek and she blushed. "Sorry. But David wasn't just a snack. He was a five-course meal, and I was tired of only looking at him from a distance, wondering what he was actually like. So, I drove home, popped the hood of my car, and tore out the first thing I saw."

We all laughed, shocked but impressed by her tenacity to get the guy she wanted. "What was it?" Lizzy asked, her face all lit up with a smile.

"I have no idea," Torrie admitted. "I just shoved it behind a bush. Then I went and told him that my car was busted and asked if I could hire him to fix it. He came over right away to look at it, and I crossed my fingers the whole time. He had to have seen that there was a part of the car literally missing."

Charlie listened with wide eyes. "Did he?"

Torrie grinned. "He asked me what had happened, and I told him that it just stopped working. He said he'd seen me drive by ten minutes ago, and he wasn't sure how a car could have been driving down the road without that part. I feigned ignorance, but then weird things started happening."

"Like what?" I asked, enraptured by her story.

"Like he came to my house every day to work on that car instead of having it taken to his house. Then, when he ordered a new part, it kept getting delayed. And even once he fixed it, something else went wrong with the car. But then one night, it all became clear."

We all leaned forward in our seats, curious to find out how the story ended. Obviously, David fell in love with her, but the how was the interesting part.

"I told him I was sorry my car was so difficult," Torrie said, smiling to herself as she put the toppings on the pizza. "And he said I could make it up to him with dinner. So later that evening he came over and when I opened the front door, he had that old car part I'd torn out that first day. It was grasped in his hands like a bouquet, with a red ribbon tied around it. And he said, 'I found this in your bushes'." She paused as we all gasped. "I was *mortified*, but then he added, 'three weeks ago'."

"So, he'd known the whole time that you broke the car on purpose?" Ariel asked, opening the oven door so Torrie could lift the heavy pizza stone into it.

"Yep. He found the part two days after I tore it out. But he never said anything because it turned out that he liked me too. So instead, he did some masterminding of his own and didn't even order the replacement part at first just so he could stick around longer. Then he pretended to find things wrong with the car, only pretending to fix it. But in the end, he didn't charge me a dime, and I walked away with a ring on my finger and a mechanic in my bed."

"Torrie!" Charlie shouted, cheeks bright scarlet.

Torrie giggled and leaned on the island, all smiles and shining memories in her eyes. "What? It's true. And breaking that stupid car was the smartest thing I ever did." Charlie rolled her eyes but couldn't stop the smile that spread across her face. "But the point is that sometimes, you have to get creative and *make* the opportunity for him. Guys are expected to make the first move, and I personally think they should. But it's a lot of pressure to put yourself out there for a girl that might tear you to shreds with a rejection." I nodded; she wasn't wrong. "All a guy needs is an opening, a little affirmation that it's safe to make the move. Because while we think we're being obvious with our subtle hints, they don't even see it. Stefan's a man, Charlie. You have to use big bold letters, not tiny little cursive. Otherwise, he won't see it and he won't act because he doesn't think you want it."

Charlie hummed thoughtfully and bit her lip. "Okay...but how do I do that? I can't be so obvious that he knows I'm in love with him. Because what if he doesn't reciprocate?"

It was a fair point. But as someone who'd just recently found love, I knew it was worth the risk. *Ugh, I'm such a sap.*

"Start by finding a way to get him alone," I suggested, shaking off my inner cheeseball.

Charlie nodded. "I can do that. What else?"

"Give him an opportunity to help you or do something for you. Like...ask him to teach you about gardening. Or offer to help him with something he's not good at. That way you'll have a reason to interact regularly. It'll show that you want to spend time with him, and it gives you both an opportunity to see how you react to each other. You'll see him watching you or he'll see you blush when he compliments you, and you'll both have enough affirmation that you like each other. Then it's his responsibility to make the move."

"You give really good romantic advice for someone who's never had a boyfriend before," Lizzy commented matter-of-factly.

I shoved her shoulder and she laughed.

"What? You said you didn't have any relationship experience before you met Chief Hohlt."

"It's true, I didn't. But you make it sound like I'm relationship challenged."

"Clearly not, since you and the Chief can't keep your hands off each other," Charlie mumbled.

All eyes turned to her, and she gasped. "Did I say that out loud? I didn't mean it rudely, I swear! I just—you two clearly love each other and have no issues communicating it. So, obviously you know how to have a relationship."

"...Thank you," I said, the words coming out more like a question.

"I'll try your advice," she added, squaring her shoulders. "But if I get brutally rejected, I'm blaming you."

I laughed, but the sound was interrupted as footsteps echoed down a connecting hallway.

"Ladies," Logan greeted us as he stepped into the room. He winked at Ariel, and she grinned like the lovesick fool she was.

"Lo, you know we love you," I started, turning to give him a mock glare, "But tonight is girl's night. Testosterone is not allowed, and unless you have a uterus and some ovaries hiding somewhere, you can't stay—"

"Good evening, Queen Caroline." My mouth snapped shut as Mikael stepped around Logan.

The older advisor looked just as grim as ever, his wrinkled face set in seemingly permanent judgment. And Volund would be disappointed to know that black was not exclusively his color. Because Mikael was wearing a black shirt under a black utility jacket.

"Good evening, Mikael," I replied, holding back a groan. "What brings you by tonight?"

"I just thought that you might like to have a copy of the minutes from the advisor meetings for the past few months," he said, handing me a bulging manila envelope. "Since you're such an involved leader."

I took the slight with a smile. "I appreciate that. I'll definitely read them before the next meeting."

Mikael smiled and glanced around at the assembled women and the food strewn across the island, judgment in his eyes. "I'm sure it's your top priority. Have a lovely evening."

Then he disappeared back down the hall.

I glared at Logan, and he held up his hands in surrender. "I tried to tell him you were busy, but he insisted that you would want the papers. And I didn't see any harm in him just dropping off the envelope."

"You're a terrible guard," I complained, snatching an olive from the can on the island. "It's a good thing we're training two more."

Logan rolled his eyes, not offended by my words. "Alright, I know a cue to leave when I see it." Then he strolled over to Ariel, grasped her face in his hands, and planted a kiss on her lips. She giggled but clutched his shirt and kissed him back.

"Get out of here!" Lizzy and I yelled, throwing bits of food at the sappy couple.

"Anything you want me to tell your boyfriends?" he teased, winking at both of us.

"Yes. Tell him I love him, he's sexy when he's pouting, and to keep his butt upstairs. I can sense him contemplating coming down here."

Logan laughed and nodded. "What about you, Liz? Anything I should tell Clint? Or Mike?"

Lizzy scowled at him so hard that Logan actually squirmed under the weight of it. Finally, he mumbled a goodbye and ran back down the hall.

"So...you never did answer our question about the boys," I pointed out, raising my eyebrows at her.

She met my gaze, not intimidated. "How are you feeling about your new guards?"

"Really?" I complained. "Evasion? It's so beneath you."

Lizzy shrugged, unmoved.

"You chose Allie and Carmine, right?" Torrie asked, opening the oven door to check the pizza.

I nodded. "Yeah. Allie was an obvious choice. She's taking really well to the training, and she's been genuinely supportive of my reign so far."

"And Carmine?" Charlie asked, wrinkling her nose in distaste. "What possessed you to choose him?"

I laughed, surprised that there was someone Charlie openly disliked. But when I considered the young man that had argued with Allie at our first training session and the arrogant way he carried himself, I wasn't surprised.

"There weren't that many people that applied," I admitted, my shoulders drooping. "And Allie vouched for him—sort of. She said he's a donkey. Fifty percent annoying, and fifty percent ass. But an honest ass. Her words, not mine."

Torrie snorted. "That's a good way to describe him. I don't think he'll betray you, but he'll definitely annoy you to death."

I agreed. Carmine wasn't my first choice, but he was what I had to work with. And at least I had Allie. She would be an amazing personal guard. Maybe even good enough to impress Morgan the Paranoid.

"How are you doing with the rest of it?" Ariel asked, giving me a knowing look. She and Morgan, more than anyone else, knew how I was struggling. They knew that making these decisions and being judged by the people my parents had wanted me to lead was hard. Harder than I'd expected.

"I'm okay. I mean, I feel good about the plan." I sighed. "We'll encourage the Alfar to engage with the other Shifter groups as much as they can to build a positive image. We're already making a plan for how to integrate ourselves into the Shifter Council, and I'm trying to decide which people I'll volunteer to be a part of Fitz's Task Force. I think it's all going to work, I just...I hate that in becoming queen and finding my people, I feel like I've started playing a role again. For years I pretended to be tough and fine on my own. And now I feel like I'm pretending to be a leader. Like I'm faking it, and at any moment, they're all going to realize it and dethrone me. Because the truth is that I don't think I'm cut out for being queen."

The silence that followed made me squirm in my seat, and I avoided everyone's gaze, feeling suddenly insecure for sharing. I was an honest person, but I was rarely ever vulnerable. I'd become more so recently, but still, it wasn't a natural instinct for me.

"Do you know what I've always hated about you?" I looked up at Ariel's rigid tone and found her blue eyes full of anger.

My sister rarely got angry with me, and it was usually over something small and stupid. But I'd never seen her look so furious. So, it seemed wisest to keep my mouth shut.

"You were always so clever, so thoughtful," she snapped, glaring at me. "No one could ever outsmart you. You were strong and capable and when I looked at you, I saw a superhero. Someone who could do anything they wanted. But for as long as I can remember, you've been surrounded by this cloud of insecurity and honestly, it pissed me off." I gaped, taken aback, but she wasn't done. "It never made sense. How could the most brilliant person I knew feel so incapable? You could do anything, be anything, and yet you lived like you had no future. No potential."

Unsure what to say, I stared at her. Confused. "...I'm sorry?"

"Don't be sorry." She reached across the island and grabbed my hand. I was surprised to find that her grip was soft. "Just please, for the love of God, stop looking at yourself like you're some kind of failure. You're incredible, Care, and I'm so sick of you not seeing it."

Now that she was finished, I let her words sink in, feeling them tumble around inside my mind. Had I really been that bad? I'd always thought that I kept my fears and insecurities well hidden. But apparently, they'd been so apparent that they went so far as to offend Ariel.

And rightfully so. I'd be pretty ticked if I watched her box herself in out of fear.

"Morgan would love that speech," I said, a little unsure. "He's always telling me to stop doubting myself. Of course, he does it much less aggressively."

Ariel smiled and squeezed my hand—hard this time. "Yeah, well, he's your boy toy. I'd be angry if he talked to you the way I do. But seriously, sis, it's not that you're not allowed to feel self-doubt. We all feel that. But you've got to stop letting it rule your life. You're a queen now, whether or not you think you should be. There's no taking it back. So, it's time to pull on your big girl panties and stop with the self-sabotage."

"Here here," Lizzy cheered, raising her soda. I raised an eyebrow at her, and she shrugged. "What? Your sister's right. I haven't known you long, but even I can tell that you're more than capable of being a good queen."

"How?" I asked. "How can you tell?"

The young assistant looked at me like I was stupid. "Isn't it obvious? Because you're already a good queen."

She held my gaze, stubborn and sure. And when the other women all emphatically agreed, nodding and giving me encouraging smiles, I started to wonder if maybe I might be cut out for this after all.

Chapter 12

MORGAN

"Which concludes the first part of the investigation for the Firebirds," Mayor Fitz read, a stack of papers in his hand. "The Task Force will continue onto the next step and hopefully within a month or two they'll be ready to start on the next faction."

"Did the Task Force find anything on the Firebirds?" Francine, the Minotaur representative asked eagerly.

Drew, the Firebird rep, stared her down, his perfect, angular features turned down into a scowl. His rust-colored hair was combed and yet still slightly messy, and the blazer and white T shirt he wore looked so effortless. But I knew Drew. He spent more time getting ready than Caroline did. And she took forever.

Not one bit of his model-like appearance was anything less than carefully planned. And I never trusted men that took that much pride in their appearance. Volund being the perfect example.

"Eager for my demise, Franny?" Drew hissed, his anger cool and slithery. I had to give him props though, Franny was a horrible nickname for the Minotaur. And judging by the flare of her nostrils, she agreed.

"You're not even going to defend yourself? Swear that you have nothing to be guilty about?" She taunted; eyes narrowed.

I glanced at Merida, the Witch representative and one of my closest friends, and she shook her head. Unlike me, she did not enjoy the constant arguments and clashes of these meetings. Care thought it was because Merida didn't like the way it stressed out Fitz. I'd been slow to believe that the two were romantically interested in each other, but as I watched Merida shoot worried glances at Fitz, I had to admit that Care might be right.

"Why should I when clearly you're the one who's feeling insecure enough to point fingers?" Drew retorted; eyes narrowed.

"That's enough," Mayor Fitz snapped, shaking his head like a tired parent. "The Firebirds are almost done being investigated. When the investigation is concluded, the results will be announced. Until then, any conjecture is a waste of time. And might I remind all of you that whether or not the Firebirds are charged with anything, every single one of you will still have your turn in their shoes. Everyone will be scrutinized eventually, so I wouldn't be so cocky, Commander Stewart. You just might be next."

Francine shut up and turned her eyes to the papers in front of her. It was the first time I'd seen anyone truly put her in her place, and it felt good to watch.

"Who will be next to face the Task Force?" Gerard, the middle-aged Hunter representative asked. Of everyone on the council, he was the oldest, but he was also the most levelheaded. He'd undergone a very scandalous time in the news a few months ago thanks to Eileen the Dragon Queen's meddling. But he and his family seemed to be thriving despite the negative attention. His disregard for public opinion was his most endearing quality as far as I was concerned.

"I don't know," Fitz replied with a shrug, tugging on the front of his suit jacket. He'd been wearing a suit to every meeting since the day I'd started serving as Berserker representative. I wondered if it was to maintain some semblance of control in this mess, or because he really cared that much about how he looked. Knowing this lot, it was probably the latter.

"How could you not know?" Chloe, the Mermaid representative asked, narrowing her unnerving blue eyes. She was the oldest council member at fifty-three, and she had a knack for looking at you as though she could see through to your soul.

I couldn't wait until she retired.

"The order of the investigations isn't chosen in advance," Fitz explained, clearly exasperated. "The next faction to be investigated will be chosen at random once the previous investigation has been concluded. So, you can all fidget and complain as long as you want, but I don't have any answers for you."

Everyone seemed to accept this—albeit reluctantly—but then I heard Francine mumble, "Likely story," as she glared at the mayor.

"Could you please act like an adult for once in your life?" I growled, nearing the end of my patience as we neared the end of the meeting.

"Like you?" she snapped, and I tensed as an evil glint flashed in her eyes. "Dating a woman half your age."

The blood in my veins turned to ice at the vague mention of Caroline. "What?"

"Rumor has it that you're dating that pretty little assistant of yours," she went on, her lips spreading into a wicked grin. "What? You didn't think anyone noticed that you brought her with you to a meeting just because she didn't come in the room?"

"Leave her out of it." Heat burned the back of my throat and if I could have breathed fire in that moment, Franny would have been nothing but judgmental ash on the table. As it was, I did feel the tingling in my fingertips that always accompanied my shift into bear form.

"Francine!" Fitz's voice boomed around the room, and I was shocked to see him standing from his seat. His palms were flat against the table, and he was wearing a scowl so deep that it turned his handsome features into something genuinely terrifying. "That is enough."

"But—"

"The only things that matter in this room," he said, cutting her off, "Are our responsibilities as leaders. Threats—no matter how veiled or vague—will not be tolerated. Remember, your positions were *given* to you. They can be taken. Don't give me a reason to ensure that you're investigated next."

I raised my eyebrows at the mayor, shocked to see him so...powerful.

When I glanced at Merida, she was likewise surprised, staring at him with a particularly infatuated look. I seriously considered taking a picture of the expression just so I could show Caroline. *I guess she was right about them after all.* Because if Fitz tried to kiss Merida right now, I had no doubt that she'd welcome it.

My anger with Francine was disrupted when my phone buzzed in my pocket. I pulled it out and felt the urge to smile at the sight of *her* name.

Red: What's wrong? Are you plotting a murder? Because you feel like you're plotting a murder. Is it Francine's? I'll help!

My fury now sufficiently muted by the sheer thought of my mate, I quickly typed back a response.

Me: Francine knows you and I are together. She's making veiled threats and generally pissing me off. So, she's pretty much just being herself.

Caroline's response was quick.

Red: Tell her I said *GIF of Eleanor from *The Good Place* saying 'ya basic'*

I shook my head, allowing a smile to tilt my lips. It was a small expression, barely noticeable, but for a man who hadn't had reason to smile in four years, it was huge. *Caroline* was huge for me. From a beast to a gentleman, a grouch to a grinning idiot. She'd turned me upside down, and I'd do anything to keep her.

Including kill Francine.

Me: *GIF of Eleanor saying 'What a dork. I love him so much'*

Red: *GIF of Chidi from *The Good Place* saying 'I love you'*

Red: *GIF of Chidi and Eleanor kissing*

I bit my lip, and drifted off, imagining me biting Caroline's. That woman was going to wreck me. And I'd be perfectly tame and completely placid while she did it.

"Their activity has picked up on the west end of town," I heard Mayor Fitz say, snapping me out my daydream. "The gambling dens are all essentially under one boss, but since they all operate independently with their own leadership, it's been hard to pinpoint who exactly is responsible."

"What kind of activity, exactly?" I asked, a pit forming in my stomach, ready to swallow me whole.

Fitz flicked his blue eyes to me, and I was surprised to see them filled with empathy. "Theft and violence have risen. We think they're cracking down on people who owe them money. But it's getting uglier."

"Have there been any deaths?" This question I asked tentatively, afraid to hear the answer.

When the gambling dens needed to get rid of one of their own, they always did it by ripping out their throat. Just like I'd done to my mother's attacker when I was ten years old.

I'd done it in defense of someone I loved. Not plotting, just reacting. But that day had been used against me, an easy game of pass the blame.

And every time a new body showed up, so did the reporters. The glares from strangers, the fear in the eyes of people who didn't know me. The whispers and news reports about the Chief who couldn't be controlled. It had been a while since the last time I'd had to survive a blow like that. And now that I had Caroline linked to my name, I sincerely hoped that those days were behind me.

But I wasn't naïve enough to really believe it.

"I'll look into it," I said, swallowing back my fear before any of these two-faced plotters could see it. If they did, it would just become another weapon.

"Because that's done you a lot of good," Drew sighed, sitting back in his chair. When he caught me glaring at him, his face went a little pale.

"I swear, I feel like a broken record," Mayor Fitz interrupted, followed by a yawn as he rubbed his eyes. "None of you have any room to throw shade at Chief Hohlt or anyone else. I'll remind you—for the *seven hundredth time*—that Shifter-on-Shifter crime is the highest kind in the region. You don't need to worry about humans attacking you. You attack each other."

No one said a word, but Fitz wasn't done. He looked around at us, a tired parent, and shook his head.

"You all seem to think that these investigations by the Task Force are some kind of game. A way for some of you to win and some to lose. Well let me kill that idea right now. Everyone will be found guilty of something during these investigations. Whether it's your finances, the enforcement of your laws, your treatment of your people. None of you will come out of this unscathed. Because this isn't an award show for a second-grade soccer team. This isn't an opportunity to get pats on the back and hear 'atta boys'. This is a performance review wherein you will be evaluated as a leader. And every single one of you will be receiving a list of ways that you can and will improve. And for some of you, you'll lose your position. So, I'd suggest you drop the shade and start worrying about how you're going to be a better leader. Because that is the goal of these meetings and this Task Force. Not to stroke your egos."

No one spoke out of turn for the rest of the meeting, and I sat there wondering which of us would survive.

Chapter 13

MORGAN

"Here, let me help," I said, grabbing the other end of the desk.

Mike tried to wave me off, holding the thing up with both arms. "I got it."

"Mike, Lizzy's in her room. She can't see you being all tough right now," I teased, not letting go of the desk. "And I have a feeling that if you damage her furniture in your efforts to impress her, she'll probably kill you."

He sighed and relaxed his grip until he only had one hand on the desk, each of us carrying one end. We were at Lizzy's parent's house, moving some of her things to the Berserker house. Since Care was living at both places, Lizzy would be too. So whatever things she hadn't taken to the Alfar house, we'd be taking to the Berserker house. Including her very heavy desk.

"So, how've you been lately?" I asked as we carried the desk out to Logan's truck.

"What do you mean?"

I noted the defensive look in my brother's eyes and watched him meticulously tie the furniture down to the bed of the truck. Mike wasn't a secretive person, but he wasn't necessarily a sharer either. I couldn't remember ever seeing him be so touchy, though.

"Mike? What's going on? You've been acting weird. Is it the Task Force?"

I hadn't heard him complain about the job since he volunteered to be the Berserker rep. But now I was wondering how well he really liked it.

"No, the Task Force has been great," he insisted. "I love it. It's been nice to have a purpose outside of...us."

"So..." I watched him tighten the tie down. Again. "What is it then?"

He finally met my gaze, his blue eyes resigned. He was a classic middle child, always trying to meet the needs of everyone around him. He was good for a joke and a smile to lift your spirits, but he also had a great shoulder to cry on. With thick brown hair that he always let grow a little long so it covered his ears, and a goofy grin accented by stubble, he was everyone's favorite therapy dog.

But I wondered who was his.

Mike was a big guy. His shoulders were twice the width of mine and he always won in any fight. But it was Clint who'd gotten all the attention growing up. Because as the baby of the family, he asked for it. But Mike never asked for anything.

"It's Lizzy," he sighed, resting his elbows on the truck, his head in his hands.

"Ah. You like her."

Mike laughed bitterly and looked at me, eyes full of tears. My big brother alarm bells went off and I stepped closer, putting a hand on his shoulder.

"Mike, what—"

"She's my mate."

I stood there, mouth frozen open, but no words came to mind except for, "Oh."

He nodded, rubbing his temple, the tears wobbling in his eyes making them seem wider. More innocent. More childlike. And suddenly I wasn't looking at my adult brother anymore. I was looking at the little kid who held Clint's face to his chest under the coffee table while I killed our mom's killer.

"Why does that upset you?" I asked carefully, knowing from experience—twice now—how confusing it could feel to find your mate. "Do you not want it to be her?"

Mike's smile was rueful, almost self-deprecating. "She's perfect, Morgan. She's clever and smart and kind. She doesn't take crap from anyone, but she's still somehow thoughtful and caring. Don't get me wrong, she scares the crap out of me. But I can't imagine it being anyone else."

"So then why…"

"I can't be in a relationship."

"What? Why not?"

Mike growled and rubbed his eyes free of tears. "Because I can't do it in a healthy way. I don't know how to stop self-abandoning. And until I figure that out, I can't be in a relationship. That's assuming she'd even want me."

I blew out a breath, trying to follow his train of thought, but feeling a little lost. "You got to help me out here, bro. What is self-abandoning and why would it keep you from pursuing her?"

"Self-abandoning is when you abandon your own needs for the sake of other people. It's when you ignore yourself and what you want or need, in order to fulfill someone else's wants or needs."

"Oh. You do that a lot."

He chuckled. "Yeah, I know. That's what my therapist tells me. I think…I think watching Mom die—it obviously screwed with all of us—but I think it made me feel like if I can help everyone and make everyone feel good, then nothing bad will happen again. And I know that that's ridiculous and not how life works, but it's hard to unravel that kind of belief when it's existed in me for so long. I'd love to pursue Lizzy—I mean, I'd also crap my pants because I've never pursued someone before." I laughed and then we both sobered. "But not only does she deserve someone who's emotionally healthy, but I can't love someone when that love makes me treat myself so poorly. I need to get through this first. To be better."

"Okay," I nodded slowly. "But why does having to wait a little while make you so emotional?" There was nothing wrong with him crying, but he seemed so heartbroken over a girl he was allowed to pursue.

"Because what if I don't get better? What if this is a battle I never win?"

Ah. I rested my arms on the truck beside him, looking out at the quiet neighborhood that many of the Alfar occupied. It was so quaint, safe and simple. So, unlike the rest of the world.

"Take it from someone who was at his lowest right before he met his mate," I said, recalling with a smile those first weeks after meeting Caroline. "It's good to try and be as healthy as you can in preparation for the right person so they can have the healthiest parts of you." Turning, I met my brother's gaze, wishing that I could just eliminate all his fears for him. Something I'd been trying to do since I was ten. And failing.

"But the thing about meeting *her*, knowing her, letting her in," I said, unable to keep myself from grinning as I thought of those early days when Care and I fought like cats and dogs. Stubborn and resistant, "Is that *she* changes you. She softens you. She makes you wiser and kinder and better. It's smart to work on yourself, but I think the most important thing is making sure that the person you're with won't take advantage of your weaknesses. Because no matter how healthy you get, you're still going to be someone who puts others before himself. You're still going to be afraid and broken because you're human, Mike. And I don't think you have anything to be afraid of with Lizzy. She isn't the type of person to use your self-abandonment for her own gain."

Mike bit his lip, deep in thought.

I was impressed that my brother was taking the time to do something for himself by going to therapy. That he was prioritizing his emotional wellbeing. But I didn't want him to give up his happiness out of fear.

"I think deep down, you're still trying to be perfect," I said gently. "Trying to control the outcome by controlling yourself. And that's not how you find happiness."

Mike stared at me, a look of surprise on his face. "Where there's control, there's no connection."

"What?"

"That's what my therapist always says. That control kills connection." He blew out a breath. "But how do I do both? Focus on learning to be honest with my needs while also trying—probably poorly—to pursue Lizzy?"

I shrugged. "Easy. You practice on her. Be honest with her, tell her your needs and wants and see how good of a mate she can be for you based on how she responds. It doesn't have to be either or, Mike."

Mike sighed, narrowing his eyes at me. "You're right. Clearly mates can change a person because I know you weren't this wise before Caroline."

I laughed. "No, I wasn't. But good women will do that to you. So, are you ready to go back in there and woo your woman?"

He turned white as a sheet. "Heck no! I'm just starting to *think* about it. There's no way I'm just gonna run right out of the gate and try to win her over. I'd fail miserably. I have to start slow, Morgan. I have zero dating experience and severe anxiety. It's probably gonna take me a good three months to get up the courage to even flirt with her."

"Oh Lord. You do realize that at some point, she's gonna realize that she can sense your feelings even when you're not together? Which Alfar can't do. And she's probably going to wonder why your eyes are always glowing."

"Yeah, but she's an incredibly focused person," Mike argued. "She might wonder, but I doubt she'll bother investigating it. She's got better things to do."

"Unless she *likes* you," I teased, drawing out the word.

Mike punched me in the arm. "She doesn't like me. Yet. And I agreed with you that I should let go of my control issues. But I get to do it at my own pace. Not yours."

I held up my hands in surrender. "Fine. I'll butt out of it. But I'm only saying that you should give yourself a little more credit. Sure, you have zero experience, but it won't matter. You're mates. You already have all the attraction and interest that's needed to get someone's attention."

"Now it's just a matter of figuring out what the heck to do with the attention once I get it," he mumbled as we walked back toward the house. "Wait." He suddenly stopped, pulling me to a halt with a hand on my shoulder. "What about Clint?"

"What about him?"

"He likes her too!"

"So? Clint likes new shiny things. It's not serious. But if I were you, I would tell him that she's your mate."

"Why on earth would I do that?"

"Because Clint may get bored fast, but we both know he likes a good chase. And who better to chase than someone resistant like Lizzy. Do you really want him to keep chasing her?"

Mike growled, though whether it was out of jealousy or frustration, I wasn't sure. "Fine. But if he breathes a word of it to anyone, you're helping me bury his body."

"Deal."

By the time we made it back to Lizzy's room where the group was packing up the last of her things, we'd made a thoroughly detailed plan for how to tell Clint about Lizzy and exactly how to dispose of his big-mouthed body if he told anyone about it.

Because that's just what brothers do.

Caroline, Ariel, Logan, Clint, Grey and Lizzy were all gathered in the small room, packing up odds and ends and bubble wrapping the breakable items.

"Looks like we need more bags," Lizzy said, looking around the bedroom, a pile of clothes in her arms.

And like the dedicated puppy he would be for the rest of his days, Mike spotted the box of trash bags on the floor, and moving faster than I'd ever seen, he pulled one out, and held it open to her.

"Oh," Lizzy mumbled, looking from the open bag to Mike. They both stood there, silently studying each other, and we all watched like it was our own personal reality show. "Thanks," Lizzy finally said, shoving the clothes in the bag.

"No problem," Mike breathed so quietly I almost didn't hear him.

"What are you getting from them?" I whispered as I made my way to Caroline.

She leaned into my side, watching the awkward couple as I slid a hand in her back pocket. Mike, true to his word, had no idea what he was doing. Lizzy had turned back to the bed to fold more clothes, and he continued standing there, bag outstretched like it was his one and only purpose in life.

"He's so into her," Care whispered sappily.

"Yeah, no kidding. What about her?"

She hummed, thoughtful. "She's...confused. Curious. Attracted. I don't think she knows what to think." Care looked up at me, smiling. "So, are we on team Mike, then?"

"Definitely. And hopefully by tomorrow there won't be a team Clint anymore anyway. Mike's gonna talk to him."

"Wow. I'm surprised."

"It's amazing what a man will do when he's found the woman of his dreams. You look gorgeous today, by the way."

She was dressed in sweats, with my hoodie hanging too big and baggy on her shoulders. Her auburn hair was tossed up in a careless ponytail and I knew by the slight shadows under her eyes that she wasn't wearing any makeup.

She had never been more perfect than she was right now. Vulnerable, open, relaxed and safely wrapped in *my* clothes. The primal part of me began to purr.

She must have sensed my attraction, because her cheeks turned pink, and she tucked her face against my shoulder. "You can't say things like that when we aren't alone."

"Why not?"

"Because I can't make out with you here."

Pride swelled in my chest, and I grinned like the dopey idiot I was. "Are you thinking of taking advantage of me Caroline Felicity soon-to-be Hohlt?" She lifted her head and poked me in the side. "Because I'm more than happy to let you."

"Alright, let's go," she shrugged, a mischievous glint in her green eyes. "My car's outside and the windows are tinted."

"...you—"

She leaned close, her lips brushing my ear. "Kidding," she laughed, kissing my cheek.

"That was cruel."

"Tit for tat, Bear Man."

"How did I—"

"'Soon-to-be Hohlt'?" she said, quoting me. "You can't tease me about a proposal like that. It's mean."

I grinned and gave her a quick peck, aware that while we might be whispering, we weren't alone. "Who says I'm teasing?"

"Don't be a Jim," she pouted, referring to the way Jim teased Pam about a proposal on *The Office*.

"If you two are done canoodling," Clint taunted from the other side of the room, "We have some packing to do."

"And some plotting," Care added, stepping away from me to grab an empty box.

"Plotting?" I asked, watching her pack up a stack of shoes.

"Queen Caroline said—"

Care cut Lizzy off with a glare. "What did I say about using my title?"

"That if I'm going to use it, it can only be during advisor meetings or for special occasions," the young assistant sighed, saying the words like they'd been repeated many times. Care nodded her agreement and continued packing.

"What did Caroline say?" Grey asked, his old school clipboard actually necessary for once since he was keeping a list of all the things that still needed to be packed.

"She said that the gambling dens were brought up at the council meeting," Lizzy explained, pausing when Mike held the trash bag out to her again to take her new stack of clothes. She blinked at him, shook her head and stuffed the clothes inside. "It sounds like they think the gambling dens are cracking down on people who owe them money."

I gave my mate an accusing look. I always told her everything that happened at the meetings, but that didn't mean she should necessarily tell other people.

"What? Like you didn't tell Grey," Care defended.

"She has a point," Grey added, shrugging when I glared at him. "You might pay me to help you, but you'd have to give me hazard pay to convince me to side against your mate."

Ariel snorted and shot a smile at Logan, who was helping her take the drawers out of a dresser.

"Fine," I sighed. "So, what plotting have you come up with?"

"Well, clearly the gambling dens are up to something," Caroline said, a little too tentatively for my liking. A subtle Caroline was a dangerous Caroline. It meant she was anticipating upsetting me.

I narrowed my eyes at her. "Uh huh."

"And we know from our stakeout that someone is paying them to attack you but not kill you," she went on, not meeting my eyes. "Clearly, they're making some big moves. But doing stakeouts and getting bits of info from council meetings isn't going to be enough. We need to get some real information."

I crossed my arms and shared a glance with each of my brothers and Logan. They likewise sobered and gave Care a knowing look. We'd been a team a while now, and we all knew that when Caroline had an idea, it was almost never good.

"What kind of sketchy plan have you concocted this time?" Logan asked, sounding mildly entertained. That made one of us.

Care shrugged, finally meeting my eyes. "It's not that bad."

Lizzy coughed and Care shot her a glare. "Sorry. It's just...it kind of is that bad."

Alarmed now, I turned to my mate. She stepped forward and put her hands on my biceps, a pleading look in her eyes.

"I swear it's not that dangerous," she insisted, but the squeak in her voice betrayed her. "I just want to get into the home of one of the den boss's and magically coerce him into answering some questions. That's all."

I stared at her for a moment, the room now completely silent as everyone waited for my reaction.

"*That's all?*" I shouted. I saw Lizzy flinch in my peripheral, but Care wasn't bothered in the least by my raised voice. She was used to it.

"Don't get all rabid old dog on me and start barking, Mor," she gently chided. "It's not that big of a deal."

"It's not—"

"This time you'll be going in with me."

I growled, not placated in the least.

"And we'll have backup close by."

My glower continued.

"I promise there won't be any fighting. Just some simple investigating."

Clint laughed, and Caroline shot him a glare. "What?" He shrugged. "Things are never simple with you, Care Bear."

Care rolled her eyes before turning them up at me, wide and pleading. "Please, Mor. We need answers. I can't live like this forever, worried about what might happen to you."

I laughed bitterly. "Welcome to my world, sweetheart. I've been worried about you since I met you."

"Yeah, but we've investigated my attackers, and we haven't found anything. But we haven't investigated yours. Please, do this. For me."

I blet out a loud breath and tried to glare at her. It was useless. She was too cute, too endearing, too loveable. "I hate how much I like you."

She grinned and hugged me tight. "I don't. It works in my favor."

Exactly. And that was the problem.

Chapter 14

CAROLINE

"Alright, the feed blocker is on," I announced, setting the electronic under the front seat of our SUV, a set of fake license plates magnetically slapped over the real ones so no one could trace it back to Morgan. "Cameras are no longer live."

"Nice," Logan nodded, readjusting the knife at his hip.

He and Clint were both dressed in black, with various weapons strapped to their bodies. They were ready for a fight, but Morgan on the other hand...

He was wearing a fancy black suit that fit perfectly to his broad shoulders, the slight taper showing off his trim waist. I'd never seen him so dressed up, but staring at him now, I decided that he needed to do it more often.

I crossed my arms and took a moment to admire the artistry that had gone into creating the body that was Morgan Gareth Hohlt. *Mm, definitely your best work, Lord.*

"If you're done undressing the Chief with your eyes," Logan teased, echoing his words from months ago, before I'd been able to admit my feelings for Morgan, "We have a mission to complete."

"Can you really blame me?" I teased, pulling a pair of sunglasses from my jeans pocket. While Morgan had to dress up for tonight's break-in, I did not. That was the perk of having shifting magic that allowed me to look however I wanted. "He's a stud. I'd have to be blind not to stare."

Morgan blushed at my praise, probably only embarrassed to be receiving it in front of the guys. "Is it really believable for me to be wearing sunglasses?" he complained as I slid them over his eyes. "It's late and it's dark out. Only an idiot would wear sunglasses right now."

"Yes, but you're part of the mob now," I argued, running my hands over his shoulders to wipe off some invisible dust. *Man, I need to appreciate shoulders more often.* "You're an idiot by default."

"Care," Morgan growled playfully, "Gambling dens are not part of the mob."

"Uh, dark suits, black sunglasses, shady meetings in public places," I pointed out. "If it looks like the mob and quacks like the mob—"

Morgan cut me off, pressing his lips to mine.

I smiled against him and wrapped my arms around his neck. "You know, I'm not usually into mafia romances," I mumbled, "Too much abuse and manipulation, but I could be into this one."

Morgan's chest rumbled and he kissed me again. Harder. Longer. Like my lips were his to taste, my hips his to hold. And he wasn't wrong.

I leaned closer, giving him better access to deepen the kiss. And he didn't disappoint.

But his brother did.

"Gross!" Clint whined, making vomiting noises. "Can we please cease the tongue lashing and get moving? I really don't want to walk away from tonight traumatized by my brother's love life instead of bullets."

Morgan finished said tongue lashing and glowered at his brother. "Then turn around."

I bit my lip to hold back a smile, but Morgan kissed the expression away. His lips were sweeter now, tamer. I kissed him back just as gently and then reluctantly stepped away.

Clint was right, we had a mission to get on with.

"Alright," I said, turning to the boys with a smile and a bit of a drunken sway. Morgan's kisses tended to have that effect on me. "Let's do this."

Without warning, I unraveled my magic, letting it ripple across my body like the lowering of a screen. It was nearly effortless for me to shift. One thought, one flip of a switch in my mind and I was someone else.

"Whoa," Clint nodded once I'd finished, clearly impressed. "You look so cool, Care Bear."

"Thanks," I grinned. I glanced down at my new body, a little unnerved to see such a large man in place of myself.

"Question, how is he supposed to get in?" Logan pointed to Morgan, who honestly still looked like Morgan, just with sunglasses on.

I shrugged. "He'll be fine. The boss will be looking at me, the terrifying underboss from the west side who's killed dozens of people and yet still somehow never been convicted of anything. Terrible man." I paused, glancing down at my own suit. "Good taste in clothes, though."

"Alright, well I guess we're about to find out if this plan will work or not," Logan nodded, turning toward the backside of the house. "We'll see you guys after."

Once he and Clint had disappeared, Morgan and I headed for the front door of the den boss's home. Needless to say, it was a fancy place, with three stories and perfectly kept landscaping. It was in a nice neighborhood on the west end of town, and we had to get past three sets of security guards to get to the front door.

But thanks to my new face, they let us through with no problems.

"Ready?" I asked, knocking on the front door.

"No," Morgan grumbled behind me. "But I guess I don't have a choice now."

"Nope." Because not a moment later, the front door swung open to reveal a middle-aged housekeeper.

"Mr. Kirby," she said, quickly stepping aside for us. "I didn't know that he was expecting you."

Arrogant butthead. Arrogant butthead. I chanted the words in my head, trying to remind myself to act like the arrogant butthead I was sure this guy was.

With my shoulders back and a somewhat bored look on my face, I met the woman's timid eyes. "He wasn't."

She seemed to go a little pale, and I felt bad for the flash of fear my response ignited in her. But then she hurried off to retrieve the boss, and I sighed.

"That was horrible," I whispered to Morgan, trying not to fidget. "This guy is such a jerk."

"Technically, you're the jerk," he pointed out.

I scowled at him.

"What? I meant—"

But before he could finish his thought, the boss of the entire west side gambling den walked in. He was relatively young, maybe forty, with a squished-looking face and a shorter stature than I was expecting.

"What are you doing here?" he asked. Then he glanced at Morgan. "And what's with the guy in the sunglasses?"

"See?" Mor whispered quietly, his voice discernable through our earpieces.

"Uh, guys," Clint said through the coms, "We might have a little less time than we planned. There are more guards back here than we were expecting."

I tried not to let my panic show in my face and rolled my eyes. "Oh, don't mind him," I motioned to Morgan, stepping slightly in front of him just in case the boss recognized the man he was actively trying to harm. "He's an idiot that I'm trying out as a favor to a friend. Honestly, I'm already regretting it." The den boss gave Morgan an unimpressed look. "Could we talk in private?" I added, hoping it didn't seem presumptuous.

The man looked me in the eye for a long moment, and I forced myself to stay completely still. If he was looking for a tell, he wouldn't find one. I'd never been caught—well, except for that time Morgan caught me—and I wasn't going to ruin my nearly perfect record now.

"Follow me," the boss said, leading the way down the hall.

I let out a silent breath and trailed behind him to a quiet study. It was nice, with lots of tall bookshelves and a roaring fireplace. The crystal chandelier and priceless antiques on the end tables were a bit much, but at least it was private.

Once the boss closed the doors, I let out a breath of relief. Phase one: complete.

"Now what is this about—"

"I'm sorry sir," I said, an innocent look on my face as I urged my magic to slide forward, "But we'll be asking the questions."

The man was rightfully confused, looking between Morgan and me. When Mor stepped forward, the boss was quick to move away from the door, though he gave us a wide berth.

"Who's paying you to go after Morgan Hohlt?" I demanded as my magic clouded around the man like a sandstorm.

Loud whisps of fear and panic brushed against my senses, and I directed my magic to latch onto them. To tug at them and goad them higher and higher. The boss's fear heightened with every brush of my power, and he stared at me with wide, petrified eyes.

"I..." he stuttered, his gaze flicking to Morgan. "It's you. You're him."

"Answer the question," Morgan barked, a pair of knives now ready in his hands and his sunglasses removed.

The den boss swallowed. "I don't know who's behind it. The head boss handles that."

He was talking about the one boss that controlled all the gambling dens. The dens were like a spider, each leg operating separately but all for the single benefit and under the single leadership of one man. Hence why they were so dangerous.

"What do you know?" Morgan sneered, stepping closer. "Quick, make yourself useful before I decide to be done with you."

"I don't know who's behind it," the man quickly sputtered, "But the boss did say that whoever it is, they're a reputable official."

Morgan and I shared a confused look. What kind of city official would stoop so low as to ask the gambling dens for help? Especially with the Task Force currently investigating all of the species leaders. Why would any of them risk getting their hands dirty right now?

"Guys," Logan's voice came over the coms, "We need to leave. Now."

Taking the suggestion seriously, Mor swung his leg out and kicked the den boss in the side of the head. The man's eyes rolled back, and he fell to the floor with a thump.

"Nice," I nodded, impressed.

Morgan dragged the man behind a couch and joined me by the door just as I was shifting into the now unconscious den boss. "Thanks. Now let's get out of here."

"Clint, Logan," I said quietly into my earpiece as we exited the study, "We're on our way out."

Despite my instincts telling me to run as fast as my legs would carry me out of that house, I walked slow and purposeful. Like I was completely innocent. Morgan strode beside me rather than behind, and I could sense the anxiety humming inside him. There was no way he was going to act like a submissive guard now. He was in total alpha male protective boyfriend mode.

I found it incredibly distracting.

"How long do you think it'll take them to find the body?" I asked.

"Stop them!" Glancing over my shoulder, I saw a handful of guards exiting the study, chasing after us.

Mor groaned. "About that long." Then he grabbed me by the shoulders and shoved me into the living room.

Not a second later, gunfire rang out through the house and bits of plaster fell off the walls where bullets punctured through.

"Okay, so maybe this plan wasn't as risk free as I initially advertised," I admitted, smiling at him. But since I was still in the body of a man, it didn't seem to be swaying him much. What I wouldn't give for the ability to employ a hair flip right about now.

But Morgan had been insistent before we came that under no circumstances was I to show my real face to anyone. I might be linked to Morgan via my fake position as his secretary, but it was a whole other thing to give people reason to believe that I was the one who was shifting my appearance.

"You think?" he snapped, eyes frantically flitting around the room. They paused on a flat screen TV that was attached to the wall. "I have an idea."

Just as the guards were rounding the corner, Morgan ripped the TV off the wall and held it by the mounting accessory on the back. With his suit jacket open, his tie now missing, and his hair a mess while he held a large TV like it was a shield, I found that my eyes were having a spasm, unable to look away. *I don't think he's ever looked hotter.* Maybe there was a way I could ensure we ended up hiding out in a locked room for a little while. Preferably one that had a table he could set me on...

"Caroline, now is really not a good time to be getting turned on." Morgan's growl brought me back to reality and I felt my cheeks go hot.

"Right. Sorry." I scrambled behind him, letting the TV block the oncoming bullets.

"But," he grunted as he herded me toward a window, "If you want to recall this scene later when we get home and reenact it with a pause for a make out, I won't fight you."

I laughed, delighted even as I was being shot at. A hot man and some good flirting will do that to you.

"Guys, how you doing? You in the clear yet?" Mor asked via his earpiece.

"Uh..." Logan grunted on the other end, and I traded a concerned look with Morgan. "Not exactly."

"So, I take it that you won't be able to help us escape through a window on the west side?" Morgan sighed, nodding toward the nearby window.

I took the cue and pushed it open. Thankfully, there were no guards on that part of the lawn right now. And since we were on the ground floor, the drop would only be about three feet.

"Sorry, man," Logan said through a series of grumbles and grunts. "We're gonna be a minute."

"Do you need backup?"

"No. You guys get out. We'll meet you at the car."

Morgan didn't waste time asking them again. Instead, he practically shoved me out the window and onto the lawn.

"Morgan!" I snarled up at him where he still stood inside.

"Sorry, I panicked," he said, throwing the TV like a frisbee at the guards who were closing in on him. "Having you and bullets in the same room seemed like a bad idea."

When he joined me on the ground, I lightly punched his shoulder. "Sweet as that sentiment is, I'd prefer you not push me out of a window next time."

"Duly noted."

Hearing the guards shout inside the house, we took off running toward the street. There was a fence we still had to jump and two sets of guards, but the SUV was now in sight.

And then I felt a bullet fly past my shoulder. I glanced back and saw at least seven guards pursuing us across the lawn.

"That's not good." I flinched as another bullet barely missed my head. "We're not going to make it to the car."

"Yes, we are," Morgan growled, stooping to pick me up.

I darted out of his reach and glared at him. "You carrying me would only slow you down and make you a bigger target. It would be better if I could carry you since I have Nephilim speed, but you're too heavy for me..." I glanced back at the oncoming guards again. "Mor, I need you to go get the car."

"Care—"

"I can hold them off with manipulation magic while you get the car," I insisted, giving him my full attention. "If we keep running, we won't make it. You go and then come back for me."

He looked like he was going to argue with me, so I stopped in my tracks and pivoted to face the guards. The magic was already at the forefront of my mind, and I easily slipped it through the ends of my fingers and down to my toes, an invisible force humming through my body.

"Go!" I shouted at Morgan as magic pulled, prodded and unraveled the emotions of the oncoming guards.

Morgan let out a loud roar, but he didn't stop me, so I assumed he did as I told him to.

"Maim him," one of the guards at the front of the group yelled.

But magic was already working its way through the rest of the guards, pulling on doubt, unraveling arrogance, and even in some manifesting a submission that didn't seem to exist before. I couldn't explain the way the power sliced through their emotions so quickly, using less manipulation and more force.

"What are you doing?" the guard giving orders snapped as the rest of the group either laid down their weapons or turned to throw a punch at their own comrade, too filled with arrogance to think straight.

When he turned angry eyes on me, I stood my ground. It was taking a bit more energy than I wanted to control six grown men at one time. But I wasn't going to back down.

Morgan would kill me if I died.

"What are you doing to them?" the man shouted, raising his pistol at me.

His emotions were a little less useful to me. There was no submission or cockiness inside him. I could have tried to create new emotions, but my power was already stretched thin. Then I noticed a bit of anger and a sense of duty in the man. *Not quite what I was looking for, but I can work with that.*

"Me?" I said, feigning innocence as my eyes grew wider. "I'm not doing anything."

The man wasn't buying it, but frankly, I didn't need him to. I just needed to keep him from pulling the trigger. And his sense of duty, of following orders and being a good soldier was more than enough for me to play with.

My magic crowded around the feeling, pushing it, shoving it, remolding it. And moment by moment, I saw the disdain slip from the man's face. Instead, he began to look doubtful, reluctant.

"You wouldn't shoot an unarmed man, would you?" I pleaded, doing my best to sound young. The other men were too busy beating each other up or running away to get involved, for which I was grateful. This man was a bigger challenge and I needed to focus.

He flinched, uncomfortable as my magic encouraged him to lean into right-eousness. And the righteous never kill the innocent. "You broke in," he protested weakly. His hands were fidgeting with his weapon now.

"No. I was invited, and then people started shooting at me."

His eyebrows furrowed, and I pushed my magic a little harder.

"I'm loved, you know," I said, sensing his resolve weakening. "I have a family. People who would be devastated by my loss. And I can swear to you that I haven't hurt anyone here today. Will you really shoot someone who didn't do anything wrong?"

The man continued to stare at me, confused. And just as he opened his mouth—to argue or give in, I would never know—a black SUV barreled in and hit him in the side.

I gasped, shocked as the man was knocked to the ground like he weighed nothing. He groaned, and I sensed his immense pain, but at least he was still alive.

Morgan stepped out of the car and walked over to the man whining on the ground.

"*No one* threatens my mate," he snarled.

"Morgan," I exclaimed, staring at the guy on the ground with wide eyes, "Wha—"

"Run!"

We turned at the shout, squinting at two figures running toward us.

"Is that—"

"I swear, I can't leave anyone alone these days," Mor growled, gently pushing me toward the car as the guards behind us continued to fight. My magic was no longer toying with them. Their testosterone did that just fine without my interference.

"I did just fine while you were gone," I protested, sliding into the passenger seat as Logan and Clint came running, a horde of guards not far behind them. I let the magic leave my body, my true face safely hidden behind the tinted windows.

Morgan pressed me back against the seat and kissed me soundly. "You put yourself in danger and forced me to leave without you," he hissed. My seatbelt clicked as he buckled me in, his eyes never leaving mine.

"Well, when you put it like that…"

He kissed me again, his hands on my face like he needed to assure himself he wasn't dreaming it. "Never do that again, Red. I'm not asking, I'm telling you. You will *never* do that again."

As much as I wanted to argue with him—if only because my nature insisted I not be told what to do—I just sat there and nodded. Because he was right. I'd be furious if he made me leave him behind.

Plus, this alpha male version of Morgan always did something funny to my sense of reason. It made me want to wear his T shirts and his ring on my finger and hear him growl *mine* any time I walked in a room.

Stupid cavewoman brain.

"I promise, I'll never put myself in danger again," I agreed, even though he wasn't asking for an answer, "Unless you're right beside me."

His expression softened and he pulled me into a hug, my face pressed under his chin. "I love you too much to lose you, Caroline Felicity."

I hugged him back. "I know."

The sweet moment was ruined when Clint and Logan yanked the back doors open, panting and flushed.

"Quit kissing and *drive*, dude!" Logan shouted, slamming the door behind him.

"Yeah, I don't know if you guys have noticed," Clint said between gasps as Morgan shut my door and went around to the driver's side, ducking a few on-coming bullets, "But we're kind of being shot at."

"Relax," Mor insisted, backing the car onto the street. "This thing is bullet proof, and the guards are on foot."

Then he laced his fingers with mine and set our conjoined hands on his thigh, his thumb rubbing my skin softly. Morgan was a sweeter man than he wanted people to believe, but I'd been dating him long enough to know that when he got touchy feely like this, it was almost always a response to anxiety. He liked touching me, but when he got scared, he *needed* to touch me.

"Now explain to me what the heck happened," he snapped, looking at his best friend and baby brother through the rear-view mirror.

Clint blushed and I raised an eyebrow. "Clint, what did you do?"

He glanced at me; his embarrassment palpable. "I got...distracted."

"He started flirting with the cook," Logan said, glaring at Clint. "He was supposed to be watching my back while I used Mike's tech to hack into the computer. But no, Clint saw a breathing female under the age of fifty and just had to flirt with her."

Clint cringed. "Like I said, I got distracted. The guards caught us, and we had to make a run for it."

"Was she worth it?" Logan taunted, clearly still bitter about being caught.

Clint smirked and held up a slip of paper. "She gave me her number, so I guess we'll find out."

But then Logan snatched the paper and tossed it out the window as Morgan sped down the road.

"Hey!" Clint punched him in the arm.

"That's for being such an idiot!" Logan shouted. "And you couldn't have dated her anyway, you moron. She caught you breaking into a den boss's house! Now do us all a favor and shut up and pout like the child you are."

Clint crossed his arms. "I don't pout." But the pucker of his lips said otherwise.

Chapter 15

MORGAN

"Can you please take something seriously for once in your life?" I sighed, feeling a headache coming on.

"I could, but I'm afraid it would kill me," Volund shrugged, dark eyes filled with false innocence.

Care and I stood just outside his room in the Berserker house. I'd been dreading coming to ask for his help—again—but we were short on options. And I'd do pretty much anything for Caroline.

Even be in the presence of Satan's spawn himself.

"I'm going to kill him," I warned Caroline, already short on patience after hearing that whoever was after me might be a council member. It was one thing for a council member to try and frame me for something, but to attack me? I couldn't think of any members who would be *that* stupid.

"Don't, you'll get blood on your shirt, and I just bought that for you a week ago," Care said, winding her arm through mine.

"You do seem to like me in Henley's," I teased, smiling when she looked up at me with mischief in her eyes.

"They highlight your strong shoulders and very firm chest," she smirked. "And you always push the sleeves up, which gives me the perfect view of your sexy forearms."

I laid my hand over hers where it rested on said forearm. "I remember how well you like my forearms. Is that all I have to do to get your attention? Flash a little arm hair and you're all mine?"

Care leaned into my side, her gaze falling to my lips. "Maybe. Why? Do you want my attention right now?"

"Oh my gosh," Volund groaned loudly, covering his face with his hands. "I'll do anything if you two will *please* stop with the lovey dovey crap. It's making me nauseous."

"Is it?" Care asked innocently. "What a convenient side effect."

"What was it you needed?" Volt growled, leveling a glare at both of us.

I rolled my eyes. I should have known asking the man a simple question would take at least an hour. Two if I decided to kill him and then had to dispose of the body. And that option was looking better and better by the moment.

"I already told you," I snapped. "We need to know what information you have on council members."

"Ah. That's right."

"*Well?*"

The Dark Elf shrugged and tugged on the sleeve of his black shirt.

"I'm afraid I'm not very well versed on the uselessness of council members," he sneered, his nose high up in the air. "I've kind of made it a point not to cross paths with them. Keeping your species a secret will do that to you."

"You don't know anything?" Care asked, and I hated the way Volund's expression seemed to soften slightly.

I didn't have any reason to think that he was interested in her romantically. He called her 'cousin' and though he looked at her with longing, it was the way a brother might miss a sister. Nothing more.

But the bear inside me didn't care that it was innocent. Possession still flared to life in my veins, and I crept a bit closer to my mate.

"Not really," Volund sighed, sounding genuinely sorry not to have more information. "I never paid much attention to them other than to make sure they were ignorant of me. From what I've gathered, many of them seem less than trustworthy. But then so do a lot of people."

The insinuating words hung between us, and I couldn't help but feel like it was bait for a trap.

When Caroline had taken Volund down weeks ago, he told her that she could trust him. That it was other people she couldn't trust. I didn't believe him for a second, but I did wonder who he was trying to throw under the bus with his remarks.

"You know something," Care said, narrowing her eyes. "What is it?"

Volt shrugged. "You didn't want to know, the last time I tried to tell you."

"No. You tried to play me last time, this time I want the truth. What are you not telling us?"

To his credit, Volund didn't look calculating. Rather, he seemed frustrated. But no matter how long we stood there, he didn't expand, and he didn't explain.

"Well, let me know when you're finally ready to be honest," Care sighed after a few moments of silence.

We turned to go but stopped at the sound of Volund's voice. "How is your investigation into the attacks coming, Chief? Find any leads?"

Slowly, I turned. But Volund wasn't smiling, he wasn't gloating. Instead, he was glaring. I couldn't remember the last time I'd seen the Dark Elf glare.

"Do you have any to share?" I asked, quickly losing my patience in the face of his endless games.

"Only that you're too trusting. If I were you, I—" he abruptly stopped and shook his head. "It's not your back you need to worry about, Morgan."

He said nothing else, so Caroline and I left and headed back downstairs. When we made it to the kitchen, Caroline hopped up on a barstool at the large white island, looking very put out.

"Why the pout, Red?" I asked, sidestepping her to get to the fridge.

"Because my self-proclaimed 'cousin' is a big fat pain in the a—" Her petulant expression softened as I set a gallon of sea salt and caramel ice cream on the island. When I produced two spoons and handed her one, she almost started crying. "Have I told you today that I love you?"

I took a bite of ice cream. "No, I don't think you have. And it's really starting to mess with my self-esteem."

She grinned and stood, dragging me over to sit on the stool instead. Confused, I watched as she tried to use a second stool to leverage herself up into my lap. After her fourth try, I chuckled and grabbed her by the waist and hoisted her up. She immediately curled close; one arm wrapped around my neck while her free hand reclaimed her spoon.

"I love you," she whispered after swallowing a spoonful of ice cream. Then she kissed me.

I kissed her back, my arm snug around her back and her body pressed against my chest. As I relaxed into her kiss, pulling her closer, I appreciated just how important it was to have barstools with backs on them. "I love you too."

"You know," she said, looking up at me with furrowed brows, "I don't think I need ice cream. You already taste like salted caramel, so I might as well just keep kissing you and skip the calories."

I smiled and shook my head. "We both know you're a beast when you're hungry Caroline Felicity. My kisses might satiate your craving, but they won't fill your stomach."

"That's true. They tend to make me hungrier—though not for food..." She gave me a coy look and I squeezed her hip. With a laugh, she took a bite of ice cream, but the sweet sound quickly faded, and the gravity of real life seemed to slip between the cracks of the silence.

"What do you think he meant?" she asked, more so playing with the ice cream than eating now.

I set my spoon down and curled both arms around her, setting my chin on the top of her head. "I don't know. Was he lying at all?"

Care seemed to ponder that for a moment, her spoon now forgotten as she lightly ran her fingers over the hair on my forearm. I smiled.

"It's hard to tell," she explained. "He wasn't lying...but I also don't think he was telling the full truth. He was anxious—and *very* irritated."

"Yeah, I caught that. Maybe he's annoyed that he's still a prisoner?"

"Or maybe he's frustrated that we don't trust him?"

I shrugged. "It could be anything. At this point, talking to him is playing a guessing game and never knowing if you're right."

"So then what do we do about the gambling dens?" Care demanded, lifting her head to look me in the eye. "They're coming for you because a 'reputable official' paid them to do it. Until we find out who that is and stop them, you're going to keep being attacked."

"Yes, but as the den member said when we so sweetly asked him, they're only supposed to maim me," I pointed out, "Not kill me."

Care tried to lift her head—probably to scowl at me—but I held her in place, liking the feel of her safely tucked in my arms. "Is that supposed to make me feel better?" she hissed once she realized I wasn't going to let go.

"Yes. Because while your attackers have previously tried to kidnap you, mine are just trying to hurt me."

This time she pinched my side until I loosened my grip, then she lifted her head and glared at me with fire in her eyes. "*Just?*"

"I'm only saying that you don't need to be worried for my life, because they're not trying to kill me."

The look in her eyes hardened. "Okay fine. Then you have no right to worry about my attackers because they weren't trying to kill me either."

"They tried to kidnap—"

"But not kill."

It was my turn to glare, but she was unbothered, cocking a daring eyebrow at me. "How's your logic feeling now?"

"Caroline," I sighed, half of me wanting to throttle her and the other half wanting to lock her in my arms for the rest of her life so I could keep her safe. "I just meant that I didn't want you to worry yourself into an early grave over these attacks. Yes, we need to stop them, but it's good to know that they won't kill me."

"If I want to worry myself to death," she argued, her voice softening as she brought her hands to my face, "Then I will. Because you're my mate and I love you. It's literally my job to worry about you, to put your needs first."

"What about my wants? Because I want you to be happy, Red."

"I'm happy when you're safe. I'm happy when you're with me. I'm happy when neither of us has to be worried."

Leaning forward, I kissed the tip of her nose. "And I feel the same way. But right now, we don't know how to eliminate either of our threats. So, the best we can do is move forward with the knowledge we have, and at least take a little comfort in knowing that our lives are not in immediate danger."

She scrunched her nose as her eyebrows drew together in an adorable scowl/pout. "Fine. But we will put equal effort into both your attacks and mine. Because if my needs and wants actually come first for you, then you'll do everything you can to ensure that I don't have to be worried about you."

"Ditto, Red. We'll focus on both of our situations, and we'll be careful for each other's sakes."

Care sighed and practically hung herself around my neck like a scarf, clinging tightly to me as she pressed her face against my skin. "Have I told you yet today that I love you?"

I closed my eyes and wrapped her up tight, focusing on the feel of her heartbeat against mine, her much smaller body cradled in mine. *Mine. Safe.* The words repeated in my head, and I let them sooth me, convincing me that even without any answers right now, we would be okay.

"No," I whispered, my fingers running the length of her hair, "At least not in the last sixty seconds. And I really need your validation at a constant rate."

"I love you, Morgan."

I smiled and breathed her in. "Not half as much or as insanely as I love you, Caroline."

Chapter 16

CAROLINE

"She's not even trying," I complained, watching Charlie standing next to Stefan, our landscaper. He was in his mid-twenties, and between his thick brown hair, chocolatey eyes and tall build, I could see what my housekeeper liked about him.

But the poor girl was barely speaking to him, let alone flirting with him.

"She should purposefully break her own car," Torrie suggested, smiling wide, her cheeks rosy and round.

She'd come outside to witness our training day solely for the gossip, with no intention of training herself. I couldn't blame her though. Alfar weren't natural fighters—and it showed.

Around fifty people were gathered in the backyard of the Alfar house under the summer heat. Since we only had Clint, Logan, Morgan and Mr. Wallace to train them, we had people come for their training sessions in shifts.

I watched as one man moved to attack Clint and accidentally tripped himself. Surprisingly, this wasn't even the worst shift.

"I don't think that tactic is going to work for everyone, sweetheart," David said, smiling down at his wife.

They were an interesting couple, with him standing at six feet two inches and shoulders nearly as wide as Morgan's, and her being only five feet tall with plump curves for days. But when she grinned up at him, sweet as a cherub, and he looked at her with pure adoration, I sighed. I could only hope that Mor and I would be as happy as they were after eight years of marriage.

"Maybe not," Ariel agreed, our group of gossip queens rounded out with her and Lizzy standing on my other side. "But if she doesn't give him some kind of sign, he's not going to make a move. He's already flirted with her three times in the last fifteen minutes, and she gave him nothing."

"I don't know," Lizzy hummed, her tablet hanging by her side in the little crossbody pouch I'd bought for her. She, like the rest of us, was wearing workout attire even though she wasn't training. But while the rest of the gossip queens had done nothing but stand around and talk all morning, I'd already trained quite a bit with the early morning Alfar shift. So, I felt justified in gossiping right now.

"What? You don't think she should give him a little more encouragement?" I asked, watching the landscaper and the housekeeper standing amongst the trainees, waiting their turn to fight Logan.

"I think she should probably learn to unclench her fists and smile at him when he's actually looking," Lizzy said, flashing her sandy brown eyes at me. "But I also think that given how long they've known each other and how often I catch him watching her, he knows how shy she is. He sees the way she tenses up and gets uncomfortable around him."

"Maybe he thinks it means that she doesn't like him," David offered.

"Wait," I turned to the valet, eyes wide. "Why don't you talk to him? See how he feels about her? Maybe you could encourage him to try a little harder with her because she's shy."

But David was already shaking his head. "No way. I don't meddle."

Torrie scoffed and rolled her eyes. When her husband raised an eyebrow, she sighed. "What about the time that girl asked you to fix her car, and you lied to her?"

David fidgeted and I smiled, immediately curious.

"You told her the part was only available through a specific place," Torrie went on, "Which it wasn't. And then you had her come out to talk about the car right when the man you ordered the part from just so happened to be dropping it off." She turned to us; eyes bright. "Turns out, this kid worked at a parts store, and he'd had a crush on this girl for months but hadn't really had a reason to talk to her yet. So, David here played cupid and *lied* to her so the guy would have a chance to meet her. Didn't you?" This question she directed at her husband.

He shrugged. "They've been married ten months now. I was a groomsman in their wedding."

"Such a softie," Harold tsked as he walked up to us, his wife beside him. I hadn't formally met her yet, but I'd seen her accompany Harold to a few functions. She was a pretty woman, with icy grey hair pulled back into a curly ponytail and a modest but trendy workout outfit on.

"Says the man who needed a tissue to blot his eyes," his wife, Angela, taunted, "When Chief Hohlt made that speech about how proud he was of Queen Caroline."

"Harold," I said with a smile, "Were you crying?"

He scoffed and crossed his arms. "Of course not...Chief Hohlt just put his words so eloquently."

I rolled my eyes and Angela followed suit. Men and their shield of masculinity. As if no one could be manly and have feelings at the same time.

"Hey Care!" I turned at the sound of Morgan's shout. He was working with Tristian and his four brothers—yep, four. Other than Tristain and Jude, there were two other men in their clan, each with a different hair color. "Can you come show these guys that move you showed me yesterday?"

"So racy, Morgan," I grinned, stepping away from the group of gossip queens. "Should we really be showcasing my make out skills in front of the children? Well, if you insist."

I hopped up to him with a smile and he gave me a quick peck. "You're incorrigible," he said, shaking his head.

"And you love me."

"Against my better judgement."

"So are you going to teach us to fight, or..." Jude interrupted, looking as put out as ever. He had his dark hair up in a man bun again today, and despite his cold reception, I didn't feel offended.

He acted like this with everyone.

"Calm yourself," Lance said, clapping his brother on the shoulder. From what I remembered, he was the second oldest of the boys. I was pretty sure he had a job in finance, but I honestly couldn't recall. But in my defense, four brothers were a lot to remember. *How am I supposed to keep all their details straight?* I was just proud that I knew all their names.

Lance had brown hair that was kept short and a clean-shaven face that showed off a very chiseled jaw. He smiled good-naturedly at the baby of the family, and I watched, fully entertained.

"Yeah, Jude," Tristain teased his youngest brother, a grin on his freckled face. "Love is in the air, brother. Don't you feel it?"

"I feel nausea," Brad, the second youngest of the boys complained. While Jude was a bit of a loner and a little enigmatic, Brad was downright surly. Maybe even worse than Morgan had been when I met him. "Can we get this training session over with?"

I exchanged a knowing look with Mor. This was going to be fun.

"He needs a woman in his life," I whispered as we walked over to retrieve my knife from where I'd thrown it about an hour ago, swearing that I was never going to work out again in retaliation for the murdering of my thighs. Funny how much one look from my boyfriend could do.

"He needs an attitude check," Morgan grumbled. "And maybe to fall on his butt a few times."

"I think we can arrange—"

But the rest of my words were lost as my fingers grasped the hilt of my pink knife and an eerie wave of cold rushed up through my body. A strange weightlessness came over me and I couldn't grasp why.

Until I hit the ground.

"Caroline!" Morgan was crouched over me in an instant, and although I saw his hands run down the length of me, looking for an injury, I couldn't feel them. *Why can't I feel him?* "Caroline, what's wrong?"

When I didn't answer him, his panic heightened. He glanced down at the knife still grasped in my numb hand and quickly kicked it away.

"Grey!" He shouted, and a moment later his Second appeared in my line of vision.

"What happened?" the older man demanded; his clipboard tossed to the ground as he also crouched over my still body.

"I don't know. She grabbed the knife and then she just went down. I don't think she can move."

I couldn't. So instead, I moved my eyes back and forth in place of shaking my head.

I couldn't feel it, but I saw Morgan pick up my hand in both of his and squeeze. "You're gonna be okay, Care. I promise."

But with my body completely still and numb, I wasn't so sure.

Chapter 17

CAROLINE

"Temporary paralysis," Mor growled, his hands rubbing up and down my arms. I curled closer to him, still shivering.

It had taken a good forty minutes for the paralysis to wear off, which had given everyone plenty of time to get here for our impromptu meeting. Unfortunately, whatever magic caused the paralysis also left me feeling bone chillingly cold. So, I sat on Morgan's lap, his body cocooning me and about three electric blankets wrapped around us.

"Like I said," Merida continued after Morgan had interrupted her—again, "The knife was jinxed."

She, along with Mike and Asher, had arrived at the Alfar house a few minutes ago. And now the entire group, including Harold, Torrie and David, were gathered amongst the expensive furniture that I was still in the process of selling off in one of the many sitting rooms.

"Jinxed to *paralyze* her," Morgan snapped.

"Mor, not so loud," I whined, covering my ears with cold fingers.

"Sorry, Red," he said—much softer now—as he pressed a kiss to my temple. "Merida, please tell me you can identify who jinxed the knife."

I didn't have to look at the Witch to know that she had bad news. I could feel her anxiety. Plus, identifying magic users wasn't a skill Witches possessed. It was, however, one that Witch Hunters possessed. But in order to hire a Witch Hunter, the Hunter would have to file a report at the Shifter Alliance building. And we couldn't take the risk of bringing attention to me right now. Not when I could lead people straight to the Alfar.

"You know I can't do that kind of magic," Merida pleaded.

Morgan seemed set to blow up at her until I pressed my hand against his chest, his heart beating under my fingers. Instantly, I felt him soften, his concern for me outweighing his frustration.

"What are our options then?" Grey asked, more worried than I'd ever seen him. In his defense though, none of us had been temporarily paralyzed before. *Something I'll be having nightmares about for a* while.

"How long was the knife out of your sight?" Asher asked, his expression slightly more intimidating than usual.

I curled my fingers under the hem of Morgan's shirt and pressed them against the warmth of his skin. He shivered at the touch but didn't complain. Normally, we were careful about physical boundaries. No roaming hands, no lights off, no removal of clothing, but all of that meant nothing when I felt like my very bones were enduring frostbite. *Give me that body, baby.* Anything to stave off the cold.

"An hour, maybe," I replied, fighting off the embarrassment I felt at being watched. It wasn't my norm to let people see me so weak. It also wasn't my norm to lean on someone else for support.

But if there was one thing I'd learned in loving Morgan, it was that there is such a thing as healthy codependency. It's when partners help each other carry burdens, when you go eighty because your partner can only give you twenty. And today, I could barely give ten.

"That's plenty of time for someone to put a jinx on it," Merida confirmed, a murderous look on her face.

Witches were the only ones who could perform spells, but they often sold those spells to non-Witches by attaching the spell to an object. The person who bought the spell would then wave that object over whatever or whoever they wanted the magic to affect.

There were a lot of rules about which objects could be used to carry spells, but not being a Witch, I didn't know what they were. I did know that selling spells was a highly monitored affair, and a jinx for temporary paralysis probably wasn't on the list of okayed spells.

Meaning that this particular jinx had probably been acquired from the black market. Which meant that whoever bought it was willing to risk going to jail in order to jinx me. *Such a reassuring thought.*

"But how would someone do it without being seen?" David pointed out, his arm around Torrie, who was watching me like I might disintegrate at any moment. The poor woman was terrified on my behalf. She'd plied me with hot tea and a plate full of scones before David convinced her to stand still.

"There were quite a few people at the training session," Clint said, arms crossed and expression hard. "It wouldn't have been too hard to go unnoticed."

"What did the cameras pick up?" Morgan asked.

Mike pulled his gaze away from the computer in his lap. Judging by the anger wafting from him, he hadn't found much. "Nothing. There's a jump in the footage. One minute Caroline is tossing her knife to the ground, and the next she's just gone."

"How would someone get into the security system like that?"

"Who has access to that room?"

"Is it hard to delete footage? Who would know how?"

All these questions swirled around me as everyone immediately began trying to solve the riddle. But all I could think was that even with all my efforts to win my people over and give them a real future—something they'd been denied in the past—they still hated me. Enough to paralyze me and risk going to prison for it. *But why?*

"What am I doing wrong?" I thought I'd whispered the question to Morgan, but when the room went silent, I realized that I'd said it out loud.

"You're not doing anything wrong, Care," Ariel insisted, giving me a stern look. "And if you use this attack as a reason to fuel your insecurities, I'll never forgive you."

I glared at her. "I'm not letting it do anything. But it is a valid question. Am I doing something that's angering people? Is there a logical reason that people want to hurt me? I'm not saying I'm a bad queen, I know I'm not..." That part was only a little bit of a lie. "But that doesn't mean I'm perfect either. And if there's something I can do to fix this, then I want to."

"You're not doing anything wrong," Torrie insisted, and although I knew she was trying to look formidable, her stern expression just made me want to laugh. "Some people are just stubborn and stuck in their ways."

"What do you mean?" Morgan asked, shifting me on his lap so he could see the chef.

Torrie shrugged, still angry. "Some people are mad that we're going public. They're convinced that we'll all end up dead or on a table being tested like rats. All a bunch of drama queens with nothing better to do with their lives."

Everyone began speaking at once, discussing the audacity of the angry Alfar who were attacking me. But I ignored all of them and looked at Morgan.

He was quiet and thoughtful, his hands moving slower as they rubbed my arms.

"What do you want to do?" he whispered.

I sighed and ran a finger across his scar, tracing his cheek. "You told me that I don't need to prove anything to anyone."

"You don't."

"Then I'm not going to. If some of the Alfar want to be mad about my choices, they can be mad. I'm not going to change my mind just because they come at me."

He nodded but said nothing. I sensed no anger in him, just a silent battle between worry and pride.

"You know I'm going to act like a bear for the foreseeable future, then," he said after a moment.

"I know. And I won't complain. You can taste test my food for me, insist that I not go anywhere alone, install new locks on my bedroom door and I won't argue with you. Because I know this is asking a lot."

"You're going to be in constant danger because you refuse to stand down," he said, slipping his arms around my waist. "I'm angry that someone has the ability to put you in that position, but I'm also incredibly proud that you're sticking to your guns."

I smiled, feeling warm for the first time since regaining my feeling. "Thank you."

"I'll try not to be a jerk about your safety, but I am going to be overprotective—*more* overprotective."

"That's okay. You love me, how could you not be worried?"

"But it's *because* I love you that I'm not going to try to change your mind or interfere with your plans," he said, leaning his forehead against mine. "Your fire keeps me warm, Care. What kind of man would I be if I tried to put it out?"

Then he kissed me, and I leaned into it, thankful that the rest of the group was too busy arguing to pay us any mind.

Chapter 18

CAROLINE

You know that feeling you get when someone's watching you? The prickles on your neck? The eerie heat of someone's eyes on your back? I had that.

Except this time, it was accompanied by a sense of attraction, desire and intense affection.

"You're staring," I whispered, fidgeting in my floor-length dress.

It was a rich Kelly green, fitting closely to my body. Just saucy enough to keep Morgan's attention, but not enough to be distracting to other people.

"If you didn't want me to stare," he rumbled, invading my space, his chest pressed against my back and his breath brushing against my bare shoulders, "Then you shouldn't have worn that dress."

I bit my lip to keep my grin from spreading.

"But I think you want me to stare, Red," he went on, slipping his arm around my waist. "I think you want to tease me."

"Now why would I do that?" I blinked innocently up at him. I'd gone for a slightly smokier makeup look than normal, and my hair was swept up into an updo, leaving a few curls to fall down my neck.

His five o'clock shadow scraped against my chin as he captured my lips with his. He looked like the devil tonight. His dark hair was combed back, and his blazing grey eyes were a stark contrast to his black suit.

And with the white scar trailing across his face and the quiet growls emanating from his chest, he would be intimidating if I wasn't so ravenous for him.

"Because you're punishing me for not proposing yet," Morgan said, bringing me back to the present. "But patience is a virtue, Caroline."

His fingers trailed down my arm before twining with mine.

"One I don't possess," I pointed out, glaring.

He smirked and dragged me forward through an open set of double doors. "And I couldn't love you more for it. It means you'll be ready to ditch this party just as quickly as I will."

"Oh, you're not getting out of this evening that easily," I said, shaking my head. "We're going to shmooze and make small talk and you're going to show off your hot girlfriend." I shrugged one shoulder, batting my eyes. "And do a little digging to see if we can't figure out which council member is working with the gambling dens."

Morgan scoffed, his expression shifting into a glare as he looked around the ballroom. "You say that way too cavalierly."

I patted his arm, attempting to pacify him. "Calm down, Bear Man. We'll get through this. No problem."

The function room on the second floor of the Alliance Building wasn't really a ballroom, but with the white linen tablecloths, the polished dance floor and everyone inside dressed to the nines, it felt like a ballroom.

Tonight, we were celebrating the one hundred and twenty-fourth anniversary of the Shifter Council. Ironic since it seemed half the council was hell bent on destroying the entire thing with their atrocious leadership skills.

I hadn't even been leading my own species for two months yet and already I could spot a dozen mistakes the other leaders made on a regular basis.

"So, you finally decided to make things official, did you?"

Mor and I turned and saw Brooks, the Fenrir representative, walking up to us. Brooks was always all smiles, with friendly eyes, a moderate build and disheveled hair. Tonight though, he'd managed to comb his mane back, and I saw a number of young women looking his way.

A man stood beside him, with wider shoulders and a pessimistic purse to his lips that Brooks lacked. But he shared Brooks' hair and rugged jaw, so I assumed they were related.

"Have you been confiding in Brooks about your undying love for me?" I teased, grinning up at Morgan.

Mor rolled his eyes and glared at Brooks. "I don't 'confide' in people."

"Really?" Brooks smiled. "Because I seem to remember you begging Merida and I for advice not that long ago."

"Is that so?" I jumped eagerly at this news. "What did he say?"

"Who'd you bring with you, Brooks?" Morgan interrupted, looking annoyed. But I felt his embarrassment, his cheeks turning just the faintest bit pink.

"This is my brother, Spencer," Brooks announced, motioning to the grumpy man beside him.

"Hi," said Spencer, clearly the verbose kind.

"Sorry about him," Brooks smiled, slinging an arm over his brother's shoulder. "He's put out about a girl."

"Says the man who brought his brother as his date," Spencer pointed out sharply.

"Yes, but we both know that I could have brought any number of women with me tonight. It's not for lack of options that I'm here with you." Brooks somehow managed to say the words without a smidge of arrogance.

"What is it then?" I asked, a sap for romance drama.

Morgan gave me a reproving look for drawing the conversation out, but the affection in his chest betrayed him. He liked my dramatic ways.

"He's a purist," Spencer said, rolling his eyes. "Thinks he shouldn't lead a woman on when he's waiting for his God-blessed mate to show up. He's a romantic fool, which leaves him in my happy company."

I smiled at Brooks, finding his and his brother's dynamic entertaining.

Brooks sighed, long and suffering. "I'm not ashamed to call myself a romantic," he said. "My brother, however, masquerades as a cynic when he's here because he's heartbroken."

Spencer scowled. "I'm not heartbroken. I don't have a heart to break."

At this, Morgan chuckled. I rolled my eyes, exchanging a tired look with Brooks. What was it with these alpha-male types and pretending they didn't have feelings?

"So, I take it I shouldn't ask what happened to *not* break your heart?" I said.

"The female species is a pain in the freaking backside," he growled.

I laughed, grinning up at Morgan. He was finally cracking a smile when a new voice interrupted us.

"Nice to see you, Chief Morgan," Lawrence, the Sphinx representative, said. He, like the other men here tonight, was dressed in a suit. He didn't have a date on his arm, and his emotions were calm and curious rather than malicious. I'd watched enough council meetings and spent enough time researching the members to know that Lawrence wasn't someone with a lot of red flags.

But that just made me want to know more.

"Alpha Lawrence," Morgan said, shaking the Sphinx's hand.

Lawrence was a big man. Morgan had more bulk, but Lawrence was taller, with a fiercer kind of vibe versus Morgan's more reclusive, protective attitude.

Lawrence had a short beard that was almost more like scruff and light hazel eyes that seemed like they saw more than they should.

"Good to see you, Lawrence," Brooks said, instantly brightening the moment with his contagious good attitude. "This is my brother Spencer, and this here is Morgan's girlfriend."

"Caroline," I said, offering my hand to the Alpha.

I felt Morgan glaring at me, but I didn't look at him. We hadn't discussed whether or not we would be telling people my real name. But it didn't seem worth it to try and hide it when any of these people could figure it out with just a little bit of digging.

"Lucky man," Lawrence said, nodding to Morgan.

I felt Mor tense beside me, but I squeezed his fingers, trying to let him know that there was no reason to be jealous. I felt no desire in Lawrence, just passing attraction.

"The luckiest," Morgan agreed, looking at me with warmth in his cold grey eyes.

"Why are you going stag?" Brooks asked, using his uncanny ability to make everyone around him feel like he was their best friend. Even Lawrence, who didn't seem keen on being friends with anyone, seemed to instantly relax.

"It's complicated," he sighed, surprising me with a small smile. "The girl I'd like to bring is...not an option right now." *I pity the woman who's running from him.* He was handsome to start with, but the smile was killer.

"Watch it, Red," Morgan whispered in my ear, releasing my hand to slide his palm along the small of my back. "I don't like to share."

"Then put a ring on it," I whispered back, taunting him.

He shook his head, a smile twitching his lips. He had something up his sleeve about this whole proposal business. I just wasn't sure what exactly it was.

"Join the club," Brooks sighed.

"You don't even have a girl," Spencer argued, hands stuffed in his pockets.

Brooks raised his hands, palms up. "Exactly! She's not an option because I can't find her to begin with."

"Boys, would you excuse me?" Morgan interrupted, tugging me forward. "I've got a date to dance with."

"Nice, Morgan," Brooks complained, smiling, "Rub it in our faces that you have a girl, and we don't."

I snickered and followed Morgan to the dance floor. The DJ had started playing a slow song, and there were a handful of couples spread out, swaying to the music.

"Did you really want to dance with me, or were you just trying to get away?" I asked as he swung me into his arms.

He hummed, one hand on my back and the other clasped around mine, leading us in a simple waltz. Or at least I assumed it was a waltz. I just tried to focus on not getting so lost in his eyes that I couldn't follow his steps.

"Both," he replied, flashing me a smirk.

I lightly pinched his shoulder. "Wrong answer. You should always say that I am your only reason."

"Caroline."

"Hm?"

He leaned close, his cheek pressed against my temple and his breath on my ear. "You're always my only reason."

I bit my lip, heat flooding my body and butterflies doing acrobatics in my gut. Then, all at once, it was like all the people in the room vanished. Like that scene in the 2005 version of *Pride and Prejudice* when Lizzy and Mr. Darcy are having such an intense moment that everyone disappears and it's just the two of them dancing.

"If you propose to me in here, I will say no," I said, eyes closed.

He laughed, his arm pulling me tighter. "Not even if I get down on one knee and give the speech of a lifetime?"

I inched back so I could see his eyes. "No. I am not sharing my engagement with a room full of strangers in a place that means nothing to us as a couple."

"But if I proposed to you in Fitz's office, that would be okay since it's the place we first met?"

I smiled, unable to keep the expression at bay. The day we met seemed so long ago now. Almost like it was completely different people who'd run into each other in Fitz's office.

"You just want to get me alone," I said, sliding my hand from his shoulder to his chest.

"Absolutely I do."

I laughed, but the sound faded as I caught sight of someone hiding behind a potted Ficus at the edge of the room. Mayor Fitz had a branch held up in front of his face, and his body was shadowed by the plant, but he was still easily recognizable.

"Want to go find out why the mayor is hiding behind a plant?" I said, nodding in Fitz's direction.

Morgan chuckled when he spotted the poor man cowering behind the Ficus. "I guess we can cut our dance short for a rescue mission."

Slowly, we made our way to the edge of the room, blocking Fitz from view as we closed in.

"Mayor Fitz," Morgan greeted him. "Hiding in the shrubbery, huh? Even I haven't gone that far to get out of conversations yet."

Fitz looked at us with terror in his blue eyes and pure exhaustion shadowing the skin beneath them. He cut a nice figure in his blue suit, and his dark hair was perfectly slicked to the side, but there was something haggard about him tonight.

"I've been followed to the bathroom five times," the mayor said frantically. "Twice by people who wanted to pick my brain to death about inconsequential political questions, and three times by women who insisted that a good mayor needs a good wife. I'm up for reelection this fall, and everyone seems to think I need to shore up my political stances and get hitched. I just want to go home, but I can't make it to the door without being proposed to half a dozen times."

"Want us to help you sneak out?" I offered, hating to see the normally confident man looking so burned out.

He stared at me for a moment, hopeful and a bit confused.

"I'm Caroline," I explained, holding out my hand. He shook it. "Morgan's girlfriend. And we would be delighted to sneak you away from all the snakes."

"You would?" he practically begged, eyes lighting up.

I looked up at Morgan and he nodded.

"Go ahead and take Care's other arm," he suggested. "We'll head along the edge of the room. I'll walk in front, so no one sees you. If I make direct eye contact, people will be quick to get out of our way."

"God bless you," Fitz said emphatically, taking my arm as Morgan stepped in front of us. "I was ready to call a police escort just to get out of here."

"Where's your security team?" I asked as Morgan led us around the edge of the room to a set of double doors.

Fitz sighed and shook his head. "I told them to give me space tonight. I figured I was safe in the Alliance Building. They're downstairs waiting in the car."

"Is that wise? Like you said, it's election season soon," I said as we stepped into the hall. There were some guests wandering along the marble floors and a few couples making out in dark corners, but no one paid us much attention.

"It's not wise, but it felt necessary. After all, it's not like I was attacked."

"Well, you were. But just by desperate gold diggers," Morgan sassed once we'd made it out onto the sidewalk.

Fitz laughed humorlessly and rubbed his hands along his face. "I'm not going to survive until reelection anyway. If the women don't kill me, the press will. The only reason they're not out here right now is because I ordered a three-block barricade. With all the attacks and blackmail lately, tonight seemed like too good of an opportunity for someone to attack."

Fitz pulled out his phone, probably to let his security team know that he was ready to go. Morgan likewise was texting Carmine to bring the car around.

"Probably a wise choice," I agreed, rubbing my shoulders against the cold. "It seems like every other week there's a new attack. I can't even keep up anymore."

"You know, if you both keep talking like that, you're going to jinx—"

Morgan paused as tires squealed on the pavement. We all turned and watched a dark van zip up to the edge of the sidewalk and come to a rough halt.

"Mayor, is that your ride?" Mor asked, stepping in front of me.

Fitz shook his head. "No."

Four men in black ski masks piled out of the van and made straight for us. Yeah, that definitely wasn't Fitz's ride.

But Morgan was ready.

He waited for the closest attacker to make a move, and when they did, he slipped his arms around them and put them in a headlock. The person whipped out a knife and I screamed a warning to Mor. Before the attacker could swing their blade, Morgan twitched his arms, and I heard the attacker's neck snap.

He let them drop to the pavement, lifeless.

One man had made a move toward Mayor Fitz, but to my surprise, the mayor seemed to handle himself just fine. If not a bit...oddly.

He pulled off his own jacket and slung it over the other man's head, holding it from the back. They looked like two kids fighting over who got the remote.

But after a moment, the other man elbowed Fitz in the gut, and Fitz dropped his hold.

The attacker swung the coat off his head and faced Fitz. But the mayor was fast. He kicked the man in the chest and the man fell back against the passenger seat where the door was still open. Then Fitz grabbed the door and slammed it against his attacker's head.

The man went still.

I stood there, watching in awe as these two men completely obliterated our attackers. But as the two of them turned to the third attacker, I sensed someone standing behind me. Carefully, I reached into the slit of my dress and pulled my dagger from its sheath.

I waited, the knife clutched in my hand, until I felt the person close in. Then, I spun and thrust the dagger upward.

My attacker grunted and danced away a step, avoiding the flash of my knife. But although I was pretty positive he was a Berserker who could turn into a massive bear, I knew he had nothing on me. I was an Elf queen and the mate of the most powerful Chief in the nation. *He has no idea what he's just stepped in.*

My adrenaline pumping, I forced my magic on him, funneling fear and doubt into his mind. He tried to resist me, his emotions demanding that I toy with them, tug and manipulate like I normally did. But I ignored the urging and pressed my magic harder.

The man cowered back a step, his hands starting to lower. I could feel the magic taking over, pressing him into submission.

But then a big furry head barreled in and knocked the man to the ground.

Morgan, in his bear form, stomped on my attacker's chest. And if the man hadn't died when he hit the ground, he was definitely dead now.

"Morgan!" I shouted, staring open mouthed as my big furry boyfriend stepped away from the dead man. "I had him! He was under control."

"He was trying to take you," Morgan growled, his breath coming out in a big puff.

"We could have questioned him."

Mor shook his big head and invaded my space, pressing his nose to my cheek. "He wouldn't have known anything. He was an underling sent here by the gambling dens. If the under boss didn't know anything, I can promise you that this idiot certainly didn't."

I tried to glare at him, but it was hard to be mad at him in this form. He was so cute and cuddly and yet still somehow majestic. His bear form was silver, bright and metallic, with beige painting his feet and snout. And his head came to my shoulder, his body bigger than natural bears.

"You killed him unnecessarily," I pouted.

Mor rubbed his fur against my neck. "He attacked you, Red. I moved on instinct, and I don't regret it. I'll never regret protecting you."

I sighed and gave in, wrapping my arm around his thick neck, my fingers running through his soft fur. His chest rumbled and he pressed closer to me.

"This is…" Fitz stared at Morgan and I, "Weird. I mean, I know you can turn into a bear, but I've never *seen* you do it before."

I stepped away from Morgan and frowned at the bodies lining the ground. "Yeah, it's hard to get used to. But don't worry, he's harmless."

Fitz raised an eyebrow. "Yeah, just a kitten."

Morgan strolled over to Fitz. To his credit, the mayor didn't shake or shy away. But he did watch Morgan's approach with wide eyes.

"Go ahead, pet me," Morgan said, nudging the mayor with his snout. "I promise I'm as soft as I look."

"Softer," I corrected, putting my dagger back in its holster.

Fitz slowly lifted his hand but froze an inch from Morgan's fur. "This isn't a test, is it? Like if I pet him, I fail—" He let out a little yelp when Morgan used his paw to push the mayor's hand against his fur.

"See? I'm a teddy bear," Morgan said dryly. "A puppy. Completely harmless."

The mayor continued to pat Morgan's head, more bemused than afraid now.

"Yeah, maybe if your name is Caroline," he sassed. "I'm beginning to think she's more than just your girlfriend."

"I'm his mate," I said nonchalantly.

Morgan turned and glared at me. "Are we just sharing that information with everyone now?"

I raised my hands and indicated to the dead attackers. "Clearly, someone already knows I'm important to you, hence why they tried to take me. What harm can it cause if they know I'm your mate?"

"A lot of harm," Morgan barked.

"If it's any consolation, I won't tell anyone," Fitz insisted. "But just so I can fully understand the conversation, who were these guys?"

Morgan and I locked eyes, and I felt the levity of the night weigh on my shoulders.

"The gambling den," Morgan sighed. "Someone's been paying them to come after me."

Chapter 19

MORGAN

Before we left the Alliance Building, we made sure the mayor didn't know *who* sent the gambling dens after us. Thanks to the dead bodies, he had to report the attack, but we convinced him not to open a formal investigation. He thankfully understood that any investigation into the attacks would probably just motivate the gambling dens to do something more drastic.

"We're home," I called out as we stepped into the dining room from the garage of the Berserker house.

"Queen Caroline, I really must reiterate that you should call us whenever you're in danger," Carmine said, continuing to lecture Caroline.

The young Alfar was a pain to work with, and he watched Caroline like it was more than just his job to do so. But he was thorough, and he'd picked up the fight training fairly quickly, so I couldn't complain too much about him. *But I will beat him to a pulp if his eyes dip lower than her face while she's wearing this dress.*

Care gave the young man an incredulous look. "How exactly was I supposed to call you, Carmine? We had four attackers, and the fight began and ended in the span of maybe three minutes."

"I doubt we could have gotten there fast enough to make a difference anyway," Allie said, glaring at Carmine.

They both looked more intimidating than usual, dressed in uniform. Both of them wore dark pants and black shirts, with a few different weapons attached to their hips. Allie's dark hair was pulled into two boxer braids, and she had a pair of aviators hanging from the collar of her shirt. Carmine's blonde hair was perfectly combed and both of them wore earpieces to make communication easier.

Care and I had forgone our own coms tonight, thinking we'd be safe in the Alliance Building. *Ha. What a stupidly hopeful thing to think.*

"Still," Carmine pouted, "They should get in the habit of calling us whenever there's a problem. It's our *job* to protect—"

"Carmine," Care said, giving him a smile so sweet it was sour, "Why don't you go and check the house for any threats? Just in case."

The young Alfar puffed up his chest like he'd been given the most important task in the world and immediately pulled out his gun and headed upstairs. "Of course, Queen Caroline."

"Of course, Queen Caroline," Allie mocked once he was gone. "Could he be more obsessed with you? It's embarrassing."

"Jealous?" Care teased.

Allie visibly shuddered. "Lord no! I'd rather have my wisdom teeth pulled without any Novocain than to have Carmine's attention."

"Drat," Caroline sighed. "I was this close to making him get over his crush. All he needs is a good rebound."

"Hold up," I said, setting a hand on her arm, "You know he has a crush on you?"

Care laughed and leaned up to kiss my cheek. "Oh, Bear Man, the fact that you think I could be so blind is truly hilarious. I can sense emotions, remember? That kid is an infatuated idiot, and it grates on my nerves." She turned a smile on Allie. "Which is why it would be great if he had someone else to focus on—"

"No," Allie snapped. "Never in a million billion trillion years. Not if hell froze over and he and I were the only two people on earth and pigs were doing flight patterns in the sky."

"You forgot 'snowball's chance in hell'," I pointed out.

Allie shrugged. "I feel like 'when hell freezes over' kind of covers that. But you're right, I can't be too careful. There's not a snowball's chance in hell that I would ever date Carmine. No."

Caroline's face drooped, defeated, and she rolled her eyes. "Fine, leave me with the overexuberant puppy."

"That puppy is going to get his tail docked if he doesn't get over this so-called crush quickly," I growled, glaring at the second floor even though I couldn't see Carmine.

"Oh, would you chill," Care smiled, leaning into my side.

I was just about to sneak in a kiss when Carmine came thundering down the stairs. "He's gone!" he shouted.

"Who's gone?" Allie demanded, immediately grasping for her weapons like it was as natural as breathing.

Her and Carmine hadn't been training for all that long, but they'd put in a lot of extra hours with Clint and Logan between practices. They weren't as efficient as me or Logan, but they were well on their way. And two half trained bodyguards were better than no bodyguards.

Carmine stopped halfway down the stairs, his face pale. "Volund."

My gut sank like lead, and Care and I exchanged a charged look.

"Grey!" I shouted, stomping down the hall. "Clint!"

I found them, along with Logan and Mike all huddled up in my office, simmering with fury.

"Where the heck is he?" I barked, barreling up to the group where they sat in the middle of my office on the couch and surrounding armchairs.

Mike cringed at the sound of my voice; his computer open on his lap. "Gone."

Care stepped up beside me, Carmine and Allie remaining out in the hall, guarding the doors. "Gone?" she parroted.

Daisy Mae, who'd been sitting next to Mike and licking his hand every few seconds, hopped down at the sight of her mother. Care absently scratched the dog's back, and Daisy wiggled, unaware of the situation.

"I went upstairs to bring him dinner twenty minutes ago," Clint said, looking like he was afraid I might pummel him. It was a valid fear. "He wasn't in his room and all his stuff was gone."

I clenched a hand around my mouth, trying to stop myself from screaming. We'd now lost Volund not once but *twice*. And with all of our security cameras and the spell on his room keeping him inside, it shouldn't have been possible for him to leave.

"How did he break the binding spell?" Care asked, leaning back against my desk like she needed its help to hold her up. Daisy, loyal as ever, curled up on her mom's feet and laid down as if she might be needed at any moment. "No one's brought him any packages, right?"

Clint was already shaking his head. "No, and we've been going over everything for the last twenty minutes since he went missing. No one's given him anything other than food and toiletries since he was locked up."

"What about the cameras?" I asked, moving around my desk to sit in my chair. My frustration pushed me to pace, but I was more likely to throw things if I was moving.

"Wiped clean," Mike sighed, fingers flying over his keyboard. Care gave me a sad smile, and even without my ability to sense anyone's emotions other than hers, I understood why. I could only imagine how guilty Mike was feeling. I had no doubt he would be carrying this baggage around for a while. But really, it wasn't his fault that Volund got out.

The Dark Elf must have had something up his sleeve the whole time that we didn't know about.

"Maybe he had a Pixie potion for invisibility?" Caroline suggested. "We didn't exactly check his luggage when we moved him back in."

"True. Or it could've been an Olfar," Clint argued, his elbows on his knees and his forehead wrinkled in thought.

But Mike was already shaking his head. "The rumor that they can produce portals is just an old wives' tale. Numerous scientific studies have been done, and none of them have attributed any portal creating abilities to those oversized magical dogs."

Olfar were magical wolves, though no one seemed to know what their magic could do. They were notoriously skittish, picky about who they liked, and—like most other magical animals—they were rarely found outside of a zoo or a rich person's home.

There were occasionally other facilities that housed them, like the Unicorn ranch just outside of Shifter Haven. The Unicorns were kind of a town nuisance since they often escaped to visit the nearest bakery. They had a major sweet tooth.

But none of the magical animals—not Unicorns, Olfar, Jackalopes or Felya—were proven to actually open portals.

"No, it's more likely that he had a Minotaur artifact again," I sighed, rubbing my temples. "It's the only way he could get around the Witch binding. He must have had it in his things the whole time."

"He was just toying with us," Care hissed, her knuckles turning white against the edge of my desk. "The whole time, he could have left whenever he wanted. So why stay up there? What did he get out of it?"

No one answered.

I'd long since stopped trying to understand the inner workings of Volund King, the great Nephilim Prince. The real concern wasn't what kind of sadistic pleasure he got from being a fake prisoner, but rather what prompted him to leave now.

"He's up to something," I hummed. "There's a reason he left now and not a week from now."

"You think he'll go after Caroline?" Grey asked, his aged face lined with worry.

I shrugged. "The only thing we know for sure that he wants is Caroline. It makes sense that he'd come for her. Why else would he leave now?"

The question hung in the air, an unscratchable itch that no one could answer. Whatever Volund was up to, I had a feeling we would only figure it out when he wanted us to...

Chapter 20

MORGAN

The walk from my car to the Shifter Alliance Building for the monthly council meetings had never bothered me. People tended to give me a wide berth, staring with wide, scared eyes. And now with it being the middle of September and the air turning crisp, people were too cold to stare for long. *Praise Jesus.*

But today felt different. There was a foreboding deep in my stomach, as if my instincts were picking up on signals that my higher thinking brain couldn't identify. The hair on my neck stood on end and I clenched my fists, ready for an attack.

"Chief Hohlt?"

I spun around fast, my hand ready to grab for the speaker's throat. But instead of an attacker, there was a woman standing there. She was holding a microphone and behind her was a man with a large camera on his shoulder.

My body tensed. This wasn't an attack. *It's war.*

I'd been hounded by the press for long enough that I knew the rabid look of hunger in their eyes. The desire to ferret out *something* regardless of if it was true, so long as it would sell. And a big bad villain who could shift into a giant bear definitely sold.

Though I never got any commission checks for all the magazines and TV spots my face had drawn people to buy. I'd sue, but then that would just be another story for them to sell.

"Chief Hohlt, what do you have to say about the recent news?" the reporter asked, holding the microphone out toward me.

She was pretty at first glance, with perfectly styled brown hair, but under the thick veneer of stage makeup, she looked like a weasel. Or maybe that was my own bias against reporters talking.

Eh. I stand by my opinion.

The woman waited for my response, and I noted that she stayed a good four feet back from me as if she expected me to Berserk out right here on the street. And maybe the me from a year ago would have. But the me today was different. Stronger. Softer. In love.

"You seem to have mistaken me for a Mermaid," I said dryly, unimpressed with this highly unprofessional bombarding, "I can't read your mind. So, if you want a comment, you'll have to explain what the heck you're talking about."

The woman visibly swallowed and glanced back at her camera man. The guy was shorter than she was, and he looked like he weighed about as much as the camera. He wasn't going to do her any good against me.

She must have come to the same conclusion herself, because she turned her attention back to me and smiled. *That won't help you either.* I couldn't have found her less charming if I tried.

"There's quite a rumor buzzing about you right now, Chief Hohlt," she said, and I stiffened as people on the sidewalk began to pause, taking out their phones to tape us.

Having been on the receiving end of more than my fair share of bad press, my defenses rose, and I felt the bear in me yearn to rip the phones out of every bystander's hand. I wanted to smash the reporter's camera on the ground, shove that godforsaken microphone into that woman's mouth to shut her up and roar at anyone who dared to speak against me.

But that would only give them something real to share with the world. Evidence, receipts, proof that The Chief was every bit the villain they wanted to sell me as. *But I'm better than that.* And my mate deserved a man who was better than that.

"What rumor?" I asked, forcing myself not to move an inch, just in case my fist decided to fly out all on its own. *Wouldn't be the worst thing to happen.*

At first, I thought that maybe the reporter was talking about Caroline. Maybe they wanted gossip about my new girlfriend. But I wasn't sure how they would have gotten that information already.

Sure, I'd brought Care to the party the other night as my date, but I doubted that the news had made it to the mainstream media already. To everyone at the party, Chief Hohlt was minorly entertained by a woman for the moment. No one took it seriously. And I trusted that Mayor Fitz hadn't told anyone that Care was my mate.

But when people began to whisper things like 'that's him', 'do you think he did it', and 'oh my gosh, are we gonna die right now?', I knew that this rumor was much worse.

"Three bodies were found late last night on the south side of town," the reporter said. "They were all slashed through the neck, as if they were attacked by something very large. A method that's long been attached to you."

I felt my face go cold and wondered if I looked pale. *Not again.*

"Are you accusing me of something?" I asked, amazed when I heard my voice come out level.

"Should I be? These men were killed using your modus operandi. Can you tell me why that is?"

My heart was pumping faster now, and I tried to take deep breaths to calm it. *I can't freak out. Not here.* "If I knew who's been framing me and why for the past decade, I would have stopped them by now."

The reporter raised her eyebrows, and I flinched as a few cameras flashed around me. "Are you saying that you would have killed them?"

"What? No—"

"Have you killed anyone, Chief Hohlt?"

I growled. "Everyone knows the answer to that. My mother's death is well known—"

"And was her attacker the only person you've killed?"

My mouth felt dry, and I squeezed my sweaty fists tighter. Normally, I batted reporters like this away with one well-placed insult. But today was different. Because this time it wasn't just about me.

My menacing reputation would become Caroline's menacing reputation. My ugly history would become her *people's* ugly history. And I couldn't let my past ruin their chance of success at going public.

I have to stop the reporter. But my usual methods—AKA being a jackass—wouldn't work this time. Not if I wanted Caroline to have a good rapport with the public.

The reporter was glaring at me now, and every bystander seemed to have the word 'guilty' flashing in their eyes as they glared at me.

I wanted to argue with them. To prove them wrong like Caroline told me to. But I couldn't figure out *how*. Not when everyone was taking one step back like they expected me to attack at any moment.

I don't know how to fix this...

Chapter 21

CAROLINE

I tried to pay attention as Millicent, the treasury advisor, gave her report of this week's financial state, but I was too busy worrying about Morgan. For the past few minutes, I'd sensed him through the mate bond, anxious and worried. It wasn't like he never got stressed, but we were rarely apart, and I didn't like not knowing what had set him off.

Pulling out my phone, I sent him a quick text, hiding my hands beneath the table in the dining room at the Alfar house.

Me: Hey, you okay?

He texted me back almost immediately.

Bear Man: Yeah I'm fine. I'll call you after the council meeting is over.

He's lying. There was no doubt about it. His stress was spiking in conjunction with his anger. But without actually being there, I didn't know what to do about it.

"Queen Caroline, I understand that your time is valuable," Mikael said, interrupting my thoughts with his heavy voice, veiled with disdain, "Which is why I was hoping not to waste any of it. So, if you're ready, we'll continue the meeting."

You can't kill him. You can't kill him. It wasn't that Mikael wasn't good at his job. He was an excellent justice advisor and always on top of it. But his dismissive attitude grated on me more and more every day.

"But of course," I said through a tight smile. I couldn't let Mikael think he'd gotten to me. It would only fuel his already problematic superiority complex. "Please continue, Millie."

"Um..." the young blonde treasury advisor stuttered, looking between Mikael and I with a bit of uncertainty. "Yes, I was just saying that the budget for the new defense division is in order and your...revenue streams are doing well."

It was no secret that Millicent didn't approve of my choice to sell off many of the expensive and excessive items in the Alfar house. So far, I'd sold almost ten thousand dollars' worth of stuff that no one needed or used. The money was being allocated to fund our new defensive division as well as to creating a public works fund that could be used to help Alfar who needed assistance. Anyone who wished to use the money had to submit an application to me for approval, and then the council and I would distribute the money together so that I wouldn't be the only one held accountable if the money wasn't distributed correctly.

"And the rooms upstairs?" I asked, flipping through my notes. They were handwritten and a little messy, and I had an array of pretty pastel highlighters and sticky tabs that only seemed to enrage Mikael and Millicent both.

All the more reason to keep writing by hand.

"Um," Millicent mumbled, looking very much like she wanted to give me a piece of her mind about my monetary choices.

I liked Millie. She was a nice person who wanted to be helpful, but sometimes her version of helpful meant trying to force others to do exactly what she thought was best. It hadn't taken her long to realize that the approach wasn't going to work on me.

"Has anyone rented a room yet?" I reiterated, giving her an innocent smile. But she wasn't fooled. Being an Alfar, she could sense the pleasure I got from pushing her buttons. But true to what I had learned of the Alfar way, she said nothing of it.

For a species that could sense the emotions of those around them, the Alfar were very polite about it. I'd gathered that it was somewhat taboo to comment on the emotions of others—they didn't even let knowing or judgmental facial expressions slip.

I wasn't nearly as well behaved. Maybe that was the Nephilim in me.

"Yes. Two people. Both small businesses," was all Millicent said.

My smile widened, though it didn't reach my eyes. "What kind?"

Millie's lips wobbled and I knew she hated that my plans were working. Being the treasury advisor, her mindset was all about saving money, not generosity. And the businesses who moved in would be paying an incredibly low rent, which I knew drove her nuts. A happy biproduct of my plans.

"A handmade pottery shop," she said, reading off of the perfectly typed notes in front of her, "And an adoption attorney."

"As for the safety regarding the businesses moving in here," Jude added, giving me a stern look—since Morgan didn't think I took my own safety seriously enough, he'd recruited Jude to be my new babysitter and make sure we took every precaution possible. They were both killing my fun. "The staircase on the east side of the house has been walled off and an exterior door has been fitted with a passcode for renters to access," he continued. "The section of the house that contains rented offices and a shared bathroom has also been separated from the rest of the house by walls reinforced with steel and every renter has undergone a background check as well as an interview with me and Mikael."

"Oh, is that all?" I mocked, mildly annoyed. I appreciated everyone's desire to protect me, but sometimes it felt like a bit much. "You didn't also install bullet proof windows that don't open just in case someone decides to sneak into the rest of the house from their office windows?"

Jude pursed his lips and then started typing away on his phone.

"Oh my gosh, are you seriously making a note to do that?" I whined.

"If you don't want me to do things, then you shouldn't give me the ideas," he defended with a shrug.

"He has a point," Tristain teased. "They wouldn't have installed the metal detectors if you hadn't made a joke about it."

I sighed, recalling the mistake that had earned me a big shiny metal detector at every entrance of the house. When I complained to Morgan that we didn't have such serious precautions at the Berserker house, he started looking into having them installed there too.

"What good is being queen if everyone else makes all the decisions?" I mumbled as the boys discussed the idea of getting some armored cars.

"If you told them no," Harold whispered beside me, "They would stop."

"I've said no."

The old man shook his head, his expression more thoughtful than I liked. "No. You complain, but you never tell them to stop."

I fidgeted in my seat. "I'm sure I've told them to stop before."

"You haven't. And I think it's because deep down, you're scared that someday someone's attack against you might be successful. And as annoying as these precautions are, they make you feel better."

I glared at him, too frustrated to admit out loud that he was right.

"There's nothing wrong with being scared, Queen Caroline," he went on in his fatherly way, "It's human nature. And it's also human nature to take comfort in being protected." He nudged my shoulder. "Don't worry, I won't tell anyone about your soft gooey center."

"Good. Because if you did, this soft gooey center would kick your butt," I threatened mildly. We both knew I was full of crap.

"Duly noted," he smiled.

I shook my head just as my phone buzzed again. I glanced at it under the table.

Merida: Have you talked to Morgan in the last half hour?

Worry immediately began to prick at my stomach.

Me: Yeah, I texted him a few minutes ago and he said he'd call me later.

Me: Why? What's wrong?

Instead of answering, she sent me a link to a news article. The headline read 'The Chief Suspect in the Newest Gambling Den Murders Has Outed Himself'.

I watched in growing fury as Morgan was cornered by a crass reporter on the street. My fingers tightening around the phone, and I imagined them squeezing her stupid neck. What kind of reporter reports on conjecture and half-truths? What kind of *person* corners someone in public and tries to dehumanize them?

And all the while, Morgan stood there on the sidewalk, eyes wide like a panicked child.

The interview wasn't long. After about a minute, Morgan mumbled an excuse about being late and disappeared into the Alliance Building. But reporters and crowds with their phones poised to record were all waiting outside the building even now.

Ready to devour him.

And there was no question about it, whoever was paying the gambling dens to get involved had definitely orchestrated these murders to make him look guilty.

They were trying to bring Morgan down, and I wasn't going to allow it.

"Where are you going?" Mikael demanded as I stood from my seat.

"To save my mate," I replied simply, shrugging. "Morgan's in trouble and the only way to help him is if I reveal myself to the council. It's going to be a mess, so until we officially go public as Alfar, everyone will need to keep their distance from me. The council will be looking for you, but so long as you stay away from me, they shouldn't be able to find you. And while we're temporarily separated, I trust all of you to keep me informed—"

"No," Mikael interrupted, standing slowly, his hands braced on the table.

I narrowed my eyes at him. "Excuse me? You can't just tell your queen no."

"No," he repeated. "Your plan is stupid."

"My plan is going to save Morgan's hide, so—"

"No, *our* plan is going to save him."

Confused, I looked around at the group. Thankfully, I wasn't the only one who looked lost as everyone stared between Mikael and I with furrowed brows.

"You have a plan to help Morgan?" I scoffed, crossing my arms. "As if you'd ever be helpful."

And then, for the first time since I'd met him, Mikael looked...sorry. I blinked; sure I was imagining it.

But there he was, looking apologetic.

"I'm aware that I've been...a pain since you arrived," he explained calmly. "But it's not because I dislike you or your mate."

"Then why?"

"Because you're young and insecure."

I laughed bitterly. "Ouch."

Mikael sighed. "I didn't mean that as an insult. I just meant that when you first came here, you were scared. You doubted yourself and I know from experience that the best way for someone to gain confidence is through adversity. Through challenge."

I stared at him, mouth agape. "So, let me get this straight. You *challenged* me at every turn so that I would, what, have to stand my ground and hold firm to my beliefs?" I asked incredulously.

Mikael nodded. "That's pretty much the gist of it."

I gritted my teeth, my pride telling me to rip him apart. To berate him and put him in his place in front of my advisors so they would all know that I wasn't to be trifled with. To be sure and make it known that Mikael wasn't responsible for my confidence as queen. That *I* had done the work to get here...

But Mikael was right.

I had been scared and insecure when I first became queen. And as much as I hated to acknowledge it, I'd needed to be challenged, to be pushed. I was stronger now, and although most of that was from my own personal growth, it was also thanks to the pushing of others. Rome wasn't built in a day, and it also wasn't built alone.

"Thank you," I finally said.

Mikael blinked, surprised. "What?"

"Let make it clear that if any of you try that kind of crap on me from now on," I said, glancing around at the other advisors, "I will ruin you. I'm plenty confident now and I don't need anyone's meddling. But..." I looked at Mikael,

"I do appreciate that you saw potential and...nourished it in your own way. So, thank you."

Mikael's normally judgy eyes softened and for the first time, I realized why he had been chosen to be an advisor. Mikael cared about the Alfar, and even though his methods could be a little tone deaf, he only wanted to help.

"So, when do we leave?" he asked.

I pursed my lips, a little lost. "What?"

"Queen Caroline," he said, smiling—but just barely, "Don't you understand? We're not just invested in the future of the Alfar. We're invested in *you*. If you put yourself at risk, then so do we."

"He's right," Tristain said, standing. "If you're going to help Morgan, then we are too."

"Dang right we are," Harold said, smiling.

"After all," Mikael added, "Chief Morgan will one day be our consort. It would be unwise to incur his wrath by not assisting his mate."

In spite of the fact that Morgan's reputation was on the line, in spite of the fact that there were droves of reporters waiting outside the Alliance Building, that we could be putting our people at risk with this hairbrained plan, I grinned.

My people believed in me, and I felt for the first time like I was ready to take on the world.

"We leave now."

Chapter 22

CAROLINE

My pink Converse tapped against the marble floor as I made my way through the lobby of the Shifter Alliance building. The receptionists manning the tall, polished counter watched with obvious interest, but none of them stopped me. I'd come in with Morgan before, so they knew who I was associated with.

Which meant that they knew better than to intervene.

I could feel their hesitation, and the anxiety rippling through the nearby guards. Not only was I linked to the 'The Chief', but I'd brought a posse with me.

Tristain, Harold and Mikael—yes, you read that right, Mikael the fusspot—had accompanied me to help Morgan. I was still trying to wrap my mind around the fact that Mikael didn't hate me. But the fact that my advisors supported me enough to come with me was kind of blowing my mind.

Torrie, David and even Jude had offered to come along too, but I didn't want to involve too many people. We needed to convince the council that the Alfar were real, but that didn't mean they needed to know how many of us there were just yet. Let them think we were just a small ragtag group instead of a full-blown community.

I only trusted the council with so many of my secrets.

"Hi, Miss. Caroline," the middle-aged man guarding the door to the council room greeted, smiling as we approached. "I'm glad you're here. Chief Morgan doesn't seem to be in the highest spirits today."

"I know, that's why I came," I said, smiling warmly at him. "I need to see him."

The man paused, filled with indecision. It was clear that he wanted to help, but he wasn't allowed to let just anyone into the room without prior notice from the council.

So, as much as I hated messing with the emotions of an innocent person, I pulled on my magic and tapped on his sense of empathy, urging it to expand.

After a moment, he sighed. "If I just so happened to turn to my left, with my key card dangling precariously from my pocket," he said, tapping the keycard clipped to the pocket on his shirt, "Then I couldn't possibly be held responsible for someone getting in."

I grinned.

The man winked and turned to the side. I quickly unlocked the door, returning his keycard with a pat on his chest. "I'll put in a good word for you," I whispered.

Then the Alfar and I slipped into the council room.

The current discussion came to an abrupt halt at our entrance. But I had just caught the words 'he should be investigated' before the silence descended. It was no surprise that Francine had been the one speaking.

A murderous look slipped over my face, and I willed my gaze to obliterate anyone who threatened my boyfriend. *Mine,* my every step seemed to hiss. My chin was tilted high, like an invisible crown was balancing on my head. *Test me, I dare you*, I thought, my shoulders back as I approached the ring-shaped table.

One by one, thirteen pairs of eyes turned to stare at me. Some widened in shock, others squinted with confusion. And some narrowed into threatening slits. Merida tried to bite back a smile, and poor Fitz blew out a tired breath like he already knew how much trouble I was going to cause.

But then Morgan turned to face me, and the rest of them disappeared.

As much as I would have loved to stick it to the rest of them for doubting Morgan's character again and again, I wasn't here for them. I was here for him. And the relief in his eyes was all I needed.

"Hi," I said, smiling at the group as I rested my hands on Morgan's shoulders. He reached up and squeezed my wrist gratefully. "I'm Caroline. Well, Queen Caroline."

Morgan's gentle caress became a tight grip, and I felt his anger flare. "I've got this, Bear man," I whispered, patting his shoulder.

"*Queen?*" Chloe the Mermaid representative parroted; eyebrows raised. "Queen of what, exactly?"

I shrugged and nodded at my posse, who stood a pace behind me, quiet and waiting. "The Alfar."

"The..." Jack the Kelpie representative stuttered. The young man was almost always full of smiles, and I was a little proud to finally shock him into a frown. "I'm sorry, did you say Alfar? As in, Light Elves?"

I smiled. "Yep."

Quiet mumbles flowed around the room, some people shocked, others scared. *Very wise.*

Satisfied with our performance, I motioned for the rest of my group to take a seat in the audience section of the room a little ways behind me. The three Alfar obeyed, but I felt their eyes on me and sensed their apprehension.

If anyone tried to mess with me, they'd have my back.

"Would you like to sit, *Queen* Caroline," Fitz asked, a little annoyed. I couldn't blame him. He probably wished we would have told him this bit of news in private, but right now I needed to make a scene. *Sorry, Fitz.*

"No, I'm good, thank you." I smiled, my hands still on Morgan's shoulders, making a point.

Normally, he was the one protecting me, standing up for me, supporting me. But today it was my turn to mark *my* territory. Morgan was *my* Chief, and it was time everyone realized it.

Fitz managed a tight smile, but the way his pen bounced quickly between his fingers gave him away. I'd thrown him off. But the mayor was just collateral damage for the people I was *really* trying to get to.

"Why don't you go ahead and explain what made you decide to join us here today," Mayor Fitz suggested, quickly taking up his role as the diplomatic one in the room.

"Sure," I replied brightly, determined to get Morgan out of this situation any way I could. "Well, as you can all clearly see, I'm quite familiar with Chief Morgan." At this, a few council members scoffed, eyeing the intimate way I touched the Berserker Chief. "We met about seven months ago, and even though he owed me nothing, he rescued me from several different attacks. He brought me into his home and protected me like I was his own, even though my presence only brought danger."

The accusatory looks around the table slowly morphed into confusion and curiosity. Encouraged, I went on.

"For months he's helped me to try and discover who's after me, often putting himself in dangerous situations to keep me safe. And when I discovered that there were other Elves still alive, he helped me find them and supported me as I took my place as their hereditary queen."

I paused, looking down at my mate. He was annoyed, for sure, and I couldn't blame him. I was revealing myself to people he didn't trust.

But I didn't care.

He'd protected me from the world so many times. It was my turn to do it for him.

"So, you decided to pop in and sing the Chief's praises?" Francine mocked, not impressed with my words.

"No, Francine," I said, purposefully dropping her proper title. Her lips curled and she glared at me. "I decided to *pop* in because I saw my protector being attacked on national television for the thousandth time. And since no one else seems inclined to speak against injustice, I will. Morgan's been accused of dozens of murders over the years, and rather than defend him, you've all allowed the accusations to go unchallenged. That ends now."

A few people—Brooks, Merida, Parker the Harpy, Jack the Kelpie and even the enigmatic Asher—looked contrite. And although I understood that they'd mostly remained silent to keep their own species out of the fight, I couldn't respect their choice.

Because what is your life worth if all you care about is preservation? Our existence isn't about comfort or even safety. It's about doing what's right when it's not convenient. Sticking up for someone who owes you nothing simply because you see a wrong that needs to be righted. Shouldering the load with a stranger because they're being wrongly attacked.

Of all the leaders in this room, Morgan was the only one I respected. Because to him, integrity was more valuable than trying to save face. *Gosh, I love him.*

"Are you threatening us?" Drew, the Firebird representative asked, leaning back in his seat as if he was in charge of this meeting.

Morgan's fingers squeezed my wrist in warning, but I ignored him. "Yes, I am. Morgan Hohlt has protected me at the cost of his own safety and reputation. I will do anything to defend him."

People exchanged wary looks, but I wasn't done.

"I have plans to take the Alfar public in the near future. It would cost me very little to move up my timeline, and I'm fully prepared to make a statement to the public that what's done to Morgan is done to me. The Alfar can be your ally, or we can be the thorn in your side. Your choice. But I caution you to choose wisely, because this man isn't just my friend, he's my *mate*. His side is the only one I'm on."

Shock practically echoed around the room. Of all the things I could have said, a threat and a revelation about my status as Morgan's mate wasn't what they'd expected. *Good.*

It was time that the council realized they weren't without accountability. Part of me even wanted to tell them that I was the vigilante who'd been cleaning up their messes for the past three years. But I didn't need to.

They already knew I had the upper hand. The respect and awe for Light Elves ran deep amongst the public thanks to our legendary history as the peacekeepers of Shifters. If I backed Morgan publicly and the other species sided against me, it could possibly start another civil war.

And everyone here knew it.

Of course, none of the council members knew what powers the Alfar had or how many of us there were. Which was why I really needed them to go along with my plan. I needed to have our species officially recognized and protected so that when people eventually realized how *un*threatening the Alfar really were, my people would be safe.

Fitz sighed and rubbed his temples. I was pretty sure that if he were alone, he would've started banging his head against the table. Poor guy. I felt a little bad for making his job more complicated.

A little.

"Chief Hohlt," the mayor said, smiling sadly at Morgan, "I would like to personally apologize for not doing more to assist you over the years. As mayor, it's a delicate thing to try and defend people without taking sides—"

"You've done all you could," Morgan interrupted, "And I know it. There's nothing to forgive."

"I appreciate that," Fitz nodded. "But thanks to the Task Force, I do have more to offer you now than I used to. As of today, I will personally divert a section of the Task Force from its investigation with the Firebirds to begin looking into the accusations against you. Queen Caroline is right; this has all gone on for too long. Either you're much more nefarious than I think you are, or someone's framing you, and it's time we find out. And for anyone who has any complaints about my decision," he gave a pointed look around the table, "Know that I that I offer you the same assistance should you ever require it."

Morgan seemed stunned into silence for a moment. I felt him warring between gratitude, anxiety, and relief, unsure how to receive the help. So, I leaned down and kissed his temple and whispered, "You're not alone, Bear Man. I'm not sure you ever have been. You just didn't know it."

Mor looked up at me, a smile fighting to take hold of his lips. "I love you. And we will be discussing this escapade of yours once we get home."

"You say discuss, I say kiss," I teased.

He rolled his eyes, and I turned my attention back to the council. Most of them were watching us with obvious shock, probably confused to see Morgan being so relaxed and affectionate. *Though maybe if you idiots had given him reason to, he would have been a lot nicer a lot faster.*

But by the looks of it, most of them were coming to that conclusion themselves.

"Alright, well now that we have that matter dealt with for the moment," Fitz said, uncapping his pen, "Queen Caroline, would you mind explaining to us any details you can about the Alfar? How many there are, where they are and what state they're in, what your plans are as their queen and how you would like to interact with the rest of the Shifter community moving forward?"

While some people looked appalled at the mayor treating me like I was any other species rep, others just seemed eager to learn the answers themselves. Sensing no immediate hostility in the room, I dropped my hands to press against Morgans chest. He covered both with his large fingers, the steady beat of his heart anchoring me.

"Absolutely," I nodded. "I was adopted, so it wasn't until recently that I discovered that I wasn't the only Alfar. Turns out that the Light Elves have been living peacefully amongst society for centuries, afraid that they might be hunted again if they came forward. As of now, not all Alfar are actively under my authority and instead living on their own elsewhere in the world, but the vast majority have opted to stay together. They've managed to integrate into human life seamlessly long before I showed up, and since I took over as Queen, we've been putting more efforts into interacting with the community and other Shifters in an effort to prepare ourselves for going public."

"So, when were you planning to go public before..." Lawrence the Sphinx began, pausing to motion a hand toward Morgan, "This debacle?"

"If I have to go public immediately in order to support Morgan, it will only up my timeline by a few months. I've been planning this move since I took over, so I'm plenty prepared," I said, taking no offense to his question. "As for how I'd like to move forward, ideally, the Alfar will function just like any other Shifter faction. I will have a seat on the council on their behalf, and we will be included in all laws, both restrictive and protective. We intend to comply with society's rules just like we always have, while being protected in the same way the other Shifters are. We don't want to hide anymore."

Fitz nodded and the rest of the council seemed to be mulling over my words, some of them looking unconvinced of my or the Alfar's innocence, and others looking merely surprised by the situation.

"What about the other information?" the mayor finally asked. "The number of Alfar and where they've been hiding."

I smiled and leaned slightly against Morgan's back. "Put the Alfar under your protective laws and I'll tell you anything you need to know."

"That's what I thought," Fitz sighed, shaking his head with a small smile, seemingly not annoyed by my refusal to explain. "Well, why don't you write up your timeline for going public and send it to me. Then we'll figure out how the council can help the Alfar transition into the public eye smoothly. Then, once all the proper protocol has been dealt with, you can explain the full story to us."

I nodded, happy that my terms were being met.

"In the meantime," Fitz continued, leveling a glare at every council member, "As always, nothing that is discussed here today will leave this room. I sadly feel the need to remind all of you that your factions are dying out because *you* can't seem to figure out how to coexist. So, here's your chance to prove me and the rest of the world wrong. Make yourselves useful as we plan for the Elves to join society, don't cause unnecessary problems, and keep your mouths shut about all of it. I'll be watching."

And although I respected Fitz for everything he'd said today, I didn't think it would do much to corral the council. It hadn't so far.

Chapter 23

MORGAN

My fingers tapped against my thighs; all the confidence Caroline had brought into the council room now gone as we drove home to the Berserker house. Care had insisted on driving, and as much as I'd wanted to argue, my growing anxiety prevented me.

Caroline had so effortlessly dealt with the council. She'd shouldered through the crowd of waiting reporters outside the building like it was nothing. And she'd somehow calmed my panic the moment she'd walked into the room.

But now...

All I could think about were the terrified faces of the people on the sidewalk. Like they'd expected me to turn into a monster right before their eyes.

And the old me would have.

I would have yelled at the reporter, glared at the crowd and stomped away, giving them every reason to believe that I was just as bad as they made me out to be. But I was different now. I didn't hide myself behind a façade—which meant that all their sharp comments and weaponized assumptions could go straight to my heart instead of getting stuck in my walls.

Stupid feelings make everything complicated.

A small, warm hand suddenly covered mine and I looked over at Care. She and I were alone in the car, with Harold driving my SUV behind us.

"Thank you," I said, realizing that I hadn't yet said the words out loud. "I honestly don't know what I would do without you."

"Don't thank me yet." She glanced at me; her green eyes wary. "We've got company."

Alarmed, I looked ahead.

At least six different vehicles were parked along the road outside our house, and a dozen reporters and paparazzi were swarming all over the yard. Their cameras swiveled toward us as we drove closer, and I wondered how they could be so stupid to swarm around a moving vehicle like this.

"Morgan?" Care asked, worried.

But I couldn't answer her. I didn't think I could speak at all.

Suddenly, I was a little boy again. Ten years old and already the man of the house. The blood was still stuck under my fingernails when the reporters had arrived to make a story out of my mom's murder.

Clint and Mike were huddled under a blanket, being comforted by Mr. Wallace and a young EMT. And I was being questioned by the police as a body was carried away in a black body bag.

Blood everywhere. The taste of it still in my mouth.

The police officer's tentative questions muddled by the shouts of reporters.

The word 'beast' uttered for the first time in reference to me.

The blood under my nails seemed to burn, branding me a monster.

And all the while I couldn't stop remembering the feeling of the man's neck ripping under the pressure of my bear teeth.

School had never been the same after that. Even as the news faded and the whole thing was declared self-defense, students still watched me from the corner of their eye. No one dared bully me, but no one wanted to play on the opposite team in gym class either, lest I kill them too.

It had been the beginning of my forever, where everyone judged me in fear.

"Morgan," Care demanded, squeezing my hand.

I snapped out of the memories, turning worried eyes to her.

She shook her head. "Not me. Look at them."

The reporters, who'd been slowing our progress to the driveway, were darting out of the way as six giant bears chased them, their roars loud enough to shake the windows. I could feel Care's joy blooming beside me. But it was gratitude that echoed inside me.

The six Berserkers herded the reporters back to the street, allowing us to make it to the garage without incident. We sat silently in the car for a moment, ignoring the sounds of the Alfar slamming their doors behind us.

"They did that for *you*," Care said, leaning over to kiss my cheek. "Not because they're afraid of you, but because they believe in you. You *earned* that by being a good Chief."

I nodded even though the words didn't quite feel true. But I'd lived long enough to know that the little voice of doubt in my mind was never truly going to go away. But maybe...it could get a little quieter.

"I love you," I said, taking her face in my hands. She slid eagerly across the bench seat of the Jeep, her hands sliding up my chest.

"And I love you, Bear Man," she whispered, smiling against my lips.

I held her close for a moment, reveling in the feel of her in my arms. It seemed like our affectionate moments were all tainted with drama these days. But who cares so long as I got to be with her?

Care hummed happily as she pulled away, setting her chin on my chest and looking up at me. "I suppose we should probably get out now. Harold, Mikael and Tristain are waiting for us."

I shrugged. "Eh, they're smart enough to know what we're doing in here even if the windows are tinted."

She laughed but didn't stop me when I went in for another kiss.

A few moments later, we stepped out of the car—with swollen lips and grins—to three grown men with their arms crossed.

Suddenly I felt like I was facing Caroline's dad...s.

"What exactly were you doing in there?" Harold asked. I didn't have to be an Alfar to know that he was thoroughly enjoying himself.

"Well, when a man and a woman love each other very much," Care replied snarkily, tugging me toward the door.

"Ew," Tristain complained, following us into the house. "I'm supportive of your guys' relationship and all, but I *really* don't want to think about the intimate details."

"I second that," Mikael added piously.

Caroline and I ignored them and made our way through the dining room toward the sound of mumbled voices. The bears who scared the reporters hadn't been my brothers, or Logan, so clearly, we had visitors.

But when we stepped into the living room, I hadn't expected to find my entire Sleuth waiting.

"What are you all doing here?" I asked, confused.

No one answered. One by one, they each raised a fist to their chests in a sign of fealty. It was a symbol rarely used except among family. Doing it meant that you were offering your respect and loyalty.

It was a vow my people had never made to me before.

"We're here for you," Mr. Wallace said from the front of the group. Even in my earliest memories of him, he'd been a cantankerous old man. But not now. Now he was a soldier awaiting marching orders.

"They came on their own after seeing the news," Logan explained, stepping toward me from the mass of bodies.

"We want to help," Trish spoke up. She was a middle-aged woman with round cheeks. I remembered her bringing us casseroles for months after my mom died. "Anything you need."

"What are our orders," Mr. Wallace asked, winking before he added, "Chief?"

Overwhelmed with emotion, I blinked at the group before me. In all my life—after my mom's death, when I became Chief, when I lost Gen—I'd never felt this level of support. And I found that I didn't know what to do with it.

But then Caroline's fingers wrapped around mine.

They were so small and slender. She had on pink nail polish today—I knew because I'd helped her paint them last night while we watched part of season eight of *The Office*. (And yes, I did cry when Steve Carell left the show. But no one but Caroline would ever know that.) And even though my hands were twice the size of hers, it was me who felt comforted and safe.

Soaking up as much of her strength as I could, I took a deep breath and faced the crowd. "It's time you all knew the full story...Caroline isn't just my mate. She's an Elf queen." It felt wrong to say the words out loud after so many months of keeping Care's identity a secret. But I knew that I could trust my Sleuth. The time for working alone was long gone.

Shock reverberated around the room, and Care gave everyone a wave and a cheeky smile. "Hi. Don't worry, I'm still a pain in Morgan's backside, so really not much has changed."

People chuckled and the tension seemed to ease from the air. Something told me I wouldn't have to use my leadership magic so long as Care was around to woo everyone.

"That will never change," I agreed, kissing the top of her head. A few of the women 'awwed' and I felt myself blush. "But we need your help. Caroline only recently learned that she wasn't the only Elf still in existence and that she's their hereditary queen. She's been planning to take the Alfar public in the coming months. But when she saw my interview, she outed herself to the council and told them that I'd been protecting her and the other Elves for months. She threatened to publicly side with me if the council didn't help to debunk the rumors about me and the gambling dens, risking her plans and her safety for me—for us."

Looks of awe shifted to Care, and she squeezed my fingers as a blush stained her cheeks. "Putting it on a little thick there, aren't we?"

"No, I like seeing you turn that shade of," I teased quietly, "*Red.*"

She glared up at me, but it wasn't anger I felt simmering inside her.

"Of course, we'll support your mate," an older gentleman said, interrupting my train of thought. "What do you need from us?"

"Well, over the last few months, someone's been hunting Caroline," I sighed. "And now that the Alfar are known to the council, I want to make sure they're as protected as possible."

I nodded for Care to explain, and she squared her shoulders, appearing every bit as confident as she had in the council room earlier.

"I've encouraged the Alfar to build relationships with people of other species," she said, her eyes scanning every face in the crowd. "My hope is that by the time we go public, the Alfar will have already built a good rapport with the people around them. But there's always the possibility that whoever's hunting me will find them, or that the other Shifters won't be very...receptive. So, if you're willing, I'd like to tell the Alfar that if they're in trouble or feel unsafe, they can reveal themselves to a Berserker for protection."

"Easy," Mr. Wallace replied, arms crossed. "What else?"

Care laughed. "My people's safety during this transition is my highest priority for now. But when we do go public, I would appreciate any public support you're comfortable giving."

The group nodded their agreement and I felt some of the tension in my shoulders release. If only I'd been able to tell them all of this sooner. But at the time, it had been more dangerous—both for them and Caroline—if they knew what she was. *Better late than never.*

"What about the news report?" Clint asked, standing by the front door. "What do you want us to do about the gambling dens?"

It was a valid question, and in the past, I probably would have said that we needed to lie low and not draw attention to ourselves. Let the news blow over and see what we could dig up about the gambling dens in the meantime.

But laying low had never served me. Because even my silence gave the media a story to fabricate. Something dishonest but dramatic enough to sell.

I've let them write my story for far too long. It was time to take the pen—and my reputation—back.

Without answering Clint's question, I let go of Caroline's hand, stomped across the room and out the front door.

The reporters weren't on the grass anymore, but they still lined the street, a bunch of dots swarming along the pavement like flies. A few of them stumbled back as I neared, but their cameras were ready and flashing.

Ignoring them, I stepped up to the nearest reporter.

"Chief Hohlt," he stuttered, his already pale, over-makeup-ed face turning whiter, "Wh-what do you say to the accusations—"

"No," I growled, "This time *I* get to talk."

Then, without warning, I stirred up my magic and let it flow through me. An involuntary sigh escaped my lips at the feel of it moving through my body. I'd been so careful for so long not to use my powers in front of people who could use them against me, determined not to give the world another reason to hate me.

But we were past that now. Now, I didn't care.

"My name is Morgan Hohlt," I began, my magic urging the reporters to let me take the lead. "Most of you probably know me as The Chief or Beast. For decades now, I've allowed the media to determine my identity and control my reputation. But not anymore."

A few of the photographers swallowed anxiously, hesitantly capturing my speech. My magic could convince them to trust my leadership, but it didn't erase their fear.

"I'm not the beast," I went on, looking into the camera of the nearest reporter. "The beast broke into my house, attacked my family and murdered my mother. The beast died at the hands of a ten-year-old boy who did his best to protect his own. Beasts ruin your families. They kill your loved ones. They tempt and steal your young. The gambling dens are the beasts, not me. And I'll admit that I haven't done enough to get rid of them. But I'm done trying to live and operate within the lines of what the media won't find villainous."

I glanced around, meeting the eyes of every camera person and every reporter. They barely held my gaze and some even trembled, but they stood and listened. "I'm not a beast," I insisted, squaring my shoulders. "But to the gambling dens, I'm about to be."

Chapter 24

CAROLINE

I watched him sitting in his desk chair, eyes glued to his computer screen. Morgan was somehow still just as sexy as he'd been hours ago during his big speech to the reporters. I'd stood back and watched him as he told the entire nation who Morgan Hohlt really was.

And the whole time, all I could think was that I desperately wanted to say that he was mine. Not just my mate, but my husband.

Even from our first meeting in the Alliance Building back in the spring, I'd known that Morgan was more than the beast he appeared to be. But I couldn't have prepared myself for the man that was sitting here now.

He was so good, so patient, so faithful and protective. Of course, he was also stubborn, argumentative, and a bit of a bear sometimes—pun intended. Morgan wasn't perfect, and I loved him for it.

"Look at my baby being all sexy and commanding, telling the world to go kick rocks," I teased, leaning against the doorway to his office. Mor looked up from his computer, rolling his eyes. "You know, I bet I can tell you what all those news articles are saying about you now."

He quirked an eyebrow, mischief lighting his face. "Oh yeah? What are they saying?"

I bit my lip to keep from grinning, twirling the green ribbon that tied off the end of my braid. My makeup was a little worse for wear after the long day, and my outfit was rumpled, but the attraction burning inside of Morgan was just as strong as ever. "Hmm..." I hummed, "They say something like, 'Morgan Hohlt, previously known to many as a beast, has made his first public announcement. Who knew that under all that intimidation was a sexy alpha male with a surprising stroke of tenderness?'"

Morgan chuckled, and I unleashed my grin at the sound. I could get drunk, high, clean and sober all on that single sound.

"Is that what they say?" He asked, smiling.

"Or some variation." I shrugged.

He sighed and shook his head like he didn't know what to do with me. It was my favorite look. The one that said I was his favorite.

"Come here," he growled, his voice deep and rough as he swiveled his chair to face me.

That was all the invitation I needed.

I scurried around his desk and slid onto his lap. His arms immediately twined around me, slipping my legs over the armrest and pulling me snug against his chest.

"This is really stupid," I warned, but the words were more or less lost as my lips found his.

He didn't complain though, his hands already on my neck and pressing against my back. This kiss was an echo of his take charge performance earlier. I felt his power as his lips commanded and teased, dancing along my jawline until they claimed my mouth again. And I gave in eagerly, clinging to his newfound confidence and the way it lit me up from the inside out.

I hummed at the gentle way he cradled my head, his fingers soft against my scalp. But then he pulled away and I made an embarrassing noise in protest.

"Don't worry, Red," he smiled, tapping on his phone with his free hand, "I'm not done with you yet. I'm just texting Logan to come get us in fifteen minutes.

That way I can don't have to worry about giving into the desire to coax you up to my room right now."

"So…" I trailed a finger over his chest, "Say you *were* going to coax me, how would you do it?"

Fire leapt into his eyes, and he tossed his phone on his desk. My eyes slid closed as he took my face in his hands.

And then nothing.

Just as I began to open my eyes, I felt the barest skim of his lips over mine. They were there and gone, barely a whisper. I whimpered, trying to pull him back to me.

"Patience, Red," he whispered in my ear, pressing a sweet kiss there. I sank my fingers into his shoulders, feeling equal measures of love and hate for this slow torture. But with every new exploration of his lips on my skin—my jaw, my throat, the spot behind my ear—I found myself falling deeper and deeper.

This wasn't just a passionate kiss between two people. Because beyond my body's initial reaction to his touch, there was something sweeter. More intimate. This wasn't a man trying to claim or impress a woman. This was a man telling his mate, touch by touch, whisper by whisper, exactly how he felt.

A kiss against my eyelid. *Beautiful.* One across my cheekbone. *Adored.* The hollow of my neck. *Clever.* The tip of my nose. *Kind.* The corner of my mouth. *Precious.* And finally, *blessedly,* my lips. *Loved.*

I kissed him back, full and sweet and tender and longing and needy and supportive. I gave him everything all at once, making this more than just a moment. More than just this feeling and this touch.

Because this feeling would fade. Just as our bodies would. The passion would temper, the desire would be less frequent, but this love would survive. Because it was built on so much more. That's what I wanted him to feel in my kiss.

"I love you too," he whispered, his breath ragged as he leaned his forehead against mine.

I grinned, playing with the hem of his shirt. He radiated joy and peace, but there was a little humor in there too. "What's so funny?"

He tucked a strand of hair behind my ear and pulled back to meet my eyes. "I was just thinking about a dream I had last night. About you."

"Oh, dirty," I teased.

He squeezed my hip. "We were lying in bed together."

"This is getting steamy." I smirked.

"Hush, I'm telling a story," he admonished with a smile. "In the dream, I let you sleep in so I could watch you sleep. You were curled up next to me. Your hair was a mess and there was a crease on your cheek from the pillow, but you were perfect." Morgan studied me, the blue ring in his eyes almost pulsating with happiness. "But then the kids came in."

I choked on air. "Kids?"

Morgan smirked and my heart skittered. "Our youngest—a boy—came in with Daisy Mae to tattle on his siblings."

"Siblings?" I parroted stupidly.

"Mhm. Then our oldest came in—another boy—complaining that his sister and his middle brother were fighting, and it was stressing him out."

"He clearly didn't get anything from me."

"He had your freckles." His finger brushed across my cheeks. "Then there was shouting—your daughter was quite the screamer." I laughed and he went on. "She and our middle son came into our room, him swearing that she was cheating at their game, and her flipping her auburn hair like she'd done no wrong."

I smiled. "Clearly my child."

"We diffused the situation by getting into a tickling war, and you and I stole a few kisses when the kids weren't looking. It was—"

"Perfect," I finished for him, close to tears. "You really want all of that with me?"

Mor captured my lips, his kiss soft and sure. "That and more."

When I leaned back, drunk on contentment, my eyes caught on Morgan's computer screen. "Wait, is that a recipe for Frank's milkshakes?"

Morgan lifted his head and glanced at the recipe and then flashed me a disarming smile. "Sure looks like it."

I tickled his neck for his snark, but he stopped me by distracting me with a kiss. Sneaky Bear Man.

"It's from an email," I said, studying the recipe again. "How did you get him to give it to you? He never shares his recipes."

"I think he has a soft spot for a man in love," Morgan shrugged. "Plus, we're responsible for about thirty percent of his income. I think he knew we weren't leaving him anytime soon."

"Or ever. Frank and I have a permanent relationship."

"I thought *we* had a permanent relationship," Morgan sassed, fingers playing with the tail of my braid.

"Yes, but Frank and I have a *business* relationship. Supply and demand. I demand, he supplies. You and I have a *personal* relationship."

"Where you demand, and I supply?" he guessed cheekily.

"Now you're getting it, Bear Man."

Chapter 25

MORGAN

"There," I said, stuffing the incriminating evidence to the bottom of the trash can that sat against the garage at the Berserker house, "She'll never find it."

Daisy Mae paid me no attention, wagging her tail as she sniffed the ground for any food I may have dropped.

This was my second secret order from Frank's this week. It was getting harder to hide my obsession from Caroline. But I had to keep it secret, or she'd never let me live it down after all the things I'd said about fast food.

"I just had to run my mouth about the health effects of deep-fried food." Daisy looked up from her scavenger hunt and licked my hand. "Yeah, I know I'm pathetic. Blame your mother."

The two of us headed for the garage door, but I paused at the sound of an engine coming down the driveway. A mid 1980's yellow pickup was driving toward us. My body went rigid at the sight of the strange car, thinking that it was more paparazzi.

But then the passenger window rolled down.

"Hey, Morgan," Mayor Fitz greeted me. I almost didn't recognize him in a grey hoodie and jeans.

"Mayor Fitz," I said, trying to reconcile the sight of him in an old beat-up truck, "I gotta be honest, I'm having a hard time believing it's you."

"Seems weird without the suit?" he prompted, smiling. Between that and his slightly messy hair, I was beginning to wonder if this was just some strange dream.

"Just a little," I admitted.

He chuckled and then we both went silent. Awkwardness stretched on for a moment and I wondered what had brought the mayor all the way out here—and in casual clothes. *Can't be good.*

"There's something I wanted to discuss with you and Caroline," he finally said.

I nodded, a little bit of unease gathering in my gut. "Sure, why don't you come on into the house."

Once the Mayor's truck was parked in the garage, I led him through the house to Caroline's office. But I froze at the sight of a picture taped to the back of her computer monitor.

"Seriously?" I complained, interrupting her discussion with Lizzy. "How long is this going to go on?"

I ripped the picture from the monitor and glared at it. After my incident with the reporters last week, a few pictures of me became fairly popular with the public.

And then came the meme.

It was a photo of me, captured by one of the reporters on the lawn that day. I was glaring down the crowd and the caption on the photo read 'When life gives you lemons...try not to drool while Morgan Hohlt makes lemonade'. The annoying part was that Caroline had been the one to make the meme.

And now it was trending.

"I have no idea what you're talking about," Care said innocently, not even raising her eyes from her notebook.

"Liar." So far, I'd found printed pictures of the meme in my bathroom, my car, inside the fridge, and taped to the front door.

Growling, I stomped over and yanked open one of her desk drawers. A stack of the memes sat on top of some office supplies.

"I don't know how those got there," she shrugged.

Unmoved by her lie, I put my hands on the desk, caging her in, my chin next to her temple. "I can feel your dishonesty, Caroline Felicity Hohlt," I whispered.

I could just see the tops of her cheekbones go pink from my vantage point. "I'm not a Hohlt."

"*Yet.* But if you don't stop with the memes, you might just stay a Birch."

Care spun her chair around, forcing me to back up a little. She looked pretty today. Not her natural, effortless kind of pretty, but her polished, boss-like kind of pretty. Every time I saw a new side to her beauty, I couldn't decide which one was my favorite.

"You wouldn't dare withhold my own engagement from me," she snapped, eyes narrowed.

"Maybe I would. Maybe that's how much I hate the memes."

She smoothed out a wrinkle on my shirt, her fingers warm against me. "And maybe I'll withhold my kisses from you."

"You wouldn't."

She quirked an eyebrow. "Maybe I would."

I stared her down, but she didn't budge. "Fine." I sighed. "Truce?"

"Truce." She smiled, holding out a hand. I shook it, barely resisting the urge to kiss her. Lizzy was used to our constant touching, but poor Fitz was not.

"Do you really hate the meme?" Care asked, drawing my attention away from her lips.

I stared at the concern in her eyes, still holding onto her hand. "I hate that the internet has it. But I like that you tease me about it."

"Yeah?"

"Teasing is half of this relationship, Red."

She grinned. "True! Okay, now that we have that settled, why don't you explain to me why Mayor Fitz is in my office."

"Right." I gave the mayor an apologetic look. "Sorry about that."

"It's okay," he replied, seeming amused by Caroline and me. "I'd be distracted too if my girlfriend worked in my house."

"You have a girlfriend?" Caroline asked, perking up in her chair.

Fitz chuckled and shook his head, his ears going a little pink. "No. Definitely not."

"Hm," Care hummed, disappointed. "Alright, well why don't you come in and take a seat? Lizzy, would you mind giving us a minute?"

Lizzy nodded, her sleek, sandy brown ponytail bobbing against her shoulder. "Sure. I'll go check and make sure the boys haven't murdered Mikael yet."

Care and I exchanged a look, knowing that Lizzy was only half joking.

My family had welcomed the three Alfar advisors into our home for the time being since they couldn't go back to the Alfar house without leading the press there. But my brothers and Logan had taken a particular interest in Mikael. And by interest, I mean an interest in pranking him. In all fairness, Mikael did prank them back, so I didn't think he truly hated it. But his reactions could be a little...violent.

"Yeah, make sure they haven't broken anything today," I called out as Lizzy disappeared from the room, shutting the double doors behind her. So far, the prank war had cost me a dining chair, three feather pillows, a stapler, and two hundred dollars in groceries. If they ruined anything from my office, I was going to kill them.

I led Fitz over to the couch and chairs that were arranged in the middle of the office, motioning for him to sit.

"So, I'm going to assume that you're not here to ask for my match making expertise," Care said, dropping a bag of mini Reese's on the coffee table as she sat in an armchair.

I took the chair opposite her, shooting her a warning look. Caroline was convinced that Fitz and Merida had a thing for each other and were destined to become a couple. And since I disagreed, we'd made a bet to see if they actually ended up together or not. And planting the idea in Fitz's head with a matchmaking scheme was cheating.

'Calm down,' Care mouthed, winking at me. 'I won't say anything.'

Why didn't I believe her?

"Are you a matchmaker?" Fitz smiled, taking a Reese's from the bag when Caroline offered it to him.

"No, she's not," I chimed in before she could answer. "She's just nosy."

But Fitz didn't seem offended by Care's inappropriate curiosity. "That's a shame. If you were, I could hire you to help me navigate through all the gold diggers and back stabbers."

"Is it really that bad?" I reached for a Reese's, but Care slid the bag away from me.

I raised my eyebrows in a silent challenge. She frowned and shook her head. I smiled and snatched one from the bag anyway. Caroline *hated* the way I inhaled her beloved chocolate. She said it was heresy not to enjoy candy as you ate it.

So, this time, I made a show of unwrapping it and bringing it to my lips. Then I ate it, one small bite at a time.

Care glared at me, but it was ruined by the smile pulling at her lips. I smirked.

"It's just because it's almost reelection season," Fitz sighed, grabbing another candy. I'd honestly almost forgotten he was there for a moment. "It'll pass."

As if sensing his distress—or smelling the chocolate—Daisy trotted over and sat at his feet, letting him scratch her head.

"Just make sure you take care of yourself," Care insisted. "This is a stressful time for you."

Fitz nodded and ran a hand through his dark hair. The move shocked me for a moment, unused to seeing the man be so...human. "I know," he agreed. "My therapist says I need to practice setting boundaries so I can stop letting people ask more of me than I can actually give."

"Do you know what you need?" Care asked, stealing a few more candies from the bag. When Fitz shook his head, she smiled. "Friends. Ones who don't want anything from you. Who can help you say no when you need to and give you escape routes from situations you don't want to be in."

A wistful expression came over the mayor's face and I felt like I was meeting a different person entirely. Not the tight laced, always-on-top-of-it man who ran the council, but a man who was tired of being alone.

"Sounds like wishful thinking," he muttered.

Care shook her head. "Maybe in the past. But you have us now."

"She's right," I shrugged, "You're one of the few people at work that I actually like. As far as I'm concerned, you're welcome to come by here any time you want. You can vent, play video games, use the gym—whatever."

"And we can make a signal for when you need a getaway at a function," Care suggested excitedly. "Like when you scratch your eyebrow, it means we need to come and save you from the conversation. And when you rub the back of your neck, it means that we need to get you out of the building. I can even get you out without being seen by a single soul. You'll be home in your pajamas before anyone even realizes you're gone."

Fitz frowned in thought, considering. Then he lifted his gaze to Caroline. "You were the one breaking into the Alliance Building, weren't you?"

I sat there, wide eyed at the turn in the conversation.

But Caroline met the mayor's look head on. "What gave it away?" she asked.

My jaw dropped. *Is she seriously admitting to it?*

"I knew something was off when Morgan started talking to himself during council meetings," Fitz replied, shrugging nonchalantly. "Then when he brought you to the Alliance Building as his assistant and you spent the whole meeting walking the third floor, I wondered if that was the connection."

"I told you that you're bad at the whole earpiece thing." Care turned an accusing look my way.

"Are you serious right now?" I demanded, shocked at the blasé way they were discussing my girlfriend's illegal behavior. "How are you not worried about getting arrested?"

"I'm not going to tell anyone anything," Fitz interrupted, turning to me. "Honestly, for a long time I've wanted to know who the vigilante was. Not so I could catch them, but so I could thank them."

I turned to Care, and her expression mirrored my own surprise.

"The vigilante brought fifty-four people to justice in three years," Fitz explained, "People that had been vetted and hired and often given positions of authority. But it took an unpaid, unsupported civilian to fix the problem that I couldn't." He paused, setting his elbows on his knees as he looked at Caroline. "Thank you for protecting our city. For doing what I couldn't. There's a lot of legal red tape that I can't cross, and even though I knew some of those people were guilty, I couldn't prove it. But you could. You did what was necessary to keep people safe, no matter the cost to yourself. I can't tell you how much I admire that."

Care was speechless for a moment, and though Fitz probably didn't notice, I saw the tears build in her eyes. I felt the gratitude burst in her chest. The person who'd worked the hardest for the safety of this city was being recognized for the first time. And then suddenly it was me who was crying.

"Did I upset you guys?" Fitz asked, looking worried.

"No," Caroline mumbled, shaking her head. "It's just...after doing it all alone for so long, it feels nice to know that somebody was on my side."

"You deserve it," I insisted, pressing a thumb to the inner corner of my eye to scoop up the tears. "You deserve to be supported and acknowledged more than anyone."

Care smiled at me, mouthing 'I love you'.

"And thank you, Mayor Fitz," she said, turning to the mayor. "For not ratting me out, and for everything you said. You have no idea how much it means to me."

"Call me Fitz," he smiled, looking between us both. "Friends don't use titles, right?"

"Heck no," Care laughed, all of us grateful for the heaviness slipping out of the atmosphere. "I honestly don't even like the Alfar to call me 'Queen Caroline'. But apparently a ruler has to demand respect, or so my advisors tell me."

"Sounds like my campaign team," Fitz groaned, rubbing his temples.

"Is that what brought you today?" I asked, curious what this was all really about. "The campaign?"

"No," he said, eyeing me. "Actually, I had a question for you."

"Okay, shoot."

"After we were attacked outside the Shifter Alliance Building the night of the party, you said you didn't know anything about why the gambling dens were after you. But since the council meeting, I started to wonder if you had more information than you let on..."

Unsure, I looked to Caroline, silently raising my eyebrows. Understanding my silent request, she studied Fitz for a moment and then nodded, indicating that his motives were sincere—at least according to his emotions.

"I don't know who sent the gambling dens," I explained, assured that we could trust him, at least with this information. "All we know is that a 'reputable official' paid them to attack me but not kill me. Caroline's also been dealing with magical boobytraps, but we don't know if the two things are connected or not."

"But both of you have been unharmed so far?" Fitz asked, looking genuinely concerned.

I looked at Care, remembering the night of her coronation when the Pixie potion she'd been slipped made her suffocate. The image of her standing there, unable to breathe, still floated through my mind, reminding me how easy it would be to lose her.

"We're fine," she assured Fitz, holding my gaze. "There's been some close calls, but nothing we haven't walked away from." Translation: I'm fine, Morgan. Stop worrying.

But she didn't understand that I would never stop worrying about her.

Fitz nodded and sat back on the velvet periwinkle couch. I had a theory that Care bought the couch because touching it was like petting a bunny, but without the risk of being bitten. It was like a magical therapy couch. Every time I sat on it, I instantly felt comforted.

"And you said the one paying the gambling dens is a reputable official?" Fitz asked.

I nodded, not liking the worried look in his eye. "That's all we know so far. Why?"

Fitz worked his jaw back and forth, his brow furrowed. "Francine was the one who called the news station to come and interview you outside the Alliance Building."

"Why?" I understood that the Minotaur Commander hated me—the feeling was mutual—but to have me cornered in public like that...

"She wants you off the council," Fitz said tiredly. "She's on a warpath to get rid of you because you shoot down all her proposals."

"That's because they're always dangerous or stupid—or both!" I huffed, annoyed that Francine's stupid ideas were what had started her vendetta against me. "As I recall, she once suggested that Minotaurs be allowed to sell their blood without having to submit records to the government. Which was both stupid *and* dangerous. It would have allowed people to create magically impervious items that could be used to commit crimes. Which is why all magic that's sold has to be documented both by the seller and the buyer. There are rules for a reason."

Fitz held up his hands in a placating gesture. "I'm not arguing with you. I'm just telling you that the reason Francine has targeted you is because you always shoot her down. Well, that and the fact that neither one of you can speak without antagonizing each other."

I rolled my eyes but didn't argue. He wasn't wrong.

"So, you think that Francine is behind the attacks?" Care asked, her forehead wrinkled in concern.

"I don't know," Fitz said, shaking his head. "It could be anyone. Maybe even someone from another region for all we know. I just find it convenient that an unknown official is targeting Morgan, and Francine—who happens to be a city official—hates him."

"It's a fair point," Care nodded, swallowing another Reese's. "There are a lot of people on the council that I don't trust, but—"

I quirked a brow, confused at her sudden silence. But as her lips kept moving and no sound came out, I became worried.

"Caroline?" I demanded, moving to crouch beside her.

She held her throat and continued to move her lips like she was speaking, but she didn't make a sound. "Can you hear her?" I snapped, looking to Fitz.

He shook his head. "No. What's wrong with her?"

I didn't take the time to respond, instead yanking the slim vial Merida had given me from my pocket. I'd been carrying it around for weeks, hoping I wouldn't find a reason to use it.

"Here," I shoved the vial into her hands, and she didn't hesitate to chug it. Once she was done, I took the vial from her shaking fingers and grasped her hands. Her worried gaze met mine, and we stared at each other, waiting for the magic to take hold.

"Well?" Fitz blurted; eyes wide as he watched us.

Care took a deep breath. "I'm okay." I sighed at the sound of her voice, letting my head fall to her knees. "It's okay. I'm fine, Mor."

I nodded but didn't move, my emotional bandwidth too strained to let the stress ease away so quickly. *I'm getting really sick of fearing for my girlfriend's life.*

"You mean to tell me that this has happened before?" Fitz gasped, and I looked up to find him watching us with an almost comically horrified look.

I looked up at Caroline, my body tight with anxiety. "Too many times."

But this would be the last, if I had anything to say about it.

Chapter 26

CAROLINE

"You're staring," I complained, sensing his gaze on my back.

"I'm gazing. It's romantic."

"It's creepy."

Silence met my ears as I continued washing the dishes from dinner. Morgan had been watching me like a hawk for a few days now, tasting all my food, checking every room before I entered it. He was driving me crazy.

Then I felt a pair of warm arms slide around my stomach and a solid chest press against my back. "Still creepy?" Morgan whispered, his lips brushing my temple.

"Yes," I stubbornly insisted, starting on the next dish.

"Red," he growled, taking the dish from me with one hand.

"Morgan—" I tried to turn in his arms, but he held me too tight. *Darn his Berserker strength.*

"I know you're mad."

"I'm *frustrated*," I corrected.

"Is there a difference?"

I pinched his side and he yelped but didn't release me.

"You're acting like you're my secret service agent," I complained, holding onto the edge of the counter.

"Sounds like a fun roleplay."

"*Mor.*"

"I know, and I'm sorry," he pleaded, setting his chin on my shoulder. "But you don't know what it was like to see you suffocate at the coronation. Or to watch you become paralyzed at practice. I've seen you injured and attacked more times than any mate should ever have to. You know how scared I am; you feel it. Those boobytraps were all jinxed so that they would only affect *you*. How could I be anything but worried?"

Sighing, I folded my arms over his and let myself lean back into his hold. "You're not wrong. But these boobytraps aren't meant to kill me, they're meant to scare me."

"Well, it's working, because they're scaring *me*."

I tugged on his arms until he loosened them enough for me to turn and face him.

"Don't be scared," I whispered, pushing his dark hair back from his forehead. "This is going to end. We're going to catch whoever's behind this and then you won't have to worry about me anymore, okay?"

He didn't answer at first, pressing his forehead to mine. "Can I show you something?"

Curious, I pulled back to look at him. "What are you up to, Morgan Gareth Hohlt?"

"Nothing you'll be mad about," he said, mischief in his eyes.

Satisfied for the moment, I let him lead me to his office. Nothing was different in the room as far as I could tell. He hadn't gotten me a puppy and I didn't spot any gift bags. *What could he show me that I wouldn't be mad about?*

"This is a good surprise, right?"

Morgan smiled and kissed me before spinning me around to face his desk. "I hope so."

At first, I didn't see anything noteworthy. All of his things were the same, organized just as they usually were. But then I spotted it.

On the end table behind his desk, there were a few knickknacks and framed photos. One of which was a picture of Morgan and his deceased wife Genevieve. At least there *used* to be a picture of them. Now, a new frame held a picture of Morgan and *me*, with me asleep on his chest.

Tears pricked the backs of my eyes and I stood frozen, swallowed up by gratitude, love, and joy.

"You didn't have to do that," I whispered, unable to speak any louder.

Morgan turned me toward him again, clasping my face in his gentle fingers.

"I know," he said, smiling tenderly. "But I wanted to. Gen is my past, and I don't want to live there anymore. I want to move on to the future—with you."

"But you're allowed to remember her and love her—"

"I know, Red." His smile widened, and I felt my body get warmer in response to the adoration in his eyes. "I'll always love Genevieve. She was the first woman to look past my reputation and see my potential. She taught me how to be gentle and how to let people in. She taught me how to love and I'll always be grateful to her for that."

His thumbs brushed my jaw, and he inched closer. "But you taught me how to accept myself. That I don't have to settle. That love can strike twice in the same place. You taught me to hope, Caroline Felicity Birch. You gave me joy when I had none and you brought life to a dead space. I will love Geneieve until the day I die, but I'm *in love* with you. And maybe now you'll understand that no matter how many years go by, I will always worry about you. Partly because I love you, but also because I've had this before and lost it. And I cannot—will not—tie ribbons to anyone else in this lifetime but you. Understand?"

I nodded, crying too hard to get a word out. All my life I'd expected to be alone. And that used to be fine. But then Morgan showed up and everything changed in an instant.

Now I couldn't see a future without him in it, couldn't imagine spending more than a few hours apart. I'd gone soft and sappy and vulnerable, but for Morgan, I didn't mind.

"I love you," I managed to blurt, his face a little fuzzy through my tears. "I don't know what I did to deserve you, but I'm not gonna question it."

Morgan's smile was wide, but there was a strange bit of anxiety lurking beneath the surface. "I love you too, Care," he said, his voice wavering just a little. "Now go look at the picture."

"But I can see it—"

"Go," he insisted.

Confused, I moved around the desk and picked up the picture frame. At the bottom of the glass was a small sticky note.

where my chesticles
first made you swoon.

I laughed, remembering the time I'd waltzed into his room late at night to demand we do a stakeout. I hadn't expected to find him without a shirt on, and I'd never been the same since.

"Your room?" I guessed.

"I don't know, let's go see," he shrugged mischievously.

Grinning, I led the way up the stairs to the second floor, opening Morgan's bedroom door. I paused on the threshold, my mind beginning to catch up with what was going on.

I was on a scavenger hunt, that much was clear, but when I saw a gift wrapped in pink and sitting on his bed, I began to wonder just what kind of scavenger hunt it was. Surely this couldn't be as big of a deal as I was beginning to think it was.

Although he had been calling me Caroline Hohlt a lot lately...

"You gonna open it, Red?" he asked, and I looked over my shoulder to find him filming me with his phone.

"First you have to tell me, is this scavenger hunt just a way to seduce me? Because it's kind of working, but I'm gonna need a ring before I start stripping."

Morgan's nerves spiked slightly, but he smiled and motioned to the gift. "If I were seducing you, you'd already be a Hohlt right now. Now open the gift."

I debated teasing him some more, but I actually really liked opening presents, so my excitement won out. I tore off the pink paper and lifted the lid of a white box to reveal a set of two matching pajama bottoms.

They were patterned with little bears, beets and tiny spaceships. The saying 'bears, beets, Battlestar Galactica' was printed all over them.

"Since you seemed to admire my pajamas so much that night you first saw me half naked," he said, smiling as I held the pants up, "I figured I'd get us a matching set."

I was about to toss them aside and hug him when I saw another sticky note lying at the bottom of the box.

> This might be the place where you
> first saw me as a man, but it was
> also where I first realized that
> I wanted to spend forever
> protecting you. Even though
> you make it an impossible job.

"Is this true?" I asked, holding up the sticky note.

"That night you came to check on me because I was having a nightmare," Morgan replied, closing the distance between us, his phone still recording, though he wasn't pointing it at me anymore, "I was dreaming that you died, and when I woke up and held you close, I knew. I never wanted to go a day without you in my arms again."

I smiled, giving him a quick kiss.

"Look at the back," he said pulling away.

Curiously, I turned the little pink note around.

> where I called your
> bluff by showing off.

I hummed thoughtfully, unsure what the note meant. Morgan took it from my fingers and slid the paper and his hand into my back pocket. "I'll give you a hint," he whispered, bringing my other hand up to feel his bicep.

I rolled my eyes even as I squeezed his arm. I wasn't about to turn away an opportunity to feel the man's muscles. "The gym, really?"

Morgan just smiled wider, kissing my forehead before leading me from the room.

A bouquet of sunflowers awaited us in the gym, right on the bench where I'd been sitting when Morgan flirted with me for the first time—well, the first time I'd noticed, anyway.

This time, Morgan said that my flustered reactions to his attempts at flirting that day gave him hope that he actually had an effect on me. That maybe he had a shot.

I kissed him just to make sure he knew how much of an effect he had on me. By the time my point had been proven, we were both out of breath and equally enamored with each other.

But the scavenger hunt wasn't over yet. There was a blue sticky note on the vase of flowers, and Mor once again instructed me to read it.

> where you only ever seem
> to be when you're recovering
> from an injury.

"I'm not injured that often," I complained, staring at him indignantly.

"You've had two concussions, almost killed yourself by using too much magic, have been poisoned twice, jinxed once, and you've come out of multiple attacks by the skin of your teeth."

"Most of those were not my fault though," I argued as we headed upstairs to my room. He wasn't wrong though. I was rarely in my room unless I was primping or recovering from something. *A girl doesn't primp as much as I do only to hang out in her bedroom.*

When we got to my room, a package of Oreos awaited me on my desk, along with another sticky note.

The scavenger hunt continued in this fashion, me finding gifts and sticky notes that led me to the next location. And like a good boyfriend, Morgan filmed the whole thing on his phone.

We went from my room—which he said was where I'd been recovering from one of my concussions, and he realized that he never wanted to go back to life without me—to his office—where we'd argued for the first time and he said I drove him crazy from the beginning, but now it was the good kind. Mostly.

We went to the stairs where he'd hidden a gift beneath the steps to remind me of the moment that I found out about the mate bond and tried to run away. It was the moment when I knew he loved me, because his feelings were bigger than my fear.

We did a little extra kissing there.

The next sticky note led us to Frank's, where the poor man *cried*, exclaiming that it was about time I found someone to take care of me. Morgan professed that the first time we stopped at the restaurant—against his wishes—was when he first realized that I had him wrapped around my finger.

Then we got milkshakes and fries and followed the next clue to the Alliance Building. To the exact spot where we first met: Fitz's office.

The door was open, and another gift was waiting, along with another sticky note. Morgan was in the middle of telling me how much I had changed his life, when Fitz walked in.

"Way to ruin the moment, man," Morgan complained, glaring at the mayor.

"Hey, I showed up at exactly five thirty, just like you asked," Fitz challenged, holding up a to go coffee cup. "I even went to go get some coffee while I waited for you to be done. It's not my fault you were late. I did as I was told."

Morgan rolled his eyes, but I gave Fitz a kiss on the cheek and tugged Morgan out of the office with me. "Sorry, Fitz, we're leaving now! Thanks for humoring us!"

Fitz requested a phone call later, asking for an 'update'—whatever that meant—and we fled the scene.

Next was the ballroom in the Alfar house. A little velvet box was waiting on the steps where I'd been coronated, and when I looked at Morgan, he nodded for me to open it. Cautiously, I opened the little box, both awed and disappointed to see a silver necklace with a bear pendant.

"This is where I first saw you stepping into yourself," came Morgan's whispered words in my ear, his arms reaching around me to take the necklace from my hands. "I remember watching you come down those stairs and thinking how proud I was to know you. You've never needed me, Caroline. You're strong and kind and smart without me. But I want to be beside you, watching you and protecting you while you take on the world."

I waited as he shifted my hair from my neck, clasping the necklace at the back. His warm lips pressed against the spot just above the chain and I closed my eyes, trying to engrave this moment into my mind.

"I want you beside me," I said, letting my head rest against his shoulder as he wrapped his arms around my middle. "Always. But you're wrong, Mor. I do need you. Sure, I was a whole person before I met you. I was happy, even in my loneliness and I felt purpose even without a partner."

I turned in his grasp, sliding my arms around his neck. "But I came alive in a new way when you came along. Single me was great, but me with you is everything."

Morgan's eyes grew warm, and we both moved so in sync that I wasn't sure which of us initiated the kiss first. All I knew was the calming, anchoring pressing of his lips against mine.

Like true partners, we led and followed, moving to accommodate the other and checking each other's desires before fulfilling our own.

But fulfill we did.

My spine was kept in place only by the strong press of Morgan's hand, and the very breath in my lungs seemed to belong to him, for he kept stealing it. But I didn't stop him. He was welcome to steal my breath, by looks or by touch, for the rest of our lives.

"Gosh, I love you," he breathed, studying me with a happiness on his face that I would do anything to keep.

"Really? The elaborate scavenger hunt and myriad of gifts didn't clue me in," I teased, smirking.

Morgan kissed the expression away and soon we were headed to the next location, the Berserker house. This clue led to the kitchen, where we had our first kiss. Morgan insisted that we come in through the front door, and as we stepped inside, all the lights were off, with only a dull glow coming from the other end of the hall.

I gave Mor a curious look, but he just urged me forward. Nervous, I walked to the kitchen. I'd barely stepped into the room when I gasped, completely taken aback.

Candles covered the dining room tables like a table runner, running along the counters, filling the island, and even lining parts of the floor. The entire room was lit with the warmth of flickering flames, and I didn't even know I was crying until I felt the tears drip from my chin.

"This way," Morgan said, tugging my hand and pulling me forward.

Mutely, I followed his urging to the sink, where a small box was giftwrapped with green wrapping paper and a silver bow. My fingers trembled as I picked it up, and I was only dimly aware of Morgan setting his phone—still recording—on the counter.

"Here," he said, turning me to face him, his hands covering mine on the little box, "There's something I need to say before you open it."

Tentatively, I met his eyes, terrified of what I might find there. Which was stupid considering that any doubts I'd ever had about our relationship had been erased by Morgan's faithfulness. All my anxieties about whether or not I could be loved had been quieted by his patience. But in the face of such a big moment, they roared loud again, making all my muscles go stiff and my lips tremble.

"Convincing you to let me love you has been a long con," he said, not letting go of my hands. "I knew from the get-go that you weren't going to make it easy. That you would need time. Which was why I kept the mate bond a secret for so long. You had walls that were put up based on people and experiences long before me, but because I love you, I had no problem waiting for you to realize that I wasn't like everyone else. That it was safe to let me in."

"How could you know all that?"

Morgan leaned forward, leaning his forehead against mine. "Because I have walls too, Red. I've used my intimidation to keep people away for a long time. I've protected myself from pain by scaring everyone away."

"But you let me in so easily," I argued. "I didn't even have to push you, you just welcomed me like I belonged there."

"Sometimes we come across people that aren't affected by our attempts at self-preservation. I tried to protect myself with fear, but you weren't afraid of me. You weren't intimidated or cowed," he said, pulling back to look me in the eye, those twin blue rings bright and constant. "You took one look at the walls I held up, tossed your hair and walked through them like they were curtains. I didn't get a chance to keep you out, Care, because you waltzed right in."

I nodded, understanding exactly what he meant. I could feel the fist of anxiety tight around my chest. It squeezed with instinct, urging me to flee, to fight, to resist the vulnerability. Nothing felt more unsafe to me than opening up all my soft and squishy places for someone to lay waste to.

But then I looked at Morgan.

It was still scary to be so emotionally naked, but only a little, because Morgan had already proven to me that he'd keep me safe. That he'd keep my heart safe.

"I didn't really let you in," I admitted quietly, sniffling as I started crying again. "In fact, I didn't even know I should be working to keep you out until you were already in. And when I felt afraid of the mate bond, I couldn't make the fear stick. Because I knew that long before I realized my feelings for you, you'd been there, watching and waiting, patient and kind while I tried to sort out my baggage."

"I don't ever let people know me the way you know me," I went on, trying not to blubber through the tears, "Or protect me the way you do, or touch me or see me the way you do. But you've proven to me again and again that you're different. Because while I was scared and confused, you were waltzing around all the breakable parts of me, protecting them fervently, and I never gave you the credit."

"I don't need it," Mor insisted, shaking his head, "I just need to know that you feel safe with me. That's all I ever want, Care."

I smiled, feeling that fist around my chest loosen its grip. "When you and I first kissed, you said that the reason you didn't want to tell me how you felt, was because you didn't want to scare me away...I promise you that no matter what happens, I'm never running from you. You *are* my safe space, Bear Man. Always."

Morgan's smile was brilliant and bright, and it filled me in a way no amount of milkshakes ever could. "Well in that case, go ahead and open it," he said, pulling his hands away from mine.

Eager and excited, I pulled off the paper to reveal a little white gift box, and inside lay a smaller velvet box. My hands were trembling by then, so Morgan took the box from my hands. Then he knelt on the ground, and my tears renewed themselves.

"Caroline Felicity Birch," he said, his voice catching as he cried too, "I was *not* looking for you." We both laughed, but quickly sobered with the enormity of the moment. "But you found me just like you were made to. You're everything I never knew I needed, and I can't fathom how I went so long without knowing you. I love you more than anything in the world, and I never want to live another day without us being partners."

Then he opened the ring box, and I reluctantly pulled my eyes from his. I gasped at the sight of the ring, a small emerald surrounded by diamonds and sapphires.

"This is what I see when I look at you," he whispered, and I was drawn in again by the face I wanted to spend forever with. "Your mischievous green eyes and the blue of the mate bond. It's what first scared me about you, but now it's what grounds me. You're fire, Red. You are life and humor and courage and kindness and strength, and I am in awe of you. There's no one else in the world I want. You're my penguin, Red." He smiled, and I returned it, the expression nearly splitting my face in two. "Will you marry me?"

Now this—not my vendetta against the Shifter Alliance or my choice to become queen—would forever be the easiest decision of my life.

"Yes."

Somehow, Morgan managed to get the ring onto my shaking finger, and I tugged him up so I could hold him. We stood there in the kitchen for a few minutes, bathed in firelight and crying as my heart burst with joy.

"Okay, my turn," I said, pulling out of his arms.

"What do you mean? Are you proposing to me too?" he teased. I shoved him, but he caught my hand and kept it, his finger running over the new engagement ring on my finger.

"No, but you gave me a speech and I always thought that the guy in the situation deserves to get a speech too—"

"Good luck topping mine," he winked, wrapping an arm around my waist. My will was too weak to fight him, so I didn't even try.

"Shut up and listen, Bear Man," I commanded, and though he smiled, he went silent. "Okay, here goes. Morgan Gareth Hohlt, did you know that your middle name means 'gentle'?"

"Yes, and I've always hated—"

"Hush," I said, putting a finger to his lips—which he promptly kissed. "It's a rhetorical question. Point is, when I looked it up after first hearing it months ago and found out that your middle name meant 'gentle', I wasn't surprised. Because your scary reputation had never once made sense to me. Sure, you're big and snarky..." I paused, skating my fingers over his cheek, "But you *are* gentle. From the beginning you've been tender with me, patient even when you were yelling." He laughed. "Calm even when I pushed through your walls like they were fabric, and you've been so good to me in my fear. So faithful."

"You drive me nuts, Morgan Hohlt. You have from the moment we met," I grinned, remembering those early days of being enemies. "In the beginning, your stubbornness and insistence on ruining my plans annoyed me. I hated how you grumbled and that no matter how hard I tried, I couldn't break you...But now, it's your constant challenge that keeps me going. I love the way you resist me, making me think in ways I'm not used to. I love that you're so protective and yet you respect my fire and don't try to put it out. And I love the way you look at me, the future I see in your eyes. It's a life I've never imagined but wouldn't trade for the world. I love you, Morgan Gareth Hohlt, and I plan on doing so for the rest of our lives."

Morgan was crying again, and I helped him wipe the tears so he could see. "That wasn't too bad, Red," he mumbled, smiling sweetly.

"Not bad? I—"

My complaint was pleasantly smothered by Morgan's mouth, and we kissed like the world was ending. Until everyone, Morgan's family, Grey, Mr. Wallace, Logan, Ariel and the visiting Alfar burst into the room and ruined the moment.

Well, not really. No one could ruin that moment, it was perfect.

Chapter 27

CAROLINE

"Question for you," I asked, leaning over so Morgan could hear me above the hum of our engagement party.

The Alfar and the Berserkers had joined forces to plan it. And although technically we shouldn't be risking a trip to the Alfar house in case the media followed us, I wasn't worried.

Morgan was so paranoid about being followed that he had four different cars leave the Berserker house, then split up in the middle of downtown and go four different directions. Then, our car drove around for thirty minutes, making confusing turns until he was certain no one was following us.

I loved him for it.

"Shoot," he said, turning from Stefan and David, who were busy talking about Stefan's new car. Everyone was dressed up tonight, and my valet and landscaper looked slick in their nice suits. But no one compared to Morgan when he was dressed in black.

We were a matched pair tonight, him in a black suit and me in a black dress. It was silky with thin straps and a simple, fitted bodice. But the skirt was the showstopper, with thick, draping black silk pooling around my feet and a slit on the left that went up to mid-thigh.

Morgan was doing a valiant job trying not to stare at the occasionally exposed skin, but I felt a selfish wave of satisfaction every time he saw it and his attraction flared.

"Are Genevieve's parents still alive?" I asked, unsure how to ask the question more delicately.

Morgan blinked, but he didn't seem offended or uncomfortable with the question. "Yeah. They live about an hour north. I uh..." he looked down, fiddling with his cuff links. "I probably should have asked you first or at least told you, but..."

Setting a hand on his arm, I waited until he met my gaze. "Morgan, what is it?"

"I went to see them the other day and told them that we're getting married. I felt like I owed them that." He gave me a sad smile. "They gave me their permission to marry their daughter and then we all lost her. I just wanted them to know that although I'm moving forward, it doesn't mean I'll let Gen's memory die."

I grinned and let out a relieved sigh. "Oh, thank God."

"What?" His brows furrowed. "So...you're not mad?"

"Not at all! I was actually just going to ask you if we should invite them to the wedding. I..." Now it was my turn to feel insecure. I bit my lip, unsure. "I had a dream last night that you and I were married with kids. And while we were all on the couch watching a movie, I saw her...Genevieve."

Morgan went completely still, but I forced myself to get all the words out. "She was smiling at us like she was happy for us. I don't think Genevieve was haunting my dreams or anything, but it did make me wonder how we could honor her. And I thought that maybe her parents would like to be honorary grandparents to our kids. I mean, you lost a wife, but they lost a daughter and everything that comes with it. I thought it might be a nice gesture..."

Morgan was silent for too long and I started to worry that I'd overstepped. "We don't have to do any of that though. It was just a thought—"

"I love you," he interrupted, grey eyes bright with affection. "And I think it's a great idea. I don't know how they'll feel about the offer, but I think it would be nice for us to ask."

I smiled. "Yeah?"

He nodded and leaned forward, his lips a breath away. "Yeah. I don't know how I got so lucky to be loved by a woman as thoughtful and kind as you."

"Cus you're a good kisser," I whispered, grasping the lapel of his jacket and tugging him to me. We kept the kiss short, aware that there were at least two hundred people crammed into the ballroom with us.

I had just turned to ask Stefan how things were going with Charlie when everyone began clapping. Confused, I looked at Morgan, but he looked just as lost as I was.

"I think that's for you," David said with a smile, pointing behind us.

Mor and I both turned and saw Ariel and Torrie wheeling out a round table. Lizzie followed behind, filming the whole thing. Meanwhile, I was distracted by the extravagant cake in the center of the table.

It was a tiered cake, and every tier was decorated differently. One level had a city skyline around it with a night sky, and another depicted a log cabin in the woods, with the silhouette of a man carrying a woman over his shoulder. The third tier was of the Alfar castle in all its glory, with a silhouetted man holding hands with a woman wearing a crown. And on the very top, instead of the traditional cake topper, there was a silver bear and a woman with red hair riding on its back, her arm up in the air like she was going into battle.

"It's perfect," I laughed, tearing up at the gorgeous cake and the array of desserts laid out around it. There was also a dessert table across the room, so no one would lack for sugar tonight.

"Is this what you want for a cake topper on our wedding cake too?" Morgan teased, kissing my temple. "Because I wouldn't mind."

I grinned up at him. "I kind of love it." Then I turned to Torrie, who was dressed up tonight instead of wearing her usual bandana and pigtails. She wore a sparkling pale green dress that offset the strawberry tint to her hair, and I noticed that David's eyes never left her.

"Thank you so much Torrie," I said, flinging my arms around her. She grunted at my sudden impact, but she hugged me back.

"You're welcome, Caroline. But I really didn't do much. It's just an orange cake with a citrus filling and a buttercream frosting with a hand sculpted topper made of chocolate. No big deal."

I laughed and shook my head. "You're incredible."

"Honestly, Ariel and Lizzy were the brains behind the plan," Torrie insisted, nudging me toward the other two women.

I eagerly hugged my sister, bending my knees a little to accommodate her short height. She was beautiful tonight in a lavender dress that was layered with tulle. I wouldn't be surprised if it ended up in some fantasy cosplay photos later.

"I'm so proud of you, sis," she said, holding me surprisingly tight for someone so small.

"For what, getting engaged? Morgan did most of the work," I laughed, still not letting go.

"I don't think that's true." She pulled back to look at me. "A year ago, it was just you and me against the world—we didn't even lean on our own parents as much as we should have. Us Birch girls were determined to take care of ourselves and not need anyone. And now here we are, loving amazing men and inviting our parents to come stay with us." She nodded her head toward Logan, who was on duty tonight, standing behind Morgan. The two were talking to David and Steffan, but they kept looking over at Ariel and I, both their gazes filled with love.

"Did Mom tell you that Dad retired?" I asked, my eyes still locked on my fiancé. *I will never get tired of that word.* Well, until I could upgrade it to husband.

"Yeah, I'm not sure it was the smartest idea," Ariel sighed, shaking her head. "You know he's gonna get crazy bored in a week."

"Eh. I give it two. Mom said to expect him to visit a lot since he's got free time."

"Maybe we should introduce him to Mr. Wallace," Ariel suggested with a mischievous smile. "They could entertain each other and get into harmless trouble together."

I laughed at the mental image of my dad—who was only fifty and always on the go—hanging out with Mr. Wallace—who was at least seventy and as ornery as could be. "That'll be a fun pairing, especially for mom."

When Ariel didn't respond, I turned back to her. She was watching me, her eyes thoughtful and a bit misty.

"What?" I asked, touching my hair self-consciously.

She shook her head. "It's just really good to see you so happy."

I sighed, knowing that of anyone, she knew the journey I'd been on.

She was there when I struggled to make friends in school. She was there when I started getting in fights because I couldn't get the chip off my shoulder. She was there when I moved to Shifter Haven, when I became a recluse, whose only hobby was being a vigilante. And she was there when everything began to change, and my heart started to thaw.

My sister had seen me at every stage, and she knew how precious this milestone was. Touched and feeling immensely grateful, I squeezed her in another hug. "Ditto, Sis...Ditto."

We hugged for a few more teary-eyed moments before I finally turned to Lizzy. My assistant was suddenly shy, studying the cupcakes beside her on the table with unnecessary concentration.

She was wearing a silk, toffee colored dress that fit snugly against her curves. Her hair was curled in that soft, retro Hollywood style and I could tell she was trying hard not to fidget with it. She looked gorgeous.

"Lizzy," I said, crossing my arms, "Are you resisting this beautiful moment of connection right now?"

She flashed her honey brown eyes at me, full of false innocence. "I would never."

"And I would never tell you that Mike is failing miserably at his job right now because he's too busy watching you."

Lizzy opened her mouth to argue with me, but I put my finger to her cheek and turned her head toward Mike. He was standing near the drink table, and to his credit, he was trying to be a good guard and watch the crowd. But every few seconds, his eyes would go back to Lizzy, his gaze desperate. Like it wasn't a choice to notice her, but an instinct.

When he realized he'd been caught staring, he didn't look away like I expected. Instead, he stared on, his blue eyes trying to convey something to Lizzy that I couldn't quite grasp. *Oh.*

I glanced back at Morgan, waving until I got his attention. With wide eyes, I mouthed my shocked question. 'Are they mates?' I pointed to Lizzy and Mike, and Morgan sighed, putting a finger to his lips.

So, they were!

I nodded to let him know I wouldn't say anything, then turned to watch the mated couple stare at each other from across the room. Clearly, Mike understood the situation, but it was unclear if Lizzy knew the truth. And as someone who'd been unaware of her own mate bond for months, I wasn't about to tell her.

Morgan keeping the truth of the mate bond from me was the smartest thing he ever did. If I'd have known too soon, I would have shut him out. I might have even run.

"Why don't you ask him to dance?" I suggested.

Lizzy turned back to me, her eyes narrowing. "You have a bet going about this, don't you?"

I gasped, pressing a hand to my heart. "How could you possibly think that I would ever—"

"Caroline."

"I bet fifty bucks that you and Mike would end up together," I shrugged, rolling my eyes. "But that's not why I think you should dance with him." She raised an eyebrow, unmoved. "I think you should dance with him because it's not every day that a man looks at a woman like *that* and she looks back."

Lizzy's cheeks went a flattering shade of pink, and she glanced back at Mike.

Twinkling lights were strung across the ballroom with fake vines of eucalyptus twined around them. Little bundles of viburnum dripped from the vines, giving the elegant room the look of being in a meadow instead of indoors. Mirrors made up the top half of the ballroom walls and tonight they reflected the fairy lights, giving the space a romantic feel.

Perfect for dancing with one's mate.

"We're supposed to be looking for—"

"I know," I interrupted her, squeezing her hand. "But just because we're on duty doesn't mean we can't still have a little fun."

She didn't commit to dancing with Mike—or even speaking with him—but she nodded and slipped away.

When I saw her pretending to look for a drink at the table next to Mike a few moments later, I grinned.

"What are you up to?" Morgan's voice rumbled in my ear, his strong hands grasping my hips.

"Nothing, just sharing the love," I smiled, turning my face to look up at him.

"Fancy way of admitting that you're meddling."

"I am not—"

"Just because they're mates doesn't mean you have a green light to push them together. Mate bonds have been rejected before."

I rolled my eyes and pointed to the aforementioned couple. Mike was clearly trying *not* to notice Lizzy. But his gaze betrayed him every few seconds, sliding over to where she feigned interest in the punch. Neither of them spoke, but they watched each other, curious but cautious.

"Not this one," I argued. "For one, they're both too smart to reject a mate bond, knowing that the rest of their lives would be self-induced agony."

"And for two?" Mor asked, watching his brother.

"Look at the way they watch each other. This isn't just a passing attraction or an innocent curiosity that they'll shrug off tomorrow. They *want* to know each other, they're just scared. I just don't know what they're scared *of*..."

"Caroline," Morgan growled, his lips brushing my skin.

"Hm?"

His hands flexed on my hips, and he nibbled my ear. "Don't push. They'll find their way to each other on their own terms."

"I'll do anything you want if you keep that up," I murmured, my eyelids at half-mast as his lips grazed the spot between my ear and my jaw.

"A dangerous proposition," he rumbled.

If only that were true. But as much as I might wish it, tonight wasn't really about us.

"Have you noticed anyone suspicious yet?" I whispered, breaking the heat of the moment.

Morgan slid an arm around my waist, his hold protective at the mention of our actual goal at this party. If all went according to plan, tonight would result in an arrest. *So much for making out under the twinkle lights with my fiancé.*

"Part of me wants to take you to your room and lock you safely away until this is over," he said, his grey eyes roving over the room. "But the other part wants you right here where I can protect you."

"You're not going to have to protect me today," I insisted, seeing suspicious faces on every guest. No one seemed particularly shady yet, but that didn't mean our prey wasn't here. "Because this is going to go smoothly."

"At the risk of making you angry with me," he said, kissing my temple, "Nothing with you ever goes smoothly."

I jabbed him lightly with my elbow.

"Chief."

Morgan and I turned to find one of the Berserkers he'd tasked with looking out for suspicious behavior standing behind us. Callie was in her mid-thirties, and she looked ravishing in a deep green dress. But the look on her pretty face was all business.

"What is it?" Morgan asked, immediately on edge.

"There's something you should see," she said ominously.

Mor nodded for Logan to come along, and we followed Callie out of the room and into a nearby sitting room. The top half of the walls were covered in expensive wallpaper that depicted a woodland scene, but thankfully the pricey furniture had been replaced with department store knockoffs and thrift store finds. I was *this close* to getting the excess in the Alfar house down to a place that didn't make me want to vomit.

But despite all the progress I'd made in creating a community that helped each other, all the work I'd done to gain my people's respect, all the planning I put into giving small businesses a leg up, and all the hope I'd put into my people, it all felt suddenly meaningless.

Because sitting on a pretty blue Victorian couch was Charlie, flanked by Clint and Grey. She stared down at her hands in her lap, her mascara smeared a little beneath her eyes. And she was cloaked with guilt.

"What's going on?" I asked, my words barely audible as Callie closed the doors behind us.

"We caught her trying to put something in the punch," Grey explained, glaring down at my housekeeper.

Merida stepped forward from behind an armchair—I'd been too focused on Charlie to notice that she and Asher were both in the room.

"It's a hallucinogenic potion," she explained, holding a small bottle. She wore a dress that was layered with tulle, and it was such a deep purple that it was almost black. She looked like all she needed was a scythe and she'd be ready to hand out judgment. I had half a mind to give her one.

"It's been spelled," she went on, "And though I'd need a Witch Hunter to tell me what specific spell was used, I'm going to assume it's been spelled to only affect you."

I nodded, slowly digesting the words. I could feel Charlie looking at me, pleading, apologetic, *begging*. But I ignored her.

This was my worst nightmare. Because the person planting the traps for all these months hadn't been just one of my subjects. She was my *friend*.

I felt betrayed, violated and...worst of all, I felt doubt. If Charlie could do this to me, then who was to say that someone else wouldn't? Maybe I wasn't as well-liked as I hoped. Maybe I wasn't as good of a queen as I tried to be...

"Care," Morgan whispered, steady at my side. His fingers wrapped around mine, sure and warm and I clung to that. To his strength. *I can do this.*

"Why?" I asked, lifting my eyes to Charlie.

She crumpled, her shoulders drooping as tears pooled in her eyes—presumably not for the first time tonight. Sympathy tugged at my gut, but I pushed it aside. I would decide if she'd earned my empathy as soon as she explained herself.

"He told me to do it," she said, lips trembling. Her words were clear even through her silent sobs and I could see her grasping for control of herself.

"He who?" Asher asked, his deep voice even and unreadable.

Charlie shrugged. "I don't know. He never gave me a name. But he knew that I owed thirty thousand dollars in student loans. He knew that I was struggling, and he offered to pay them off. I wasn't making much before this job and I got so sick of always feeling smothered by my debt. So, I did as he asked."

I said nothing, my fingers squeezing Morgan's so hard that I was surprised he didn't complain.

"He said that all I had to do was scare you," Charlie continued, her blue eyes earnest. "He gave me each boobytrap one at a time as he wanted them done, and I put them wherever he told me to. I tried to test them on myself before I gave them to you, but then I realized that they were all spelled to only react to you..."

"How did he contact you?" I asked, not ready yet to let in any kind of warm feelings where she was concerned.

Charlie answered quickly. "He called me each time he had a new trap, and then he would leave the items in a post office box downtown. He paid me through a wire transfer, but only after I called him to tell him what each trap did to you and how you reacted to it."

"What do you mean, how I reacted?"

"He wanted to know how you were emotionally." Charlie's brow furrowed, her eyes searching the air like she was looking through her memory. "He didn't say what he was hoping for, but he was always interested in how the traps affected you as queen. If they motivated you or scared you."

My jaw went slack and the hairs on the back of my neck stood on end, instinct telling me to prepare for battle. *It can't be... He wouldn't...*

I growled and ground my teeth, feeling the urge to hit something. *He absolutely would.*

"What?" Morgan whispered, not understanding my sudden rage.

"Volund," I hissed. "It's Volund."

"But why would he—"

"Because he lost the fight," I snapped. "He lost the upper hand and he had to get it back by messing with my head."

"But how would he know about the Alfar?" Clint asked, hands braced on the back of the couch.

"The Nephilim make great spies," Grey ground out, glaring into space. "He's probably had them watching us the whole time."

"And we visited the Alfar neighborhood for weeks before Harold ever approached us," Morgan added, his own anger mounting at the realization that Volund could be behind it all.

I listened as the group continued to bicker about Volund's possible involvement, only halfway paying attention. *What could Volund's end game be?* It didn't make sense...

But my thoughts were interrupted when Charlie caught my gaze, her eyes widening dramatically in a silent plea. Curious, I nodded and turned my attention to Clint and Grey.

"I'd like to talk to her on my own, girl to girl," I said, motioning for Charlie to stand.

"Are you sure?" Mor asked. His expression said he was concerned, but his emotions said he was curious. *Thank God for the mate bond.*

I kissed his cheek for sensing that there was more to it and smiled. "I'm okay, I promise."

He nodded and no one argued as I led Charlie to the edge of the room, a few yards from the rest of the group. The others watched us but continued to talk amongst themselves, only minorly concerned that I was semi-alone with my housekeeper. She wasn't exactly much of a threat.

"What is it?" I asked, crossing my arms. If she was about to beg that I let everything slide, she would be greatly disappointed.

"First of all," she said, a little timid, "I want to say that I'm sorry. What I did was wrong. Those boobytraps genuinely scared you and Chief Hohlt, and some of them even could have hurt you if they'd gone wrong. I was selfish and I let my desperation rule me and I'm sorry. I don't expect forgiveness or to evade punishment. I just needed to say that I'm sorry."

I eyed her, noting that she didn't give me a sob story about her unfortunate financial position or feed me a line about how desperate people often make rash decisions because of their circumstances. She didn't explain away her behavior or try to make me feel sympathy. She simply owned her choice.

I couldn't help but respect her for it.

"Is that why you wanted to speak to me alone?" I asked coolly. I could appreciate her apology, but that didn't mean she was off the hook. I'd been paralyzed, magically asphyxiated, and struck mute. I would have justice for that.

"No." She shook her head and turned her body slightly to the side. Then she carefully withdrew an envelope from the pocket of her dress and handed it to me. "I wanted to give you this. It's from him. He wanted me to leave it on the gift table, but I never got a chance. I don't know what's in it, but I imagine there's a reason you and Chief Hohlt are supposed to read it when you're alone."

I glanced at the envelope, careful to keep it out of sight of the group.

To the happy couple,

Read me when you're alone.

I stared at the elegant handwriting, recognizing it immediately. *Volund.* His penmanship was annoyingly perfect, and I could hear his smug voice in my head as I read his words. The question was whether or not I should do as he asked and read it with only Morgan present...

"Will you..." Charlie stuttered. "Will you tell Steffan what I did?"

"No." I looked her in the eye, letting my empathy stand beside my judgment instead of one overruling the other. "You will. I'm not going to rat you out, Charlie. I get it, you were in a tough spot and Volund offered you a way out. But you could have come to any one of us in the house and we would have gladly helped you figure out what to do about your financial situation. Especially Steffan."

She hung her head, her brown curls tumbling over her shoulder. "I know. It's what I regret most; lying to him."

"So, fix it. Tell him the truth."

"He'll hate me."

I shook my head and put a hand on her shoulder. "I don't hate you and I'm the one you wronged. I can guarantee that Steffan won't hate you either. Like me, he'll be hurt and disappointed. You're going to have to work to earn both of our trust back. But it doesn't mean you can't do it. It does, however, mean that I can't have you working here. No one will find out what you did, they'll just think the traps stopped. And I'll write you a good reference letter. But I do encourage you to tell Steffan the truth. If you really love him, honesty is the best way to show it."

She nodded, fresh tears dripping down her cheeks. Her remorse was heavy, and I was struck by the level of self-loathing rippling from her.

Giving into my softer side, I hugged her, shooting Morgan a look over her shoulder to let him know everything was fine. He nodded; his expression filled with pride.

"For what it's worth, I forgive you," I whispered to Charlie, holding her tight.

"You can't—"

"I can. It's my forgiveness to offer. But you have to take it, Charlie. You have to move forward and forgive yourself. And the first step is being the person you want to be. Which I hope is someone who's honest and selfless and good."

She nodded against my shoulder. "It is."

"Then guess what?" I pulled back and gave her an encouraging smile. "You've already got one out of three. Because you *are* a good person. You're just...a good person who screwed up and did a bad thing. The good thing is that life isn't about the mistakes we make, it's about what we learn from them."

"Oh, I've learned a *lot*," she said in a self-deprecating way, rolling her eyes.

"So go use it." I gave her one last hug. "And maybe in a few weeks you and I can go to tea together."

She stared at me like I'd lost my mind. And maybe I had. But I was glad that it wasn't my people's doubt or hatred toward me that led Charlie to set those boobytraps. It was Volund, and that was an enemy I knew how to face.

"Are you sure?" She asked, eyes wide.

I gently squeezed her arms. "Yeah, I'm sure."

She nodded, still dazed by the offer. I looked back at the group, everyone shocked to see us hugging—except for Morgan whose lips were twitching in the ghost of a fond smile.

"Clint, would you escort Charlie to her room without making a fuss?" I asked. Then I turned back to Charlie. "I'll give you two days to get your things together and say your goodbyes. Remember, you're still welcome here, you just can't be on staff."

She sniffed the last of her tears away and nodded. "Thank you, Queen Caroline. For everything."

I smiled at her and headed for the door, holding out my hand for Morgan. He followed me without question, linking his fingers with mine. "I'll see you guys tomorrow," I said, leading us from the room.

No one protested our escape and Morgan followed silently at my side up the stairs to my room, the envelope pressed safely between the folds of my skirt.

But I didn't let myself relax until I'd locked the door behind me and felt its solid surface pressing into my back.

"Care, what's going on?" Morgan finally asked, his hands on my cheeks.

I didn't answer, instead handing him the envelope. He stared at it for a moment before looking back to me, his eyes lighting with anger. "Who gave this to you?"

"Volund via Charlie," I growled, my own frustration rising to match his. "Should we open it?"

Mor was quiet for a moment as he considered the envelope. "I doubt he did anything magical to the contents and it doesn't feel like there's anything other than paper inside."

"So..." I raised my eyebrows and Morgan sighed, ripping the envelope open. I came to stand beside him as he read it out loud.

"Caroline and Morgan," he read, "I'm sorry I couldn't come in person to congratulate you on your engagement. I didn't think it wise to give you an opportunity to lock me up a second time. But I still wanted to give you a gift.

For Caroline, an apology." Morgan scoffed and I rolled my eyes. "As if he would even know an apology if it bit him in the ass."

"Just read it," I sighed, wanting to get this whole thing over with.

"I'm sorry for the things I had your housekeeper do," Morgan read, his tone snide, "But I promise it wasn't selfishly motivated. You were born to be a queen, Caroline. You just needed someone to push you out of your own self-doubt. So, I created a fictional nay sayer to give you the motivation you needed. But I am truly sorry for the fear and pain I'm sure my actions caused. But from what I gather, you're quite the queen now. You're welcome."

Morgan dropped his hand, the paper crinkling as he tightened his grip on it. "That pathetic little worm! He thinks he can actually take credit for *your* accomplishments? I swear if I ever see his stupid face again—"

"I know, I know," I assured him, taking the letter. "You can pummel Volund later. Right now, I want to know what else he said."

I scanned the letter until I found the spot where Morgan had left off. "To Morgan, I offer evidence." I glanced up at Mor, both of our foreheads wrinkled in confusion. "Enclosed, you will find a series of emails from Francine to an unknown email address. She's been plotting to take you down for months. I'm sure you'll be quick to lay blame at the feet of the gambling dens or even myself, but I encourage you to broaden your thinking."

Finished with Volund's letter, I flipped the page to the emails. They were incriminating for sure, but they didn't give any clue as to who Francine was contacting. But then I flipped to the next page.

It took me a moment to realize what I was seeing, the numbers meaning nothing until I noticed the dates. My heart seized in my chest, and I stared at the page, trying to force it all to make sense. "That can't be right," I breathed, scanning the lines over and over again. But they remained the same.

"What?" Morgan snapped.

I hesitated, unsure how he would react. Sensing my worry, he took the pages from my hands and quickly scoured them. I saw the moment it clicked. The moment that he realized the implication of the document.

His face went slack, and he stumbled back a step, slowly shaking his head. "This is fake," he snarled, crumpling the paper in his hand. "He's trying to mess with us."

I didn't argue with him, too overcome by my own emotions to insist that he face his own. Fingers shaking, I texted Lizzy and Mike and asked them to come upstairs. They would be able to check the validity of the pages. *I hope.*

By the time they arrived, Morgan was pacing, anger roiling off of him like steam, and I'd twisted my engagement ring on my finger so many times, I worried it would leave a scorch mark on my skin.

"What's going on?" Lizzy asked, looking between Morgan and I warily.

I wordlessly handed her the crumpled pages, waiting for her and Mike to realize the heaviness of the information.

"It can't be real," Mike argued after a moment. He seemed so sure. Like there was no question that this information could be authentic.

But I was an Alfar. The appearance of emotions meant little to me when I could *feel* the doubt lingering inside him. It was the same doubt that drove Morgan to pacing right now.

"Can we find out if it is?" I pleaded, forcing my panic not to show.

Morgan was too distraught to notice that it remained in my feelings, but Lizzy eyed me with concern. She felt the doubt in the room just as well as I did.

And it didn't bode well.

Chapter 28

CAROLINE

"How are you feeling?" Morgan asked.

I raised an incredulous eyebrow at my fiancé, and he scowled.

"Just because I can sense you," he whispered, tangling his fingers with mine, his voice too low for everyone else in the room to hear, "Doesn't mean I don't want a verbal answer, Caroline. So, how are you feeling?"

"Anxious," I sighed, looking around the living room at the Berserker house. Merida, Asher, Logan, Ariel, Mike, Lizzy, Clint and Grey were all present, though they didn't yet know why. Tristain, Mikael and Harold were also in the room, standing off to the side and just as anxious as we were. "This can only go two ways."

"Does one of them end up with you and me making out?"

I gaped at Morgan, shocked that he could crack a joke at a time like this. If things went the way we feared, he would be devastated.

"What is wrong with you? You've been touchy feely and flirting all day," I said, eyeing him with concern. "Aren't you...upset?"

"Do I feel upset?"

"You feel...anxious and very affectionate."

"Both right." He stepped closer, nuzzling my hair.

Thankfully, we were standing at the back of the room next to the hallway and everyone was too busy watching the TV to notice us.

"Are you using me as a distraction?" I demanded, the words coming out thin and breathy as Morgans's lips found my neck.

"Are you opposed?"

I bit my lip and shook my head, not pushing him away when his hands landed on my waist, drawing himself closer. But after a moment, he lifted his head and those beautiful grey eyes bored into me.

"Our entire world—my entire world—could implode in a matter of minutes," he gently reminded me. "And at the end of it all, all we have is you and me. Right now, I need that. I need something to cling to, to keep me afloat. I need *you*."

I let myself take a moment to study him, my eyes running across his white scar, the strong line of his jaw, the rumpled look to his dark hair, the sturdy line of his shoulders, and the vulnerability in his eyes.

To some degree, Morgan would always be that ten-year-old boy who felt alone. Who was desperate for comfort and light and happiness in his life. And for the rest of my days, I was determined to bring as much of it into his world as I could.

Sliding my arms around his neck, I reached up on tip toes and kissed him. "I promise you that whichever way this turns out, you and I are going to end the day with smiles and laughter. I'm going to make sure of it, whether I have to kiss you or tickle you to accomplish it."

Morgan smiled, running his nose against mine. "I have never loved you more than I do right now."

"Ditto. And I promise to love you even more tomorrow."

"Deal," he whispered, leaning down to kiss me again.

I was actually starting to think this whole distraction thing had some merit to it when Logan shouted for everyone to quiet down. Morgan and I turned, his arm sliding around my waist, and we watched the TV.

Where our faces were staring back at us.

"I'm here in the Shifter Alliance Building with breaking news," a young male reporter said to the camera, Morgan and I sitting across from him in one of the conference rooms. "Where a new Shifter species has just come to light. Yes, you heard that right. Apparently, an unknown Shifter species has been living right under our noses, and I have the exclusive interview."

The reporter turned in his chair and faced Morgan and me. He'd been much nicer than the woman who'd cornered Morgan on the sidewalk—which was why we'd offered him the story. He had a much kinder reputation that we hoped would work in our favor.

"Why don't you start by introducing yourselves," Grant, the reporter, suggested.

"I'm Morgan Hohlt, Chief of the Shifter Haven Berserkers," the TV Morgan said, his hand holding mine on my knee.

"And I'm his fiancé Caroline," the TV me said, allowing for a dramatic pause, "Queen of the Alfar."

Pandemonium broke out in the living room, everyone shouting, asking questions, and standing to their feet as they berated us for going public. Everyone was some varying shade of shocked, anxious and minorly annoyed.

The only ones who weren't surprised by the announcement were Lizzy—since she'd been the one to get the appointment with the news station for us—and the other Alfar.

"You went public without telling any of us?" Mike sputtered, sending an accusing look at Lizzy. She just raised an eyebrow at him.

"I serve my queen, not you," she shot back.

"They told us," Mikael added with an arrogant shrug. Harold slugged him in the shoulder, but the persnickety Justice Advisor was unrepentant.

"Of course, they did," Clint sneered with narrowed eyes. "It's *about* you."

"We didn't tell anyone other than the Alfar because it was important that it be a surprise to Francine," Morgan lied smoothly. But I felt the words stick in my gut, knowing *why* they weren't true.

The group continued to bicker about who should have been told, but I ignored their words, focusing instead on the emotions. Anger was building in the room, along with hurt and confusion. But there was curiosity there too, and a bit of fear...

"Caroline." I turned at Asher's whisper. He was standing at the mouth of the hallway, just behind my shoulder.

And for the first time since I'd met him, his emotions were clear. *Hesitation. That can't be good.*

"What is it?" I asked eagerly, turning to face him.

His dark eyes flicked around the room, and he pushed an impatient hand through his black hair. "I found a location."

I straightened; eyes wide as adrenaline already began to flow through my system. "You're sure?"

He nodded. "I debated whether or not to tell you."

"Why?"

Asher sighed, his expression—clear for once—darkening into...worry? Something told me that having Asher's first discernable emotion be worry was *not* a good thing.

"Because I have a gut feeling that this fight of yours is going to end at this location," he explained, his voice a little heavier than normal. "It's not a magical feeling, I have no reason to feel this way."

"But you do."

He nodded and I let his words wash over me, bringing more weight to my decision. But at the end of the day, I needed this madness to end. I didn't care at what cost.

"Let's end it."

Chapter 29

CAROLINE

"I can't believe he encroached on my territory like this," I complained, taking my frustration out on Morgan's hand.

"Ow," he said, deadpan, flexing his fingers around mine.

"Sorry. I'm just so annoyed. This is *my* people's neighborhood. Just who the heck does he think he is having his creepy hideout here?"

Creepy probably wasn't the right word for Volund's base of operations. It was settled in the neighborhood where most of the Alfar lived. It was a quaint street with fluttering oak trees and kids playing basketball in their driveways.

The house we now stared at was on the larger side for the area, with a manicured lawn and a fresh white paint job that looked crisp against the black trim.

From what Asher said, it sounded like Paul had played a big part in finding this location. I made a mental note to give my sweet homeless friend a bonus for the find. Just as I'd planned, Paul had slowly become my employee, getting real paychecks instead of a fifty-dollar bill for keeping me appraised of the goings on in town. It had taken a little more work than I anticipated to get him to allow me to pay him a legitimate salary. But eventually I convinced him.

It gave me some comfort to see him meandering along the sidewalk a few houses down, pretending not to notice us. As per usual, he'd insisted on being close by in case I needed him.

"He's a softie for you," Morgan said, kissing my temple.

"He has good taste."

"He absolutely does. Now we just need to convince him to take a room at the house."

I eyed my fiancé, finding a sliver of joy in the midst of a truly ugly moment. "You'd invite him to live with us?"

"Would that be okay?"

"More than okay." I smiled and he returned it.

"I really hate to rush this along," Clint interrupted, his voice coming through our earpieces, "But we should probably get this thing over with."

"Fine," I sighed, letting Morgan pull me along the walkway to the front door.

He knocked on the big oak door, and we waited in silence for someone to answer it. Morgan and I's anxiety hummed together, buzzing loudly in the back of my mind.

Somewhere down the street, a lawnmower could be heard, and I could just make out the shouts of the kids playing basketball a few houses down. It was a cruel mockery considering the conflict we were stepping into.

Suddenly the front door swung open, and I looked up to see Volund standing there. He was impeccably dressed in all black, and his dark hair swooped low on either side of his face, perfectly styled. *I shouldn't have expected anything less.*

"Long time no see, Cousin," he said, a Kai Parker-esque smirk spreading across his face.

"Not long enough," Morgan interjected snidely.

Volund chuckled, unperturbed by my fiancé's unfriendly attitude. "Won't you come in? You'll have to forgive me for the state of the place seeing as how I only had a twenty-minute warning." He stepped back to let us by and Morgan and I stepped inside.

Volund led the way into a large living room, which only contained a black leather couch and a wooden coffee table. It definitely wasn't Volund's style to be so sparse.

"Why am I not surprised that the only pieces of furniture you own look more expensive than my car?" I sassed, too on edge to play nice today.

"What can I say? I'm a high quality man who appreciates high quality things." He shrugged, but it lacked his usual swagger. The light streaming in through the large windows highlighted the dark circles beneath his eyes and the angry tilt of his lips. He was almost as tightly wound as Morgan and me.

I could feel the stress buzzing through both of our bodies, keeping the adrenaline high and my shoulders tight. I felt like a child about to get their first shot, a three second span of pain looming on my horizon with the same gravity of a ten-year sentence. *Please let this happen quickly,* I prayed.

"Is that what made you squat here? Because it was fancy?" Morgan mocked, gently squeezing my hand in a silent show of comfort. I squeezed him back, knowing that we both needed the encouragement today.

"The quality level certainly enticed me," Volund smiled, the look never reaching his eyes. "But its proximity to Caroline's people is what sold it. Now, shall we get down to business?" he asked, splaying his fingers with a flourish.

"By all means," I grumbled, eager to be done with the whole thing.

"Alright then." Volund sighed and turned his head to the side. Morgan and I watched him, confused.

But then *he* walked in.

"You have an annoying habit of playing with your food," Grey admonished, glaring at Volund as he stepped up to the Nephilim's side. "The world is not your stage, and you are not a thespian."

"A man can dream," Volund said, smiling sardonically.

Bile rose up in the back of my throat as I stared at the man who'd pretended to be my friend and Morgan's Second. I'd expected to be angry when I came here today, but the rage I felt boiling in my veins was almost more than my body could hold. And all the hurt and betrayal that initially flooded my system quickly faded with every pound of my heart, leaving me with only vengeance to keep me company.

"You're angry," Grey sighed, almost annoyed. "You'll get over it."

Then, as if on cue, five large men stepped into the room, taking a hold of Morgan's arms and sticking a needle in his neck before I even registered what was happening. His body slackened a little, and the men's grasp seemed to be all that was holding him up.

"What was that?" I hissed, not taking my eyes off of Morgan until he looked at me. His eyes were a little slow to find me, but they were clear.

"The same potion that attacker sprayed you with in the alley," Grey said matter-of-factly. "Although a little less strong. Morgan should be able to speak just fine."

"Jackass," Morgan spat, fury blazing from his eyes.

"Sounds fine to me," Volund snickered.

For a split second, Grey's nonchalant demeanor cracked. Just a little.

He eyed Morgan with the tiniest bit of sorrow, a glimmer of humanity spilling through. But then the crevice filled right back up with an arrogance that was unparalleled in its simplicity. It wasn't the self-importance that made a narcissist, but rather the self-righteousness that made dictators.

"Why?" Mor ground out between clenched teeth, his nostrils flaring and his eyes not leaving Grey's.

Grey straightened his shoulders, clasping his hands behind his back. "It's nothing personal. I did everything to serve the Sleuth."

"You faked being our friend to serve the Sleuth?" I scoffed, the man before me unrecognizable.

"We are friends, Caroline," Grey insisted calmly. "That was all real. I've been on both of your sides from the beginning."

"Explain," I growled, *this close* to unleashing the entirety of my magic on his ugly mug of a face.

He studied me for a moment, perfectly composed and thoughtful. Like he hadn't just revealed himself to be our enemy. "You needed me. You both did."

Morgan snarled and Grey shifted his gaze to him. "The gambling dens were taking over, and the Berserkers were one bad press release from an uprising. Your image was bad enough to make them hate us, but not bad enough to make them respect us. So, I did what I had to. I framed you."

I could feel the shock reverberate through Morgan like a slap to the face. Vibrations of hurt and confusion rumbled through his body, and I saw him blink back the moisture gathering in his eyes.

"Are you telling me that you aren't just in league with Francine, but that you've been plotting my downfall from the beginning of this whole thing?" He demanded quietly—deathly quiet.

"Yes. I did all of it. I got Eileen the Dragon Queen to frame you for Caroline's heists. I organized the kidnapping attempts and Volund's sudden appearance. I made a deal with the gambling dens to come after you. I planned everything, pivoting when necessary to get the job done."

"Why?" Morgan asked, a detached look coming over his face.

"Because you needed to be either a victim or a monster to the public," Grey explained simply. "You were never going to get their respect unless you provoked sympathy or fear. So, I orchestrated scenarios that I hoped would make you into a terrifying hero or an innocent who faced adversity. You needed a stronger image to keep the Berserkers from becoming social pariahs, so I gave you one."

"And me?" I asked, unable to separate the face of the man before me from the one who'd watched *The Bachelor* with me and pigged out on junk food. He was both friend and enemy and my brain couldn't process the overlap. "What did you gain by giving me to Eileen to barter with? Why set up kidnapping attempts?"

"Let me explain this in the simplest terms," Grey sighed tiredly, looking from Morgan to me and back again. "I gave Eileen the idea to blackmail Morgan because I thought it would trigger him into becoming a stronger leader. When I realized who Caroline was, I pivoted. I told Eileen that there was a Nephilim and that if she could catch it, she could make a pretty penny. She, of course, didn't know where the information came from, but she followed it."

"Morgan had to kill the attacker she sent to the house," I shouted, angry at his callousness. "That's on you."

Surprisingly, he flinched. "I didn't like that loss of life either. Which was why I told her not to try coming to the house again. The original plan was for Eileen to *attempt* to sell Caroline to the highest bidder and for Morgan to thwart her in a grand display of heroism. But that blew up in my face." He turned a glare on Volund.

The Nephilim prince stared at me, devoid of remorse, almost proud of himself. "I didn't trust you with her," he said, flicking his eyes to Grey. "So, I tried to buy her out from under you."

That shocked me and I stared at the man who claimed me as a cousin, not sure I really knew him at all.

"When the whole thing with Eileen fell to pieces," Grey went on in an unfeeling manner, "I decided it was time to employ Volund. When I first began looking into Caroline, I found Volund lurking around. Which was how I discovered that she was an Elf."

I shot a look at Volund, realizing that when he said he'd watched me for a few months before we met, he hadn't been lying.

"He and I struck a bargain. He would help me kidnap Caroline," Grey nodded at me, "And I would ensure that the Elves were welcomed into society. He wasn't supposed to reveal himself to you and become our house guest. That was him going rogue." He scowled at the Nephilim again.

Volund shrugged. "Still didn't trust you with her."

"In the end, I made it work," Grey sighed, rolling his eyes. "Volund would kidnap Caroline and then Morgan would make his media debut as a hero against unknown bad guys who either died or escaped. Thus, setting the two of you up quite nicely with the media and giving the Nephilim a clean slate and a few allies to enter society with. It would've played out well with the public if all had gone that smoothly."

"But nothing went as planned," I surmised, putting the pieces together in my mind. "You tried to get us to trust Volund with that attacker who broke in through the kitchen, didn't you? But it didn't work. Volund was never going to get me alone. So, you freed him, knowing that we would go after him."

Grey nodded, showing neither pride nor pleasure.

"But we beat him instead of the other way around," Morgan said, following my train of thought. "And since you knew you couldn't immediately spring him from the house without notice, you employed the gambling dens."

Grey smiled almost sadly. "A man who would move heaven and earth for his mate and a woman who would burn the world down for hers would make quite the story. There's nothing people love more than a good power couple."

"So, what now?" Morgan asked, a defeated tone to his voice that shredded me. My strong, resilient boy was obliterated, and it was all Grey's fault.

As a rule, I tried not to waste energy on hate. It's a dark, heavy thing that infects a person. But in that moment, I *hated* Grey for breaking my mate's heart. *He'll pay dearly for it.*

"Now I get you both to agree to never speak a word of any of this," Grey replied tonelessly. "Then we'll stage a brief kidnapping, a heroic rescue, and the Berserkers will be on top where they belong. No more scraping the bottom of the barrel for respect. No more disdain in the eyes of strangers. No more prejudice. It'll all be over."

Ah. *So, the rumor is true.* "You're part Sphinx," I said, seeing him in a new light now that all my fears had been proven true. "That's why you don't ever shift into your bear form, because it's not as bulky or large as the rest of the Berserkers, right?"

"You're not surprised," Grey said, eyes narrowed.

"You were one of my most trusted friends and now it turns out that you've been betraying me the whole time," Morgan interjected with a shrug. "You could tell me anything at this point and I wouldn't be shocked. I am curious though how you expect to get us to agree to a Sphinx binding. You have to have a willing participant in order for the binding to take."

"You'll be willing here shortly." Grey nodded to Volund, and the Nephilim prince took a knife from his belt. "With some motivation. Volund, please show them what will happen if they refuse the binding."

"So much for cousins," I hissed at Volund as he stepped up to me.

"Stop pretending it's a shock," he sassed, rolling his eyes. "Drama is supposed to be *my* thing."

"I have feeling you're going to be plenty dramatic even without my interference," I retorted dryly.

His lips slowly turned up and light finally entered his eyes, bringing a glimpse of the intolerable man I'd originally met. "Correct."

I winced instinctively as he swung his knife, but the blade didn't meet with my skin. Instead, it swerved backward.

Into Grey.

Chapter 30

MORGAN

Earlier today...

"Paul thinks he found Volund's hideout in the same neighborhood where most of the Alfar live," I heard Asher whisper to Caroline, everyone else still too busy arguing to hear him.

"You found Volund?" I demanded, turning to hear him better.

Care nodded, taking a deep breath. "Now we just have to decide what to do about it."

"Did you sense...anything?" I asked hesitantly. The whole point of going public today without warning our friends was to see how they reacted to the news. To see if Volund's evidence was real.

Along with the letter he left for us at the engagement party, he'd included a printout of emails between Francine and an unknown email address, plotting my demise. As well as Grey's bank statement. According to it, he was making wire transfers that happened to line up with the dates that I was attacked. Lizzy and Mike were able to get into Grey's bank account and confirm the payments, but I didn't consider it damning evidence yet. *It can't be.*

Volund *had* to be lying.

"Everyone was shocked when they saw the news report," Caroline said cautiously, watching me like I might break at the slightest provocation. And she wasn't wrong. I felt like I could shatter with the touch of a finger.

"And?" I prompted, needing to know for sure.

"And while everyone seemed minorly annoyed that they hadn't been warned about the announcement, Grey was furious...and scared."

"He's also gone," Asher pointed out.

"What?" I spun around, my eyes desperately searching for my Second. For the man who'd made my promotion to Chief feel seamless when it should have been a mess. The man who'd seen me grieve my wife and struggle to carry the worries of the entire Sleuth on my shoulders.

But he was gone. Something told me he'd been gone for a while.

"It doesn't mean he's guilty," Caroline pleaded gently, setting her hand on my arm.

"It might as well." I shook her off and paced to the front door and back.

The rest of the room grew suddenly quiet as everyone began to realize that something was wrong. But I ignored them all, my skin crawling with the sting of betrayal. I felt violated and angry...and yet a small part of me still hoped that somehow, we'd been mistaken. That Volund was lying.

Caroline explained to the group what was going on, and I vaguely registered that Logan and Clint immediately rose to search the house for Grey. But they wouldn't find him. *The Grey we know is dead.* My friend and my enemy couldn't live inside the same body, and I refused to sully the memory of my confidant by thinking of him as this warped new version.

"We should storm the place," Harold was saying, his usually relaxed face now screwed up in anger. The rest of the group argued about the suggestion, some saying that we should break in and take Volund, others saying we should wait and see what the Nephilim prince did next.

But I couldn't keep track of their suggestions. My brain was spinning too fast, and then suddenly my heart was beating to match it. An ache formed in my chest, sharp and painful, and I clutched my shirt, trying and failing to steady my breathing.

"Morgan," Caroline's voice called. It took me a moment to register that she was standing in front of me, her hands on my face.

"I can't—"

"I know," she nodded, her green eyes a little hazy to me right now. "I need you to focus, okay? Look at me, you see the blue rings in my eyes?"

I blinked away the fog, watching those twin blue rings stare back at me. "Yes," I gasped between panicked breaths.

Oh my gosh, that's what this is. A panic attack. "I'm having a panic attack."

"I know," Care nodded, grabbing one of my hands and placing it against my neck where I could feel my blood pumping too fast through my veins. "Which is why you need to calm down. Let's start by counting backward, okay?"

I wasn't sure if I verbally agreed or not, but then Caroline was counting. "Count with me, Bear man," she pleaded gently. "Slow and steady. Thirty, twenty-nine, twenty-eight..."

"Twenty-seven," I rasped, my breathing still too shallow.

Care nodded, grinning wide, but I felt her worry, sensed her pain coming alive in response to mine. As we continued to count backwards, I focused on her. On the concern, the love, the loyalty I felt pouring out of her.

And slowly, beat by beat, my heart began to slow back down to normal.

"Thank you," I said, my voice finally clear now that I could breathe and the fist around my heart wasn't squeezing so tight.

"Always," she replied, her eyes still brimming with worry. "You sure you're okay now?"

I pulled my hand from her grasp and set my fingers instead on her neck, feeling her pulse thrum softly beneath my skin. Pressing my forehead against hers, I took a deep breath, letting myself focus on her scent. Floral and fruity. *Caroline.*

"I'm okay now," I whispered, capturing her lips in a kiss filled with gratitude. She kissed me back, but I could sense her hesitation, concerned that I would break again. I pulled away, meeting her gaze so she could see my progress with her own eyes.

"If this becomes too much, I'm dragging you out of here," she threatened fiercely.

I smiled and kissed her again. "I'll hold you to it."

She gave me one more stern look before stepping back. But she didn't go far, dropping her hand to link it with mine.

"So, have we decided on a plan?" I asked, blinking around at the rest of the group, slightly embarrassed that they'd all borne witness to my freak out.

"No," Mike replied, his voice heavy and his expression filled with an anger I'd never seen from my well-adjusted brother before.

"We could call him," Lizzy suggested tentatively. All eyes turned to her like she'd lost it, but she turned the electronic tablet in her lap so the rest of us could see the screen. "I asked Asher for the address, and it turns out that there's a home phone registered to the house. So instead of trying to agree on whether or not someone should go spy on a home that's possibly inhabited by Dark Elves and our potentially traitorous friend, perhaps someone could just call first to see if anyone answers."

No one spoke for a moment, all of us overcome with shock at the surprisingly logical solution. Mike stared at Lizzy where they sat beside each other on the couch, his face now bright with awe instead of dark with anger.

"That's brilliant," he exclaimed.

Her cheeks turned a faint shade of pink and she let loose a small smile. "Thank you."

"What's the number?" Caroline asked, her phone poised and ready in her hands.

A few moments later, everyone gathered close as Care pressed call, the ring loud and clear over the speaker. We'd agreed that she alone would do the talking, but I was prepared to break that promise if Grey answered the phone. In fact, I was prepared to do a lot of things if Grey answered.

"Hello?" It wasn't my second's voice on the other end of the line, and I felt my shoulders droop with relief. I'd been prepared to deal with him now if I had to, but I really didn't want to do it over the phone.

"So, you're a squatter now, huh?" Caroline sassed, speaking into the phone. "And in my neighborhood no less. Talk about a lack of boundaries."

"Ah, dear cousin," Volund replied, a smile in his voice. "I see that you got my letter. Congratulations, by the way. Your kids are destined to be both loud and violent with you and Morgan for parents."

I went stiff at the mention of the letter and the evidence it contained against Grey.

"About your letter," she said, all business, "Why did you send us Grey's bank statement? Why out him like that and why now?"

There was a pause, and Care and I exchanged a curious glance. Volund was *never* at a loss for words. *Something's off...*

"Do you remember what I said to you right before you kicked me in the face and took me prisoner?" he finally asked, his voice lacking its usual nonchalance.

"You told me it wasn't you that I couldn't trust," Care hummed thoughtfully. "But if that's true and you're as innocent as you claim, then why all the cloak and dagger? Unless..." She paused, a light coming into her eyes. "You're all cloak and no dagger."

This time, Volund didn't respond at all, and the resulting silence was charged and tingling, filled with implication. Everyone in our circle glanced at each other, confused but patient. We all trusted Caroline, and she knew what she was doing.

"I've always felt like I was missing something with you," she said, staring at the phone like she could will Volund to appear. "A page missing from the book, or a piece gone from the puzzle. There's something about you that doesn't add up...and you call me cousin."

"So?" Volund deflected warily. "We're both Nephilim."

"True, but I don't think that's it. You yourself said that you watched me for a few months before I met Morgan. That you planned to offer me a home with the Nephilim so I wouldn't be alone. And if that's true—"

"It is." The Nephilim prince's words were quick and firm.

"Then what you did by bribing Charlie to set traps for me wasn't an act of cruel manipulation. You really were trying to help me gain confidence as queen."

I couldn't tell if Care believed her words or if they were just bait to hook Volund. But I hoped it was the latter. There was no way I was about to forgive the man for paralyzing, suffocating and muting my fiancé—even if they had been temporary scenarios.

"You've always been capable," Volund insisted, "You just needed to believe it."

"Physically harming her and making me watch was the best way you could come up with to accomplish that?" I demanded, breaking my promise to keep my mouth shut.

Care smacked my chest and glared, but I wasn't sorry. No one hurt my mate and got away with it.

"Ah, Morgan." To my surprise, Volund didn't sound nearly as arrogant as I'd expected. In fact, there was almost a bit of shame to his voice. Just a little. "I should have assumed that you were on this call too."

"Give me one good reason not to drive over to that house and rip your sorry excuse for a spine from your back," I growled, my nerves coming to the end of their frayed edges.

"Look, I've probably gone about things in the wrong way—"

"Probably?" I snapped. Care elbowed me and sent me a warning glare.

"I was aggressive, and rash and I should have approached the whole situation better," Volund sighed, sounding tired. "But I only acted the way I did because I didn't know if I could trust Morgan. From the beginning, I wanted to offer Caroline a home. But then she met Morgan, and by then I—ugh!" He broke off into a fit of growls and snarls, clearly frustrated. "When I revealed myself to you in that alley, I did it because I wanted to make sure that Caroline was safe in your house. That those around her could actually be trusted. Should I have been more upfront and less evasive? Probably. But there's not a lot I could do about it..."

"What do you mean?" Care asked, eyebrows puckered. "Why couldn't you be more straight forward if all you wanted was to help me?"

Silence echoed and no matter how long we waited, Volund never answered.

"Volund, I'm going to ask you a few things and I need you to be completely honest with me," Care went on, determined.

"I won't lie," he promised quickly.

"Have you ever intended me harm?"

"No. All I've wanted was to protect you."

Caroline met my gaze, and as much as I wanted to argue that Volund was dangerous, even I was starting to doubt that belief. At least where Caroline was concerned.

"Did you hire the gambling dens to come after Morgan?"

"No."

"Did you lose that fight at your house on purpose?"

This question surprised me, and I watched my mate's face in confusion. The fight at Volund's house back in July had almost killed her. She had to use all her magic and drain herself of energy to put him down. *What is she getting at?*

"Yes," came Volund's response.

"Why?" she asked, not surprised by his answer.

He sighed heavily. "Because I was never your enemy, and I knew that I could do the most help by removing myself from the chess board."

"And who's pawn were you, Volund?" she asked. He didn't answer. "Volt, were you working alone?"

Again, no answer.

'What are you doing?' I mouthed, not liking where she was going with these questions. Volund is Innocent Lane led straight to Grey is Guilty Boulevard, and I didn't know if I was ready to go down that road.

'Trust me,' Care mouthed back, her green eyes boring into me. And since I couldn't argue with that, I kept my mouth shut.

"Are you alone right now?" She said to Volund, continuing with her questioning.

"Yes," Volund quickly replied. "Although probably not for long."

"Merida," Care whispered to the Witch as she muted the call, "Could he be cursed not to answer certain questions?"

"I don't think so," Merida shook her head. "Curses usually have to do with reprimands or retribution. When I cursed Volund not to harm you, it was a consequence, a punishment. I've never heard of someone being cursed to keep quiet."

Care nodded and unmuted the phone.

"Volt, are you cursed?"

"No," he answered, his voice gaining strength, almost sounding excited. *Maybe she is onto something...*

"Could be a Sphinx binding," Mike supplied, his forehead heavy with wrinkles.

"If it is, he had to make it willingly," Lizzy added, meeting his gaze.

"He might have been tricked into it, thinking the Sphinx meant well," Mike argued.

Lizzy nodded. "True. And if it is a Sphinx binding, then he wouldn't be able to so much as hint at whatever secret he swore to keep."

"That would make sense," Care agreed, biting her lip. "If he made a deal with a Sphinx, thinking that it would be an equal, harmless bargain only to later find out that the Sphinx's plans weren't what he thought they were, he wouldn't be able to talk about it. And he's answered every question except for the ones about who he's working with."

"You think he's innocent. That he's under someone else's control." I didn't pose the words as a question. I could feel her emotions, I already knew that's what she thought.

"It makes sense, Mor. He's never felt evil to me. Arrogant and annoying, yeah, but never *bad*. Even when we fought at his house and he taunted me, using my birth parent's faces to mess with me, it never felt real. It felt like a performance. Almost all of my interactions with him have felt that way. Like he was putting on a show for someone else's benefit."

I tapped my thumb against my thigh, unsure what I thought. I had to admit, here in the safety of my mind, that Volund had always seemed more an actor than a truly depraved villain. But thinking that he could be trusted was a whole other ballgame. Because it meant that Grey couldn't be.

"I know you don't want to think about it," Caroline whispered, speaking only to me, "And I don't either. But those payments in Grey's account matched the payments that the gambling dens received. He ran the moment that news report aired and...have you ever seen him shift?"

"What?" I growled; my patience incredibly short as I realized that the time for hope was quickly fading.

"Grey. Have you ever seen him shift into bear form?"

I'd known the man for nearly a decade. I'd seen him angry, happy, tired, disappointed, but... "No, I've never seen him shift." And now I couldn't help but wonder why. Was it because his bear form looked different? "You think he's a Sphinx."

"At least part Sphinx. It's possible, right?"

I didn't answer. The crazy notion that my Second was actually part Sphinx and plotting behind my back suddenly sounded...not so crazy. *No. Not Grey.*

"Volt?" Care said, having unmuted the phone again, "Did Grey bind you to a secret?"

And there it was again, that blasted silence.

I shook my head, refusing to believe it. Mike, Clint and Logan likewise shared looks of stubborn disbelief, but when Asher shot us looks of pity, I felt my confidence crumble. Everyone else in the circle—Ariel, Lizzy, Merida and the Alfar—all seemed to be watching us Berserkers with varying degrees of sympathy.

I was starting to feel sick.

"Even if he's telling the truth," Mike argued, pain and frustration in his eyes, "Even if Grey is guilty, we have no proof other than a bank statement that's too vague to hold up in court, and Volund can't testify."

"So, we get a confession from Grey." Caroline shrugged like it was an easy answer.

"How are we supposed to—"

"Volund," Ariel interrupted, stepping closer to the phone, "You said you don't expect to be alone for very long, right?"

"...yeah," the Nephilim replied warily. "Why?"

"Getting a confession might not be that hard," she said, ignoring Volund's concern. "All we need is to get him to talk, and I'm pretty certain we know where he's going to be."

Caroline's eyes widened and she looked up at me, silently waiting for my opinion. After all, it was *my* friend we were talking about. And even as the pain continued to burn through me, I knew we had no choice.

"Alright, Volt," I groaned, "How are your acting skills?"

Chapter 31

CAROLINE

Currently...

"What are you doing?" Grey gasped as Volund pulled his knife free from the traitor's shoulder.

"Picking a side," Volund shrugged, stepping up beside me. The gambling den members froze as they watched the scene play out, seeming unsure if it was worth their effort to step in or if they should make a run for it.

"How?" Grey snarled, pressing a hand to his shoulder with surprisingly little urgency. "You can't—"

"Out you?" Morgan snapped, gaining back some of his usual vigor. "Turns out that even a Sphinx binding isn't perfectly infallible. But the real question is, does it even matter when the entire country now knows what you did?"

Grey went completely still, his eyes flicking anxiously between Morgan, Volund and me. It was the first sign of panic I'd seen in the older Berserker, and it only seemed to grow when the front door banged open, and Logan, Mike, Clint, Paul and a few other Berserkers stormed the room, easily pulling the gambling den members away from Morgan.

"Say hi to America, Grey," I taunted with a vicious smile, unclipping the microphone from the inside of my leather jacket. "You're on national television."

Grey stared at the microphone for a minute. And then I sensed not defeat or disappointment settling inside him, but acceptance and even relief. When the ghost of a smile flickered across his lips, I felt my stomach sink. "Fine. Take me to Niffleheim, then," he shrugged.

"You shouldn't be this cavalier..." I shook my head. "You're happy about this. This whole thing works perfectly with your narrative, doesn't it? You'll be the villain and Morgan and I will be the power couple who saved ourselves from you. Right?"

Morgan moved closer, crossing his arms like he was restraining himself from using his fists. "Are you seriously still plotting, even now?" he demanded incredulously. "This is you pivoting to make sure the Berserkers come out on top."

"Like I said," Grey sighed, remorseless, "You need me."

"No." Closing the gap between us, I stood toe to toe with the man who'd fooled us all. "You don't get to win. Not after what you did."

And then, as simple as a breath, magic flowed out of my body, grasping onto Grey. This time, I didn't just tug and pull and manipulate. This time, I yanked, molded and forced his emotions to do my bidding.

New feelings manifested wherever I thought to put them, and his entire emotional landscape became my garden, pruning, planting, cutting, burning as I pleased. Where there was a seed of remorse or regret, I didn't bother to grow it bigger and stronger. Instead, I obliterated everything in my path, funneling Morgan's every emotion from the mate bond into Grey.

Betrayal. Pain. Confusion. Disappointment. Sorrow. Grief. Anger. Rage. Insecurity. Vulnerability. Shock. Fear.

I poured all of them into Grey, Morgan's raw, brutal feelings sprouting up inside him like weeds, devouring all his happiness, all his satisfaction, all his pride. Now all he felt was Morgan.

Grey cried out and staggered to his knees, clasping his head as if to stifle the pain.

"Should we stop her?" I faintly heard Volund ask.

"Not yet," came Morgan's steady reply.

Grey gasped, looking up at Morgan with tears streaming down his face. Finally convinced that he fully understood the consequences of his actions, I stepped back, fumbling blindly for Morgan's hand.

It wasn't until his fingers laced through mine, holding me close and steady, that I felt the magic release, leaving me feeling a little cold.

"You okay?" Mor whispered, the fingers of his free hand on my chin. I met his gaze and nodded; not sure I was quite capable of words just yet. "What did you even do?"

"I gave him your emotions," I breathed once I could finally speak.

"But I thought you couldn't create feelings, only manipulate them."

"She's queen," Volund said, as if this was explanation enough. When Morgan and I gave him blank looks, he rolled his eyes. "Elf rulers don't have the same limitations as their subjects. While my people can only shift into people they've seen before, I can look however I want. And while your people can only manipulate feelings, you can create them. It's an inherited gift, but it comes to full maturity once you become the official ruler."

"Huh." That explained so much. Why there seemed to be times in the past when I did more than just nudge people's feelings and why it only seemed to happen sporadically before now. "That's new information."

"I can't believe you didn't know that," Volund scoffed, arrogant as ever.

"Hello, orphan, remember?" I complained, slugging him in the shoulder.

He grasped the appendage dramatically. "Ow! Was that completely necessary?" I smiled. "No, but it was fun."

"Morgan," Grey pleaded, his voice broken and uneven. We all turned to the middle-aged man who still knelt on the floor. He looked so different from the perfectly controlled man that I'd thought I knew. So raw.

"I...I'm sorry. So sorry." He didn't try to excuse himself or explain away his behavior—he'd done plenty of that already. And as the words left his lips, I felt the sincerity. Not because my magic made him—the magic was already gone from his mind. But because he understood now, the pain he'd caused. And that was all I really wanted.

Morgan watched Grey for a moment, still kneeling on the ground like a man about to be executed. And in a way, Morgan could choose to slay him or set him free. I wasn't sure which outcome I was hoping for.

I waited silently as the two men stared at each other, feeling Morgan's heavy emotions battling against his determination to be better than the man before him. And when he extended a hand to Grey, I'd never been more proud.

Grey stared at it for a moment, before taking it and letting Morgan pull him to his feet. Grey sobbed with his shoulders back, still holding Morgan's gaze, stern even in his regret.

"I forgive you," Morgan's deep voice rumbled, the words slow and heavy with certainty. "You love the Sleuth, and for that I can't fault you. But you've proven that you're untrustworthy, and that to you, the ends justify the means. You'll go to court for what you've done, but I'm not going to hold any ill will for you. Because I have to hope that someday, you'll be different, you'll be better."

Grey nodded, his own emotions—unencumbered by my influence—filled with only remorse and regret, no arrogance or apathy left behind. They might find him later when he was alone, but at least I could rest easier knowing that he understood the pain he'd caused.

"And Volund?" I asked, staring Grey down, my own feelings less abrupt than they had been only minutes ago. "Will you free him from the binding?"

Grey stared at me for a moment, a silent pleading echoing from his eyes, begging me to understand. And against my better judgment, I did. "It was all real," he said to me, quiet but insistent.

"I know."

Nodding, he turned to Volund. "You owe me nothing."

Volund glared at Grey, shrugging like he was releasing tension in his shoulders.

"Well?" I asked.

"Grey's a freaking jerk who tricked me into a binding by telling me that he'd help the Nephilim go public if I helped him with his plot and promised to never reveal his involvement," Volund ranted. "Which was why it took me so flipping long to explain myself, because I couldn't do it without revealing Grey."

Grey said nothing in response, standing silently as Morgan pulled out a zip tie and bound his wrists. He handed Grey off to Callie and two other waiting Berserkers, entrusting them with his custody.

"Well, shall we go introduce me to the press?" Volund grinned, providing a perfect distraction from the residual heavy emotions. "I'm sure they'll want to know all about the man who risked his own life and saved the day. I wouldn't be surprised if I have my own action figure soon."

"Action figure or voodoo doll?" I mumbled, following him and the rest of the group to the front door.

Morgan snorted beside me, releasing my hand. "If he's half as annoying to the public as he is to us, it'll be the latter."

Thinking that he was falling behind to talk to his brothers and Logan, I didn't pay too much attention. But when I stepped outside and saw the waiting news crew watching us with open mouths and wide eyes, I turned back.

Morgan had shifted into bear form, his hulking body nearly looming over his brothers. His silver fur glinted in the sunlight, shining like metal. The beige on his snout and paws almost looked like gold as it too caught the light.

And then those steady grey eyes found me, and I smiled.

From a man who hadn't shifted in the presence of another in twenty years to a man who did it in front of a crowd of strangers. And it was no secret to me why he was doing it. Because if the world saw the region's scariest man tamed by a frilly woman, it would simultaneously soften his image while bringing an edge to mine.

"Very crafty," I said as he walked up to me, pressing his head against my belly. I laughed and scratched behind his ears.

"I don't know what you're talking about," he promised, feigning innocence.

"Morgan."

He lifted his head to look at me. "Hm?"

"I trust you."

His entire countenance softened at the callback to the heist at the hotel months ago, when he'd shifted for the first time in decades. I'd trusted him then, but it was nothing compared to the trust I had in him now. Because now I trusted him with more than just my life. I trusted him with my heart too.

"In every form," I swore, kissing the soft spot between his eyes.

A rumble echoed from his chest, almost like a purr. "Do you have any idea how much I love you?"

"So much that you're going to offer to let people take selfies with you," I teased, turning so we could walk to the sidewalk side by side.

"I'm not doing that."

I just winked and jogged toward the reporter.

"Caroline!" Morgan roared.

I felt the fear and anxiety of the news crew and the crowd that had begun to gather beside them. But as they watched me nuzzle the giant bear and heard us banter, their worries slowly began to fade, and one by one they smiled.

And the man whose reputation was built on fear, slowly became known for the love he showed his mate. And the woman who'd once believed she had to do everything alone, found herself leaning on her friends, her newly reformed enemies, and the love of her life.

Chapter 32

CAROLINE

"I can't believe you actually stood there and let them take selfies with you," Clint laughed, holding onto Mike to keep himself upright.

"He even let that little boy sit on his back," Logan added, slapping Morgan on the shoulder as he chuckled.

"I took a video of it as blackmail," Asher admitted nonchalantly. Morgan glared at him, but Asher wasn't bothered. "You never know when it'll be useful."

"I'm going to kill all of them," Mor growled as we walked up the wide concrete steps to Asher's house, where Ariel and Lizzy had been hiding during our showdown with Grey.

They'd both been highly offended by the suggestion that they needed a babysitter. But since Ariel had already been kidnapped once, I insisted. When Asher offered to have them wait at his house, protected by his guards and his older brother, I accepted on their behalf.

The place was massive, hidden back in the trees on a hilltop in the middle of town. It was all concrete and glass, layered like a short, stout Jenga tower, with the roofs of each offset level flat and wide like landing pads for helicopters.

"You're not killing anybody," I said, tightening my hold on his arm. "You're a hero now. You finally have a *positive* image to protect. But Asher," I tapped the Wyvern on the shoulder, "I would love a copy of that video."

Morgan's eyes narrowed into slits.

"What?" I shrugged. "Seeing you be sweet with all those kids today kinda does it for me."

He shook his head but lost the battle against an indulgent smile. "You're incorrigible."

I kissed his cheek. "I know."

"Please, I am too tired to hear you guys flirt," Mike complained halfheartedly. "I'm getting a cavity just by listening to it."

The biggest Hohlt brother might pretend to be annoyed, but he couldn't fool me. He was eager to get through Asher's front door and see Lizzy—I could sense it.

"Yes, let's just get this over with so I can go back to my quiet existence," Asher whined as he opened the large front door.

"You'll miss us," I smirked, and though his emotions were still all but silent, I did catch the slightest twitch to his lips. *I'm calling it a smile.* "But remember, you're always welcome at the Alfar or Berserker house. Pop in anytime."

Asher just rolled his eyes, but I knew he'd take me up on the offer someday. Everyone needed friends.

We all followed the Wyvern into the house, the rest of our crew off seeing to other things. Merida had helped the Berserkers make sure Grey was properly arrested and contained, while the Alfar were at my house prepping for the press conference we'd be holding there tomorrow. And Morgan and I had decided to let Volund go.

I invited him to come by the Berserker house later after he'd briefed his people about Grey, but he hadn't given me a straight answer. And despite the parasite he'd been for the past few months, I hoped he'd show up.

"I don't know why she keeps trying with him," came Lizzy's voice from further in the house, drawing my attention. "He's clearly using her to make Brittany jealous."

"Yes, but you're forgetting the horde of producers that are telling her that he's into her," argued a male voice that I didn't recognize. "Their sole job on this show is to manipulate the cast members into doing stupid stuff. Like dressing in a giant hot dog suit."

"I love Logan, but you couldn't pay me to dress up in costume like that in ninety-degree heat," Ariel commented, a smile in her voice.

"Oh really?" Logan said with a grin as he waltzed into the room. "What about that costume last week? You didn't seem to have a problem wearing that one."

The rest of us entered the room and I looked around in awe at the large space and its floor to ceiling windows that offered views of the surrounding trees and the tops of some of the taller buildings in the city. And despite the mix of white, concrete and angles in the house, the furniture was surprisingly cozy.

Sitting curled up on a large couch were Ariel and Lizzy, a giant bowl of popcorn between them and *The Bachelor in Paradise* playing on the TV. And on a loveseat nearby was a man I'd never seen before but safely assumed was Asher's brother. His hair was much lighter than Asher's nearly black locks, and this man wore his a little shorter but just as messy. He shared his brother's dark eyes and fierce bone structure, but where Asher frowned, this man was quick to smile, and I had no problem sensing his cheery attitude.

"Lo?" Ariel grinned when she spotted Logan, and she launched herself from the couch, running toward him at full speed. As if they'd practiced it, he opened his arms—squatting a little because, hello, my sister was barely five feet—and she jumped into them.

She clung to him like a koala, and I smiled, watching their sweet reunion. Morgan, however, pretended to gag when they shared a—perfectly appropriate—kiss.

"Oh, shut up," I said, leaning into his side. "I kiss you in front of people all the time."

"Yeah, but I'm not watching it, I'm doing it."

"Fair point." Now that Ariel was standing on her own two feet, I cast a glare on both her and Lizzy. "I can't believe you traitors are watching BIP without me!"

Lizzy cringed and opened her mouth—probably to apologize—but Ariel interrupted her. "Don't you dare say you're sorry, Lizzy. They abandoned us here while they went off on a mission, and we had no choice but to entertain ourselves. Consider it the price you pay for cutting us out."

"Says the woman who got kidnapped last time," I scoffed.

The playful argument probably would have continued, but the man on the loveseat stood and walked over to join the conversation. "So, this is the Elf Queen who's caused all this chaos. I'm James," he smiled, holding out his hand, "Asher's big brother."

"*Older* brother," Asher corrected in his usual enigmatic way. "Although people usually assume it's the other way around. Can't imagine why."

"Because I'm more fun—obviously," James grinned, shaking my hand, "And you're Caroline."

I opened my mouth to reply when hot jealousy rippled behind me, and a hand pressed against the small of my back. "My mate," Morgan clarified—because clearly no one would possibly know we were mates after having seen *two* news reports where Morgan broadcasted it.

"Possessive," James nodded, offering Morgan his hand the same way he'd done to me. "I get it. I'd be the same way."

"Hm," Mor grunted, shaking James' hand—thankfully he didn't break it.

"Sorry we watched your show without you," James said, shoving his hands in his pockets. "I suggested it, so it's really my fault."

"I'm not totally sure I understand the obsession with that show," Lizzy added, folding the blanket she'd been using and repositioning the throw pillows, "But it's entertaining."

"I'll make you a fangirl yet, Lizzy," I smiled, trying to think of future *Bachelor* nights with new friends instead of past nights with old ones.

Normally, this would be the moment when Clint would insert himself into the conversation and try to get Lizzy's attention. But I'd been recently informed that Mike had told his younger brother about the mate bond, and Clint—not a complete caveman—immediately backed off so Mike could pursue her himself.

Which he was apparently attempting immediately.

"I had a coat..." Lizzy mumbled looking around the room.

"Here," Mike offered, grabbing the jacket off the back of a chair.

Lizzy stared at the coat for a few moments, her curiosity and attraction merging into something deeper. If she didn't already know that they were mated, she'd figure it out in a month. The connection between them was so strong I could almost see it.

"Thank you," she finally whispered.

But when she reached for the coat, Mike kept it out of reach. "Here, let me help." He motioned for her to turn around.

With her expression carefully guarded, she silently turned her back to him. He took his sweet time helping her into the jacket, and I wished just this once that I could read minds instead of just feelings. *Oh, to know what they're thinking right now.*

"How long do you think it'll take for them to start officially dating?" Morgan asked, his hand warm on my waist.

"They're both so cautious...I'm gonna say two months."

"Are we talking about Mike and Lizzy?" Logan whispered, him and Ariel leaning close, "Because I totally want in on that bet."

"Alright, how long until they get together?" I asked.

"Mm...a month," he said, smirking as Lizzy turned around, her eyes wide at finding Mike standing so close.

"I'm betting on three months," Ariel hummed, watching the couple. "I don't think Lizzy will move quickly."

"What about you, Asher?" I whisper-shouted to the Wyvern King.

He was standing off to the side, his brother speaking with Clint about some kind of manly topic that I had no interest in. Asher seemed not to hear me at first, but then he let out a dramatic sigh and stepped up to our group.

"You mean, how long do I think it will take Mike and Lizzy to act on their painfully obvious feelings?" he asked, deadpan.

I smiled. "Yes."

He quirked an unimpressed eyebrow. "Six months."

"That long?"

"Have you seen how much Mike struggles to speak to the woman? I'll be surprised if she doesn't make the first move."

"Well, if you're right, we'll all owe you ten bucks a piece."

"No, you'll all owe *me* ten bucks," Logan sassed with a smirk. "Ow!" he suddenly exclaimed, looking down at my suspiciously innocent sister, who smiled sweetly at him.

"Us," she corrected him. "They'll owe *us* ten bucks."

Logan shook his head as we all started heading for the door. "Nope. Until we say, 'I do' what's mine is *not* yours you little imp."

"It is if you want to kiss me again."

As the couple continued to banter and the rest of the group smiled and laughed, I looked up at Morgan. He was watching me with a thoughtful look in his eyes and a private smile on his lips.

"What?" I asked, trying to read him.

"We're gonna be okay," he whispered, the blue rings in his eyes winking at me, promising me forever.

"Yeah," I nodded, smiling against his lips as he kissed me, "We are."

Chapter 33

MORGAN

"*I learned a while back that if I don't text 911, people will not return my calls,*" came Michael Scott's voice from the TV above the fireplace in the living room of the Berserker house.

We were four episodes into the extended, superfan version of *The Office* episodes for the night, the coffee table filled with assorted junk food and everyone nursing food babies in their bloated bellies.

"I just realized something," Care said, all snuggled into my side, her knees up to her chest and her head on my shoulder. "Volt, you're totally Michael Scott."

Volund turned in his armchair and glared at Caroline.

Honestly, I was surprised he'd showed up tonight. When we left the house where Volund had been squatting, Care had invited him to come over, but part of me wondered if we'd ever see the Nephilim prince again now that he was free of Grey's binding.

I should have known better. He was a celebrity now, there was no way he'd leave that behind willingly.

"I am *not* Michael Scott," he insisted, now dressed in loungewear—a matching black set. "I am not some overgrown child who makes a dramatic scene about everything."

As if choreographed, everyone's heads turned toward Volund, all of us holding back smiles.

"I need a little refresher," Logan chirped sarcastically, Ariel sitting on the floor in front of him, her back against his chest and his legs on either side of her. "Who was it that cried when we played tag?"

"Volt," Clint supplied cheerily, working on his fourth ice cream sandwich.

"You call that playing tag?" Volt demanded loudly, and Daisy Mae rose from the floor, tail wagging, to investigate. "You turned into bears and chased me around the yard like an animal! And the only reason I cried was because you *tore* my favorite workout shirt!"

Daisy must have deemed Volund likeable now, because she hopped up in his chair and sat on his lap like she was a house cat. When she started licking his face, he raised his chin as high as he could to avoid her.

"Cousin, control your wild beast, would you?" he pleaded, voice cracking with fear.

Daisy, the terrifying attack dog, licked his neck until she realized he was never going to give her access to his face. Then she laid down in his lap, perfectly content.

"Seems pretty controlled to me," Care smiled.

Volund continued to mumble nervously about the consequences should Daisy ruin his clothing, and the rest of us rolled our eyes. Lizzy and Mike were also present—albeit on separate couches, proof that this particular relationship would be moving at a glacial speed—but the Alfar had finally been able to move back into their own homes.

Now that the public had seen me in my bear form, seemingly kept in check only by Caroline, everyone knew that an attack on the Alfar would be an attack on the Berserkers. *We might actually enjoy some safety for once.* And with Caroline and my reputations melding together thanks to our two news reports, my mission to deal with the gambling dens didn't feel quite so farfetched. I wasn't naïve enough to believe that the gambling dens would ever completely go away. But they were about to get a whole lot smaller.

"I get it, I was a jerk for months and now you're all getting your revenge," Volt continued, narrowing his eyes at the rest of us. "This is you guys getting back at me for being the *pretend* bad guy."

"Pretend?" I scoffed, only halfway watching the TV screen as I trailed my fingers through Caroline's loose hair. "So, I must have imagined Caroline suffocating at her coronation."

"I said I was sorry—"

"I must have *imagined* her becoming paralyzed during training," I went on, still holding a teeny tiny grudge.

"Morgan," Care pleaded quietly, nudging me with her elbow. "New beginnings, remember?"

I sighed and turned to Volund. "Fine. I'll forget the boobytraps, but in return, you owe me one favor of my choosing."

Volund—not a complete idiot—paused as he considered my offering. "Nothing physically harmful, and nothing that would require me to ruin my clothes."

"Deal."

"Deal."

"Question," Logan asked, throwing a piece of popcorn at the Dark Elf, "Aren't your people kind of freaking out right now since you just took them public? Are they not bothered that you're here with us instead of being with them?"

Volund shrugged, his hand hovering above Daisy like he wasn't sure if it was safe to touch her. But when she continued snoring, he tentatively patted her back. Daisy wagged her tail, stretching out on her side so he could reach her belly.

But Volund just stared at her like she might grow tentacles and attack him at any moment. "They're actually glad to have me gone for the night. Apparently, I've been an anxious, nagging old lady lately. Their words, not mine."

"Fretting over my safety, were you?" Care sassed with a wink.

"I'm sure he's driven his people mad with all his worry for his dear cousin," I teased before kissing the smile from her lips. It tasted like cookie dough. So, I kissed her again.

Everyone turned back to the TV, and I watched with perfect contentment. I had my family around me, my girl in my arms, and a reputation that was finally worth protecting. What more could I need?

Chapter 34

CAROLINE

Two months later...

"Okay, can I take this off now?" I whined, reaching up for the blindfold.

"No!" my mom shouted, batting my hand away. "Just wait two more seconds."

"This is a good surprise, right?" I asked warily. "Because you're not traditionally supposed to blindfold someone before giving them bad news."

My parents had arrived last week for Morgan and I's wedding. My mom had gone wedding dress shopping with Ariel, Lizzy, Merida and I, and her and my dad threw us a barbeque to celebrate the engagement. They'd been in and out of town dozens of times in the last two months, but now they were staying for two weeks until the wedding. And since they'd already bought us a professional grade milkshake maker as a wedding gift, I knew this surprise couldn't be a present, which had me feeling anxious.

When no one answered me, I started to panic. "Mom?"

"Okay, now you can look," Dad said from my other side.

I carefully pulled off the blindfold and blinked against the bright sunlight. We were outside, that much was clear. But it took me a moment to realize where we were.

"Mr. Finch?" My old neighbor was standing in the front yard of my old house, next to a for sale sign. "What's going on?" But then I noticed the red banner across the sign that read 'SOLD'.

"Wait, did you buy my house?" I asked, confused as I looked between the old man and the house I used to live in. "Why? You lived right across the street."

"He didn't buy it," Mom explained, watching me with a bit of trepidation. "We did."

Unsure if I heard her right, I looked at my dad. But he just smiled, his blonde hair completely white now and the wrinkles around his eyes deeper than I remembered. The three years I'd spent as a vigilante seemed like a lifetime now and I wished I could get some of that time back with them.

"Your mom finally retired, kiddo," he said, squeezing my shoulder. "We decided that we wanted to be closer to you girls, and when we saw that your old house had gone back on the market, we thought it might be nice to keep it in the family."

I stared, dumbfounded. "You...you bought my house."

I looked at the empty driveway where I'd first introduced Morgan to Mr. Finch, and we pretended not to be infatuated with each other. The dent in the siding by one of the front windows was still there from when I'd once thrown a rock because the racoons ate my DoorDash meal before I could get to it. (I didn't throw the rock *at* the racoons—*I'm not a barbarian*—but I needed to throw *something* after losing my milkshake to rodents.) And the tree in the front yard still bore the little green ribbon I'd used to tie a bird feeder to one of the lower branches.

"Is it okay that we bought it?" Mom asked, and I turned to find her brown eyes wide with nerves. She looked just like Ariel, with big eyes and an innocent curve to her face, but she had brown hair instead of blonde. I'd always had a hard time finding a reason to be mad at her. "We don't want to infringe on your space, but—"

I cut her off with a tight, bone crushing hug. "I love it, Mom."

"Really?" she insisted, hugging me back just as tight. "Because we don't want to overstep."

"You're not. I missed this house and knowing that it will still be in the family makes me so happy."

"And I'm sure seeing your favorite neighbor more often is a big bonus," Mr. Finch teased, a hand on his hip like he was posing for a photoshoot.

"Don't speak for me you old coot," Mrs. Finch said with a smile as she crossed the street. "We both know I'm Caroline's favorite."

"I'd be willing to share the position if you'll share a kiss," Mr. Finch said, wagging his eyebrows beneath his beret.

I laughed, cocooned between the arms of my parents, and I realized how desperately I'd missed this. The last three years had been my time to grow, but now I was ready for family, for roots.

"We missed you, baby girl," Dad whispered as Mom cried; I held them tighter.

And as I looked at the pink front door that used to contain my entire life, I felt encouraged to know that my life had since grown too big to be contained anywhere.

Chapter 35

Morgan

"Which way, left or right?"

"Uh..." Wallace closed his eyes, squinting as he focused.

"Left or right, Wallace?" Clint demanded loudly, tapping the back of Wallace's seat.

"Left!" Wallace shouted, and I took an abrupt left turn halfway through the light.

We'd been driving around for half an hour now, trying to locate Mr. Wallace's missing mate. Well, she wasn't really missing. He just didn't have the nerve to introduce himself when he first saw her, therefore intentionally letting her get away. But since he'd recently reclaimed his intelligence, we were using his connection with her through the mate bond to hunt her down.

"You know, she might have lost her marbles a little after all this time with someone else's feelings in her brain," Mike mused from the backseat. "Especially if she doesn't know that she's bonded to you."

"Or she might have just grown numb to them over time." Wallace sighed in the passenger seat, looking out the window with a dejected look on his face.

"Hey, don't despair," I insisted, patting his knee as we drove along a road that led to the west end of town, small shops and quaint old houses lining the street.

"We have no idea how she'll react. At the very least, she knows how you feel, and that's half the battle right there."

Wallace nodded but didn't seem fully convinced. I didn't push him—and thankfully, neither did my brothers—letting him guide us further through town, hoping that whoever this woman was, she wasn't on the move.

"What now?" I asked at the next stop sign.

Wallace didn't answer.

"Wallace?" Clint asked, leaning around the seat, "Hey," he said when he saw the panic on the old man's face, "It's going to be okay. We're going to find her."

Wallace shook his head. "We did."

"What?"

Mr. Wallace pointed to a small two-story house set close to the road, a low iron fence lining the small yard. It was cute with its scalloped trim and fish scale siding, and a happy yellow front door.

"I can't do this," Mr. Wallace shook his head as I parked along the curb in front of the house.

"Yes, you can," Mike argued, both him and Clint leaning an arm on the console to see him. "I know it's scary and you think that maybe the mate bond made a mistake, that maybe she'll be disappointed that it's you, or that maybe the bond is somehow one sided and she never felt it for you." Mike paused, grasping Mr. Wallace's wrinkled, gnarled hand, and I wondered if he was saying the words as much to himself as to Wallace. "But the magic of the mate bond is bigger than that. It wasn't the mate bond that failed you years ago, it was your own fear. Don't be the reason you're unhappy. Not again."

Mr. Wallace sighed thoughtfully.

"Remember what you told me," I said, grabbing his shoulder. "Don't lose her because you're too stubborn to get out of your own way."

"Okay," he nodded, squaring his frail shoulders. "I can do this."

Then he stepped out of the car, Clint and Mike catcalling after him. He made it to the short gate that blocked the walkway to the front door and then turned around.

"Well, aren't you coming?" he snapped.

"You want us to come with you?" I asked incredulously. Surely, he didn't want the three stooges up there when he finally met his mate.

"Do you think I want to do this alone?"

The three of us boys shared confused looks, but we followed the old man's orders just like he'd raised us to. None of us made a peep as he knocked on the yellow front door, standing behind him like a posse of bodyguards.

When the door swung open, it took me a moment to realize why the woman on the other side looked so familiar.

"Irene?" I blurted, staring at the woman that Caroline and I had met in the elevator at Volund's apartment. "What are you doing here?"

The older woman's face brightened as she smiled at me, recognition dawning in her green eyes. "Morgan! I've seen you on the news. Sounds like you finally got you head out of your bum and got the girl."

I grinned, chuckling along with my brothers. "Yeah, I'm the luckiest guy on the planet. I'm marrying her next week."

"Congratulations!" She gave me a hug and a kiss on the cheek. "But that can't be why you're here..."

Her eyes flitted hesitantly to Mr. Wallace.

The man was bright red, and his hands were shaking, but he met her gaze head on. "Hi, I don't know if you remember me—"

"Remember you?" Irene huffed, folding her arms. "How could a woman forget the mate that walked away?"

"How did you know he was your mate?" Clint asked, leaning around Wallace. "Are you a Shifter?"

"No, but my son in law is, so I know what the signs of the mate bond are. And I know an avoidant man when I see one." This comment she directed at Wallace.

He flinched at her words, but he didn't cower. "I'm sorry I walked away. I was stupid and scared and so wrapped up in grief..."

Irene's wrinkled face softened, the previous fire in her eyes dimming to a kinder warmth. "I know. I felt it. Did you lose someone?"

Wallace nodded. "My wife Gloria. She was my first mate and losing her was...brutal. So, when I met you, I was determined not to lose twice. I figured if I never had you, I couldn't lose you."

Irene sighed and shook her head, which was much shorter than mine, but only a few inches below Wallace. "That's a fool thing to think, you know that? You made a decision that not only affected you but affected me too. You're not the only one who's lost a spouse. My husband's been gone nearly a decade now and not a day goes by that it doesn't haunt me. But I never would have made that decision without you."

"I know, I—"

"Irene, who's at the door?" Esther came plodding down the hallway, and the moment she caught sight of me, she grinned wide. "Well, it's lover boy himself! How are you?"

I quickly explained that Care and I were getting married, and then that Wallace was here to speak with Irene.

"So, you're the idiot who made her cry for years," Esther growled, her eyes roving up and down Wallace and coming up unimpressed. Irene tried to tell her to calm down, but Esther wouldn't have it. "No, it's my right as your sister to demand that he make a fool of himself as recompense."

"Fine." Wallace nodded his head. "I'll do anything. I'll do whatever foolish things you want, and I'll even post it on the internet. Just please say you'll come to the wedding with me. Then, if you can't stand my presence after that, you don't have to see me again. But at least this time, it'll be on your terms, not mine."

Esther looked like she had a million other things she wanted to say—and insults she wanted to throw—but she waited silently for her sister to decide.

Irene studied Wallace, and an unspoken conversation seemed to flow between them. She fiddled with her fingers, bit her lip, and shifted between feet. Then she finally nodded.

"Alright, I'll go. But Esther gets to decide how you make a fool of yourself."

Esther grinned maniacally and Wallace swallowed. "Deal."

Chapter 36

CAROLINE

Every little girl dreams of her wedding day. The dress, the groom, the flowers, the seating arrangements, the guest list, the lighting and the playlist.

Okay, so maybe not all little girls dream of their weddings in as much detail as I had, but I'd always been a girly girl. I loved picturing my wedding day when I was a kid. It was the one princess daydream I had that was actually realistic.

Ha. Joke was on me. I'd skipped princess and gone straight to queen.

The backyard of the Alfar house was completely transformed for tonight's occasion. Twinkle lights and vines had been strung across the yard, with strands of white and pale pink flowers trailing down.

A wooden archway stood on the stone porch, wreathed in greenery and flowers, with chairs settled in the grass to watch the ceremony. Further back toward the river were long wood tables with runners of greenery and white flowers. A buffet of burgers, fries and milkshakes sat near a wooden dance floor, the lowering sun reflecting off the water nearby.

It was an extravagant affair, but with Lizzy's help, we'd managed to get most things on sale or at a discount. But I wasn't too concerned with the budget. This was going to be my only wedding. I wanted to remember it in every sparkling, shining, vibrant detail.

I watched through the window as Ariel, Lizzy and Merida fluttered around in their mauve bridesmaids dressed, taking care of a few last minute details. Mostly, they were bossing around the boys.

Mike, Clint and Logan were Morgan's groomsmen, and Volund was set to be our ring bearer. He'd be walking down the aisle with Daisy Mae and I although he'd complained plenty, I was pretty sure he was actually excited to be included.

My parents, Mr. Wallace and Irene, along with Genevieve's parents and her sister were all mingling together, and I smiled at the sight. I hadn't been sure that Gen's family would want to be involved in Morgan's future if it included someone new. But they'd been moved to be invited. When we visited them to tell them we were getting married, Genevieve's mom even hugged me and told me how happy she was and that she liked to think that a part of Gen lived on in me.

We'd both cried.

Most of the guests had arrived and were mingling in the yard. We'd invited all the council members—except Francine.

As I watched the smiles and laughter outside, a peace settled in my gut. Everyone I loved was in the same space, about to celebrate the love Morgan and I had built. *Speaking of Morgan...*

I turned from the window and stalked through the house, following the sensation of guilt and fear that was emitting from my mate. Whatever he was up to, he wasn't supposed to be, and I was going to catch him.

"*Are you serious?*" I demanded as I came upon him hovering over a takeout bag on the desk in my office, his mouth full of fries.

"Caroline," he squeaked guiltily, trying to swallow the fries but choking instead. I waited as he coughed to clear his throat, tapping my foot impatiently. "I can explain."

"Can you? Because from where I stand, you *lied* to me. For months you've complained about Frank's food. I can't even count the number of times you've whined about how unhealthy it is. You even refused to get it for me!"

"Hey, I only refused to buy Franks *once* and that was because we didn't have time," he defended, though the effort was made a little less effective by the burger that he pointed at me.

I stomped toward him, shoving a finger at his chest. "You secretly like the stuff that you gave me so much crap for and you never told me!"

"I'm sorry," he pleaded, wisely holding out the fries. I grabbed a few. "I shouldn't have lied, but after I'd made such a big deal about the food being chemically dangerous—"

"You're such a drama queen about health."

"—I didn't want to admit that I was wrong because I knew you'd gloat," he finished, shrugging shyly.

"How often have you eaten it without me?"

He dropped his eyes and rooted through the empty bag, avoiding me.

"Morgan Gareth Hohlt," I demanded, grabbing his arm, "How often?"

"...About twice a month."

"Ugh, I cannot believe—"

"I know," he grimaced.

"That you would order *my* favorite food," I continued.

"Care, I'm sorry!"

"Twice a month, and not ask me if I wanted anything!"

Morgan lifted his eyes, a slow smirk growing on his lips. "I should've known that would be what bugged you the most."

"Yes," I agreed, grinning, "You should have."

We stood there watching each other for a moment, and I took the opportunity to appreciate his appearance. Dressed in a black tuxedo and bow tie, with his dark hair combed back, he looked like a spy. *A sexy spy.*

I laughed. Here I was, a reformed spy herself, about to marry the man who'd once captured me. If I'd heard the story about anyone else, I would've been concerned. Who the heck marries the person who captured them and kept them prisoner?

Me.

Because while Morgan had only kept me a physical prisoner for like three days before we struck more of a partnership, he'd held my heart prisoner since day one. Well, probably more like day twenty. *Close enough.*

Morgan seemed to notice my ensemble for the first time too, his eyes skating over my entire body, leaving flames and shivers in their wake.

The dress I'd chosen was a gauzy white ballgown, with pink applique roses and little bits of greenery embroidered here and there along the skirt, mostly flowing over the bodice, which fit me like a bustier. Wide bell sleeves went to my wrists, my skin visible through the fabric, and my shoulders were left bare.

The back of the dress was my favorite, so I twirled for Morgan, allowing him to see the gauzy bow that was tied at the bottom of a shallow V cut. It was a ridiculously girly dress, for a ridiculously girly girl.

When I turned back to Morgan, I suddenly wondered if my loosely curled updo was too much. If the wispy pieces we'd left trailing down my neck was over the top, or if my smoky eye makeup wasn't as flattering as it'd been in my bedroom earlier.

"Red."

I looked up at the sound of his voice, deep and rough with the scrape of desire. A storm whirled in those grey eyes, the blue ring around them reassuring me that this was it. That he wanted me as much as I wanted him.

"I..." he trailed off, his Adam's apple bobbing as he swallowed and took a step toward me.

I stood completely frozen, scrutinizing his face as he tossed the burger aside and reached out a hand to run it down the soft material on the skirt of my dress. When his warm palm pressed against my waist, his thumb skating across my ribs, I shuddered.

Feeling suddenly weak, I grasped the lapels of his jacket and tugged. Morgan laughed, letting me yank him closer even though we both knew I'd never be able to overcome his Berserker strength.

"Eager are we, Mrs. Hohlt?" he teased, his smile like temptation incarnate.

"I'm not Mrs. Hohlt just yet," I reminded him, just barely restraining myself from the desire to bury my fingers in his hair. "But I'm *very* eager to marry you. And for all these guests to go away so I can have you to myself."

Morgan growled, his arms wrapping tightly around me.

"Care, a man can only handle so much. And if you keep looking at me like that, my self-control is going to crumble like a cookie."

"Mm, a very yummy cookie," I smiled teasingly, my fingers tracing the neckline of his jacket, his skin soft and smooth. "Let it crumble, Bear Man. We both know I'm not afraid of the calories, and after finding out about Franks, I don't think you are either."

"Not with this particular cookie anyway." Then he swooped down and kissed me.

Kissing Morgan had been fun from the get-go, but this kiss was different. This kiss knew something that all the other kisses didn't: that this kiss was forever. No more girlfriend or fiancé. I was about to become 'wife'; *his*. And I couldn't wait.

"Consider the cookie crumbled," I gasped, pulling back so I could actually breathe.

"It's your fault," he rumbled against my throat, trailing sweet kisses.

"Me? What about you in that tux? How was I supposed to resist that?"

He laughed, lifting his head to meet my eyes. His were a little less fiery now, or maybe just more contained. His hold on me loosened and he grasped my face between his gentle hands.

"I love you, Caroline Felicity Birch," he whispered, "And I trust you in every way."

I grinned, remembering the beginning of our story. Back when the trust we built was a surprise, something I hadn't seen coming. Now, Morgan was my mate, my safe space and soon he'd be my husband. Because of his love, I'd realized that I was strong and capable and a force to be reckoned with all on my own. But because of his faithfulness, I'd come to understand that I didn't need or want to be those things alone.

"I love you, Morgan Gareth Hohlt, and I trust you," I replied, clutching him close again, "In every form."

A gentle smile cracked his rough exterior, and I felt that profound sense of home in his arms.

"You and I are going to live a very complicated, very dramatic," he teased, squirming when I pinched his side, "Very *happy* life together, Red. No matter what happens."

"Life can throw a lot of things—we know better than most."

"True," he nodded, and my eyes fluttered closed at the feel of his breath on my lips. "But one thing I've learned is to *never* underestimate you, my ribbon-wearing vigilante."

THE END

Keep reading to get a sneak peek at the next Shifter Alliance series!

Taylor:

August, two months ago...

"I know, I wish you could come too," I murmured to the yowling ragdoll cat that was perched on the top of my ratty old couch—a beige yard sale find from last summer.

But Pitt was not placated by my promises, batting at my hands as I dug in the dish on the table by the door for my keys. I laughed and scrunched his fluffy little face in my hands, kissing him between his brown ears. He was a beautiful cat, with a thick light beige coat that faded to white on his belly. His eyes were shadowed with dark brown, and his mouth and snout were white, all contrasting against his big blue eyes.

The little brat had me wrapped around his finger and he knew it.

"Okay, I have to go or I'm going to be late. And we both know that as much as Frank loves me, he's going to lecture me for at least an hour if I'm late again."

Before Pitt could decide to launch himself at me, I slipped out the door of my apartment, locking the scuffed white door behind me. I would have preferred to paint it a prettier color, but the landlord was adamantly against making permanent changes—even though I'd promised I would paint it white again if I ever moved out.

Which wasn't likely unless I somehow came into a miraculous inheritance. "Not happening," I snorted.

"Talking to yourself?"

I flashed a glare at the man leaning against the railing of the long balcony a few feet away. My next-door neighbor was dressed in the same faded leather jacket as always, and I was forced to wonder once again what kind of attachment a person could have to such an unfortunate item of clothing.

His brown hair was slicked back like he fancied himself a young John Travolta, and he had a cigarette in one hand and a newspaper in the other.

"Oh, did you finally learn to read?" I snapped, tossing the tail of my blonde ponytail over my shoulder. "Your teacher must be so proud. What are you, a quadruple senior now?"

"I would gladly go back to high school if you were the teacher," he retorted, that one perfect eyebrow rising on his forehead.

"And I'd have you arrested for sexual harassment. Man, what a dream it would be to be rid of your presence while you rotted in prison."

I turned and headed toward the stairs, my well-worn converse tapping against the fake turf that was straining against the staples that kept it attached to the floor.

"So, I take it you haven't heard."

I sighed, letting my head fall back as I closed my eyes. I'd been up all night looking over the requirements for the criminal justice program at the local university. I'd already taken all the classes I could at community college, and now it was time to see if I could afford the cost of the required university. The odds were *not* in my favor.

"What, Blake?" I groaned, not turning to look at him.

"The news about the tournament," came his voice right next to my ear as he held out the newspaper in front of me.

I was too distracted by the article to complain about his nearness—though I did note that for someone who smoked as often as he did, he never smelled like smoke.

"They've finished designing it?" I mumbled, skimming the words on the page. The Dragons had been without a leader for months now, waiting for the other kings and queens of the region to plan the tournament that would decide our area's next leader. Honestly, it had been nice not having anyone in charge for a while. There was no one to enforce the tyrannical rules Eileen had imposed during her reign.

"The tournament starts in a month," Blake said, pulling the paper back and tapping me on the should with it. I glared up at him, but he just smirked, his brown eyes smoldering at me. "Crazy huh?"

"Crazy," I mocked, hiking my bag further up my shoulder, "That the leaders in our region did their job? Yeah," I rolled my eyes, "Super crazy."

Then I started stomping down the narrow staircase, a single light flickering on the wall, too dim to really help my descent much. When I heard a second set of steps following right behind me, I ground my teeth.

"Do you seriously not understand boundaries?" I complained, pressing the fob on my keychain to unlock my crappy blue car that sat five spaces down.

"No," he came up beside me, an innocently confused look on his face. "I thought you already knew that."

"What do you want, Blake? I'm tired and I'm late."

"You should enter."

"Enter what?"

He bumped my shoulder and smiled. By some miserable twist of fate, he was one of the few men of my acquaintance that was taller than me. At five feet eleven inches, I'd gotten used to towering over most people ages ago. When I dated someone, it was an added bonus if they were taller than me.

But with Blake it was just annoying. The jerk always leaned close and narrowed his eyes like a Chad Michael Murray wannabe just to make me feel small. I hated him for it.

"The tournament," he said, and I stopped, turning on the sidewalk to face him.

"You think I should enter the tournament to become our next queen?"

He shrugged. "Yeah."

I stared at him for a moment before I shamelessly cackled, bending over to catch my breath. The laughter went on for a few moments and he just watched, arms crossed and unimpressed.

"That's a pretty good joke." I patted his arm and walked to my car. "Who knew you could be funny."

"I'm being serious, T. You should enter it." I almost believed him, the look in his eyes lacking any mischief for once. But then I reminded myself of all the things he'd done to make me miserable in the years that we'd been neighbors. The loud music, the banging on my door at godforsaken hours, the times when he borrowed my car without asking or stole my DoorDash orders before I could get to them.

"Yeah, you, serious." I snorted and opened my door. "Totally believable. Hey, tell your sister I said 'hi' and that I'll come see her tomorrow."

"Why don't you ever come see me, T Bird?" Blake asked, his signature lopsided smirk back on his face.

"Because I don't like you." Then I waved my fingers at him and got in my car. But as I backed out of my space, pressing play on my phone to turn on some music, I couldn't quite shake the way his brown eyed gaze made my heart twitch uncomfortably in my chest.

It's just indigestion. It had to be...

Taylor and Blake's story will be the next series in the Shifter Alliance universe, and if you want to stay updated on when it comes out, be sure to subscribe to my newsletter and find me on social media :)

Hi! Thank you so much for reading the final chapter of Morgan and Caroline's story! I'm so sad to see this story end, but so pleased and so proud of how it all came together. And if you're hoping to find out what happens for Taylor and Blake, keep on the lookout because their book is coming next in the Shifter Alliance.

And if you're attached to any of the side characters from this book, chances are, either a trilogy or a standalone is in the works for them. **BUT** if there are any specific characters you want to see get their own story, please feel free to send me an email or send in your suggestion on my website! I have lots of plans for the Shifter Universe, but I always want to keep reader's preferences in mind!

And for those of you who like short stories starring characters you know, extra scenes, and fun behind the scenes things, you can always check out the newsletter! And if you're interested in chatting with other readers (or me), you can join my private Facebook group. There's also my Instagram page and YouTube channel. Or if you just care about the books, that's fine too! I'll see you in the next one!

Thank you for reading,

Rachel

When you join my newsletter, you get my novella *The Grinch Next Door* for FREE! You also get access to short stories, extra scenes and more!

Join at rachelescott.com

Also by Rachel E Scott

Contemporary
The Grinch Next Door

Fantasy
Legends of Avalon: Merlin
Legends of Avalon: Arthur

A Tale Of Ribbons & Claws
Stale-Mate
Bond-Mate
Check-Mate

Welcome to Autumnvale
Book One Coming Autumn of 2024

Plot Twist
Bonding With the Bodyguard (Coming winter of 2024)

Acknowledgments

Somehow, writing a book is much easier than writing my acknowledgments. But we're going to give it a shot!

Thank you to my family for always supporting my crazy dreams. Maybe they just realized that like John Locke, Rachel doesn't like being told she can't do something. Wise of you all. But regardless, you've carried so much of my load, and my poor back would've broken without you!

Also, a huge thank you to my friends, Beth, Melody and Jennie! And to my friend Leigh, who was my awesome beta reader! These books wouldn't be the same without you! I want to list all of my lovely bookish friends here, but it would take almost an entire chapter. So I'll just say that if you've kept in contact with me, cheered me on, given me advice, or sent me funny reels and memes to keep me going, you're counted in this category and I'm *SO* grateful for you!

And thank you of course to the One who gave this passion to a child (kind of irresponsible really. This creative streak got me into a lot of trouble as a kid). But really, thank you God for storytelling, it's my truest love in the world.

And last but not least, thank you to my babies Daisy Mae and Marshall Moose. Now that Daisy has gotten her own trilogy, it's time for me to brainstorm other pets in my life to include...

And thank you reader for reading this book! If you get the chance, please leave a rating or review (especially on Amazon)! Reviews mean so much to a self-published author like me! And even if you don't review, thank you for reading this trilogy—the first one I have ever completed. Just the fact that you chose this story means the world to me.

Until next time,

Rachel

About the Author

Rachel is an author of both contemporary and fantasy stories. She's a *The Office* enthusiast, a *The Lord of the Rings* superfan, and a sucker for all things geek. She reads anything with some clean romance—bonus points if there's some snarky MCs, funny side characters, and a happy ending. Rachel is dog obsessed, and two of her series even include her dogs (Daisy Mae appears in *A Tale of Ribbons & Claws* and Marshall is in *Legends of Avalon*). This hobbit author and her dogs spend lots of time writing, walking, and of course, watching *The Office* and *The Lord of the Rings* and *The Hobbit* appendices.

***

Where to Find Me

RACHEL E SCOTT

Website: rachelescott.com

Instagram: @res_writer_chick

YouTube: Rachel E Scott

Facebook Group: Rachel's Party Planning Committee

Newsletter (keep up on upcoming releases): sign up on my website

Follow me on Amazon

Podcast: Good On Paper (available wherever you get your podcasts)

Made in United States
Troutdale, OR
04/01/2024

18867697R00206